JOURNEY
to
PARADISE

Paula Greenlees has an undergraduate degree in English and European Thought and Literature, and a Masters Degree in Creative Writing. She spent three years living in Singapore surrounded by the history and culture that provided the inspiration for her first novel, *Journey To Paradise*.

JOURNEY
to
PARADISE

Paula Greenlees

PENGUIN BOOKS

PENGUIN BOOKS

UK | USA | Canada | Ireland | Australia
India | New Zealand | South Africa

Penguin Books is part of the Penguin Random House
group of companies whose addresses can be found at
global.penguinrandomhouse.com

Penguin
Random House
UK

Published by Penguin Books in 2021
001

Typeset in 11/15 pt Palatino
by Integra Software Services Pvt. Ltd, Pondicherry

Printed and bound in Great Britain by Clays Ltd, Elcograf S.p.A.

The authorised representative in the EEA is Penguin Random House
Ireland, Morrison Chambers, 32 Nassau Street, Dublin D02 YH68

A CIP catalogue record for this book is available from the
British Library

ISBN: 978-1-787-46616-6

www.greenpenguin.co.uk

For J, E and I

One

Despite the fog, the train journey from London to Southampton had been surprisingly easy. Even her parents had arrived on time. Miranda looked about her at the other passengers standing on the quayside, catching sight of the *Queen Mary* through the grey swirls of cloud that obscured the ship. Like her, the other passengers were surrounded by their suitcases and wrapped in their winter coats and hats. A man stood close by, cheeks reddened by the wind, blowing on his bare hands to keep them warm, and a woman tightened a hand-knitted scarf around a small boy, who wriggled away from her overprotective hand.

Miranda knotted her coat belt to keep out the tugging wind and noticed just how much her hands were shaking. She dug them into her pockets, hoping that no one would see, but she needn't have bothered. Her husband, Gerry, was glancing towards the gangplank and her mother was pulling something out of her bag.

Immediately, she recognised her grandmother's writing case. It was made from maroon calfskin and inside there were sheets of paper textured roughly, like tree bark, and envelopes that were lined with silver paper that crackled to the touch. The case was such a lovely thing.

'I knew you always liked it,' her mother said. 'And I thought you could use it to write to us, let us know how you are.' Her voice quivered and the words caught in her throat before drifting away; her gaze fell from Miranda's face to the ground.

'She'll be fine,' her father said. 'There will be so many new things to see, she probably won't have time to write.'

Gerry glanced at his watch then touched her elbow, lightly nudging her away. 'Darling, we'd better get a move on.'

She took the case and hugged her mother while she wiped away the tears that she didn't want her mother to see.

'Please. Don't worry about me,' she whispered, 'I'll be all right. But you won't forget, will you? About the flowers?'

'White roses. Every week.' Her mother squeezed her back. 'I promise.' She kissed Miranda on the cheek. 'I guess you had better go,' her mother sighed. 'Take care, darling, won't you?'

After they had set sail, Miranda sat by their cabin window watching as the bustle of the port receded behind her. How strange it seemed, at the age of twenty-eight, to be leaving England for the very first time; it surprised her how the people on the quay grew smaller as well as the buildings, and they were quickly absorbed by the grey. Yet still she watched, hoping to get one last glimpse of the thin line of land on the horizon so that she could say a final farewell to home, but it had faded from view and there was nothing left to see.

Gerry tried persuading her to join him for a stroll.

'Just around the upper deck. It would do you good to get some fresh air.'

'No. I'd rather unpack first.'

After he'd gone, she stood for what felt like an age by the window in their cabin fiddling with her locket. She loved tracing the scrollwork and feeling the heavy weight of gold in her hand. It was shaped like a heart and Gerry had given it to her on the first night of their honeymoon three years ago: she had never seen anything quite as perfect, and she had vowed to always wear it. Now, she opened it and took out a lock of baby-soft hair.

Time passed. How difficult it was, so much harder than she had imagined, to leave. Her thoughts turned to the flowers she had placed at Henry's grave that morning, the whispered words, then on to her parents. She imagined her mother and father's return to London, and Socrates, her cat, purring on her mother's lap. He was so young and lively, such a typical tabby, that he'd be bound to be puzzled by where on earth she and Gerry had gone. And then she thought of the work that she had left behind: the Women's Volunteer Service – the WVS – and the volunteering she used to do at the hospital, long after the war had ended. Would the other women miss her, she wondered? How she longed for their evenings chatting – during the last few months, it had been more of a salvation for her than any of them could possibly have known.

The cabin door opened. 'Guess what?' Gerry said, leaning against the doorframe. He brought a draught of cold air in with him and his hair had been blown about by the wind.

'First night and we're on the captain's table.'

She smiled. Even now, after three years of marriage, the blue of his eyes still caught her off guard and she saw him as others must do – handsome and successful. Sometimes, she couldn't quite believe that a man like him had chosen her for his wife, and seeing him now, standing there, gave her a feeling like tumbling through the air. Even with his windswept hair and his crumpled linen jacket, he had an air of confidence about him that authority brings. He wore it like armour, she thought, and nothing seemed able to pierce it.

'Wouldn't it be better,' she asked, putting the curl of hair away and snapping her locket closed, 'if we dined alone? It's been such a long time since it's been just the two of us.'

'But it's such an honour,' he said.

'There'll be other nights, surely?'

'Maybe,' he shrugged. 'But I've seen the guest list for tonight, and they're a pretty impressive bunch, I can tell you. Sir Lim Bo Seng, he's a head of the Bank of China, and Beryl Keppel.'

'The socialite?'

'Yes. Imagine.'

She could see how excited he was to be invited, and yet she really wanted a quiet night. There would be other occasions, she was certain, but she also knew that, once his mind was made up about something, she would be unable to change it.

'Fine,' she said. 'But let's not make it a late night.'

*

She wore her best navy silk dress and sat between the captain, who was wearing his dress uniform, and Lim Bo Seng, a quiet, serious man in his fifties. She wondered which knife and fork to use and which glass was for white wine or red. The food was rich – terrine of pork, sole meunière, and chocolate mousse or apple charlotte, followed by stilton and port. When they'd finished, a band struck up and they danced – a waltz, the foxtrot, even an attempt at the tango – until suddenly it was well past midnight.

When they finally got to bed, Miranda couldn't sleep. Despite her earlier reservations, she had enjoyed the evening. And it struck her anew that Gerry's new job in Singapore as a colonial officer meant she would be meeting important guests like Lim Bo Seng and Beryl Keppel on a regular basis. It was both thrilling and terrifying at the same time: so many complicated rules, such as which way to pass the port – was it to the left or the right? She never could remember, and she didn't want to let Gerry down by showing herself to be a fool.

At three o'clock, she switched on the bedside lamp, got up quietly so as not to wake Gerry, and sat at the desk where she'd left her grandmother's writing case. Loneliness and uncertainty rose through her and the desire to be close to her parents and all that was familiar caught her off guard. She picked up her pen, wanting to write to them, needing to be close, but all the words she'd been wanting to write thundered around in her head, making her temples throb.

The writing case made her think of her granny – what a character she had been, with her hat and mink coat. She'd always kept a bag of peppermints in her crocodile-skin handbag and her handkerchiefs always smelt of eau de cologne. Sunday afternoons weren't Sunday afternoons without Granny calling for tea – salmon paste and cucumber sandwiches, sponge cake with strawberry jam, tea poured from mother's best teapot into fine bone china cups. There were conversations about neighbours that she listened to from under the table while she played with her dolls. *That Mrs Morris! Well, you reap as you sow. Or Have you heard about Shirley Watkins? Nothing better than she ought to be.*

She glanced across at Gerry sleeping. His mouth was open and a small bead of saliva clung to his lower lip. She couldn't let him down, not now that his career in the Colonial Office was taking off. And what was more, there was the secret she carried with her every day, the one that she could never let him know. It shamed her to think of the small items she'd stolen from the shops after Henry had died, the caution from the policeman, the spiralling of her emotions that had led her down such a stony path. The pain of it still stung, and she wondered if the humiliation would ever go away.

A burst of laughter from a couple passing on the other side of the closed door made her lift her head. She imagined them – the man wrapping his arm around the woman's waist, them kissing, their faces shining with love. Her eyes smarted with tears. How could this new life in Singapore possibly undo the past? She knew she had to try to forget her mistakes, however hard it might be, but she wasn't certain she could be the wife that Gerry needed in Singapore. She needed to ask her mother's advice, but all she could do was stare at the open writing case as the words in her head stuck fast and her pen hovered over the paper.

'Miranda, what are you doing?'

There was a rustle of sheets as Gerry sat up.

'Nothing.'

'Well, switch off the light and come back to bed, then.'

She hesitated, then placed the lid back on her pen.

The next day the case lay open and forgotten. Another day passed and Miranda put the case in a drawer.

In the weeks that followed, she distracted herself by reading, sewing or playing bridge. On other days, she'd sunbathe or attend the ladies' exercise classes on the upper deck while catching passing glimpses of Morocco and Egypt. When they reached the Straits of Malacca, she started packing. Finally, their cases were locked and waiting, so Gerry searched for a porter.

She rested against the rail, her dress sticking to her in this new, humid heat. It was so different to the dryness of Alexandria, where the desert crept into her lungs, and different, too, to the cloying heat of Calcutta, where the smell of spices thinly disguised the stench of human waste.

England seemed another world as she watched the mesmerising blues and greens of the sea, the hills in the distance and the unfamiliar buildings looming into view. Never had she imagined Singapore to be like this. And it wasn't just the land – the water was heaving with boats carrying huge bags of rice or crates of bananas, with children swimming in the water and men hauling fishing nets on to the quay.

The cry of a heron startled her, and she lifted her head. She followed its flight as it dipped and dived up the Singapore River and as it moved towards the shore, over the sampans and junks and the crates of bananas, then as it darted beyond the crumbling tenements and rows of washing hanging on long poles, like festive banners welcoming the *Queen Mary* in.

The port was full of even more activity – yet more men in fishing boats tugging in their catch, trishaws and bullock carts transporting strange-looking fruits and vegetables, labourers staggering beneath the weight of heavy baskets on their backs. As she noted the rainbow clothing of the local women, she could hear the distant jingling of temple bells, and the aroma of spices that punctured the air made her giddy.

Her gaze turned to a group of children who were playing close to the nets while their mothers chattered and washed clothes in the dirty water. She lit a cigarette and watched. It made her think of Henry and the softness of his hand in hers. Her whole body ached at the thought and she longed to know how big his hand would have grown by now.

A shadow fell at her feet. It was Gerry, with his hands in his pockets and a frown on his face. She drew her gaze away from the harbour.

'I've been looking for you everywhere. Ready?'

Uncertain and excited, she nodded.

'Good. I've found a porter to carry our bags. We'd better get a move on. There's quite a queue.' He headed towards the passengers filing down the gangway.

While standing in line, passengers began to throw coins into the sea. As they fell, men and boys from the sampans jumped into the air or dived into the water to catch them.

'What's going on?' she asked, leaning over the hand-rail to get a better look.

'It's for good luck. The Chinese are the most superstitious creatures on earth.'

She watched the coins tumbling and falling.

'Gerry?'

'Mmm?'

'I don't suppose you have a penny, do you?'

He raised an eyebrow and dug around in his pocket, then jingled some coins in his palm. 'I didn't think you believed in all that good luck nonsense.'

'Well,' she replied – she tossed the coins into the sea, and as they fell, she glanced back at the children and mothers on the shore – 'I don't suppose it can do any harm.'

Two

It took an hour to disembark, then they had to queue to get a landing card and make their way through customs, but at last they arrived on shore and started to search for their driver among the crowd of passengers, jostling trishaws and bullock carts. Miranda spotted a Chinese man in his early forties leaning against the textured bark of a towering coconut tree. The feathery fronds cast a welcome shade over the baking ground. He was holding a piece of card with their name on it, and close by a Vauxhall – the latest model J, with four doors and a shining spare wheel fastened on to the boot – glinted in the sun.

'Goodness,' she said. 'That must be our car. It's a bit showy, don't you think?'

'Come on.' Gerry led her by the elbow. 'You'll have to get used to the finer things in life now. And don't forget, the driver will help us with our bags.'

'Captain Lewis?' The man bowed. 'My name is Jinhai. I am your driver.'

Gerry shook his hand then instructed Jinhai to load their cases into the boot of the car. Miranda watched, aching to help with the smaller ones. When their luggage was loaded, she took her cue from Gerry and settled into the back with just her handbag.

Moments later, they were off, and their car wound through the narrow streets away from the port. She clutched her bag and studied the crumbling buildings and the locals, who shouted and pushed through the market stalls lining the pavements. Trishaws and bicycles wove between women carrying wicker crates containing chickens, their feathers fluttering as they squawked, or strange vegetables in rattan baskets, children were crying and beggars limped on crutches. A bullock cart trundled along ahead of them. All the while, the unbearable heat mingled with the sulphurous stench of rotting eggs, which filtered through the open windows of the car.

Miranda lit a cigarette then leant back, her dress sticking to the seat.

'So, are you going to tell me what you wished for?' Gerry asked. 'A Packard? One of those beautiful black-and-white mansions they have here? Or maybe a team of servants pandering to your every need?'

'You never take me seriously.'

'I'm only teasing you.'

Gerry leant forward to speak to their driver, a butterfly of sweat already staining the back of his shirt. 'How far is it, Jinhai?'

'Not far-*lah*. Maybe forty minutes.'

'Good.' He wiped his forehead with the back of his hand. 'It's really hard to breathe in here.'

Miranda threw the cigarette out of the window. Even the streets were so different to how she'd imagined them: there were shacks everywhere, the pavements crowded with people, and heat was pushing in from all directions. There was so much colour too – such a contrast to the greys and browns of London streets. As she inhaled, she tried to untangle what the astonishing scents were. Something floral. Could it be jasmine?

'Don't you think it's all so exotic?' she asked.

And she really did like everything, even the smell of tobacco in the car, the sweat clinging to the leather seats and the humidity. It didn't matter to her that the car was insufferably hot because all of it was utterly intoxicating.

'Besides, it's interesting, don't you think, the first time you see a new place?' She leant a little closer to the open window, allowing the breeze to cool her face. 'Like reading a new book or watching a movie. You never know exactly how it's going to unfold.'

'You're an insufferable romantic.' Gerry slumped back next to her. 'I just want to get on with it: get there, unpack, sort myself out.'

They drove on, over the river and past huge, white Neoclassical buildings, their images reflected in the water's edge.

'Government building.' Jinhai explained, before they drove on into a leafy residential area, where towering palms obscured mansions at the end of winding drives.

'Are we here yet?' Gerry leant forwards again. 'Is this Alexandra Gardens?'

12

'No. This is Tanglin.' Jinhai said. 'Rich people live here. Your house is not so very far.'

They carried on. Jinhai manoeuvred the car between bicycles laden with mangoes and watermelons, and then they continued towards a collection of wooden huts whose roofs were made from palm leaves.

'This is a kampong,' Jinhai explained, gesturing to the village. 'Malay people live here.' He slowed the car to avoid a procession of chickens running in front of them. 'Not everyone in Singapore lives in big houses.'

'Indeed,' Gerry said. 'But it's like that everywhere, isn't it? The same is true of England.'

Jinhai clicked his tongue.

Close to the car there were groups of Malay women hoeing the ground or loading vegetables into baskets on their backs. Although she had read many books about Singapore in preparation for her new life here, and had held numerous conversations with other passengers on the journey out, it surprised and delighted her that Singapore was a visible melting pot of cultures – Malay, Chinese, Tamil, she simply couldn't wait to discover them all.

The women stopped and watched the car pass, some leaning on the handles of their hoes. From underneath the wide brims of the bamboo hats shading their faces, Miranda could see their skin was burnt and wrinkled by the sun. She smiled and gave them a little wave, but the gesture was met with cold, unsettling stares, and one of the women took a step forward and spat on the ground.

Twenty minutes later, their car slowed as they entered a palm-lined avenue. Miranda slid closer to the edge of her seat; they were surrounded by almond trees and mimosa, bougainvillea and banana trees, their huge branches spread out like giant fans, and dotted between them was a collection of colonial-style bungalows. The car pulled into a driveway.

'Is this our house, Jinhai?'

'Yes, Mrs Gerald.'

She turned to Gerry. 'It's huge! Twice the size of our old house at least. And look at the verandah running all the way around it.'

'It looks a bit rickety, don't you think? And a little dark, surrounded by all this jungle?'

'Not at all. I love it. I simply can't *wait* to get out and explore.' Her hand pushed open the car door.

'The thing I'm looking forward to the most is a bath – either that or sleeping in a decent bed. After six weeks at sea, I believe I have forgotten what it feels like.' Gerry yawned as he spoke.

Jinhai unloaded their cases as a Chinese woman shuffled towards them from the house. She couldn't have been more than five feet tall and her gently creased face was topped with a tight knot of hair. She wore a white tunic with buttons running down the front and black ankle-length trousers.

'Welcome. I Mei Ling.' She bowed, then gestured for them to enter the bungalow.

14

'Mrs Lewis.' Miranda held out her hand, which Mei Ling didn't take. 'But you must call me Miranda, and this is my husband, Gerry.'

'Captain Lewis.' Gerry gave Mei Ling a curt nod then turned to Jinhai. 'Bring the cases up to the bedroom.'

They followed Mei Ling past a bed of scarlet peonies, while, behind them, Jinhai pushed their cases on a trolley. An aroma crept towards Miranda, exotic and yet slightly familiar – she'd smelt it at church once and guessed it was a type of incense. At the base of the steps was a low table, on top of which were three Chinese figurines and a collection of fruit and cakes, piled high and set next to smouldering sticks.

'What are all these for?' she asked, pointing at the fruit.

'For house god, Mrs Gerald. To keep evil spirits away. And to make the house lucky for your arrival.'

'I told you, didn't I?' Gerry's whisper was dismissive. 'Superstitious to the core.'

'I think it's lovely,' she whispered back, then she turned to Mei Ling. 'Thank you. I'm sure that it will bring us lots of luck.'

'I bring you tea after journey?' Mei Ling indicated a sofa and a set of cane chairs.

Miranda glanced around her and at the garden, which was a patch of bleached grass surrounded by coconut palms, mimosa bushes and a nutmeg tree with orchids hanging in pots from the branches, then back at the bamboo blinds hanging from the verandah. There was a plate of strange pink cakes, as well as teacups and a jug with a familiar pink rose pattern on it, similar to the ones in her mother's kitchen at home.

Excitement fizzed through her and she longed to explore all the new and exotic elements of her new home.

'It all looks delicious, but we'd love to see the bungalow first.'

She followed Mei Ling up the steps and was startled by a nearby pair of gold-and-blue parrots that squawked loudly and flapped their wings at her. She turned and grinned at Gerry as he followed her into the hall, where there was a thick white envelope propped against a large arrangement of creamy orchids.

'How beautiful! It's very thoughtful of you, Mei Ling.'

Mei Ling shook her head. 'No-*lah*. I didn't do.'

Gerald ripped open the envelope. 'It's from the Metcalfes. They've asked us for drinks tomorrow. And they've left us a book.' He picked it up and turned the pages.

'Oh, how wonderful! Last time she wrote to me, Georgina said she'd arrange a welcome party for us. I can't wait to see them again. It's been so long.' Miranda placed her hand on Gerry's arm and read the book's title: *The Stranger's Guide to Singapore*. 'How thoughtful of them. But do come on, let's look around the house!' She tugged the book from him and closed it.

She led him by the hand through a corridor where their footsteps echoed along the tiled floors, then she pushed opened a door to a large room where louvered French windows opened out on to the lawn. Close to the window was a large, freshly polished teak table and eight chairs, along with a sideboard with six empty cut-glass decanters that gleamed in the afternoon light.

'Goodness me. A proper dining room.' Miranda squeezed his hand. 'Isn't it lovely? Do you think we'll have lots of proper dinner parties?'

Gerry ran his hand over the surface of the table. 'You know, I don't think you should be overly familiar with Mei Ling.'

'Why on earth not?'

'It's just not the done thing here and you have to make sure that she respects you.' He gave her hand a little squeeze. 'It's different to England, where one might have a cup of tea and a chat with the daily. She's a servant, something that you'll have to get used to, not a friend.'

'But, surely, it can't hurt to be civil?'

'True. But like I said, it's not like home. You both need to know your place.'

'You make it sound as though I'm Princess Elizabeth, not a civil servant's wife.' She walked into the sitting room, where there was a rosewood table with chips in the veneer.

'All of it standard government issue.' Gerry joined her and flopped into an armchair. 'Sturdy and serviceable, but unattractive, a little bit like me,' he said with a wink.

'Don't be stupid, darling.' She kissed him on the cheek. 'It's all absolutely adorable and even better than I'd imagined.'

He kissed her back.

'And,' she continued, 'I can always make some cushions or hang new curtains. Make it more homely.' She stroked the faded curtains. 'It wouldn't take much.'

'Of course. You should do whatever you like to make you feel at home, darling, but labour's cheap out here and you can get anything made, so you won't need to do a thing yourself.'

'But I like sewing!'

'Suit yourself,' he sighed.

They continued through to the bedroom on the ground floor, which was large, airy and painted a soft white.

'My goodness, this is amazing!' she grinned.

There were starched sheets and crisp white pillowcases on the bed and a mosquito net tumbled in swathes from the ceiling. It looked so relaxing and clean.

Gerry sank on to the bed while she went to the window and looked out.

'Now, *this* is absolute bliss,' he said. 'I could drift off right away.' She turned to see Gerry peering up at the ceiling fan whirring above him, and she noted how the pillows were already squashed.

'Honestly, you've made such a mess.'

'Come on, old girl, feel how comfy it is.'

'No. Not yet. I want to explore the rest of it.' Impatience bubbled as she turned and walked across the hall tiles, before she pushed open the mesh door that led outside. The parrots were back, sitting together on the rail, nodding and bobbing as she settled into one of the cane chairs beneath the wooden awning.

At the bottom of the garden, she noticed what looked like an old tumbledown summerhouse, now covered with vines and creepers. Above it, there was a large tree with pink buds that were reaching out towards the sun. The branches created a vaulted ceiling between their bungalow and the neighbouring one and she wondered when it would all burst into life, taking into account that there were no seasons, as she knew them, in Singapore. The surrounding trees and bushes were menacing, much bigger than she was used to, and beyond the garden, the heavy jungle hung back as though ready to creep out when no one was aware. The shrieks of monkeys penetrated through the trees along with the birdsong, while, from the kitchen, she could hear the clatter of plates, and Mei Ling's high-pitched voice and Jinhai's low reply.

It was paradise.

Gerry came out carrying *The Stranger's Guide* and sat next to her.

'Thought I'd have a quick read.'

And so, for a few moments, they sat side by side. It had been such a long time since they'd sat like this, just enjoying the moment together, relaxed and happy in each other's company. There was much to look forward to, so much hope for the future, that she couldn't help but smile.

But then the cry of a baby filtered across from the neighbouring bungalow. Instinctively, Miranda tensed. Gerry shifted in his seat before lifting his head to glance across the garden. Miranda searched his face to see if he'd heard it, but he didn't look back at her. He seemed a million miles away, then he sighed and lowered his eyes, concentrating on his book once more.

The baby was wailing now. She clenched her hands, digging her nails into her palms. Gerry licked his finger and turned another page. Surely he could hear it?

'Gerry?' She reached out a shaking hand to touch his knee. The baby's shrieks and howls were so loud she couldn't stand it any longer. But still he ignored her.

'I'm going to unpack.' She stood, her knees shaking, waiting for him to join her, but he shook his head. She ran back into the house, the door banging behind her as she retreated.

In their room, she sank on to the bed, curling up around a pillow, which muffled the sound of her sobs; she longed to feel the gentle touch of Gerry's hand on her shoulder, but it never came. After a time, she calmed. If the baby was still crying, it was too far away for her to hear. Miranda lay clutching her tear-stained pillow, listening to the sounds around her: the monkeys calling in the trees, the buzz of the ceiling fan, the drone of a mosquito overhead, but all she could think about was that night, the way the north wind had cut at her face as she had run, hugging Henry to her chest. She remembered how a man had shouted at her as she passed him, knocking his paper to the ground. She hadn't seen him and didn't care. All that mattered was to get to the hospital.

Breathless, she had pushed through a pair of large double doors, and, in her confusion, she headed up the stairs, not down. She turned, her coat swinging around her knees. In the casualty room, she was dazzled by the brilliant lights and saw a nurse come towards her. The woman stared at Henry, and her fingers automatically touched his neck.

'Please!' Miranda screamed. 'I only left him for a minute. Oh God! Tell me that he's breathing.'

'I'm so sorry,' the nurse had said, her face revealing what Miranda had feared the most. 'He wouldn't have known a thing.'

The memory sent her heart racing. Shutting out the past was going to be harder than she thought. She sat up and opened her locket to look at Henry's photograph; her hands were trembling and her chest felt tight. Sometimes, she convinced herself that if she were only able to sleep for long enough, on waking he'd be there and everything would be as it had been before – a futile wish, she knew. She wiped her eyes, closed the locket and studied the room.

Jinhai had placed their cases at the bottom of the bed. She forced herself to her feet, opened her case, took out a battered tin box and gently laid it on the bed. She lifted the lid as though it were porcelain and took out a small, white-handled hairbrush. Every time she held it or ran the soft, fine bristles against her cheek, she tried to capture the feeling of the weight of his head in the crook of her arm. She smoothed out a pair of faded yellow booties with blue ribbon running around the top and lifted them to her nose, then she placed them next to his hairbrush. Finally, she lifted out a silver thimble she had stolen from an antique shop, a man's pocket watch and a small jug with a chip in it she had taken from the Peter Jones in Sloane Square. As she turned the thimble in the light, she examined the hallmark and wondered again why she had taken it. There was no real value to it, after all, but holding it in her hand always helped to remind her of that dark place she had found herself in and then dragged herself away from after Henry died. Strange to think, now, that taking these things had made her feel better. Was it simply the dare or the thrill of it? Or was she trying to get caught, wanting someone to scoop her up and really take notice – of her?

Carefully, she returned everything to the box and locked it: this was a part of her life that Gerry didn't know about. And, for both their sakes, she had to keep it that way.

Opposite the bed, there was a dressing table with two long drawers. She opened one and put the box inside. Her reflection looked back at her from the mottled mirror; so pale, as though all those weeks at sea or sitting in the sun had counted for nothing.

For a few moments, she leant against the dressing table, then slowly she began to unpack. First, she placed her hairbrush and a bottle of perfume on the dressing table, then a collection of framed photographs: Gerry at the Sidcup Hunt; one of them all at Henry's christening, a couple of photographs of them on their wedding day. Gerry looked so smart in his officer's uniform. She ran her finger over her image, outlining her wedding dress made from parachute silk, looking for signs of the tell-tale swell that she'd hoped only she could see. Finally, she shook out her dresses, hung them on the hangers in the wardrobe and closed the door with a gentle click. Everything was organised, and the room looked neat, as though it had been staged. She straightened her dress and took a deep breath, scanning the room: she needed to put on a brave face and not spoil their first night in their new home.

When she re-emerged from the house, it was close to seven. Gerry was sitting in the exact spot where Miranda had left him, still reading the guidebook. The sun was fading from red to orange, casting fiery light between the leaves of the trees. As she sat next to him, he looked up. Gerry looked happy and relaxed and Miranda attempted to return a smile, wondering if he could tell she'd been crying, or if he'd ask her where she'd been.

A light evening wind was blowing, and she caught the aroma of jasmine mingling with mosquito coils, the endless thrumming of the cicadas – an invisible wall between them and the darkness of the jungle – but he didn't ask her how she was. He never seemed to, these days.

A bottle of whisky was open on the table, a good two inches down, as well as two glasses, one empty and another half-full.

'Chin-chin!' Gerry said brightly, pouring her a glass, then he clinked his own against hers. 'I think we're going to be very happy here, don't you?'

She took a sip of the whisky and watched as the sunlight began to fade over the trees. For a moment, stillness settled around her, making her feel calm and happy once again, but then the mocking screech of a monkey startled her as it ripped from the depths of the inky trees.

Three

Miranda held the Metcalfes' invitation. The last time she'd seen her friend Georgina had been two years earlier, shortly after Henry had been born. Georgina had told her, between Henry's screams, how wonderful Ingrid Bergman had been in *Joan of Arc* and about the new Margarita cocktail Peter had bought for her at The Connaught. There had been a slight shift in their friendship, she recalled – brought on, no doubt, by Miranda's all-consuming motherhood and Georgina's responsibilities as the wife of a senior civil servant before the Metcalfes' move to Singapore. It seemed so long ago now, a different time, a different life. And now, as she put the invitation down, more than ever she missed what she knew she could never have again – their youthful evenings at dances and their laughter in the midnight air.

'What time are we leaving?' she asked Gerry, who was changing in the dressing room.

She started to apply a layer of lipstick, only to discover that it had melted on the journey. Honestly. The heat was impossible; she'd only been in Singapore for a few days and had spent most of it permanently flushed.

'I told Jinhai to bring the car round for quarter past.' Gerry came in from the dressing room still knotting his bow tie and paused. 'Is that what you're wearing?'

'Why?' She frowned. 'What's wrong with it?'

'Wouldn't the blue be better? Less dressy.'

'Yes, but this is my favourite frock.' She smoothed the red silk at her waist and viewed her profile in the mirror. 'And I like the cut of this much better.'

'Well,' he pulled his dinner jacket from the hanger on the back of the wardrobe door and brushed the collar, 'I suppose it doesn't matter much. Look, I'm sorry. You look lovely. I can hear the car. We'd better go.'

They drove west, bumping over potholes. Miranda fanned herself as she looked out at the Malay villages, kampongs Jinhai had called them, and the banana trees and pineapples growing at the side of the road. It surprised her that pineapples grew from the ground, as she'd always imagined that they grew from trees. There was so much fruit everywhere, just for the taking, and she resisted the urge to ask Jinhai to stop the car to allow her to pick some. Old war habits die hard, she mused.

Gerry took a hip flask from his pocket, unscrewed the top and took a large sip.

'Want some?'

'No.' She shook her head. 'And you ought to be careful, you'll be drunk before you get there.'

'I'll be all right,' Gerry said, leaning his elbow against the door with the unscrewed flask in his hand and staring out of the window. Silence fell between them.

'You like Singapore already?' Jinhai asked.

'I think so,' she said. 'Although we haven't had much time to explore it yet.'

'Last boss say Singapore is very different to England. He said, "England rains all time." I think maybe here better. Hot.'

'Yes. It does rain a lot back home. And it's cold too.'

They travelled on, Jinhai indicating points of interest along the way. 'Here's Raymond Road' or 'This one's Kandang Kerbau Hospital – KK we call it.'

She thought of what Gerry had said, about not being too friendly with the servants. Jinhai was clearly intelligent and expecting her to respond to his comments. Perhaps Gerry had got it wrong, but it made her feel a little awkward to be chatting away while Gerry was sitting next to her, especially as he wasn't joining in the conversation.

After a mile or two, she heard the banging of drums and cymbals. Coming towards them was a band of men holding a strange collection of instruments, while others in the crowd were wearing white clothing and following a turquoise wagon decorated with bright pink and white paper flowers.

'Is it some kind of a carnival?' she asked, as their car slowed to a halt.

'No, Mrs Gerald. Not a carnival. A funeral.'

How could it be a funeral? She peered across as the turquoise hearse drew parallel to them. Lying in the middle of a pile of toys and paper money was the body of a child.

Instinctively, her hand found Gerry's arm, but his body stiffened, and he moved his arm away.

'Gerry?'

He pulled out a packet of Lucky Strikes and struck a match. It sparked and fell on his lap. The smell of sulphur drifted towards her.

'Damn!' He swiped the match away. 'Bloody thing!'

He lifted his head. It always startled her, the way he did that, looking directly into her eyes. The blue was so intense. Violet, they called it, but she always thought it was more magical, like lapis lazuli.

Those eyes – they were what had attracted her to him in the first place.

She had been standing in Trafalgar Square among the crowds waiting anxiously for Churchill's announcement to begin and her nerves had got to her as she waited. She'd pulled out a packet of cigarettes but hadn't got any matches.

'Excuse me, have you got a light?' She'd approached a couple of officers standing close by. The nearest soldier to her had several medals clipped above the left breast pocket of his service jacket and a blaze of red velvet flashed along his lapels. He'd been chatting to his neighbour when she'd interrupted them, but as he lifted his face towards hers, she caught the mesmerising blue of high summer.

'Allow me.' He'd flicked open a silver lighter and cupped his hands around her cigarette, protecting the flame as the loudspeakers began to crackle and a deep hush fell over the crowd. 'Sometimes it can be a bit tricky.' His long vowels were soothing, his voice confident, belonging to another world.

'What do you think he's going to say?' she whispered, as interference broke across the square from large loudspeakers.

'Sssssh!' A woman in front of her turned around and glared at them. Gerry winked at her just as Churchill's voice drifted across the crowd:

'Yesterday morning at 2:41 a.m. at Headquarters, General Jodl, the representative of the German High Command, and Grand Admiral Doenitz, the designated head of the German State, signed the act of unconditional surrender of all German land, sea, and air forces in Europe to the Allied Expeditionary Force, and simultaneously to the Soviet High Command.'

'Is it finally really over?' she gasped. 'I can hardly dare believe it!'

'Yes. Thank bloody God, yes!' He'd picked her up and swung her around while all about them a roar surged over the square. They spent all night celebrating, dancing in Soho at Sonny's Jazz Bar, and as he walked her home in the early morning light, whenever she caught the blue of his eyes, it was as though she were tumbling through the air all over again. Ever since, they'd found it hard to be apart.

But now, as she looked across at her husband, it seemed as though the blue that once sparkled so clear and bright seemed to fade at stormy moments, like the sky darkening on a winter's day.

She took the matches from him. 'Here, let me help you.'

They drove on. The kampongs gave way to the large black-and-white houses, so distinctive to Singapore, which sheltered among the drowsy jungle. Halfway along Tanglin Road, they turned right into a driveway lined with royal palms, their branches swaying like ostrich plumes.

The driveway cut through terraced lawns until they reached the steps of a house. At the far side of the building, covered walkways joined smaller structures to the main body of the house. She could make out five people on the terrace, holding glasses and laughing.

'I didn't know there would be other people.'

Gerry held the car door open for her as she stepped out. 'Is that a problem?'

'No.' She shrugged, but the truth was she'd rather be seeing Georgina alone. After all, it was the first time they would be together since Henry had died.

They made their way over to the group, where she could see Georgina's slim form. Her friend was smoking a cigarette from a long tortoiseshell holder, and Miranda noted that she'd had her hair cut in a sharp bob. Georgina lifted her head as they approached and large diamond drops flashed from her ears.

'Miranda!' Georgina's face lit up.

'Georgina!' They embraced, kissing each other on both cheeks. Georgina wore loose black silk trousers, and a thick rope of pearls swung against a cream silk shirt with a mandarin collar; she looked even more beautiful and glamorous than Miranda remembered.

'It's *so* wonderful to see you. And you look fabulous! When did you get your hair bobbed?' Miranda asked.

'Oh. A few months ago. My hair couldn't cope with this blasted heat.'

'Miranda, Gerry!' Peter strode towards them. He was a little older, perhaps a bit plumper than Miranda remembered. 'Good to see you. Let me introduce you to the others. This is Longland Mackintosh, head of the rehousing programme, and Dickie Fraser, second in command. And this chap is a doctor – Nick Wythenshaw. Wythenshaw's doing some medical report work for us. Thought it would be good for you to meet a few chaps before you start work.'

'Lovely to meet you,' she said, as Longland shook Gerry's hand then hers.

'An absolute pleasure, my dear.' His grip was firm, and it dug her diamond ring into her finger. She tried not to wince.

'Gin Fizzes?' Peter asked.

'Please.' Miranda nodded as she shook hands with Nick Wythenshaw; his grip was also firm, but lighter. She looked up into his face and their eyes met, like sunlight catching a window. The impact startled her. He let go of her hand, but the warmth of his touch still lingered, like the residual heat of the sun.

A servant brought the drinks around on a tray.

'Thanks.' Gerry took a glass, then handed it to Miranda before turning back to Peter. 'So, give me the lowdown. What's Ambrose Hawkins like? I've heard he's a stickler for detail.'

'A. H. is all right.' Longland produced a cigar and concentrated on lighting it for a moment. 'But this social welfare plan of his is coming up against a bit of a wall. The governor wants more facts. That's where Nick's a real godsend, aren't you?'

'Thanks. But I heard you did a good job, Gerry, for Bevan's lot,' Nick said.

'Slum clearances in Birmingham, wasn't it?' Dickie swiped away a mosquito that had landed on his neck.

'Both, really – advisory.'

'Another drink – Gerry, Dickie?'

'Go on then.'

'Miranda?'

'I'm fine, thanks.' Miranda stood on the periphery, clutching her glass. 'Still got plenty.'

'Telephone, madam,' a servant informed Georgina, who then followed him into the house. She returned a moment later.

'Damn it. Two of my guests can't make it. Charlotte and Andrew Yeardley. They live close to you – thought it would be good for you to meet someone over your way.'

'Just us two girls, then,' Miranda smiled. 'Like the good old days.'

'Come here!' Georgina said, tucking her arm into Miranda's. 'I've *so* missed you!' she whispered into her ear, then dragged her away from the group and towards the house. Gerry gave her a gentle nod as they left.

'You know, I've been desperate to get you by yourself – how are you?'

'Surviving,' Miranda sighed, and not wanting to dampen the moment, turned her face away.

'Really? Are you sure?' Georgina continued. 'You know,' she paused, her voice almost a whisper, 'that I wrote to you at the time, but I can't imagine what it must have been like for you. Just awful. I wish I'd been there for you in person.'

Miranda clenched her jaw. Although she'd known this moment would be coming, she didn't want to talk about it. Not here. Not now – for, if she did, she knew that the tears would never stop.

'I'm coping, just about. You know – it *is* good to see you.' Miranda squeezed Georgina's arm, struggling to get her equilibrium back. 'It will be like old times, won't it?'

'Likewise – but I hope you don't mind me saying, you're looking awfully thin.'

'Six weeks of constant sea-sickness won't have helped,' she joked.

Georgina opened the front door, revealing a hallway with an impressive collection of artwork on the walls: a few portraits, a couple of landscapes, an abstract painting she didn't much like, all of it startlingly beautiful. Persian rugs in blue and red lay on highly polished marble floors and small palms in blue-and-white Chinoiserie were dotted between rosewood cabinets, while an antique carriage clock ticked softly on a chest of drawers. The swan's neck curve of a staircase rose up from the hall, to where she imagined a leisurely corridor leading to large bedrooms with sumptuous bathrooms, luxurious toiletries and armfuls of orchids.

'My God – it's amazing, Georgina. It's like something from *Gone with the Wind*! You're *very* lucky.'

'I know. Peter's uncle said we could stay here until he gets back from Malaya. After that, it will be Alexandra Gardens for us too, most likely. Come – look in here.'

They entered an oval room where French windows opened into an inner courtyard. In the centre of the room, eight rosewood chairs were arranged around a rectangular coffee table, which was covered in magazines and books. Whisky and sherry decanters glinted, along with cut-glass tumblers perched on a polished bureau.

'It reminds me of Howdean,' Miranda said. 'Do you remember when we did a midnight raid on Mrs Joseph's office and drank all that sherry stashed in her desk?'

'Just a bit,' Georgina grinned. 'Do you think they ever worked out it was us?'

'Probably. But she wasn't supposed to have it there, was she? Bloody dipsomaniac. But this is beautiful – how on earth did it survive the Occupation?'

'The servants hid most of it. Apparently, Chang Chang buried all the silver under the rosebushes. Come on! Let's have a drink.' She poured two generous gin and tonics, then raised her glass. 'Only way to prevent malaria. They say it's the quinine, but I think it's to relieve the boredom.'

Miranda's eyes wandered towards the piano. There was a framed picture of a man in full evening wear and a woman wearing a long silvery dress with gloves that reached up to her elbows and a diamond necklace glittering at her neck. The next photograph was of soldiers taking part in some kind of military ceremony on what looked like a parade ground.

'Don't say you get bored in a place like this? Isn't this Mountbatten?' She picked up the photograph of the military scene.

'Ah. Yes. Such a scandalous occasion that was.' Georgina's eyes lit up. 'Some people think he's too liberal, you know.'

'Why?'

'The Supreme Commander – honouring the Communists. It ruffled a few feathers, I can tell you, giving the commies a medal from the British Government. A cunning man, Mountbatten – it was a clever calculation to get the commies on our side. It even worked for a while.'

'And now?'

Georgina frowned. 'There have been a few nasty incidents recently. There was a rumour that the Brits have been creating a black market for rice here and roadblocks were put up at the docks to stop the locals storming the containers of rice just in from Malaya. A few got shot. Peter thinks the communists are behind it; propaganda, you know, inflaming the situation.'

'The locals must be desperate if they did something like that.'

'I wouldn't feel sorry for them. They hate the Brits, Miranda. Don't be deceived that they're glad to have us here running their country. Not only do they resent us, but they can't forgive us for the Occupation. Not after we let the Japs march right in over the causeway. See that photograph of Peter's aunt?'

Miranda picked up the other photograph. 'Yes?'

'She spent two years in prison at Changi. Almost bloody well killed her. The Japs rounded up all the women and marched them through the streets. They were desperate for water and not one single local helped them. Some even applauded.'

Georgina shrugged, her diamond earrings swinging. 'But this is a bit serious for a welcome evening, don't you think? What did you think of the book?'

'Gerry's had his nose in it since we arrived. And thank you for those fabulous orchids.'

'My pleasure. But, well, you'll let me know if you need any help or advice, won't you? Or if you're feeling a bit down.'

Miranda replaced the photograph – she didn't want their conversation to return to Henry. When she kept Georgina talking about other things, it was like re-living a happier section of her past. Surely there was something she could say to contain the moment or to keep the conversation light?

'Actually,' she said, grasping at the first thing that came into her head, 'Gerry needs some new suits.'

'Try Wing Loong's down at Dhobi Ghat. Peter says it's better than Anderson & Sheppard, but don't forget to barter.'

Georgina put down her glass. 'I think we'd better go back. Chang Chang's supposed to bring out some nibbles, but she gets a bit confused and we don't want the men getting too drunk, now do we?' She gave Miranda a wink and tucked her arm back into hers as they joined the others outside.

Back outside, she noticed that Gerry's face was already flushed and that his speech was slurred: she'd been right, he'd had too much to drink in the car before the party and she remembered that he'd started before they'd left home.

'Perhaps we shouldn't stay too late,' she whispered, slipping her hand into the crook of his arm, but he looked at her with such affection she couldn't be cross with him for long.

At dinner, she sat between Peter and Nick Wythenshaw.

'So,' she said to the young doctor once they had sat down, 'you're a doctor *and* you do medical research?'

'I'm a paediatrician, a children's doctor, really. The research is a side-line, but it helps to highlight issues, such as which diseases need focusing on and where we can get funding. It can be pretty desperate here at times.'

'How interesting. A children's hospital.'

'Well, it's more of a Catholic mission, really, and there's an orphanage attached to it. About a third of our numbers are made up by children with no one else to look after them.'

'Goodness. I used to volunteer at the local hospital during the war – mainly injured soldiers, though.'

'Really?' he asked, and his face lit up as he smiled. 'Do you miss it?'

'Yes,' she nodded.

When they had finished eating, Georgina stood up and announced she was going to play some music on the gramophone.

'I've got the latest Bing Crosby singles,' she said, 'as well as a Buddy Clarke. I insist that we all have at least one dance before the end of the evening.'

'That's not fair!' Peter said. 'There are only two ladies.'

'Count me out,' Gerry said. 'Think I'll sit here and watch.'

'Peter, you must dance with Miranda. I'll dance with Dickie.'

'Just the one,' Dickie said.

Peter took her by the hand and led her to a space on the floor, where they danced quietly to Crosby's crooning. Georgina looked even more beautiful in the softly lit room and Miranda envied her elegance, the way she carried herself with such ease.

The music stopped and Georgina put on another record.

'Right, we have to swap partners now.'

'Not me, I'm done in.' Dickie sat down on the nearest chair. 'Nick, be a gent, would you, and dance with Mrs Lewis? Can't let a lady dance alone, you know.'

Miranda glanced across at Gerry – he seemed to be dozing and she knew it was time to get home, but Nick had stood up and held out his hands to her, inviting her to dance.

'I'm not much good either,' he said, 'but if you lead me, I'll do my best.'

'Ah – this one's easy,' she said, as the music crackled into life. 'You just move around slowly and act like Fred Astaire.'

'More like Charlie Chaplin.' Nick took her hand and followed her lead, only tripping over her feet twice.

'Well,' Gerry stood up, swaying a little, when the music stopped, 'it's been a fabulous evening, but I think it's time for us to say goodnight.'

It was midnight by the time they arrived back at the house. Gerry missed the top step up to the verandah, then crashed into the cane chairs.

'Thank you, Jinhai, I think I can manage him from here,' she said, struggling.

'If you can't manage, you let me know-*lah*.' Jinhai bowed, then left them alone.

'Sssh! Gerry, this way.' Miranda guided him to their room, sitting him on the edge of the bed.

'Can you help me take off my shoes?'

'You've left them outside.'

'Have I?'

'Yes.'

'Ah. What are these on my feet, then?'

'They're your socks. How about some coffee, or some water?'

'Coffee or water,' Gerry said. 'Water or coffee. I don't know, you decide.'

She went to the kitchen, and, when she returned, Gerry was slumped on the bed with his mouth open, snoring. He looked unfamiliar, a stranger. The thought unsettled her. I suppose we don't know anyone as well as we think we do, she mused, placing the glass of water on the bedside table. She pulled off his socks and took off his tie, then she got ready for bed and switched off the lights.

In her dream, she was walking along the edge of a cliff above a deep valley in Singapore. Gerry was walking several paces ahead with a rifle slung over his shoulder. She was carrying something that was wrapped in layers of cloth; the weight made her clumsy, and she tripped against a stone. She landed on the path, then rolled towards the edge of the cliff. Words stuck as she tried to call Gerry. He strode ahead.

The ground started to crumble, and she fell. Miles beneath her lay the valley floor. She floated down towards it as if supported by an invisible parachute, and the wind carried her towards a river stretching the length of the valley between the toy-like trees.

The bundle slipped from her arms. She grabbed at it, but the cloth unwound and a small silver thread, like the string of a balloon, trailed from it. The dark, oval eyes of a child looked at her from the bundle. She swiped at it, but it spun and spiralled to the ground.

She plummeted, the wind roaring in her ears, but then, before she hit the ground, she jolted awake, and focused on the green fluorescence of the alarm clock and the hands pointing to half-past three. The bedroom was bathed in the half-light of the full moon, and all she could hear was the thrumming of crickets. Gerry lay on his side; she could just see his outline under the mosquito net and his chest rising and falling in the eerie light.

Heat prickled her skin, her head ached, and she needed a drink, so she went to the kitchen and filled a glass with water. In the moonlight she could see the trays that Mei Ling had already laid out for breakfast; a tea towel was draped on top of the crockery creating ghostly bumps.

She wandered outside to the two-seater sofa, where she curled up, half-listening to the pulsing chirp of crickets, longing for the warmth of the sunrise. But a mist hovered over the garden. She imagined it rolling in from the sea, long fingers of vapour creeping across the lawns and paths, trailing along the roads and on into the city, shrouding Singapore with a suffocating blanket. She dozed, imagining a cloud invading the island, creeping forever inwards and enveloping her in the mist.

Four

The following morning, Jinhai drove them to Dhobi Ghat.

'We'll walk from here,' Gerry said. 'Do a bit of exploring. You can wait for us over there.'

'Yes, sir. I'll wait under that tree until you're ready.'

They left Jinhai and the Vauxhall in a side street and walked along the path next to the Stamford Canal. Red, pink and green garments floated in the water, like giant water lilies.

'You can see why it's called Dhobi Ghat, can't you?' Gerry looked up from *The Stranger's Guide*. 'It means "washing place" in Hindi.'

There was such energy emanating from the groups of women pounding sheets against the stepping-stones, along with shouting from the washermen she knew were called *dhobis*, who were wearing nothing but loincloths. She loved the busyness of it all and the cacophony of voices, and she wished she could capture it for ever: the colours, the scent of jasmine and the streams of other *dhobis* balancing baskets of laundry on their heads.

Excitement bubbled everywhere. From the riverbank, a group of urchins threw stones, which landed in the water with heavy plops. She couldn't help but smile. One of the boys caught her looking. He hesitated for a moment, then ran towards her.

'We'd better get a move on,' Gerry glanced at the boy, 'if we're going to Wing Loong's before lunch.'

But she lingered, and the boy came closer, holding out his hand.

'Memsahib…'

It was difficult to tell how old the child was: his features appeared too big for his body, and there was hunger in his face – sharp as knives.

'Here you are.' She fumbled in her bag and dropped a few cents into his palm. 'Buy yourself something to eat.' Then she turned to catch up with Gerry. He was nowhere in sight.

Miranda dodged bicycles and rickshaws travelling in all directions, crossed the street and took in the scene around her. Despite her hat and the shade spanning the pavement from the awnings, she was sticky and uncomfortable. She had no idea where Gerry was, and none at all about where to find Wing Loong's.

After a moment, she saw him walking a few hundred feet ahead of her. Relieved, she pushed past the shoppers and hawkers crowding the pavement. He turned a corner, then another, but then she caught his face in profile and realised it wasn't him.

The sun was blistering, and all the unfamiliar streets looked the same. She dabbed her forehead with her handkerchief; this was the last thing she needed, even though she longed to explore, to try on the rattan hats hanging from doorways, to run her fingers through the trays of spices spread out on stalls spilling on to the streets. Why hadn't Gerry waited for her? She knew he'd be cursing that she'd gone and gotten herself lost. She thought of going back to the car and waiting for him there, but she couldn't remember where they'd left it. It might be better, she thought, if she made her way back to the canal – surely he'd come back to look for her? She took another turn, but realised she was now completely lost.

'Dhobi Ghat?' she asked a thin man carrying buckets of water. He shook his head, muttering something in Chinese and nodded in the direction of a path.

Uncertain, she followed it. The roads became alleys, and shops gave way to shacks. Finally, she entered a large open area where bougainvillea mingled among the boughs of trees that cast shade across the street.

In the shadows, she saw a group of hawkers selling papayas and mangoes. She crossed towards them. A young Malay woman sat on her haunches, and four or five small fish were lying on the pavement, slowly cooking in the ambient heat. From a sarong tied between the lower branches of a tree, a baby was crying, and a little boy was trailing a stick about in the dirt.

The woman stood up as she approached.

'You wan' buy-*lah*?'

'No, thanks. I don't suppose you can tell me how to find Dhobi Ghat?'

'Lady, you buy. Fresh pomfret very good. I give you best price.'

She looked at the pomfret. The heads were buzzing with flies, and their glassy eyes had turned opaque in the heat. The smell made her queasy. She shook her head.

'Fifty cent.'

She turned to go, but the boy ran by her side, still dragging his stick.

'Lay-*dee*, fifty cent! Fifty cent *onleee*!' He wiped his nose with the back of his hand, looking at her, his dark lashes crusted with sleep. She ignored him and strode on.

'*Please*, lay-*dee*, buy fish,' the woman called. 'My son sick. I mus' buy medicine.'

Miranda came to a standstill, halted by the pain in the woman's voice. An image of how still Henry had been that awful day, of how cold his skin had felt as she had touched him flickered in her mind. She retraced her steps back to the woman squatting in the shade.

'How much did you say the fish were?'

'One fish, fifty cent only. Very nice. Fresh this morning.'

'All right, I'll take them all.'

The woman picked up the pomfret from the pavement and wrapped them in old newspaper. 'You nice lady, I give you all two dollar.'

Miranda took the packet from her and handed her a note. 'Dhobi Ghat?'

'Very close, lady, just five-minute walk.' The woman pointed over Miranda's shoulder.

As she left, she heard the woman calling: 'Lay-*dee*, you give me too much money-*lah*.' But she walked on, pretending that she hadn't heard. She found a quiet place

44

at the canal away from all the bustle and sat on the bank holding the packet of fish. The paper was wet, and the moisture leaked on to her hands, so she threw the packet as far as she could into the water. Minutes passed. She listened to the shouts of the *dhobis* calling to each other and to the chatter and laughter of the women on the bank and wondered how long it would be before she would make a group of friends herself and settle properly here in Singapore. Real friends, that was, not merely acquaintances – people who would understand her and with whom she could relax, not just the important contacts that Gerry wanted her to make.

'There you are! Where the heck have you been?' She jumped as a hand touched her shoulder, lifting her thoughts back to the present and to the men and women in the water.

She looked up to see Gerry, his frame silhouetted by the sun.

'Miranda? Where've you been? I've been looking for you everywhere.'

'I'm sorry, I got lost. I came back here and was watching all the activity. I was miles away.'

'Well, I reckon we should find somewhere to get a drink now. This heat is blistering and both of us will have had too much sun.'

She nodded. 'Good idea. That would be nice.'

'Come on.' He took her hand, pulling her to stand. 'I saw some expats at that café over there – might be a good place.'

They found a table.

After the sun on the canal side, sitting under the covered walkway was like dipping into a cool stream. The café was noisy, and she could hear music on a nearby radio. Sinatra – it seemed so out of place. A fly landed on her collar. She swiped it away.

'Here, shall we try this?' Gerry took a glass of tea from the *chai-wallah* and placed it on the table in front of her.

She examined the milky brown liquid, the droplets clinging to the side of the glass, then lifted it and sipped. It was warm and sweet, with a hint of something spicy: cardamom. Gerry dropped a few cents into the man's hand.

'You know,' she began, 'I really do like Singapore, but watching the *dhobi*s made me think about the women I used to volunteer with at home. We used to have so much fun, and it meant so much to me after Henry died. Coming here – it's made me feel mixed up and unsettled again. I wonder if there isn't something I can do?'

'Like what?'

She leant forward, her elbows on the table.

'I could volunteer again. At a school or a hospital. Doesn't that doctor we met work at a children's hospital? I'd love that, and I might make some friends.'

He was silent for a moment, took a sip of his tea, then said, 'It's an admirable idea, but we've only just arrived. Don't you have enough to do, settling in?'

'Of course. But what about after that?'

'Give it some time, Miranda.' He took her hand. 'You're still fragile. And while it's a very noble thing to do, the nurses here, well, are they the right kind of people?'

She frowned. 'The "right kind people"? What on earth can you mean?'

'Look,' he tapped the ash forming on the end of his cigarette to the ground, 'coming to Singapore is a great opportunity for us both. You've already had a taste of that on the ship. Besides, Longland said, if I play my cards right, I might get a promotion in six months. You have to remember that as we make new friends, how important it is to move in better circles. The ex-pat society here is so much more conscious of status – just think what it will look like if my wife's working. I can't allow it.'

He lowered his voice as he glanced about, then he lifted his face a little shyly to hers, the blue of his eyes shining, 'And, who knows, we might even try for another baby?'

His words felt like a ball slamming into her stomach.

'You know I'm not ready for another baby.' The thought of it horrified her – of course she loved him, more than anything, but even the idea of sex, of being so intimate, was something she wasn't ready for. In fact, the idea of it sickened her.

'But I thought, coming here, we could start to try again.'

'Gerry—' she shook her head. 'You know I want to, but I need more time.'

He sighed and his features sagged, then his gaze turned to the street for a moment before he turned back to her.

'So that's it is. Volunteering's the answer, is it? Not even a shred of ambition to try to better yourself? We have to move forward – I won't allow you to wear yourself out on things that aren't important. And what the hell is the point of everything I've done to get us here if we simply return to square one?'

'Isn't what I want to do important? And I do have ambitions: a need for a purpose other than parties and lunches and whatever else it is that expatriate wives do with their time. Can't we at least talk about it?'

'No.' He withdrew his hand from hers. 'That's the end of it. Do you hear? I'm not having my wife let me down before we've even got started. Now,' he glanced at his watch, 'we're running behind as it is, we should get a move on.'

'I don't see why you can't think about it – even if it's when we're more settled.' Disappointment made her voice rise a tone.

'Sssh. People are looking at us.' His jaw clenched and he shook his head. 'Come on. I think we should go.'

'Well, I'm not ready.' She gripped the edge of her bag. 'You're always dismissing me and what I want. Why can't you consider my feelings for a change?'

'For goodness sake! When do I *not* do that?' He stood, scraping back his chair, and left.

Minutes passed. Anger and frustration exploded in her head. She finished the dregs of her tea, trying to compose herself, and when she was a little calmer, she took a compact and a lipstick from her bag and was re-applying her makeup when one of the other expats in the café asked for the radio to be tuned to the World Service. After a moment, she heard the clipped tones of a newsreader's voice from the wireless.

48

'Mr Anderson of Johor Province, his wife and four children are thought to have been shot in their sleep. Plantation workers were also found dead or injured, and buildings were destroyed by fire. The Colonial Office is warning expatriates in Malaya to be extra vigilant.'

Icy fingers seemed to tickle her neck at the thought of all those children ... but she couldn't allow herself to spiral. She snapped her bag shut. Really, she ought to find Gerry. He was probably right. She needed to settle here first – make the contacts, then friends would follow. She could always bring it up again later when they'd had a chance to settle and he wasn't so anxious about his job.

He was standing in the shade on the street, turning the pages of his book. At her approach, he lifted his head, but he said nothing, and they walked on together in silence through the maze of covered pavements, taking in the piles of Chinese slippers and the rolls of fabric stacked outside the shops. She searched his face, hoping to catch his eye so that they could talk, but he stared straight ahead, casting his eyes occasionally downwards to check the map in his hands.

Five

The following week, Georgina arranged to collect Miranda at eleven to take her to Holland Village.

'It's where all the expats go,' Georgina had explained. 'There's a little shopping centre and back streets with local shops selling everything you could possibly need. We could go for a bite to eat after.'

But instead of being ready, Miranda sat on the bedroom floor with her battered tin box. However much she had tried to silence the past, flashes of it kept returning like waves crashing on to the shore. She picked up Henry's brush. How soft the bristles were, reminding her of his baby-soft head and the aroma of talcum powder and shampoo after she had bathed him. The brush had been a gift from her parents: ivory handled and silver backed, but yet no bigger in total than her hand; such a delicate and beautiful object. She ran her thumb over the bristles; his scent still lingered and it almost choked her as she recalled the last time she had used it. It had been the morning of his funeral, before his coffin was sealed, and when she could finally pull herself away from stroking his hair, she had placed the brush gently in her handbag.

There had been a dozen or so people at the church; she remembered her parents, as well as Gerry's, his sister and a few friends.

Impossible as it had been, she tried not to cry as she followed Gerry into the church. He carried Henry's coffin, his jaws set and his face staring resolutely ahead, but grief consumed her as her sobbing ricocheted around the silent church. Her hands hurt so much as she dug her nails into her palms and she could feel her legs shaking.

Back at their house, guests, tea, cake and sandwiches appeared from nowhere. People wanted to speak to her, to tell her how sorry they were. All she wanted to do was to push them away, to be left alone with the emptiness consuming her. Then Lily touched her arm, her head held high and proud like a thoroughbred.

'I'm so sorry, Miranda. You do know that we are both devastated, don't you? A sudden death – so cruel.'

Lily. Miranda had never been certain of her mother-in-law's feelings and was taken aback by her comment. The ill-disguised disdain she had shown Miranda when she'd started walking out with Gerry was palpable and little had changed after Henry had been born. Unlike her own parents, she hadn't given up her time to spend it with the new baby. In fact, she'd held him for as short a time as possible at the christening and had hardly visited after that.

You could have shown more affection or support, she wanted to scream. *Welcomed me as Gerry's wife, shown me at least once that you were pleased to be grandparents.*

But the words stuck in her throat and all she could do was shake her head. She opened her bag to take out a handkerchief, and as she reached inside, her fingers had grazed the bristles of his brush.

And now, as she placed the brush back inside the tin box, she wondered again why Lily had never liked her nor shown much interest in Henry. How easy it would have been, even if it was only for Gerry's sake.

She stood up and put the box back into her dressing-table drawer. It was a good idea that Georgina was coming to take her out. A day catching up on old times and buying knick-knacks for the house was just what she needed to chase away the ghosts of the past. But as she pulled on a yellow striped sundress, she sensed the stubbornness of her mood and she prayed that it might lift.

After a time, she heard the crunch of gravel. She picked up her hat and bag, then made her way out to the car that she knew was waiting for her on the drive.

'Don't you look a picture!' Georgina smiled, as her chauffeur opened the car door to let Miranda join her on the back seat. 'I've asked Adi to take us to Holland Village first – there are some glorious lamps and fabrics there. Then, if you're up to it, how about Orchard Road and C. K. Tang's?'

'Sounds perfect.'

'You know, I keep pinching myself that you're here.' Georgina beamed. 'So much has happened since we left school, hasn't it? But here we are like two old pennies that have turned up in the same place. Incredible, really.'

Miranda glanced at Georgina's face. She was right: time had passed and so much had changed for them both, but good friends, real friends, could pick up anywhere – and Georgina had always been the best.

They drove for about twenty minutes, away from the expanse of bungalows set in the leafy jungle, along palm-lined roads. She leant close to the window, enjoying the warmth of the sun on her skin and the gentle breeze ruffling her hair.

All along the roads, people had set up stalls: *chai-wallahs*, newspaper stands, vegetable or fruit stands, all mixed up with washing hanging on poles stretching across the street. Like a kaleidoscope, the colours were clear and strong, and appeared to keep changing form or shape as the car drove along. The Chinese women wore mainly black or white, she noticed; the Indians, meanwhile, wore jewel-like saris – she loved watching them all going about their shopping or chattering in tongues she couldn't understand. Outside in the sun, the women appeared leisurely, enjoying their chores, unlike the hurried shopping in the rain or cold she was used to on London streets.

The car slowed as they reached a settlement that spanned across both sides of the road. Hugging one pavement, there was a row of small houses with gardens at the front, on the other, a double-storied building with a parade of shops standing on the curve of the road.

Miranda continued to examine it – everything was all so fascinating, she didn't want to miss any of it. And she tried not to be distracted by Georgina's chatter about which hardware stores were best for household goods and where to buy the best silk lampshades. Miranda nodded; she should have been excited about the shopping, but her mood suddenly became flat and stubborn once again.

Adi parked the car and, as they walked towards the row of shops, Georgina linked her arm in Miranda's. Adi followed in tow, to carry their shopping.

'Now, welcome to Aladdin's Cave!' Georgina gestured towards the row of buildings ahead. 'Where would you like to begin?'

Miranda took in the shops. They didn't look very promising; the buildings were tumbledown and men wearing sarongs chatted to each other on the pavements outside. A few European women hung around the entrances to the shops with nervous expressions on their faces.

'Some lamps would be good, and some fabric for cushions – the ones in the bungalow are past it.' She pulled out a list from her bag. 'I was thinking of greens or blues. What do you think?'

'Let's see what they've got.' Georgina guided her to a shop in the middle of the row. Miranda gasped as they went inside. There were lamps of all shapes and sizes, and each of their bases seemed to be made from what looked like old Chinese artefacts – some were porcelain vases, others brass figures – but then the shades were ever more glorious. She'd only ever seen conical-shaped ones at home in England, but here they came in all designs, some were even shaped like pagodas.

'Heavens! These are extraordinary.'

'They're all silk,' Georgina said, picking up a large boxy shade.

Miranda glided through the aisles, picking up shades and bases. Georgina was right, it was just like Aladdin's Cave. Eventually, she chose three lamps and shades, then they pottered around examining local goods, in case there was anything else that took her eye, until she discovered a collection of Chinese watercolours.

'I like these,' she said. 'The colours are exquisite. I could put them in the sitting room and pick out the emerald and cobalt for cushions.'

'A deep ruby too, perhaps, to set them off?'

'Or gold?'

Time passed quickly as she examined each painting then settled on two, which she put to one side. Georgina was looking at jade ornaments, which ranged in colour from pale white to the darkest of green.

'The darker colour is the best,' Georgina explained. 'And jade, of course, is extremely lucky.'

'I like these earrings.' Miranda pointed to a pair of droplets

'Why don't you get them? But you know you'll need to bargain the shopkeeper down?'

'Really?' Miranda hesitated. 'I don't know how.'

'It's easy. Start below half-price then walk away if he won't play ball. Or ask for something else to be thrown in.'

Next to the earrings was an ivory tie-pin. It would make a lovely present for Gerry, she thought, so she decided to try her hand at bargaining.

'How much? For all of this – the pictures, the lamps and the earrings?'

'Five dollars,' the shopkeeper said.

'Oh,' Miranda feigned disappointment and made a pretence of looking in her wallet. 'That's more than I wanted to pay, especially as I want to get that tie-pin for my husband. Could you possibly add it in?'

The shopkeeper shook his head and so Miranda snapped her wallet closed.

'Well, I think I'd better leave it.'

Georgina took her arm and they walked towards the door, but as they reached it, the shopkeeper called out, agreeing to her offer.

She paid and, as the shopkeeper wrapped the items in brown paper, Georgina squeezed her arm.

'Oh my goodness!' Miranda laughed, as they left the shop. 'That was *such* fun!'

'Yes, it always is when it works like that.' Georgina smiled but her face was glowing from the humidity. 'How about we get a cold drink? I don't know about you,' she said, 'but I'm parched. Adi – take all this back to the car, please, and then come back and get us from the hawker stand along Holland Avenue.'

'Hawker stand?' Miranda asked.

'Street café to us.'

Georgina led her to the hawker stand, where they could sit in chairs on the wide, covered pavement that ran parallel to the shops.

'This area is gloriously cool.' Miranda flopped on to her chair. 'It's so good to get out of the heat. What a good idea to cover the pavements like this.'

'It's called a five-foot way,' Georgina explained. 'It's designed to hide the shops and to keep everyone cool when walking, but the locals keep setting up shop in them.'

A Chinese man approached them and asked what they would like.

'Two mango juices, please.'

'Are you sure this place is safe?' Miranda's gaze followed the man, who walked towards a basket of mangoes and a small table of glasses soaking in a bowl. 'Clean, I mean?'

Georgina smiled, and put her hand on Miranda's. 'Of course. And just you wait until you taste the mango juice.'

Their drinks arrived and Miranda sipped hers through a straw with caution.

'My goodness, I've never had anything like this before – it's like a really thick, sweet orange juice. Thank you so much. I really needed all this today.'

'It's my pleasure. Now, tell me, how are you and Gerry settling in?' Georgina asked.

Miranda frowned, and the mango juice seemed to stick in her throat.

'Something wrong?' Georgina said.

Miranda took another sip of her drink as she thought. Right now, she realised she wanted a friend to talk to.

'To be honest,' she twisted the straw in her glass, 'I'm finding it harder to adjust here than I thought.'

'It takes time.'

'I know. But already there's something about being here that has unsettled me, which, at the same time, seems to have changed Gerry in a different way. I can't really explain.'

'Why don't you just try?'

'Well,' she took a deep breath, 'after Henry died, I found it helpful to volunteer at the local hospital. I'd even thought about training to be a nurse. I didn't really tell Gerry about it, but when we went to Dhobi Ghat the other day, I had an idea about doing something similar here – it would give me a purpose and I could make friends. When I asked him about it, he wouldn't even talk about it. He's more concerned about his career and what people will say than how I feel.' She jabbed the straw hard into her drink. 'I don't understand what the harm would be, do you?'

'It's different out here, Miranda. And you know what men are like – he probably wants to simply look after you and doesn't like the idea of you working; it's a bit emasculating, don't you think, for men if their wives have to go out to work?'

'But it's only volunteering!'

Georgina raised her eyebrow. 'But why do it? There's so much else to do here and so many people to meet, shops to discover – and then there's the Tanglin Club. You haven't even been, have you? It's such fun, and there are so many opportunities to socialise with other Englishmen's wives who have found themselves out here. Embrace it and enjoy it. None of us know how long it will last.'

Miranda paused for a moment, forming her thoughts. Could she tell Georgina how ill she'd become after Henry had died? How she had lost herself, wandered around London, taking tiny things that didn't matter from the shops? That volunteering had helped keep her on a better path?

Georgina was resting her hand on Miranda's. 'I know it's tough coming out here, especially for us women, and goodness knows that you've had more to cope with than most, but he's right. You need to support Gerry in his job. He's got a tough role being in charge of the new social housing programme – there will be days when he's dead on his feet, others when you'll have to entertain important guests. Take my advice and put this notion to bed – in a few weeks' time, you'll be so busy, you'll see that I was right.'

'Perhaps.' She smiled, but Miranda couldn't help feeling disappointed that even Georgina didn't see the situation as she did.

'Good!' Georgina lifted her glass. 'Now finish that drink – we've got plenty more shopping to do.'

Miranda returned home laden with bolts of silk, pictures and lampshades, along with a promise from Georgina that next time she'd take her on a tour of the financial district along Battery Road, and Raffles Place, before hitting the jewellery quarter.

'The buildings are impressive in that part of town,' Georgina said. 'And there are some wonderful jade and pearl shops, if you know where to look.'

Miranda spent the next hour placing lamps on tables and pictures on walls, mulling over the day. Then, later, she found a piece of blue ribbon in her sewing box and used it to tie a bow around the boxed tie-pin.

As six o'clock approached, she changed into a white linen dress, mixed herself a gin and tonic, and then she waited for Gerry in the drawing room while listening to a record on the gramophone – Glen Miller, *In the Mood*.

She looked out of the window, sipping her drink, slowly swaying from side to side in time to the music. Again, her thoughts turned to Georgina – how good the day out had been, and how nice it had been to have her spirits lifted. Dancing like this, sipping a drink and listening to music, brought back memories of the days even before she knew Gerry, of the times when she and Georgina used to go out and dance until dawn. Perhaps, after all, she ought to let go of the idea of doing things just for herself – get her satisfaction and fulfilment from being a full-time housewife.

A footstep fell and she turned her head. Gerry.

'Is it a party for one, or can anyone join in?'

She swivelled around and watched him pouring a drink.

'It's a party for two now,' she said. She went to him and kissed him on the cheek. 'Good day?'

'All right. Lots of paperwork. Looks like you've had a busy day too.' He gave a nod at the silk she'd laid out on the sofa. 'Like the lamps too.'

'I went shopping with Georgina. I can't tell you how much she knows about Singapore – all the best shops and places to eat.'

'I bet she does.'

Gerry sat down in an armchair and stretched out his legs. She waited for him to settle, then she sat on the arm and placed her arm loosely around his neck and took his gift from her pocket.

'I bought you a present,' she said.

'Oh, sweetheart, you needn't have done that.' He opened the box and took out the pin. 'It's beautiful.'

He lifted his face to hers and she bent to kiss him.

'Shall I put it on for you?'

'Go on!'

He pulled her towards him, and she fell into his lap and both of them laughed. It was a perfect moment, reminiscent of when they had first met – deliciously long evenings curled together on the sofa or in bed. There was a time when nothing else had mattered but the two of them and the invincibility of their love. But as she sat on his lap, a niggling doubt grew, and, however hard she tried, she seemed unable to push it away.

Six

The last outpatients had left St Augustin's Mission Hospital, and the corridors were empty. Although technically off the clock, Nick Wythenshaw still had paperwork to get through, but as he sat at his desk, he pushed the pile of folders in front of him to one side and re-opened the letter that he'd been carrying around with him all day. Each time he read it, it was as though a scorpion had stung him and the pain coursed through him all over again.

My Dearest Nick,

I hope that this letter finds you well. I know that you said you wanted me to give a little more thought to us deciding to end things, and that we said we wouldn't write for a while, until we were certain, but there is something I have to say. You see, I feel that I need to be more honest with you. I really hope that you won't take what I'm going to say too badly, but it has been torturing me. I don't know where to start, if I'm honest, and it really pains me to tell you that I've been walking out with someone else. His name is William Harvey, and one thing led to another and now I'm expecting. William's a lovely man, and he's going to do the honourable thing – Nick, I'm so sorry to tell you in this way, but we're going to get married.

I know that this will be the worst kind of blow to you, but I want you to know that I did, and perhaps I still do, love you.

Nick scrunched up the letter and let it drop. The news had floored him: Daphne, the love of his life, soon to be married and expecting another man's child. Of course, it had been foolish to expect her to wait when he'd come out to Singapore two years earlier, but he'd always nurtured the hope that ... he wasn't entirely sure what he'd hoped. But this – with a baby on the way. It was difficult to believe.

He took a deep breath and looked out of the window, trying to calm his feelings. In less than a minute his world had irretrievably shifted. From the window, he could see an orderly sweeping leaves, bougainvillea petals floating through the air like confetti, but all he could think of was the image of Daphne in a wedding dress in the arms of a man he couldn't visualise.

What was the point of any of it? he wondered. All he'd ever wanted to do was to make sure that he could provide for her properly before she came out here. They'd both agreed it was for the best. Now he could see that he'd got so busy with work that he'd probably become too distant, and she might have taken it as a sign that he wasn't ready to commit.

Now the career that he'd been trying to carve out for them both suddenly seemed meaningless. What was he going to do? Was his life always destined to be filled with sadness? It had been bad enough when his brother Freddie had died, but Daphne, his childhood sweetheart, had pulled him through it.

He ran his hands through his hair in frustration. It was one thing on top of another. Apart from Daphne, while the take up for smallpox vaccinations was growing, there wasn't enough money from the social welfare plan for both the smallpox vaccinations and the tuberculosis screening programme, so it was proving impossible to balance the books. As far as he could see, the Mission needed more cash if it was to continue at the level it was currently operating at, and that was before the children's free meals were taken into account. No doubt Alice Matthews, the centre's manager, would be on his back again, with more messages of gloom and doom from the board meeting. What the hell was he going to do?

Get a grip, man, he told himself. He clutched the side of the desk as he remembered the advertisement he'd read earlier that day for medical staff in the Philippines. Was it time for a change, or would he be running away again?

He opened the drawer of his desk and took out a copy of *The Medical Weekly:*

Staff needed for Children's Hospital Project in the Philippines – including builders, community developers, medical and nutritional staff, and teachers of English.

64

It was a similar advertisement that had brought him to Singapore. Now, after nearly two years, he wondered if it was again time for a change. He'd given so much of his time to St Augustin's, but his faith in the system, let alone his belief in his own abilities, was beginning to dwindle.

Nick heard hurried footsteps in the corridor, and Nurse Li, a Chinese woman in her early twenties, who was wearing a white uniform and a starched nurse's cap, appeared at the door. He pushed the copy of *The Medical Weekly* back into the drawer.

'Dr Wythenshaw, Sister Bryant says come quick.'

'Why? What's wrong?'

'You best come straight away.'

Nick followed Nurse Li to the ward, where six beds were arranged on either side of the room. In each lay a boy between eight and twelve years of age. Above the patients, mosquito nets were rolled up and tied to the ceiling, like the folded sails on a boat. Sister Bryant, the ward sister, stood next to a young boy who was lying with his eyes wide open. It was Chen, the boy with advanced tuberculosis of the bones. A thin line of blood trickled from his mouth, pooling on the white sheet.

Nick felt for a pulse, noting the flexibility in Chen's joints, the way his jaw had relaxed, and how his body had lost all of its muscular tension. He placed his ear close to the boy's mouth and listened for a moment, then stood up straight and shook his head.

'Time of death,' he looked at his watch, 'five forty-seven.'

Sister Bryant nodded briefly and pulled the curtain around the bed.

'I'll write the certificate before I go home,' Nick said softly, before glancing back at Chen.

Sister Bryant was brushing the boy's hair lightly with her fingers. 'Dear God,' she crossed herself, 'I claim him for the Kingdom, and I release his spirit to you. I cover him in the blood of Jesus. And in Jesus's name I pray.'

Usually their religion wouldn't bother him, but today he felt tempted to tell Sister Bryant that he didn't damn well believe in God, and that, as Chen was Buddhist, all her prayers were lost on him. Then he felt irritated with himself for being uncharitable; after all, once the orphaned boy was buried at the municipal graveyard at Bukit Brown, no one would think about him again. Chen, like all the other children, deserved this one last moment of tenderness and respect.

He went back to his desk and signed the death certificate, then made his way out towards his Jaguar roadster, which was parked beneath a banyan tree. A twenty-first birthday present from his grandmother; he knew it was extravagant to have had it shipped out to Singapore, but it kept him connected to a happier past. For a moment, he paused and sat in the driver's seat thinking about Chen, then he turned the ignition and drove away from the hospital into the maze of streets that made up Tanjong Pagar market and out towards Raymond Road. As he reached the long stretch of open track hugging the coast, he put his foot down hard on the accelerator.

Twenty minutes later, he arrived at Alexandra Gardens. The lights were on again in number five, where the Lewises, the new couple he had met at the party the other evening, lived, and he thought he saw movement on the verandah. The roadster clambered up the drive towards Belvedere – the red Malacca-tiled house that he shared with fellow doctors Charlie Moffatt and Brendan Watts. In the distance, he could hear the thud of tennis balls on rackets and the occasional burst of laughter. He looked at his watch: twenty-five past six. It would be getting dark in half an hour, by which time Brendan and Charlie would have finished their game.

On the terrace, Khalish, the houseboy, was splashing water on the rolled-down chick blinds to cool the rooms inside. Khalish raised his hand at Nick in greeting.

Nick got out of the car and made his way towards him.

'Evening, *tuan*,' Khalish said, as he placed the bucket on the ground. 'Nice day. Not many mosquito.'

'That's good. Do you think it will rain later?' Nick smiled. Khalish was one of the orphanage's success stories. Riddled with worms and malnutrition and weighing less than five stone at the age of fourteen when he'd been admitted, Nick had doubted that Khalish would survive. But here he was, determined to make the most of his chances, learning English in his spare time and even wanting to become a teacher.

'No, *tuan*. The flowers on the rain tree are still open. I tell you before, rain only coming when the flower be close.'

67

'When the flowers are closed,' Nick corrected.

'Yes, *tuan* – when the flowers are closed. Would you like that I get you something to drink? Water? Whisky soda?'

'Thank you, but it's all right, Khalish. I'll do it.'

The first thing Nick saw when he entered the house was the pile of letters on the hall table. He flicked through them absently: bills and medical journals, a letter from England. He poured a whisky from the drinks cabinet and went to his room, where he threw his keys and post down on to his desk, sat down, picked up his pen and began to proofread the report he'd typed the night before:

The death rate in Singapore is currently twice the pre-war level. Most diseases are caused by malnutrition and poverty. By the time patients seek help from Western medicine and hospitals, diseases, such as tuberculosis of the bone, have reached an advanced stage. We are trying to tackle the issues in various ways. A mass vaccination programme has been offered at St Augustin's along with screening and feeding the children. The centre examines, on average, 875 patients and provides 2,600 free meals each month. While this is admirable, the social welfare budget doesn't cover the expense, and the centre is receiving more and more children at its doors every day.

Although education is a key factor in improving standards, 95 per cent of locals are illiterate. Any progress requires a three-pronged approach. Firstly, by teaching the locals to speak English as a common language; secondly,

*through better living conditions; and finally through
teaching the local women to become nurses. In doing this,
the nurses can reach out to locals in a way that, owing to
suspicion of Western medicine, Europeans can't.*

He could hear the door opening, Charlie cursing and
Brendan laughing, followed by the clink of a bottle on glass.

'Want a drink, Wythenshaw?' Brendan called.

'Already got one, thanks.'

'Well, come and join us, then!'

He got up and leant in the doorframe. Charlie was rubbing his hair with a towel and it stood up like a brush.

'Thought we'd go to the Capitol later. They're showing
The Third Man. Do you want to join us?

'I don't think so.' He took another sip of his whisky. 'I
think I'll get an early night.'

'Come on, don't be such a miserable old sod.' Brendan
grinned. 'I know you're working on that paper, but even
Einstein needs a break.'

'Sorry, I'm just tired.' He rubbed his eyes. 'But you're
right. I'll join you.'

'Thought we could go to the Sea View after, get a curry
and grab a couple of drinks,' Charlie added.

Nick didn't want to go, but the three of them had
formed a bond as expats away from home, buoying each
other up when their spirits weakened. Perhaps all he
really needed was a good night out. He nodded.

'God, I'm a bit sick of curry, aren't you?' Charlie lit a
cigarette. 'Could kill for some fish and chips. Last time I

had them was in Brighton – a November weekend with a lady friend.'

'Honestly!' Brendan rolled his eyes. 'Bet that's not all he's pining for!' he winked at Nick.

'What about you, Wythenshaw?' Brendan asked. 'What do you miss?'

Daphne.

'Oh, I don't know – everything and nothing.' That was true, in a way, but, still, he couldn't get her image out of his mind.

'Well, I don't think it's such a bad old life out here. Apart from the lack of girls, that is.' Charlie grinned.

Brendan threw a tennis ball at Charlie, 'For goodness sake – trust you!'

Charlie threw the ball back. 'Wythenshaw, you all right to drive us again?'

If he was being honest, Nick was increasingly unhappy with them all squashing into the front of a car that was only made for two, but not wanting to be a killjoy, he nodded and said, 'Sure.'

Feet away from the Sea View Hotel, pale moonlight illuminated the waves breaking on the shoreline. Nick made his way with Charlie and Brendan to a table on the long verandah and sat beneath the electric fans. While the waiter brought them cold beers, Nick listened to the soothing rhythm of the water and to the monkeys chattering in a nearby grove of coconut trees.

'That was the best film I've seen for a bloody long time.' Brendan leant forward as the waiter placed three bottles of Tiger beer on the table. He took a bottle and gulped a third of it down.

'It was certainly atmospheric, but could have done with a spirit level on the camera.' Charlie turned to him. 'What do you think, N. W.?'

Nick's thoughts had kept flicking away from the black-and-white images on screen to the memory of Daphne; the ring he'd never bought but had always thought that one day he might place on her finger.

'N. W.?'

He looked up. Charlie and Brendan were waiting for him to say something.

'Well,' he began, 'I've always liked Orson Wells – *Citizen Kane* is one of my favourite films.' His knew his reply was weak and non-committal.

'I think the atmosphere was spot on – captures post-war Vienna brilliantly,' Brendan added.

'Been, have you?' Charlie winked at him.

'No, but I have an imagination – unlike some.' Brendan smiled, then picked up his menu. 'So, are we all having curry?'

'Oh, go on, then.' Charlie leant back in his chair, 'And let's have some more beers while we're at it.'

'There's a cabaret later.' Brendan closed his menu and signalled to the waiter. 'Billie Jackson's on her way to Oz for a Christmas show. Heard she's pretty good, actually.'

'Why not?' Nick agreed, but his heart wasn't in it. Everything felt out of kilter – like the oddly presented images in the film.

'Do you ever wonder if you've made the right choice?' Nick asked.

'It's too late now,' Charlie joked. 'Order's been placed.'

'Not the food. I mean about coming out here, instead of joining a practice back in England.'

'No. Never.' Brendan paused for a moment. 'What's brought this on?'

Nick hesitated, weighing up in his mind what he wanted to say; he didn't want to tell them about Daphne, nor that he was toying with the idea of leaving Singapore, but they were looking at him, expecting him to give an explanation for his throwaway thoughts.

'I was meant to take over my father's practice in Harley Street,' he began. The others leant forward. 'But I didn't want to. It wouldn't have worked, working with my father's rich female patients when there's still so much to put right for the poor children of this world. When this opportunity came along to come out here, I had to take it. I guess I didn't think of the consequences.'

'But isn't that why we're all out here?' Brendan said. 'Our careers lead us to places we wouldn't expect and that means we have to make some difficult sacrifices.'

'Don't you ever wonder if it's the right decision? My mother said I was running away. What if she's right – if I'm out here burying my head in the sand?'

The alcohol was making Nick pensive and wistful and he wondered if the others were feeling the same way.

'Perhaps we all are. But the rewards are different, though, aren't they?' Brendan leant back in his chair, as though assessing him. 'Whatever the cost – personal or otherwise.'

'I suppose.' Nick paused. 'But sometimes things get to you, don't they? Once in a while, a death or lack of funds or medicine makes you so angry, so frustrated.'

'Yes.' Brendan nodded in agreement. 'But you've got to let it go, old chap, try not to care so damn much. We're just cogs in a wheel. Remember – patch them up and send them home.'

'But what if I want to be part of a bigger picture?'

Brendan and Charlie exchanged a glance. 'Look,' Brendan began, 'all this stuff you're doing – the government papers, the extra hours – it's wearing you out. No one's saying stop caring, but it's like you're on a one-man crusade to nowhere. Why don't you get a job at the hospital with us? We could do with more doctors like you at Kandang Kerabu.'

'Like I said, obstetrics is my father's thing, not mine.'

'No, but the hours are shorter, and the nurses are pretty.'

'True,' Charlie added. 'But he's got to do what he feels is right.'

Brendan took a long sip of his beer and then their eyes met for a moment. It was as though Brendan was searching his soul for some deeper meaning.

'It's not easy.' Brendan dropped his voice a level. 'I understand what it's like – running away from the past, living in the shadows.'

Nick felt the hair follicles on his neck and arms contract. *Freddie*. Could Brendan know about his death, or how much Nick blamed himself for what had happened? It was impossible, surely, but it had made the papers at the time, with his father being an eminent doctor.

'You know what your problem is, don't you?' Charlie passed a packet of cigarettes around. Nick took one, noticing that his fingers shook. Charlie held up a lighter. 'You're an idealist.'

Nick was about to protest when the waiter approached the table with their plates, a large bowl of rice and another of curry, and Nick found that he no longer had the energy to keep up their debate.

'Mmm. This smells good.' Brendan held his fork above his plate. 'And for once the rice doesn't appear to be mixed with tapioca.'

After they'd eaten, Brendan asked, 'So, how about the cabaret?' He wiped his fingers on his napkin. 'I'm sure we can still get a table.'

Nick shook his head. 'No. Not yet. I need some air. I think I'll go for a walk along the beach – I'll join you later.'

He made his way along the sand. There was music in the distance and lights were blazing on the ships out at sea. He took his shoes and socks off and began to walk along the edge of the water. The light of the full moon reflected on the waves cast a kind of brightness, like a ghostly version of daylight.

Nick sat down and looked out towards the ships. Singapore was safe for now, but this small island, like him, had experienced so many changes – the scars were still raw for them both. He lit a cigarette and watched the glow of the tobacco burning in his hand, then he took his wallet from his pocket and pulled out Daphne's picture; her image looked surreal in the light. He traced the outline of her face with his finger, the way her hair curled around her shoulders. He would always love her, but it was time to let go.

He ripped up the picture, tearing it again and again, allowing the pieces to scatter over the incoming waves. As they fell, they mingled with the blue flashes of phosphorescence in the water and he watched as the fragments of Daphne disappeared among the dancing sparks of blue.

Seven

There were grey smudges of cloud in the sky, and despite the fans, the air felt as thick as a woollen blanket. Miranda sat pinning the cushion cover that she was making with the fabric she'd bought in Holland Village. The wireless was on and broadcasting *The Pantomime Quiz*, her favourite programme; she'd been amazed when she'd managed to find it and tune in. She smoothed out the wrinkles in the silk and threaded a needle. Sewing soothed her, the fine details forcing her to focus on something other than unpicking her feelings.

In London, she'd always sewn in front of the fire with Socrates curled up at her feet, and she kept expecting him to appear at any minute. Now, she was experiencing a different kind of heat, heavy and foggy; one that made her listless and tired. She looked up at the jungle, hoping to catch sight of the two parrots and the monkey who visited regularly among the trees, but all she could see was layer upon layer of impenetrable foliage.

She sighed and turned up the wireless, then glanced at her watch. It was only ten o'clock. There was still plenty to do to get the bungalow spruced up; a lick of paint, new cushions for verandah chairs that she'd bought in a rattan store she'd discovered on a return visit to Holland Village. She was toying with the idea of doing up the tumbledown summerhouse she'd noticed at the bottom of the garden; the chairs would look perfect in there.

From the kitchen, she could hear Mei Ling moving about, the clatter of plates and then a tap running. Should she make Mei Ling some tea? It wasn't that long since Mei Ling had returned from the market. Miranda had quizzed her about the unfamiliar groceries in her basket – the strange green vegetable that curled like an exotic fleur-de-lis: *kai-lan*, Mei Ling called it. Miranda tried to help put the shopping away, but Mei Ling's face had set, as though offended.

'No-*lah*, Mrs Gerald, I do.'

Since then, she'd decided to stay out of Mei Ling's way, and she was alert to the slightest sound and movement in the garden. She lifted her head. Footsteps were crunching along the path and then there was a knock on the door.

She heard shuffling along the corridor, and, a moment later, Mei Ling announced, 'Mrs Gerald. Someone's come to see you.'

A woman, about Miranda's age, with blonde, shoulder-length hair, came towards her. Her face was tanned and freckled and the aroma of musky perfume wafted towards Miranda.

'Hello,' the woman said, holding out her hand. In the other arm, she held two magazines. 'I'm Charlotte Yeardley, your neighbour. You must be Miranda?'

Miranda smiled. It was a relief to have a visitor, especially one her own age. She stood and shook Charlotte's
hand. 'Yes. How do you do?'

'I'm sorry I haven't been before.' Her cut-glass accent
hinted at shooting parties and debutante balls. 'We were
supposed to come to Georgina's party but my little boy,
Jack, has been unwell.'

'I'm sorry to hear that. I hope he's better now?' She
looked to see if Charlotte had the child with her.

'Oh. He's not here. He's been teething, you see, and my
amah finally got him down an hour ago. When I left them,
he looked dead to the world.'

Miranda stiffened. All the pleasure of meeting Charlotte
slipped away as she pictured Henry, the way he had lain
unnaturally still in his cot, his head turned to one side.
She tried to blink the image away.

'May I?' Charlotte indicated a chair and sat down.

Miranda composed herself. 'I'm sorry.' She attempted
to focus. 'Yes. Of course. Mei Ling, do you think you
could bring us some tea?'

'That's kind,' Charlotte sat back in the chair, 'but I'll
have to get back to Jack in a minute. Oh, I forgot. Would
you like these?' She held out the magazines: a *Marie France*
and a *Vogue*. 'A welcome present, if you like. They're like
gold dust here,' she smiled.

'Thank you.' Miranda took them and held them in her
lap. 'How kind.'

'Not at all. And you must let me know if there's anything you need. Andrew, that's my husband, said your

husband works in a different department to him at the Office. Social housing department, is that right? How's he finding it?'

'Fine. There's a lot to get to know in any new job – but I think the challenges here, such as persuading the locals to accept the plans, add an extra dimension,' Miranda replied, but all she could think about was Henry: the residual warmth of his cheeks on her trembling fingers and her shock at the shadow of blue around his mouth. Charlotte was talking about Jack. Instinctively, Miranda asked, 'How old is he? Your little boy?'

'Seven months. It's such a lovely age,' Charlotte carried on, smiling. 'He's beginning to sit up and, apart from the teething, he really can't stop beaming.'

Miranda dug her nails into the covers of the magazine. 'Excuse me.' Tears smarted and her nose started to run. She fumbled around in her pocket for a handkerchief and blew her nose. Charlotte sympathised about summer colds, and Miranda nodded, half-listening, as Charlotte started to tell her where the best places were to shop.

'Amazingly enough, there is a supermarket here called *Cold Storage* that sells American produce. Rice is rationed, as there are still sanctions in Malaya, but, thank goodness, there's no limit on spirits. Gin is *so* cheap.'

Miranda tried to concentrate, but it was as though the conversation, Charlotte, the morning, everything, existed in a world beyond her own. Eventually, she noticed Charlotte looking at her with a puzzled look on her face. As their eyes met, Charlotte's glance flickered away to her watch.

'Goodness! Is that the time? Jack will probably be awake now. Oh, before I forget – a couple of girlfriends are coming over for lunch tomorrow. Nothing fancy. We get together about once a month or so for a catch-up. Would you like to join us? Say twelve for twelve-thirty?'

'That would be lovely. Thank you.'

Miranda walked her to the door and watched as Charlotte and the blue of her linen dress receded as she returned to her bungalow next door. It was lovely to be invited, and to have the prospect of meeting some new friends, but the thought of meeting Jack unsettled her once more and, by breakfast the next morning, she had worked herself into a panic.

'I don't think I can go, Gerry.'

He peered at her over his paper. 'Why ever not?'

She tried to explain: it wasn't that she was ungrateful about the invitation; she knew she should be glad of the company. And it wasn't that she found Charlotte intimidating, or even that she was nervous about meeting Charlotte's friends. It was Jack.

He turned another page. 'You should go.' He didn't look up. 'I've bumped into Andrew at the Office a couple of times already. Nice chap. I actually suggested they should come around for drinks sometime, so it's wonderful that you're already making in-roads with his wife.'

'But—'

'Look, you need to start making an effort.' He folded the paper and took a final sip of tea. 'You'll enjoy it once you're there.' He squeezed her hand back. 'Once you get yourself dolled up, you'll be fine.'

Miranda blushed. She had already applied her make-up and done her best to set her hair. Gerry's voice was kinder as he stood. 'I'd better hurry. See you later.'

As she listened to his footsteps fading, then the door closing, she cradled her head and listened to the tick-tick-tick of the clock. *Come on*, she told herself. *Don't be so pathetic. It's only a lunch. What on earth can go wrong?*

Motes of dust danced in front of the wardrobe as she hesitated over which dress to wear – cotton floral seemed too casual, red silk too suggestive of the evening. She pulled a pale-blue linen dress off a hanger and closed her eyes, heat rushing to her face. It was the dress she'd worn to Henry's christening, the one that her mother-in-law had taken an irrational dislike to.

As she touched the fabric, she caught sight of her reflection: there were dark circles under her eyes and her night-dress hung loosely from her shoulders, and she heard in her mind Lily's bitter words once more. 'That dress, I don't know why you wear it. It makes you look so pale,' she'd said. 'And with your hair, your complexion, surely a stronger colour would be better?'

Although she hated to admit it, she could see now that Lily had a good point, although she hated the way Lily spoke to her in such a patronising way, as though she were child or someone who hadn't been brought up properly and constantly needed to be corrected or told how to do things.

From the bedside table, she picked up Charlotte's copy of *Vogue* and read 'Dressing for a man's Eye'. The sultry gaze of Veronica Lake, wearing a coral evening dress, stared back at her from the cover; her long hair was curled up in the latest style. She could do that, she thought, fashion her hair like Veronica Lake's. In England, she'd have thought it too showy, inappropriate somehow, but Singapore was a fresh start, a chance to try something new. She remembered packing a deep-red lipstick in her cosmetics case. She could pluck her eyebrows, and ring the changes with her own coral day dress by tying it with a navy belt instead of the usual coral.

An hour later, she examined her reflection in the mirror with surprised satisfaction. Was it too much, she wondered, as she viewed herself from the side? She didn't want to look like she'd gone over the top or never went anywhere, but, on the other hand, it was nice to be dressed up, plus it gave her a confidence she hadn't felt before.

Buoyed, her steps were light as she approached Charlotte's bungalow, and she heard the welcoming sound of women's voices and laughter trailing towards her from beyond the building.

'Hello!' she called.

'We're out here!' A breathless voice and then Charlotte appeared; her face was flushed, and she held a glass in her hand. She looked elegant in a crisp white cotton dress, which look whiter still against her tanned skin. 'Come and meet everyone.'

Charlotte led her by the arm to the other women, who were sitting on the verandah at a table that overlooked the lawn.

'Everyone, this is Miranda Lewis. Miranda, this is Mary Hutchinson and Jane Curtis. We're drinking pink gin. Would you like one?'

'I'd love one,' she said, and took the glass she was offered, glancing at the other guests. The women were all as well-groomed as Charlotte – thank goodness she'd made the effort to get dressed up.

'Now, why don't you sit here?' Charlotte indicated a space between Jane and Mary.

'Charlotte said you've only just arrived.' Jane made way for Miranda. 'Settling in?'

'I think so.' Miranda sat down and took in the others. Jane was a gaunt woman with chestnut hair, and amber eyes like a cat's. Mary was rounder, jolly-looking, with red hair and a freckled face. Miranda placed them both in their mid-thirties.

'We were just discussing the Christmas do at the Tanglin Club.' Mary began. 'Are you going to go?'

'No,' Miranda said too quickly, and then seeing the expressions of the women, hesitated. 'I'm not really a Christmas person.'

'Not a Christmas person? I've never heard of that,' Mary said incredulously. 'And Christmas in the tropics is so different to the cold, miserable ones in England.'

'Oh, but you *must* come,' Charlotte said. 'You can't miss all the fun.'

'Lots of fun,' Mary smiled. 'And it's an opportunity for you to meet everyone. It really is the only time when we all get together in the same place.'

'Do you remember last Christmas?' Jane giggled. 'When Reginald Turner arrived a day early for the fancy-dress party?'

This was met with a wave of raucous laughter. Jane turned to Miranda, clutching her side, and gasped, 'It was hilarious! He came as a mummy! All wrapped up in lavatory paper. You should have seen the look on his face when he found out.'

'Poor man,' Mary said. 'He must have been so embarrassed.'

'Not as much as his wife. Poor Elsie really isn't very well,' Jane said. 'Everyone seems to think she's losing her marbles too.'

'Anyone like a top-up?' Charlotte asked, still laughing as she poured more gin into their glasses. 'Miranda?'

'Please,' Miranda nodded. She took a large sip, listening to the other women. The conversation moved on to an animated discussion over where it was possible to get a decent haircut in town.

Well, she thought, this lunch wasn't so bad after all. And all the women seemed pleasant, laughing and joking, happy in each other's company. Perhaps it was a combination of the gin and the confidence that came with her new look, but she was definitely easing her way in with this group in a way she never could have imagined in England.

The conversation turned.

'Have you been following the stories about that Muslim girl?' Jane asked Miranda. 'Marion something?

'Martha,' Mary said. 'Martha Hollande.'

'That's it. In all the papers,' Jane continued. 'Seems when the Japs invaded over in Malaya her Dutch father was sent to a labour camp, but he managed to leave her with a Muslim family for safekeeping. The father thought he'd never survive the camp, but he did, and of course he wants her back. And now, the Muslim family claim she was legally adopted. The whole thing's going to the Supreme Court here in Singapore.'

'Well, if she was adopted legally, I don't see how they have a case to answer,' Charlotte said.

'But don't you think it's better if she's with her own kind?' Mary said.

'Do you mean the people who brought her up?' Miranda joined in. But Mary's expression told her that was not what she had meant by 'her own kind'.

'I don't understand – wasn't the occupation in '41?' Miranda continued. 'That's almost eight years ago now. Surely she must be able to make up her own mind?'

Mary glanced at Jane for confirmation, 'I think she's only about thirteen.'

'Yes. Thirteen.'

'Apparently, they can get married at that age, Muslims,' Jane said. 'Seems far too young to me; they're only children. All the more reason to, you know, be with us.'

'I'm not sure I agree with anyone being married at such a young age, but as for Martha, shouldn't she be with

85

the family she's known all her life? Surely it would be awful for her to be taken away and live with people she really doesn't know at this age?'

'Well, if you ask me it's not a good environment for children if they marry their young off like that – it's like going back to the Middle Ages,' Jane snapped.

'I agree with Miranda,' Charlotte interrupted. 'I don't think girls should be married so young, and I also think that all children are better off staying with the people they think of as family.'

There was an uncomfortable silence.

'Still, there's not a lot we can do about it, is there? However, I *can* offer you all another drink,' Charlotte said, and smiled as she stood and walked over to the drinks cart, on which there were several bottles – whisky, gin, vermouth and half a dozen cocktail glasses, along with a cocktail shaker.

Jane shot a look at Mary, who gave her a thin-lipped smile. A moment later, Charlotte's *amah* brought out plates of prawns in a salad, and thin slices of bread and butter. Miranda was hungrier than she'd expected, and the gin was beginning to give everything a light, fuzzy edge.

'Goodness. I don't know how you do it,' Mary began. 'I haven't seen prawns this size for years. And this salad looks impressive. Is that pawpaw *and* pineapple? Where did you get them?'

'Well,' Charlotte picked up her knife and fork, 'they're not black market, if that's what you mean. Suyin bought them from her cousin's fish stall on Sultanate Road.'

'I'm sure she didn't mean that,' Jane smiled, placing her hand on Charlotte's.

'Is the pineapple home grown?' Mary asked. 'We've pawpaw, but no pineapple.'

'And bananas, I seem to remember.' Jane turned to Miranda. 'It's a bit like home, I'm afraid. There are still some things we grow and have too much of, so we all end up swapping goods.'

'In London, my husband tried to grow potatoes once. He dug up the back garden and the whole lot went rotten in the rain,' Miranda said.

'Thank goodness we don't need to deal with all that damp and miserable fog any more. It's been a while since I lived in England, but I still remember it well,' Jane chimed in.

'Where have you lived?' Miranda asked her.

'Hong Kong when I got married. Sydney for a year or two, then here. My parents are from Norfolk, but I went to boarding school in Kent. Queen's Gate. Do you know it?' Jane poured out a glass of water from a chilled bottle on the table and passed it to Miranda.

'My goodness. That's where my mother-in-law went. Lily Lewis now, but Lily Griffiths as was.'

'Good heavens!' Jane looked up. 'What a bloody marvellous coincidence! She's my mother's best friend.'

Miranda's face twisted and she hoped that Jane hadn't noticed.

'It's a small world, the expat community, isn't it?' Mary gave her a wry smile. 'So, Miranda, tell us all about yourself'.

'Well,' Miranda looked up, wondering how well Lily and Jane's mother really knew each other, but everyone fell silent, waiting for her to reply. She cleared her throat.

'I've spent most of my life either at boarding school or with my parents in London. When I was young, I always wanted to be a teacher, but when the war started, I joined the WVS. Gerry and I met on Armistice Day, and we married soon after.'

'That's so romantic,' Charlotte said.

'Yes, it was.' A twinge of regret swept over Miranda as she recalled the headiness of their early relationship.

'What about family? Any children?' Mary asked.

It was the question she always dreaded, and usually she said a simple 'No'. If she was to know these women, to have them as friends, however, she should tell them about Henry, but she knew what would happen: there would be shocked silence, followed by clumsy sympathy, faces looking down, no one knowing what to say. She braced herself, not wanting to start with half-truths, but knowing it was best to get the facts out into the open air.

'Actually,' she began, but Suyin returned to the table and started to remove their plates. A moment later, she returned with a pineapple cake and some strange green squares, which looked like stiff leaves folded into small parcels.

'Goodness, Charlotte. You have surpassed yourself this time. Pineapple cake *and* tapioca parcels.' Mary's face lit up. 'I just love the taste of palm sugar; it's so sweet.'

'Thank you, but, really, it's Suyin who should be getting all the credit.'

'Miranda, what would you like?' Charlotte cut the cake and placed a slice on a bone china plate. 'Pineapple cake, tapioca parcels or both?'

'Ooh ... I don't know. They both look impressive, perhaps the green one, the tapioca parcel, but could I nip to the lavatory first?'

'Of course – it's through the hall and to the right. Probably in much the same place as yours.'

She stood in the hall. The furnishings in Charlotte's bungalow were much finer than her own. A large Indian rug lay in the middle of the floor and there was a carved rosewood desk displaying a collection of cloisonné figures and silver-framed photographs: Charlotte and Andrew's wedding day; a bundled-up Jack in a christening robe. She stepped forward and picked up the christening picture, peering at Jack's barely discernible face, and Charlotte's beaming smile and protective gaze.

Resentment flashed through her, followed by guilt. She put the photograph back as curiosity burned. His bedroom must surely be along the corridor. Would it be any harm to take a look?

'Are you lost?'

She spun around. It was Jane, watching her.

'You've just passed the bathroom.'

'Oh. Have I?'

She turned back. Jane had an expression on her face, weighing her up, the way a cat might look at a mouse.

On her return to the other women, Miranda noticed their fleeting glances followed by Mary pinching her lips and shaking her head slightly. Jane looked at her, but no one spoke, although she was certain they'd been talking about her before she came back to the table.

'I suppose we'd better get off,' Jane said. 'Delicious lunch, Charlotte.'

'Yes, it's been super.' Mary stood.

'Thank you so much,' Miranda joined in. She turned to Mary and Jane. 'I hope I'll see you again soon. It's been so lovely meeting you both.'

The women nodded and walked out to the drive. Miranda followed, waiting awkwardly while Charlotte bid Jane and Mary goodbye.

'Thank you for coming.' Charlotte turned to Miranda. 'And do call around any time that you want.'

'Thank you.' Miranda's head was throbbing. The gin was stronger than she had thought, making her head woozy, and although she was glad of its anaesthetising effect, a new wave of insecurity washed over her, threatening to leave her vulnerable and exposed once more.

Eight

Dear Mother and Father,

I've been so busy since I arrived. We went to a drinks party at Georgina's when we first got here, and the following day Gerry and I went on a trip to Dhobi Ghat. I'm enclosing a snap of the river – can you believe the locals do all their laundry there? Mountains of it! Yesterday I went to a lunch at Charlotte, my neighbour's house and met a couple of other expat women. So, you see, I'm settling in!

I'm glad to hear that Socrates is well, but I do miss hearing his little miaows and having him curling up on my lap while I sew by the fire. I've no pets here, I'm afraid, but there are two parrots that we've christened Gin and Tonic, and a monkey who creeps up to the house. I've called him Tommy. He's such a tinker – yesterday he stole all the eggs from the kitchen!

Miranda tapped the end of her pen rhythmically on the desk, thinking hard. She was desperate to write about her true feelings, but also fearful of revealing too much to her parents. Getting the balance right was always trickier than she thought.

I want to let you know that, although I miss you both very much, and that my thoughts often turn to Henry, I believe coming here will help me to put all the terrible events behind me. I know I have never explained everything fully, but I do believe the time has come to leave these memories in the past. Henry's death, although difficult, I will try not to blame myself for – and you are right, I see that I do need to be kinder to myself.

As for the time I was so ill, you were both so supportive and I have never really thanked you enough, especially for not telling Gerry about that awful incident with the police.

I did toy with the idea of volunteering at a local hospital here, but Gerry has made me realise that this isn't the right thing for me. I need to move forward, not backward, and as you can see, we are moving in good circles and I hope that this will enable Gerry, in time, to make contacts and get the promotion that he deserves.

She paused, re-reading the words that she had struggled for so long to write, then signed off, satisfied at last. After, she folded the letter and sealed it, then wrote a thank-you letter to Charlotte for the lunch the previous day. It didn't seem right to ask Mei Ling to take the letter over, so she made her way to Charlotte's bungalow with the intention of slipping it under the door.

Charlotte was sitting on the verandah, drinking tea, as she approached. She looked lovely in a pink silk tea dress embroidered with white sprigs of flowers. A pair of large, rose-tinted crystal pear-shaped drops hung from her ears and a pearly-white clutch lay on the chair next to her. She caught sight of Miranda and waved her up.

'I did so enjoy the lunch,' Miranda said, sitting on the chair opposite. 'And meeting Mary and Jane.'

Charlotte's lips pinched together, and Miranda wondered if she'd caught her at a bad time.

'I'd better let you get on,' she said, taking in Charlotte's attire once more. 'I'm sorry, you look like you're going out.'

'There's no hurry. I'm taking Jack to see a specialist at Mount Elizabeth in a bit. He's still waking at night, although typically he's fast asleep right now. I thought it was his teeth to start with, but they've broken through. I really don't know what it could be.'

'Have you tried clove oil? Or letting him chew on a cold carrot?'

'I've tried everything. To be honest, I'm at my wit's end.'

'Does he have a good routine? It helps if they don't sleep too much during the day.'

'Yes. I think so.' She picked a piece of invisible fluff from her dress. 'You seem to know a lot about babies.'

Miranda paused. Had Charlotte guessed, she wondered? She braced herself to explain but the telephone rang and, a moment later, Charlotte's *amah* came out.

'Mrs Yeardley,' she said, 'it's the receptionist from Mount Elizabeth. They say you can't go today.'

'What? Oh, honestly.' Charlotte stood up, frustration on her face. 'You'll excuse me, won't you, Miranda? I'll be back in a moment.'

Miranda waited. She could hear Charlotte's voice rising and falling, a hint of anger in her tone. A mosquito landed on her leg. She swiped at it but missed and knocked over Charlotte's teacup instead.

'Oh my goodness!' She managed to stop it rolling to the ground, but the tea had spilled everywhere. What an idiot she was! She'd have to go and get a cloth before Charlotte returned.

But, inside the house, curiosity about Jack took hold once more. Charlotte was still talking on the telephone, the *amah* was in the kitchen. There was no one about.

Time seemed to lengthen as she made her way towards the nursery. The door was only half-open, but she could make out shapes in the darkened room: a nursing chair, a chest of drawers that had been painted white, and, in the corner, away from the draught of the fan, a cot with mosquito netting.

The child was lying on his stomach, his face turned away from her. The two whorls of a double crown were visible in his white-blond hair. She crept towards him, giddy with the agony of it, dizzy with the scent of talcum powder. He was thinner and longer than Henry. A dribble of saliva rested in the corner of his mouth. She wanted to reach out a hand to wipe it away, to pick him up and inhale the milky, powdery softness of him. She lingered, standing by the cot, then she lifted the netting and ran her fingers through his hair.

'Miranda?' Charlotte stood in the doorway; her features were clouded with concern. There was agitation in her voice as she stepped into the room. 'What on earth *are* you doing?'

'Nothing.'

'It doesn't look like that to me. Jane said she caught you snooping around yesterday. I wasn't prepared to believe her, but now, well ...'

'I ... I'm sorry. I knocked your tea over, and I was looking for a cloth to wipe it up with.'

'Oh, come on. You don't expect me to believe that, do you?'

Jack stirred.

Charlotte sighed. 'I really don't know what to make of this.'

'I can explain.' Tears blistered. 'I just wanted to have a look at Jack.'

'He would have woken soon enough.'

'I know,' her voice sounded hollow. 'I think I'd better go.'

Charlotte nodded and moved away, letting her step through the door and out of the bungalow.

The shame was painful. Miranda's heart beat so loudly she was certain that Charlotte would be able to hear it too. How stupid she could be. Charlotte would always be doubting her, not quite trusting, watching her actions. Miranda could imagine her discussing the matter with Jane and Mary, them all being quick to judge. Integrating with these women had been within her grasp, and with one action, she'd blown it all away.

*

'Morning, *tuan*. You wake early.' Khalish held a small basket as he walked away from the hens. Nick could just about see in the dawn light that there were five or six eggs clustered like dirty stones at the bottom. 'Would you like me to make you coffee?'

'Morning, Khalish. I thought I'd get some exercise first – a quick run up to Bukit Kalang. I might even get a good view of the sunrise.'

He hadn't been able to sleep, and he'd given up trying at six-thirty, so he'd got up, pulled on his shorts, an old top and a pair of plimsolls.

'Why for you want to go *run*?' Khalish looked puzzled.

'I used to do it when I was in the army, to keep fit.' He demonstrated a star jump and laughed at Khalish's bemused expression.

'You not in army now.'

'No.' But today he felt as though he were ready for combat of a different kind; although he wasn't certain yet what it was.

'I'll be back in an hour or so, Khalish. I'll eat breakfast at eight.'

'Yes, *tuan*.'

He began slowly, running along the garden path, then past the government bungalows and up towards the ridge leading to Bukit Kalang. The combination of humidity and being unfit was making running harder than he remembered. He placed one foot in front of the other, but despite the shade of the bamboos, it was as though he were running through something thick and sticky. The path narrowed, and he had to push back branches as he ran. Overhead he could hear the chatter of jays and the click-click from monkeys as they shrieked warning.

He ran on, determined and panting, his body dripping with sweat, until he reached the summit, where he flopped on to the ground. Below him, there was the ridge, and beyond that, miles and miles of jungle covered in trailing wisps of mist. From the horizon, orange and pink bled into the clouds and a stork flew across the emerging sun. He sat up and watched the progress of the sun rising. It was majestic and glorious, a full-bodied red that infused the sky with fingers of vermilion.

The sun's warmth caused the mist to disappear. Parakeets screeched overhead, and he heard the high-pitched call of a mynah bird. A crested grebe flitted from the trees, and he watched it dart between the bamboos and banyan trees. Strands of wood smoke were visible from kampongs hidden in the canopy below. To the west lay the city and the Singapore River. If he squinted, he could see how it snaked out towards Clarke Quay and the sea. To the east was Tanjong Pagar, where the hospital lay, and beyond it was Bukit Brown, where the municipal graveyard was. He felt a prickle of guilt thinking of Chen and his pauper's burial, and he wondered when it would be.

As he sat, he leant forward and hugged his knees. Close by he could hear the sound of running water. A waterfall, perhaps, feeding into the MacRitchie Reservoir? The view was so beautiful and full of emerging activity. He wasn't sure he could leave Singapore, but, equally, he wasn't sure if he could stay. Why had he become a doctor? What was he going to do with the rest of his life? He had asked himself those questions a thousand times, and here, with this panorama beneath him, the scent of wild jasmine and the chattering monkeys, he asked them once again.

In one of the plots of vegetation among the scattered huts below, he caught sight of an elderly woman with a young child. They looked like they were hoeing or digging, the child running backwards and forwards towards her. He must have been a similar age, five maybe six, the first time his grandmother had shown him the green daffodil shoots pushing through the grass beneath the sycamore trees at Coombe, her home.

'Remember them, Nicky, the bulbs we planted in the autumn?' Her voice was so clear in his head and he could almost feel the pressure of her hand on his.

'In a few days, the flowers will open. Won't that be exciting?'

It was thanks to her that his love of nature had begun, and the spring flowers always made him think of her. He'd almost forgotten those holidays at Coombe, kneeling at his grandmother's side, planting seedlings, weeding out dandelions, constructing cloches and collecting plump berries from the raspberry canes. Now he longed for it, that connection with the earth, the promise of all new things.

But he ought to get going. He'd have to be quick if he were to get back to Belvedere for eight, let alone get to St Augustin's by nine. If he got to St Augustin's early, he'd call in to see Alice Matthews. She would know more about Chen's funeral, and if he had time, he might pay a visit to Bukit Brown.

Running down was difficult, and his knees began to ache as he went. After a hundred yards, he took a path to his left, scrambling between the bamboos and straight towards the sound of water running. He headed towards the sound, his thirst gripping like a fever. As he pushed aside the dripping palm leaves and parted the tall sticks of bamboo, he found a pipe jutting out of the hillside. The water seemed clean, so he splashed his face to cool down. As he did so, the leaves parted and the black-and-yellow head of a mangrove snake flashed towards him, forcing him to spring back in shock, his heart pounding.

Jesus! He ought to be more careful. Next time he'd wear better shoes, and bring a compass and water with him. A stout stick would be a good idea too. He scrambled on back down the hill, leaping to avoid puddles of swamp water, but as he landed, he turned on his right foot, and a sharp searing pain ripped through his ankle.

'Damn!' he yelped. He tried to put his weight on his foot, but the agony was too great. 'Bugger!'

He limped towards a tree stump, sat down, took off his plimsoll and sock and began to examine his foot. There was already swelling around the lateral ligaments. It could be that the anterior fibres were torn but he hoped he hadn't damaged any of the small bones. What he needed was an ice pack, or at least to keep his foot raised to stop the injury bearing the full twelve stone of his weight.

He glanced about for a stick to support his weight and hopped towards a piece of broken bamboo. He tested it; it would do. He then took off his top and soaked up the water from the swamp with it to bring down the swelling of his throbbing foot.

How bloody stupid he was. He, of all people, should have known better. Other than Khalish, no one knew where he was. Something rustled in the undergrowth nearby.

'Hello!' he shouted. 'Is there anyone there?'

The bamboos rustled again, then nothing. It was probably another snake. He pulled the damp top over his body and leaning on the cane, he hobbled down the slope. For an hour he limped, sweating and cursing, until, finally, he emerged from the jungle. Through the palms he saw the government bungalows of Alexandra Gardens, but further still lay the red Malacca-tiled roof of Belvedere.

'Jesus! It's bloody miles away.'

The temperature had to be around ninety, the sun was burning his back and his lips were cracking. He had no idea what the time was, ten, ten-thirty? He felt dizzy and he feared he'd get heat stroke if he didn't get back soon – the trees in front of him seemed blurry. He hobbled towards the nearest building, the pain in his ankle shooting up his calf.

In the drive, he was relieved to see a woman sitting on the verandah with her head in her hands. It was the woman he'd met the other evening at the Metcalfes' party, Miranda Lewis.

Nine

'Excuse me!'

Miranda lifted her head, squinting as her vision re-adjusted in the sun. A man was limping towards her, and as he hobbled closer, she could see that it was the doctor with whom she had danced at Georgina's party.

'Are you all right?' Miranda asked, as he finally reached her. 'Come on, sit down.' She stood to help him. 'What happened?'

'I've messed up my foot. Twisted it running down the hill.'

She frowned. 'Well, you'd better let me have a look.' She undid his plimsoll and gently pulled it off to see the blue hue of a bruise forming. 'That needs ice. Stay there, I'll get some.'

She went into the kitchen and emptied ice cubes from the tray into a tea towel. Nick was probably thirsty, she realised, as she filled a glass with water. A few moments later, she returned and squatted down by the chair, placing the glass on the floor and the tea towel of ice on his foot. Her hair grazed his foot as she leant forward. Carefully, she placed the wayward lock behind her ear.

'Ouch, that's bloody cold!' Nick winced.

'That's the point, isn't it? It will bruise even more if I don't.'

He groaned.

'Doctors make the worst patients,' she grinned. 'Come on. Lift it up. Put it on this other chair and rest it.'

He placed his foot on the chair she pushed towards him.

'I'm glad you were out here,' he said. 'What were you doing?'

She sat down on the floor near him, crossing her legs.

'Nothing. Just thinking.' She shrugged. The last thing she wanted him to know was that she'd been upset and dwelling on her disastrous lunch.

'You ought to be careful.' He rearranged the icy towel. 'There's all sorts out here. Last week, my houseboy found a cobra on the balcony.'

'You're a fine one to talk.'

'I suppose I am. Can I?' He indicated the glass of water.

She passed it to him; condensation slithered down the glass on to his fingers. Long and sensitive-looking with the nails chewed down.

'How's it feeling?' she asked. 'Has the ice helped?'

'A little bit. It isn't throbbing so much.'

'You won't be able to run on that for a few days.'

'I know. Let's see if it's any better.' He tried to stand up. 'Sh-ugar!' She could see how much the pain seared his tendons and clouded his features.

She weighed up the situation: she'd really wanted to be left alone, but he clearly couldn't walk back unaided.

It was annoying, but at least it was a distraction from her own melancholy. She'd have to help him.

'I'll ask Jinhai to drive you home; you shouldn't walk on it yet.'

'I don't want to be a nuisance.'

'Don't be so daft. Where is it that you live?'

'Belvedere – it's at the top of the hill.'

She stood up and went to find Jinhai at the back of the house, where he was sitting down on the verandah steps with Mei Ling. There was a newspaper on his lap, and a pot of jasmine tea and a plate of what looked like rice cakes were between them. They seemed to be having a heated debate about something.

'Jinhai, I need you to bring the car around straight away. My neighbour has hurt his foot and we need to take him home.'

'Of course, madam.'

Miranda returned to Nick, who held the tea towel and ice in one had while he examined his injured foot.

'Jinhai's bringing the car. Can you lean on me to get there?' She stood next to him, her hand held out.

'I think it's better now.' He hobbled towards her, placing his hand on her arm. He was heavier than he looked, and her arm muscles strained with his weight.

'There's no need to come with me,' he added, as he leant into her for support.

'I think I will. Just to make sure.'

Jinhai had brought the car and, although it was only a few feet away, he continued to use her as a support as they made their way to the car. She opened the door, and he sat on the back seat with his leg outstretched.

'Do you know Belvedere, Jinhai?' Miranda sat in the seat next to her driver.

'Yes. House at top of hill.'

She turned to say something to Nick as they swung out of the drive and she couldn't help noticing the rise of his nose, the sharpness of his jaw, and the perspiration beading around his forehead.

Jinhai drove slowly up the hill to Belvedere and then both he and Miranda helped Nick into the hall.

'Can you wait in the car for me, Jinhai? There's probably someone at home to help.'

'Are you sure, madam?'

'Yes. Thank you.'

When Jinhai had returned outside, Nick tried to walk on his own.

'Careful,' she said. 'Don't put your weight on it.'

'Honestly, my foot is much better. I can stand on it, see?' He let go of her arm and hobbled ahead to the living room. A houseboy was sweeping the floor and he lifted his head as they entered the room.

'Khalish,' Nick flopped down into a rattan chair, 'can you get some water to drink? I've hurt my foot, and Mrs Lewis had kindly brought me home.'

Khalish nodded, and despite his obvious concern, immediately did what Nick asked.

Miranda could see that Nick had overdone it. Despite the comfort of the rattan chair, perspiration poured from his forehead and sweat had soaked through his clothing. She saw him shiver.

'What about some ice?' Miranda asked. 'Wouldn't hurt to put another pack on it.'

'I don't think it needs it.' Nick wiggled his toes.

'Here you are, *tuan*.' Khalish returned with two glasses of water. 'Can I get you anything else?'

Nick shook his head.

'What about work?' she asked, glancing about the room.

He examined his foot for signs of swelling. 'Should be all right to drive, and I'll be at my desk for a good part of the day.' He put his foot on the floor and stood, testing his weight. 'I think it will be fine.'

'I don't think so.' She picked up her glass of water and took a gulp. 'There's no way I'm letting you drive yourself to the hospital. Jinhai will take you – I insist.'

She could see that Nick wasn't happy about her suggestion, but at last he agreed to it.

'I'll need to get changed first.' He levered himself up.

'I'll wait.'

Nick hobbled out of the room and, while he was gone, she gazed around her. There were four tennis rackets propped against the wall, three different types of panama hats on the top of a bookshelf. The bookshelf housed a collection of books – medical journals, a couple of Agatha Christies – along with a large conch shell that reminded her of her childhood trips to the sea with her father; how happy they'd been collecting shells in a bucket while he explained what they were called. On the shelf, there were also some clam shells, a calico scallop, a shark's eye moon shell that she recognised from a book she'd read about shells, and others that she didn't know. One curled and spiralled like a horn, the colour of a lobster, while another was shaped like an olive, as dark as chocolate. Her attention was taken by a pair that looked like figs, small and delicate with a purple hue. She picked them up and examined them, wondering where they had come from and who the collector was.

A little guiltily, her attention wandered to the remainder of the bookshelf. Still clutching the shells, she glanced at photographs: a man she didn't recognise sat on a picnic rug with his arm around a pretty blonde woman in a nurse's uniform. Another doctor, she guessed; one of Nick's housemates? Her gaze fell on another frame – a group of young men and women and, in the middle of them all, she recognised Nick, smiling and flanked by women. Could it be that one of them was his sweetheart?

From a distant room, she heard the sound of water flowing. He was evidently showering. She put the shells back and pulled out a book about plants and trees in Singapore, then she sat in the rattan chair he had vacated to pass the time reading. As she flicked through the pages, a folded letter fell out and landed on the floor. She picked it up – she knew she shouldn't, but she couldn't help opening it.

'*Dear Nick*,' she read, then the signature at the bottom: *Daphne*.

She toyed with the idea of reading the letter, but she hurriedly slipped it back as she heard Nick's limping footsteps returning.

'Ready?' she asked.

He nodded.

'I'll put this back.' She stood and returned the book to its home.

'Here,' she offered him her arm, 'let me help you back down the steps.'

'Thank you for all your help,' he said, as they inched towards the car, which Jinhai had parked beneath a large tree whose shade sprawled across the oven-like ground. 'I feel such an idiot. But, honestly, you really don't need to take me.'

'I'm not doing anything,' she said. 'And, in any case, it could have happened to anyone.'

They set off. The car was roasting inside, and the roads turned from tarmac to dust as they journeyed towards Tanjong Pagar. As they drew closer to St Augustin's, the car hit a bump in the road, covering the windscreen in a coating of dust. Jinhai turned on the wipers to clear it, but they smeared opaque stripes across the glass instead, and for a moment the wheels spun before the car lurched sharply forwards again. Nick cursed. The movement must have jarred his ankle, and as Jinhai carried on driving, with the car stopping and starting, caught between trishaws and labourers who were all heading through ramshackle market stalls set up between banana trees and shacks, she caught him wince on more than one occasion.

Eventually, they turned into a collection of single-storey buildings beyond the bustling market, past a hand-painted sign propped up against the wall. The lettering was faded and peeling, but she could just make out the wording: *St Augustin's Mission Hospital*.

'This is it,' Nick said.

The forecourt was busy with people crowding around the doors. All faces turned towards the car as Jinhai slowed and parked in the shade of a palm tree.

Nick sighed.

'Are you sure you're up to this?' Miranda asked.

'Oh, I'm absolutely fine,' he replied. 'Once I'm inside, I'll find a walking stick or something.'

'Do you want me to help you?'

He shook his head. 'I'll get one of the nurses to do it – they know better than I do where all the equipment is kept.'

Miranda felt eyes watching the car from all around the courtyard.

'There are so many people here,' she said. 'I had no idea it was so busy.'

'Every day the queue in the morning seems to be longer, the needs of the people greater. And it isn't just families that come – look over there.'

Her eyes followed to where he indicated. A little away from the crowd, a girl of about seven stood alone; her grubby dress was hanging loose.

'Where are her parents?' she asked.

'Poor kid probably hasn't got any.'

'Are there many like her?'

'Too many and not enough money to go around. I'd better get on now. Thank you once again for your help.'

Miranda watched him hobble across the courtyard and push open the door to the hospital. He stood a foot taller than the locals crowding around him, and, like the Pied Piper, he led the groups of children, who trustingly followed him in.

Ten

Back at Alexandra Gardens, a letter was waiting for Miranda on the rosewood table. She recognised the small, neatly formed script as her mother's. She picked it up and sat on the verandah with it on her lap, surreptitiously checking the garden to see if there were any of the snakes or creepy-crawlies lurking nearby that Nick had warned her about before ripping the letter open.

Dear Miranda,

It was lovely to get your postcards from Alexandria and Bombay. The scenery looks absolutely unbelievable, but I'm not sure that I'd like all that heat.

You must have arrived in Singapore by now, and I do hope that your new bungalow is just as charming as you expected. Do let me know what it is like and I'm certain that you will settle and have a good crowd of friends soon.

Now, don't go worrying about Socrates either, as he's settling well. And guess what, he's discovered the remnants of that old summerhouse you used to love playing in as a little girl. I wonder sometimes if he can sense you there – I'd have to say it has become a favourite haunt of his …

She certainly *did* remember that summerhouse, although she can't have been much more than about six or seven at the time her mother described. It had been in a terrible state when she'd found it: overgrown, the roof had been patched and the door nailed down. But, still, she'd crept inside, pushing away the hanging spider-webbed curtains with a stick while the soles of her sandals scrunched against crisp leaves and the decaying bodies of beetles and flies.

Every day over the summer, she'd returned. First, she'd taken a pan and brush to sweep away the debris. Next, she took an old blanket, after that a tea set, some books and a teddy. She used to lie there for what felt like hours, eating apples or turning the pages of a picture book, listening to the birds singing or the wind stirring the leaves in the tree overhead.

That summerhouse, she remembered, had been a perfect world, a glorious escape, and she had loved it. If only she had somewhere like that to hide in here in Singapore, somewhere all of her own. She'd already been planning on doing up the old summerhouse at the bottom of the garden next, but she'd been so busy shopping, making curtains and getting the bungalow into shape that, apart from the chairs she'd bought in Holland Village, she hadn't got very far.

Inspired, she folded the letter and placed it inside the envelope, then made her way to the summerhouse. The front was completely covered in creepers and she couldn't open the door. She peered through one of the windows, wiping away the dirt with her lawn cotton handkerchief. There wasn't much there – a pile of leaves, some children's wooden building blocks scattered across the entrance, a chair turned on its side, a few broken bits of china – but the structure looked solid and dry.

Earlier, she had tied up her hair, pulled on a long-sleeved blouse and a pair of black slacks, so all she needed now were a pair of stout shoes and Jinhai's machete. She made her way back to the house, determined to make a start on clearing the summerhouse right away.

'Mrs Gerald, I take to bottom of garden.'

Jinhai insisted on carrying the machete until they reached the summerhouse. Something rustled in the undergrowth.

'You sure you want do this, Mrs Gerald? Best watch out – plenty snakes. Mosquito also. Only last week I see big python and cobra nesting over there.'

He pointed in the direction of the space between them and the neighbouring bungalow – a small patch of scrub-land dotted with banana trees. She paused for a moment – she'd never seen a snake, but remembered again what Nick had said. She recollected that they liked to live in the under-growth or that sometimes they liked to bask in the sun. But, although she didn't like the idea of it much, she knew that she was bound to come across one sooner or later.

'I'll be careful, Jinhai. Thank you.'

With him gone, she parted the leaves and set about hacking back the foliage, dragging the branches on to a heap on the lawn. After twenty minutes, she'd cleared enough space to push open the creaking door, which scattered the leaves and building bricks across the floor. In a corner, a huge spider hung in menacing silence. A mosquito bit the back of her neck; she swiped at it and lit a cigarette, hoping that the smoke would keep the bugs away.

It was better than she'd imagined.

That afternoon, she used all her energy to get the summerhouse cleared of vines and creepers.

The next day, as she was sweeping, she heard a car driving past, and when she looked, she saw Jane inside. Miranda lifted her hand to wave, but then hesitated and turned her head away. A knot tightened in her stomach as she wondered what Charlotte would say about her. Later, she heard Charlotte and Jane in the distance, and she wondered if they were talking about her. She carried on sweeping with hard, sharp strokes, quelling her unease, then she gathered up great bundles of debris. When she had finished, she brushed her hands on her trousers, satisfied with all her hard work.

That evening, when she'd finished, she showed Gerry her handiwork.

'What do you think?' she asked. 'I found these old rattan planters chairs in Holland Village a few days ago and Jinhai painted them for me.' The chairs were now white, with ruby-coloured cushions she'd made from the leftover silk from the sitting-room renovations.

'It's lovely.' Gerry beamed as he sat in one of the chairs. 'And now that you've got everything looking so nice, we could ask some people around. I think we owe the Metcalfes, don't you? And you could ask Andrew and Charlotte from next door.'

'Oh.' Miranda bit her lower lip. She hadn't told Gerry about the incident at Charlotte's and the shame of it washed over her all over again.

'What's the matter? You've gone as pink as the inside of a watermelon!'

'I don't mind asking the Metcalfes, but do we have to ask the Yeardleys?'

'Why?' He frowned. 'What's wrong with them?'

'Well,' she took a deep breath and sat down on the chair next to him. The chair creaked as she pulled her legs to her chest and rested her head on her knees, not wanting to look at him. 'We had a bit of a thing.'

'Honestly, Miranda, already? You women – you've hardly been in Singapore long enough to start a feud. What was it about?'

'I don't want to talk about it.'

'Well, whatever it is, I don't care. You need to make amends. They're our neighbours here and you can't afford to be on bad terms with people like that.'

'I like Charlotte,' she began. 'But her friends, they're not my kind of people.' She lifted her head to look at him. 'Wouldn't it be better for me to make friends I feel more comfortable with?'

He thought for a moment.

'Miranda, you don't need to tell me what happened, I'll respect that, but, honestly, we've only been here a couple of weeks. Word will get around that you're awkward or difficult, when we should be socialising, making the best of our opportunities here. Take her some flowers or something, clear up the misunderstanding and start again.'

He got out of the chair and walked to the doorway, then turned to face her.

'Darling, I'm a pretty lenient chap on the whole. Perhaps I've allowed you too much freedom, but now isn't the time to test my patience.'

'Ugh!' she groaned, as she sank into one of the chairs. How could he not even see it from her point of view? Honestly, sometimes he could be so frustrating.

The following morning, she retraced her steps to the Yeardleys' bungalow, half-hoping Charlotte wouldn't be there, and dreading it, in case Jane or Mary were.

She knocked on the door and waited, listening to the hammer pound of her heart.

Suyin opened the door.

'I've come to visit Mrs Yeardley. Is she at home?'

'Yes. She here. You best come in.' Suyin opened the door wider and led Miranda to the sitting room, where she sat on a coral-coloured sofa, which was stacked with turquoise, lemon and green cushions. As she waited, she fiddled with the fringe of one of the cushions until, at last, she heard Charlotte approaching and lifted her head to see her standing in the doorway.

'Oh,' Charlotte said. 'I wondered if it might be you.'

Miranda examined her expression, trying to work out if, behind her mask of well-bred politeness, she was still angry.

'I've come to say I'm sorry.'

Charlotte raised an eyebrow, but Miranda was relieved when she sat down in the chair opposite the sofa.

'I feel as though I need to offer you an explanation.'

'Go on.'

'I'm not really sure where to start.' She twisted the cushion fringe in her fingers once more. 'But it's harder than I ever imagined settling out here, and as soon as I think I'm doing fine, something always trips me up.'

'What do you mean? I don't understand.'

'Your baby. Jack. He's so much like my Henry.'

'Henry? Who's Henry?'

It was no good. Her shoulders began to shake and the pent-up grief began cascading out.

'Are you all right?' Charlotte asked.

She wiped her eyes with the back of her hand, realising that her face was wet with tears.

'Oh, Miranda!' Charlotte's arm was around her. 'What is it? Whatever is the matter?'

'He was my son. He ...'

'Your son?' Charlotte looked puzzled.

She took a deep breath in. 'We had a baby.' Her words were slow and deliberate, heavy with her grief. 'He died.'

'Oh my God, Miranda. I'm so sorry. I had no idea.' Charlotte's expression softened and suddenly she was handing Miranda a handkerchief. 'When?'

'Just under a year ago.'

'Do you want to tell me about it?'

'It was so sudden.' She shook her head, her hand over her mouth, as though it could plug the pain. Charlotte squeezed her hand as she waited for her to calm.

'I understand if you don't, but, if you feel like it, I'm told I make an excellent listener.'

Miranda nodded her appreciation.

'Can I get you anything?' Charlotte asked. 'A cup of tea, or a glass of water perhaps?'

'No.' Miranda wiped her nose.

Charlotte touched her lightly on the elbow. 'I see that now, and I can see that it must be terribly difficult for you – coming out here, seeing Jack for the first time. I can't imagine what it must be like to lose your child.'

'But I shouldn't have gone snooping around your house, should I?'

'Well,' Charlotte took Miranda's hand and squeezed it, 'Jane did say she saw you wandering around the bunga-low at lunch the other day, and as we don't really know you, it's easy to form the wrong impression, isn't it?'

Charlotte patted Miranda's hand. 'This probably doesn't help in the slightest, but there are so many things happening here – lunches, dinners, bridge, tennis, swim-ming – you'll get to meet people and you'll find you're so busy that, before you know it, you'll be calling this place home. Perhaps I overreacted.'

'Rather easy for you to say.' Miranda released her hand from Charlotte's. 'This environment seems pretty natural to you.'

'Well, it's true: I do like being social and entertaining. Look, we'll put this incident behind us, shall we, and start again? And I do hope that you'll be able to spend some time with Jack and me, now that, well, you know.'

Miranda nodded, understanding without her needing to finish. She appreciated the lack of pity in her eyes, the empathy that only a mother could know.

'In that case, perhaps you can join us for drinks one evening?' Miranda was glad now that Gerry had suggested it; it gave her an excuse for showing Charlotte that she, too, was keen to start again. 'What about Friday?'

'Six o'clock?'

'Perfect.'

The visit hadn't been a complete disaster, then. In only an afternoon – in just a few minutes, in fact – a person she hardly knew had shown her more understanding than her husband ever had. Perhaps everything would be all right after all?

Eleven

That evening, she decided to try hard to be the perfect wife, one who was more like Charlotte; composed yet fun, a gracious host who was at ease with guests and loved entertaining. Miranda was finally acknowledging that it was, at least in the short term, the key to fitting in and making new friends. She had been given a second chance, and she was going to make a go of it. Miranda had never been a natural cook, but if she were to get the hang of her new resolution, she could begin by preparing dinner and impressing Gerry.

'Have we got any potatoes, Mei Ling? And carrots?'

'Yes, Mrs Gerald. Plenty in larder. But why for *you* wan' cook?'

'I thought it would be nice, that's all, to make a special effort. Can you buff up the silver cutlery and put our best wine glasses on the table?'

'But it only Wednesday-*lah*,' Mei Ling frowned. 'Next you wan' I use best tablecloth.'

'Well,' Miranda smiled, 'that's not a bad idea.'

At seven o'clock, she lit the candles on the table and waited in the living room for Gerry to come in. An hour passed, then another. When she finally heard the dull rumble of the car pulling into the driveway, the candles had burned half down their wicks. There was a hint of whisky on Gerry's breath along with the smell of cigars on his clothes. His hair was sticking up in certain parts, as though he'd been running his hand through it.

'Is everything all right?' she asked, searching his face for clues, but he went straight to the drinks cabinet.

'Do you want to talk about it?' she continued.

'No,' he said curtly.

'Did something happen?'

Gerry sighed and said, 'I'd rather forget about it.'

'Oh. Perhaps we should eat, then? You might feel better for a meal.'

'I'm not hungry.'

'But it's meat and potato pie!' She thought of all her effort – the pie keeping warm in the oven. 'I've held it back for ages.'

He poured out a whisky, knocked it back, winced, then poured another.

'No. I think I'll just have a soak in the bath.' Gerry turned to leave without looking at her and retreated to the bathroom, slamming the door.

She waited, then followed and listened. There was water running; she could hear him getting into the bath. This was so odd – not at all like him.

'Gerry? What's the matter?'

He didn't reply.

She went to the kitchen to take the pie out of the oven, and after a time, she returned and tried again.

'Gerry, what's wrong?'

The water sloshed about, then the door pulled open. He'd wrapped a towel around his waist, but water was dripping everywhere.

'You really want to know?' His tone seemed bitter.

'Yes. Of course.'

'Well,' he folded his arms, 'a couple of nights ago, in a village in Selangor called Batang Kali, something rather dreadful happened.'

'Go on.'

'There was a massacre.'

'Another guerrilla attack against the British?'

'No,' he paused.

'What, then?'

He ran his hand through his hair. 'A group of female plantation workers were killed.' He took a deep breath, then continued. 'Twenty-four women, children and their babies were hacked to death in the fields where they worked. We saw the report and photographs this morning.'

'My God! Who would do such a thing?' It was appalling and it sickened her to think of such barbaric actions.

'It was us. Well, the Scots Guards. And that's not the worst of it. The people were completely innocent, and the bastards acted without any orders.'

'Good Lord! Oh, Gerry – that's appalling. I don't know what to say.'

'There's nothing to say.' He brushed past her and walked towards his dressing room. She stood at the door, watching as he banged the wardrobe doors and drawers.

It was hard not to picture the women and children, butchered where they stood, and then a thought occurred to her.

'But what about the men from the village – where were they? They must have gone mad when they found out.'

'They were working on another part of the plantation. We haven't told them who it really was. Believe me, it's better that way.'

'But won't they want some kind of justice – or revenge?'

He shook his head gently. 'They can't have it.'

'What do you mean?' She tried looking him in the eye, but he wouldn't meet her gaze.

'Come on, Miranda. Think about it. What would happen if news like this got out? The locals are only just beginning to trust us again after the Occupation. Something like this would set relations between them and the Brits back beyond repair. There's been a round-robin at the Office telling us all to go lightly on whatever projects that we're doing – to keep a lid on it all just in case the locals resist our authority.'

'Do you honestly think you can stop it?'

'It's the Colonial Office's job to make sure it doesn't go further.'

'You mean a cover-up, don't you?' The idea that the CO would even consider the idea repulsed her, let alone that Gerry would go along with it. 'How could you think of doing such a thing?'

Gerry shrugged. 'The housing development programme I'm in charge of is highly sensitive. To stop overcrowded living conditions and the spread of disease here we have to create goodwill to get the locals on board. All the negotiations we've made with the Chinese will just go to pot if this news gets out. We simply can't allow this to happen, whatever the cost.'

'That's no excuse. What if it had been me? Wouldn't you want justice? Remember how you felt when Henry died? You were devastated – those poor people will be feeling the same.'

'It's just the way it is, Miranda. Just forget about it. I wish I hadn't told you now.' There was a long silence before Gerry said, 'On second thought, maybe I will have some of that pie.'

He left the room and went to the kitchen. Miranda didn't join him. The thought of eating after what Gerry had just told her suddenly made her feel sick.

She couldn't sleep that night. Snippets of the day replayed in her mind, like images on a moving screen. Jack seemed to turn into Henry, and Jane and Mary's features took on a sharpness in the dark that hadn't been there in the daylight. She turned and tossed, trying not to imagine the women and children killed at Batang Kali, but she couldn't get them out of her mind. She kept visualising them lying where they had been slaughtered, and it was as though she were there, hovering over their mutilated bodies, trying to make sense of it all, attempting to block out the mothers' screams as they desperately tried to protect their young.

How could anyone do such a thing? she asked herself again and again.

And now the government, her husband, wanted to cover the whole thing up.

Shame and anger twisted and tightened within her.

A clock struck two. She could have cried with frustration. Exhausted, she switched on the bedside light and lay in bed, watching the fan spinning overhead.

'Can't sleep?' Gerry mumbled. He rolled towards her and placed his arm around her. She could feel the warmth of him, the stickiness of his skin against her own. He began stroking her hair and kissing the side of her throat.

'No. Gerry, *please.*'

'Come on, old girl.' She could feel him; how much he wanted her.

She pulled her head away as he began to kiss her and shoved aside his hand, which was slipping between her legs.

'Gerry, for God's sake, stop it.'

'Why can't you ever relax?' He turned away, his back resolutely towards her, and thumped his pillow into shape far more than it needed.

She wondered if she should have let him continue: they still hadn't made love since Henry had died, but the idea was overwhelming and made her panic. What if they had another child? And then, if anything happened to that child, she didn't know if she could bear it. She hastily climbed out of bed and mumbled something to Gerry about deciding to sleep in the guest bedroom. He didn't follow her. She lay down, her mind racing, and after a few minutes she heard the sound of Gerry snoring. It was hard not to picture him lying close to her, but on the other side of the wall. She rolled over, as far away from him as she could. Sleep came in fits and starts and she was aware of the darkness shifting into lighter shadows, and then daylight came, with the ring of his alarm, the squeak of the bedsprings as he moved on the bed, the flush of the lavatory and water running in the shower. She sat up, pulling the sheet around her body, listening. Waiting. Then, she got up and pulled her dressing gown on.

Gerry was in the dressing room, his eyes focused on the ties hanging in the wardrobe.

'Gerry?'

Their eyes made contact briefly, then he turned his head away.

'We need to talk,' she said, as gently as she could.

'What about?' Still, he didn't look at her. She waited, picking at some loose threads on her dressing gown.

'You know what about. Last night.'

She watched him pull a paisley tie off the rack.

'I've told you before – I'm not ready,' she continued. She really did want to make him happy, but now, particularly after last night, the thought of being intimate seemed like a form of self-betrayal.

'I thought you wanted it – the candles on the table, the way you'd done your hair. What did you expect me to think?' He knotted his tie.

'Not that.'

'Come on.' He stepped towards her, catching a lock of stray hair. 'It's been so long.'

She recoiled.

'What's the matter with you?'

'Nothing.'

'That's not what it seems like to me.' He sighed. 'What's happened? When we first met, we couldn't keep our hands off each other.'

'Things have changed.'

'Obviously.' There was such a look of hurt in his eyes. 'Is it me? Or something I should have done?'

'No.' She shook her head. 'I love you.'

'I know, but I have feelings and needs too.'

'Of course you do.'

'And it's so cruel, you know. Playing with a man.'

'I don't mean to.'

'For God's sake,' he was shaking his head, a thread of saliva on his lip. 'What's wrong with you, then?'

'Look,' she interrupted, 'I'm trying to explain.'

'What is it, then?' He was frowning.

'I'm frightened,' she murmured, 'that if we have another baby, I'd lose it too. I simply can't go through all of that again.'

'But the chances of that happening are a million to one.'

She didn't know whether that was actually true or not, and she wondered if he'd ever understand what she was going through. There was no doubt in her mind that he thought he loved her, but it occurred to her that, now, it was some other Miranda that he needed. He kept wanting her to move on, to change and be different, but, to her, love meant you had to take the rough with the smooth, grow together and support one another through the good times and the bad.

She shook her head. 'I know that, but it doesn't mean I'm not frightened and confused. You know I need your love, but not the rest of it. Not yet.' She shuddered and shook her head.

'*You're* confused? What about me?'

'This isn't all about you.'

'No,' he looked straight at her, his voice hard. 'You're right. But it isn't just about you either. It's about the both of us. Sometimes, even you have to make compromises.'

'I know, I know.' Of course she did. Her mother had told her all about that when she and Gerry had first married, and soon after she'd read all about it in an article in a women's magazine: always greet your husband at the door when he comes home from work, it had suggested, even if you don't feel like it. He'll be tired from a day at the office and will look forward to coming home to a smiling wife and food on the table, and, remember, don't trouble him with your little worries of the day. Another article, she remembered, said that a man's physical needs might be greater than a woman's, and to remember it was his right, and the wife's duty to oblige. But she'd never seen an article teaching you how to repair a relationship after the death of a child – was she supposed to bury her feelings and shut her eyes to his advances? Well, she didn't want it to be like that, lying in bed, staring at the light fitting or the suitcase on top of the wardrobe during their lovemaking. That certainly wasn't right either.

'I do love you.' She lifted her hand towards him. 'Just give me more time.'

'Fine,' he nodded; there was impatience in his tone. 'But I don't know how much longer I can take this.' He picked up his jacket from the back of the chair and pulled it on, then he pushed past her.

'Ugh!' She buried her face in her hands. If only they could find a middle ground. After a few minutes, she followed him to the dining room, where Mei Ling had already set the table for breakfast.

She sat opposite Gerry, toying with a teaspoon while she watched him unfold his newspaper.

'Perhaps we should both try harder to understand each other?' she began. 'You could start by telling me more about your work. What about Batang Kali? I don't agree with what you have to do, but all of this must be distressing for you. I have no idea what it must be like, the type of things you see every day.'

'No, you don't.' He looked up from the paper. 'It's not always pleasant.'

'And there seem to be more attacks happening in Malaya.'

'Yes.' He glanced back down at the paper and turned a page. 'Some particularly nasty ones recently – not only on plantation workers, but also on the British.'

The door opened and Mei Ling entered.

'Morning, Mr, Mrs Gerald. I make you boiled eggs as a surprise.' She placed a tray with eggs, toast and a teapot on the table, then left.

Miranda took the teapot and poured out the dark brown liquid into two cups, followed by condensed milk, which was all that kept well in the heat, and watched the white mingling with the brown.

Gerry cracked open his egg. 'Too damn soft, again. Can't you show her how to do it properly?'

She glanced up at him; he was picking out a piece of shell from the soft yolk.

'Eggs can be tricky.'

'They can't be that damn hard.'

She buttered her toast, wondering if he'd ever tried to make them.

He pushed his plate away. 'Look, I'm going off to work. None of this is getting us anywhere.'

'Hold on.' She swallowed a mouthful of toast. 'Before you go, I want to tell you about my visit to Charlotte yesterday.'

'Fine.' He paused. 'Go on, then.'

She really wanted to tell him about Jack lying in the cot, the urge to pick him up, to stroke his head, to hold him in her arms and inhale the essence of him, but she knew she had to find a middle ground between them. The kind of wife he needed was one more like Charlotte, so she'd have to try to be like her, however hard it might be.

'It was good, actually. And I've asked Charlotte and Andrew around for drinks on Friday night – like you suggested. You could ask Dickie and Longland, make a party of it?'

'Good.' He gave a nod of his head, then stood. 'At least there's something for me to look forward to.'

After he had gone, Mei Ling placed a handful of envelopes on the breakfast table. They were mainly for Gerry, but there was another aerogramme from Mother.

Mei Ling waited. 'Why didn't you eat what you cooked last night? I saw the bin this morning, you threw nearly all of it away.'

Miranda raised her head. 'Mr Gerald was late, and it had spoilt by the time he got home.'

'Shame not to eat.' Her gaze shifted from the table to the floor and she shuffled awkwardly on her feet. 'Maybe next time if you don't want it, you'll give it to me? My father is sick. I think he'd be happy to eat it.'

There was a hint of embarrassment in Mei Ling's voice, which mortified Miranda.

'I'm sorry, Mei Ling. I didn't think.'

Mei Ling turned to go. Guilt crept over Miranda. She'd had no idea Mei Ling's father was sick, nor how old he was. In fact, she knew nothing about Mei Ling's life beyond the bungalow. How could she never have asked?

'Is he very old, Mei Ling?'

Mei Ling drew herself tall. 'He nearly eighty.'

'But that's not all, is it? You said he was sick.'

'Yes, Mrs Gerald, he is sick.'

'Why don't you tell me? Go on, please.'

Mei Ling hesitated then began. 'The Japanese soldiers took lots of Chinese people to prison for no good reason. My father was one of these people. The soldiers beat him many times. They broke his arm and leg. He cannot work for a long time after. Now he can't walk any more, so I, Mei Ling, and my big sister must take care of him.'

'Mei Ling, that's absolutely appalling. I had no idea. Please, you must let me know if there's anything I can do.'

'Why did the British people let the Japanese people come to Singapore in the first place?' Mei Ling snorted. 'Now everything's no good.'

Miranda thought about what Gerry had said about the housing programme and the attacks in Batang Kali.

'But we're trying to make it better here again – it will take time.'

'Maybe it's too long a wait for my father.'

'Oh, Mei Ling!' She could see film forming across the woman's eyes. 'Why don't you take the morning off and spend it with him? There are plenty of eggs, and I think some fruit, as well as some biscuits. Take those with you.'

Mei Ling's gaze met hers. 'You sure, Mrs Gerald?'

'Yes.' She smiled. 'Quick. Before I change my mind!'

Once Mei Ling had left, she sat for a while. Of course, the Japanese occupation had been awful, she knew that, but what she hadn't appreciated was the depth of anger the locals still harboured against the British for allowing the Japanese to march unchecked over the causeway. There was still so much she had to learn about Singapore, and she wondered if she'd ever understand the people here.

After a time, she picked up the aerogramme from her mother and ripped it open.

My dear Miranda,

It was so delightful to receive your letter and snaps. I still have to pinch myself to think of you living half the way around the world. Every day, with rationing and goods in such short supply, I think of you living such a life. To have the constant, all-year-round sunshine sounds like bliss, especially when I think about all the snow we had last winter. I can still recall January '47 when the snow was so deep that, even with all the manpower to help, the trains got stuck and the country seemed to come to a standstill. Our dear king and the princesses visited South Africa, do you remember? And I suppose that's how I think of you, like the young princesses and enjoying a glamorous life such as theirs.

Miranda smiled at her mother's comparison, knowing that nothing could be further from the truth. She carried on reading.

But you'll never guess what, the other day I received a letter from Lily Lewis. She was asking all about you and Gerry. Can you believe it, she hasn't received a single letter from him since you left?

Actually, Miranda could. Gerry had never been the best of writers.

Anyway, last week I went to her house for afternoon tea. Such a lovely house near Cadogan Square. Such a beautiful lemon drawing room with silk curtains and damask on the sofas. There were cakes to die for. Not sure how she managed all that on rations, but one rule for the rich, I suppose. We spent ages talking – seems she has a friend whose daughter is out in Singapore. Jane, I think? I wonder if you've met her. Anyway, I took your letters to read selected parts from as well as your photographs. She really was thrilled to see them.

Miranda froze. To start with, she didn't like the idea of her mother sharing news and information with Lily. Her mother had always been impressed by Lily, had been charmed by her manners, dazzled by her wealth and connections. Miranda had never been able to make her mother understand just how cold and calculating Lily could be. Her mother-in-law had never liked her, and Miranda didn't trust Lily's motives for inviting her mother around. She was being a busy-body, most likely. But a horrible thought dawned. What if Jane had alerted Lily to something about Miranda? Was Lily spying, looking for an excuse to dish the dirt on her? And what if her mother let something slip out? The thought of it getting back to Singapore panicked her.

She folded the letter, wondering what to do. Her mother could get carried away in conversations and was especially influenced by those whom she considered her betters. There was only one thing for it, she'd write a guarded letter sandwiching a request for her mother to be careful what she shared with Lily between descriptions of the party she was going to hold in the summerhouse and an account of a recent trip to Holland Village.

But her mother's letter had unsettled her more than she thought. She tried to push her anxiety away, but it wouldn't leave. To settle her thoughts, she decided to call on Charlotte to test if there was anything amiss in Charlotte's attitude towards her. She could make up an excuse about some advice she needed for her party; the perfect excuse to call round and assess Charlotte's reactions.

Charlotte was sitting in the garden when she arrived, feeding a bottle of milk to a fretful Jack.

'He's even more restless today. I don't know what to do.' Jack batted the bottle in Charlotte's hand. The young woman looked exhausted. Miranda noticed the dark shadows below Charlotte's eyes; she knew all about those sleepless nights.

'No luck with the doctor, then?' she asked.

'No.' Charlotte sighed.

'I'd give him some more gripe water. Can't do any harm, and he'll grow out of all this crying in the end, I'm sure of it.'

'That's a good idea. I think I've got a bottle somewhere.'

'I can hold him while you look.'

Charlotte hesitated and Miranda noticed a tightness in her face, as though she didn't quite trust Miranda.

'I haven't forgotten how to hold a baby,' she said, with a good-humoured smile as she held out her arms to take Jack.

Charlotte handed him to her. Miranda stood, shifting his body in her arms. His mouth bobbed on her shoulder as he bawled. She jiggled him, leaning her head against his, pressing her hand tight against his back, then gently swayed from side to side.

'Here it is.' Charlotte returned and took Jack from her, then gave him a spoonful. It soothed him, and after a time he fell asleep

'You look tired,' Miranda said, watching Charlotte place Jack in a Silver Cross pram. Charlotte tugged the mosquito netting over the top but continued to rock the pram gently.

'I must admit, last night was bad. All this crying is taking its toll on me.'

'If you need a break, I could look after him.'

Charlotte pursed her lips for a second. 'That's very kind, but Andrew said we should get another *amah*. I've resisted the idea up to now, but with help being so cheap, he has a good point.'

Miranda nodded. In London, she had struggled: washing nappies, cooking meals, feeding Henry even when her nipples were so sore. Charlotte was lucky.

'I've actually called to pick your brain,' Miranda began. 'It's about my party. I have to admit I'm a bit of a novice cook – there wasn't much scope for entertaining back home, and you seem so experienced. Should I cook something and, if so, what?'

'That would be nice. What about some vol-au-vents? Or some cheese straws? I could bring something sweet, if you like, but, really, don't go to too much trouble. Food doesn't last that long in the heat, and then, of course, there are always the ants.'

'They seem to get into everything, don't they?'

'Here's a little trick I've learnt, if your *amah* doesn't know it already. Place everything on a plate on an upturned bowl in a bigger bowl of water. The ants will drown long before they can get to the food.'

'That's so clever. And so simple. Thank you.'

Charlotte peered into the pram and her features relaxed.

'Thank goodness. He really is asleep.'

'Well, I'd better let you get on, then,' Miranda said. 'I know how precious the time is when they're sleeping.'

As she walked back home, she mulled over their conversation. Charlotte couldn't have been kinder or more helpful. Clearly, there was nothing to worry about there. She was being paranoid about Lily and Jane. There was so much distance between England and Singapore, and, after all, it was just as much in her mother's best interests to keep Miranda's secrets hidden, wasn't it?

Twelve

Nick ran along the paths winding between the bungalows. He'd been for another run, but his foot hadn't healed completely and it had taken him longer than he'd expected to get down from Bukit Kalang. He was a little short of time before he had to head off to St Augustin's for an emergency meeting that Alice had called. It annoyed him that Alice, in her role as manager, always seemed to arrange meetings on his day off, summoning him as though he were an afterthought.

Ahead of him, he saw a figure walking. Miranda. He hadn't seen her since he'd hurt his foot, and he felt a little guilty for not having thanked her.

'Hello,' he called.

'Hello.' She turned, her face marbled by the foliage overhead. 'I see your foot is better.'

'It seems to be. I've just been up the hill again. Thank you so much for helping me the other day. You were a life saver.'

She smiled and her face glowed a gentle pink.

'So,' he asked, aware that he needed to get on, but he lingered, noting the lustre of her hair, how it seemed to be lit from within. 'Are you all settled, do you think?'

'I think so. The house looks quite different now. Really cosy. And I rescued a summerhouse that was falling apart at the bottom of the garden. It's a little retreat.'

'Well, I know I've told you about the snakes, but look out for scorpions too. They like to hide in dark corners and under cushions.'

'Are you trying to scare me?' she asked, grinning.

She was very pretty, he thought. The dress she was wearing enhanced her silhouette and the sun had brought out a scattering of freckles across her face. There was a mole on her neck and a bead of perspiration curled into the curve of her throat. He fought the urge to wipe it away.

'Well,' he said, shifting on his feet. 'I'd better get on, I suppose.'

'Me too.'

She set off but then turned on her feet to face him.

'You know, we're having a few friends over for drinks tomorrow evening. Why don't you join us – six o'clock?'

He straightened up. 'Tomorrow?' He'd been looking forward to a quiet evening to himself, but her smile lured him. 'I think I'm free, but let me check first.'

'Good,' she said, as she touched the locket nestled at her throat. 'It would be lovely if you could join us.' This time she left.

He watched her retreating. From this angle she could so easily have been Daphne, right down to the slim shadow walking awkwardly behind her, and he realised how much he missed Daphne and female company.

Back at Belvedere, he quickly bathed and changed, knowing that he was definitely going to be late.

Alice was in full flow when he pushed open her office door. Tall and thin, with greying hair and grey-blue eyes, he placed her in her mid-fifties, and there was something about her that put the fear of God into him. Perhaps it was the way she knew everything about everyone or the way she moved around the medical centre? You never knew where she might be, but you could be certain she was only a few feet away. It was as though she moved through secret corridors and glided through walls. Today she appeared more intimidating than ever.

All eyes lifted towards him as he settled into an empty seat in the corner of the room, but hers were the most piercing.

'I was just reporting from the board meeting last week.' Alice turned to him. 'Owing to the increased number of patients arriving at the centre, the board are going to enforce some radical action regarding budgeting. I know, Dr Wythenshaw, that you've been trying to liaise with the Colonial Office to raise more funds. How has that been going?'

'Yes. I met Longland Mackintosh a couple of weeks ago.' Nick glanced up, turning his thoughts to the meeting in the room. 'As many of you know, the Colonial Office is implementing a social welfare plan here in Singapore, similar to the one in England. I've been providing data for them, in the hope of getting some more funds in this direction, but I'm afraid it's not amounted to much.'

'That's a shame.' Alice's lips thinned. 'Unless we can find a way of generating a more substantial income, the board will have to make further cuts. I think we all know what that means.' Hawk-like, she glanced about. The discomfort in the room deepened.

'What about fundraising?' one of the nurses asked. 'With Christmas coming up, we could organise a charity lunch?'

'I suppose that's a good idea, but if you have the time to plan it, let me know.'

The nurse shook her head.

'In that case,' Alice picked up a manila folder from her desk and opened it, 'I've received this letter from the Supreme Court. Some of you may have heard of Martha Hollande?'

'The Malayan girl?' the nurse next to him asked. 'The one whose natural parents are fighting against the people who adopted her?'

'*Allegedly* adopted her,' Alice said. 'The case has become more complicated. It's too intricate to explain here, but, in a nutshell, she's been made a ward of court and a safe house is needed. They've approached the centre and, after some consideration, I wondered if we should take her in. Any objections? The remuneration would be worthwhile, I think.'

'Doesn't that go against the principles of the centre, taking what is essentially a private patient?' Nick asked. 'We only treat those who have nowhere else to go.'

'Well, in a sense, she doesn't, does she?' Alice's look was blistering.

'But she'll take a bed from someone who needs it more.' He looked at the others, appealing for their support.

'It's an exceptional set of circumstances. I'm sure it won't happen again. Well, if there are no other objections, I think we should go ahead, don't you?' The others nodded. 'Dr Wythenshaw, could I trouble you to sign the admission papers?'

'Can't it wait until the morning?' he snapped, irritated that he'd been overruled. 'It *is* my day off.'

'Of course, but better to get it out of the way, don't you think? We never know what tomorrow might bring.'

'All right.' He took the folder from her and signed the paperwork with an angry flourish.

'Are there any other items to discuss?' Alice's voice cut through the silence. He handed back the folder and crossed his arms. Someone coughed. 'In that case, I'll call the meeting to an end.'

He was annoyed with himself. He was spineless. Why couldn't he stand up to her more? All he wanted to do was to get the hell out of there and drive fast along the coast road with his foot pressed hard on the pedal. As he got ready to leave, Alice called him back.

'Here,' she slid a letter towards him, 'I want you to look at this.'

He glanced pointedly at his watch, then picked up the paper.

Dear Miss Matthews,

I appreciate your cooperation in agreeing to look after Martha at the Mission Hospital and Welfare Centre, in what is a highly unusual set of circumstances. As you know, Martha is currently a ward of court, and while permanent custody for her is being arranged, the Supreme Court has ruled that she must remain in Singapore.

As part of the evidence for this case, we need a thorough and discreet medical report. Can you present this at your earliest convenience, please?

He snapped his head up, even more annoyed. 'Good God! You've accepted the offer already!'

'I had no choice.'

'So, what was all of this, then?' He waved the paper, indicating the meeting that had just ended. 'A bloody charade?'

Alice sighed. 'As I said, it's an unusual set of circumstances.'

'I think you owe me an explanation.' He pushed the letter back, then sat back firmly on a chair in front of her desk. 'Go on, then, I'm looking forward to hearing what you have to say.'

'Fine. Both parties are playing every trick in the book. Look, not many people know this, but she's recently been married to a Malayan cousin and the court needed to ascertain, without delay I might add, if the marriage has been consummated. It's pivotal to the case.'

'This isn't ethical. I've got a good mind to rip up the admission papers here and now.'

'Come on. Show some compassion. She's just a minor, and a confused and frightened one at that.'

'All right.' He shifted his body forward. 'I'll agree to this admission on the condition that it's a one-off.'

'Good.' Alice placed the letter back in the folder and stood up. 'I'll take you to meet her, then.'

'What? You're telling me she's here already?'

'There was nowhere else for her to go.'

As he stood, he pushed back his chair, scraping it loudly against the floor. 'This really is the bloody limit.'

'Dr Wythenshaw, protocol is protocol, I know, but how would it appear if we turned away a high-profile case like this?'

'This really *is* against my principles and my better judgement.'

'I know. But it really is necessary. Please come. She's a lovely girl.' Alice stepped out of the office and he followed her to a small, faraway room.

Martha was sitting on a chair, wearing a loose top, trousers and a hijab. It wasn't her youth that struck him the most, nor was it the pale strands of hair escaping from the fabric on her head. It was the colour of her eyes.

They were startling – as blue as a sea-polished piece of glass.

'Martha? This is Dr Wythenshaw.'

The blue eyes flickered towards him again, not fully comprehending. Lines of confusion puckered her brow.

'She probably only speaks Malay and doesn't understand us,' he said. 'Can't you see, she's completely terrified?

You should have asked one of the nurses to sit in with her instead of abandoning her like this.'

'She's not abandoned.' Alice shook her head. 'Anyway, the nurses don't know she's here yet and, even if they did, they don't have enough time to be at her beck and call. Besides, she's got things to occupy her.' Alice indicated the books and the sewing on the floor.

She might not be abandoned, he thought, but she needs some love and affection to keep her happy.

The following day, he was still fuming when he arrived at St Augustin's. Alice had really got under his skin this time, and he needed to calm himself down before they crossed paths again. As he made his way from the car park, he could see a light on in the centre's chapel. It illuminated the stained-glass windows, and he could hear the organ playing and the sound of singing. Nick could never fathom how the schedule of the nuns and their religious community married so smoothly with the life of the hospital, but it did.

Inside the corridors, the smell of disinfectant was overwhelming. Nurses mingled with women and children, guiding them to different rooms or corridors. A baby screamed and a toddler ran towards him, a thread of mucus hanging from his nose. He'd never seen the place so busy. It was going to be a very long day.

'Here you are.' He gave the boy his handkerchief. 'You can keep it.'

The boy smiled and ran back to his mother, clutching the handkerchief and wrapping his arms around her sari-clad legs. She lifted her eyes towards Nick; dark, soul-searching eyes, tinged with yellow: hepatitis, liver damage. He suspected she'd not have that long to live.

At the end of the airless corridor, he turned right and pushed open the door to his office. It was humid inside, the desk fan inadequate for the space. He looked at his list for the day: a vaccination clinic in the morning, followed by ward rounds, then screening the new patients. He wouldn't be home until late.

There was a knock at the door.

'Come in!' he called, still reading his list.

'Good morning, Dr Wythenshaw.'

Nick lifted his head. It was Alice. Today she was wearing her nurse's uniform, and a silver cross hung from her neck. In one hand she held a pen and in the other a piece of paper.

'We have a busy morning ahead of us,' she began. 'Firstly, here's the report from the board meeting. I'll let you look at it, but the long and short of it is that the news isn't good – if we carry on spending at this rate, we're going to have to make some serious cuts. Read it and get back to me later. Secondly, we're offering X-rays today. Short notice, I'm afraid, but after a bit of luck, we managed to get hold of a mobile unit. We can kill two birds with one stone, which will save some money. Since half the patients are here for the smallpox inoculations, we can do them at the same time.'

'Yes. I saw the chaos in the corridor.'

'Thirdly, you'll have to halve the amount of time you spend with each patient if we're going to get this done smoothly.'

'I'll try.' He tapped his fingers on the desk, wondering how he would achieve this.

'And then send each patient straight to the mobile unit, which is out beyond Ward D. We can't have them hanging around outside for too long; the last thing we need is patients going down with heat stroke.'

'Got it.'

'Well, make sure you do. I've lived here for most of my life and I still don't underestimate the sun.' Her tone was dismissive – he hated the way she spoke to him as though he were a fool.

It was after seven by the time he'd finished at the hospital and he walked slowly away, mulling over the day. The sun had already set behind the roofs as he made his way across the forecourt towards his car. He noticed that the chapel lights were still on and he decided to go in.

It had been a long time since Nick had believed in God, but, from time to time, he liked the comfort of the chapel. It was dim and smelt of incense: sandalwood mixed with bergamot. He always enjoyed walking along the empty aisles, looking at the Stations of the Cross; he found it oddly comforting and evocative of his school chapel – a mixture of his old life and his new. Towards the back of the building there was a statue of the Madonna with the

Infant Christ. Someone had recently hung a chain of jasmine around her neck and a pot of incense burned at her feet. He smiled. It reminded him of that Christmas term at Ampleforth when he was fifteen, before Freddie had died, how he'd decorated the Madonna with tinsel and drawn a moustache on the Baby Jesus. It was funny to think of what a tearaway he used to be. He sat down in a pew at the back and looked up at Mary's angelic features: the perfect image of a selfless mother. It made him think of his own mother, and her face on the day he was expelled knowing that she'd always wanted him to be more like Freddie when he was alive. 'For the love of Christ!' she had yelled, her face twisted with anger. 'After all that good money we've spent on fees! How could you? Why can't you at least *try* to take a leaf out of Freddie's book?'

Was that when he began to lose his faith? There wasn't one moment he could point to. However, whatever doubts he had been experiencing were certainly consolidated by the war – being confronted by the awful, dreadful waste of life. And, of course, there was losing his brother, Freddie. In the early days of life without Freddie, he'd only felt anger. Later, he'd sometimes felt the urge to pray, but each time he tried he had been consumed by his fury, desperately demanding an answer, and it had been no use.

A door clicked open, then he heard footsteps to his right. A shadow fell and he turned to see a stout, European man standing close by. His hair was silvery-grey yet luxuriously thick and his face was crimped with gentle lines.

PAULA GREENLEES

'Good evening.' The man's voice had a hint of Irish in it. Southern, Nick thought, or possibly Dublin. 'Are you all right there, or can I help you?'

'Good evening,' Nick replied.

The man settled into the pew next to him. 'I'm Father O'Donald, and you must be the young doctor whose car I've been admiring, parked beneath the tiger palms?'

'Ah. Yes, I am.'

'I've heard all about you from the nurses.' He smiled at Nick knowingly.

Nick felt himself blush. Since Daphne, he'd been shy of the veiled invitations from the other nurses, their suggestions that he join them in the staff canteen, the outings to the beach.

His mind turned to Miranda, the way the light filtered through the trees, speckling her complexion, the aroma of her perfume lingering behind her.

Perhaps it was time to take the nurses up on their invitations.

Thirteen

More than anything, Miranda wanted her drinks party to be a success. She spent most of Friday preparing egg vol-au-vents and cheese-and-prawn sticks while Mei Ling made sweet-potato dips with papaya jam.

'How's your father?' she asked.

'He liked it when I saw him the other day.' Mei Ling smiled. 'Big surprise. Thank you for letting me go. We played mah-jong with friends.'

'I've seen you playing that with Jinhai. Is it a good game?'

'*Very* good.' Mei Ling smiled again. 'Maybe I can teach you?'

'Yes. Why not? I'd like that, but I'm afraid I wouldn't understand any of the Chinese characters on the tiles.'

'Not too hard, Mrs Gerald. I teach you those also.'

Later, they swept the summerhouse clear of ants and beetles, placed tea lights in jam jars, and jasmine and camellias on the table. Mei Ling hummed as Jinhai brought out bottles of gin and vermouth, along with slices of lemon and a selection of glasses, a bucket for ice, then finally her gramophone and a collection of records, which he placed on a table on the grass.

By six, everything was ready, and she sat in the summerhouse with a large gin, feeling pleased with her efforts, but also a little nervous. Despite it being the end of the day, the heat was still overpowering, and she was glad of her drink and the fan she had brought with her. As she waited, she heard footsteps scrunching along the drive. It was the telegram boy.

'Mrs Lewis?' he asked.

'Yes.' Even now, so long after the war had ended, the arrival of a telegram stirred up fear within her. She took it from him.

WILL BE LATE. G

'Oh, for goodness sake! And tonight of all nights, and he doesn't even have the decency to call me.' She took another slug of gin, wondering what could have happened. No explanation. Just a curt message. She stood up and flicked through the stack of records next to the gramophone before selecting one and placing it on the turntable.

Perry Como's voice filtered across the garden, and she clutched her glass, listening to the words and looking at her handiwork. Everything was perfect: Mei Ling had placed the canapés on the table and covered them with damp tea towels, and the centrepiece of jasmine and camellias smelt heavenly. Candles flickered in glass containers, like glowing flames of hope. It all looked lovely, but now the sense of something akin to a broken promise hung over it all.

She turned away.

Footsteps fell, then a shadow fell across the path, and a woman cleared her throat. Miranda lifted her head. It was Georgina.

'I simply adore Perry Como! And my goodness! Everything looks divine, but, I'm sorry, Peter's going to be late.' She was wearing a midnight-blue dress and her diamond earrings glistened in the candlelight. 'Seems like there's been another emergency. All hands on deck.'

Miranda groaned – that meant everyone, Dickie and Longland too. 'Gerry's just sent a telegram. Do you know what's going on?'

'No, but I wouldn't worry about it. It happens all the time. You'll get used to it.'

Miranda glanced with disappointment at the candles burning down and at the flowers she guessed would wilt before the canapés were eaten. 'Can I get you a drink? Or something to eat?'

'Gin and a little ice, please.' Georgina sat down. A fretwork of stars was beginning to form behind her, lacing the sky with silvery-gold. 'You look done in,' she said. 'Have you been at it all day?'

'Mei Ling and Jinhai helped.'

'You should let them do more for you. Don't underestimate the heat – it takes weeks to get acclimatised.'

'It wasn't that hard.'

'Perhaps not – but remember you've been through a difficult time. You mustn't overdo it.'

Miranda sighed.

Georgina edged forward. 'It was lovely to see you the other day. Tell me, how are things with you and Gerry? Given up those ideas of changing the world?'

'You mean volunteering? Yes. I'm going to take everyone's advice and treat this like a long holiday on a tropical island.'

Georgina nodded. 'Joking aside – that's good.'

Miranda grinned. 'Now, you tell me about you.'

Georgina leant back in her chair and took a sip of her drink.

'Well,' she said. 'I've had a letter from my sister in London. My niece, Poppy Fanshawe, remember her?'

'Mmm. Most certainly do. At Howdean, isn't she?'

'Not any more. Just turned twenty and is proving to be a flighty thing. Apparently there's some unsuitable romance going on and my sister wants to get her out of London. In fact, God forbid, she wants *me* to take her under my wing.'

'Really? What are you meant to do with her out here? And how did she grow up so fast?' Miranda mused. 'I still remember her in pigtails and petticoats.'

'I know. I think I'll have to get Peter to get her a job in the CO. They're always looking for secretaries, but, honestly, I think it's a terrible idea. All those men.'

'Goodness. A bit like out of the frying pan into the fire, I'd say! But I can't see it being a problem. Most of the men there are either old or married, surely?'

'I suppose.'

Charlotte arrived, carrying a plate of what looked like lemon meringue pie. She was flustered and breathless. 'I am *so* sorry I'm so late. Even though we've got a new *amah* for Jack, he still wouldn't settle.' She put down the pie on the table and took the gin Miranda held out to her. 'And then I was listening to that terrible news on the wireless.'

'What news?' Miranda glanced across at Georgina's blank face, then back to Charlotte.

'You mean you haven't heard?' Charlotte raised an eyebrow. 'The Malayan high commissioner's been assassinated.'

'Bloody hell!' Miranda gripped her glass.

'In Malaya – near KL. Some ghastly guerrilla attacks. And poor Lady Montieffe was with him.'

'My God. That's awful.' Georgina frowned. 'I hope she's not, you know ...'

'No. She's all right. Well, as much as she can be, given the circumstances.'

'Honestly, it makes you wonder what's going to happen next if even the high commissioner isn't safe.' Georgina's frown deepened. 'I hope Peter's uncle is all right.'

'Where's he based?' Charlotte asked.

'Just south of KL. Small rubber plantation.'

'Had any trouble?' Charlotte's expression was one of concern.

'No. Not really. A few workers have had stones thrown at them, but nothing more.'

'It's pretty worrying, isn't it, this whole situation?' Charlotte continued. 'It's as though one's always looking over one's shoulder, not knowing what to expect next.'

'But Singapore's safe, isn't it?' Miranda looked from Charlotte to Georgina.

'I hope so, but who knows?' Charlotte said.

'I don't think we've got anything to worry about,' Georgina replied. 'There's the causeway between us.'

'Didn't keep the Japanese out, though, did it?' Charlotte said.

Silence fell between them. They sat waiting among the flickering candles, which cast gloomy shadows on the summerhouse wall. Miranda wished the men would hurry up. Three, four times, they saw headlights pass the drive, each time they strained their heads in unison, searching for a sign of their husbands, but the beams travelled on, and their eyes searched for the comfort of each other again in the darkening light.

After a time, the drone of a car engine grew louder. Miranda watched as blazing headlights slowed then turned into the drive. It was Nick. Miranda hadn't been certain he'd come, and she was delighted when she saw the shape of his sports car, then his tall, lanky figure as he approached.

There were a million other places Nick should have been. To start with, he was exhausted, and he'd also had another altercation with Alice. Lastly, on Monday evening he had to get a finalised report to the CO. Longland had arranged to meet him at the Civil Service Club to discuss it over drinks after work and he ought to give it one last look before the weekend shifts began.

What he wanted was a soak in the bath, then to sit in his room, quietly reading a book, but he knew Charlie and Brendan had company: some doctors and nurses from KK, and he'd had enough of hospital talk for one day. But if he were to be totally honest, there was something about Miranda that fascinated him – was it her smile, or the coy turn of her head, the way she parted her lips when she was thinking, revealing the soft line of her mouth? He could still feel her hands around his shoulders as they'd danced at the Metcalfes' party, the soft brush of her breath against his neck. It stirred up the still raw and painful memories of Daphne, feelings that he thought had died within him, except worse, because Miranda was a married woman – surely it would be better to stay away?

But he was here now, walking towards her door. He could see lights flickering in glass pots around the perimeter of the summer house, then Miranda came forward to greet him.

'Nick! I wasn't sure that you would come.' The half-light cast dark shadows beneath her eyes. 'You know Georgina, but this is Charlotte Yeardley, my neighbour.'

'Delighted.' He shook her hand.

'I'm sorry – there aren't any men here yet. You must have heard the terrible news?'

'Ah. Yes.' He took the glass she offered him.

'About the high commissoner?' Charlotte said. 'Simply ghastly.'

'Yes. It's terrible.' He'd heard it on the wireless in his office before he'd left work.

'It's shocking,' Charlotte continued. 'And *so* unnerving.'

'We've all been saying how the communist activity seems to be getting worse.' Miranda was clutching her glass. 'And now this. It makes you wonder what will happen next.'

'I wouldn't worry too much,' Georgina said. 'There's nothing you can do about it; unless you decide to leave, of course.'

'They've been calling it "The Emergency" for ages now,' Charlotte continued. 'If it's such an emergency, I wish they'd damn well get on with sorting it out.' Her face flushed.

'But that description is only for insurance purposes,' Nick said. 'Manufacturing companies – tin mines, plantations, things like that, can't claim compensation from their insurers unless Lloyd's decide that the fighting over here is a war. The definition's simply a loophole.'

'What? You think it's a war? I wish someone would damn well clarify the situation. Well,' Charlotte looked into her drink, 'I'm sick of it. It makes you wonder when all this damn fighting will ever end. Years and years of it. Haven't we all had enough?'

'I'm sure it won't last much longer,' Georgina said. 'Here. Top up?'

Nick held out a glass and watched as she poured in some vermouth. What they all needed was a diversion.

'Well,' he glanced about. 'That's a rather fine gramophone you've got there. Shall I choose some music?' He flicked through the stack of records. 'Charlie Parker, Crosby, Peggy Lee, Nat King Cole? What's it to be?'

'Bing Crosby,' Georgina said. 'Something lively.'

He took the record out of its thin, papery sleeve and placed it on the turntable, watching as the needle settled into the groove. He would have to stay until the men came, he decided. Keep the women calm. They were discussing a lunch at their club. He was only half-listening as he helped himself to the food laid out, then he sat down. The women, too, made an effort, picking at their plates. Miranda poured out another round of drinks, which quickly disappeared. The women complained how humid it was, and how their hair seemed to frizz or go flat in the heat. Time moved slowly.

Nine o'clock came. Then ten, followed by ten-thirty. Still, the other men didn't arrive. The women were worried. He could see their determination not to mention it, the frowns marking their foreheads and the furtive glances at their watches. Even he was getting concerned. Around eleven, Charlotte decided to leave. Georgina went with her.

'I suppose we ought to go in.' Miranda knocked over a glass as she stood.

'Shall I walk you up the path?' he offered, wondering if she were drunk.

She nodded. Perhaps he should take her arm. 'How about some coffee?' he suggested.

'No. It will keep me awake all night.'

'Tea?'

'Yes, tea. Good idea. Mei Ling will get some.'

A small Chinese woman was sitting on the verandah, and she rose from the shadows as they approached.

'Could you get Mrs Lewis some tea, please?' he asked, as he slipped his arm around Miranda's waist to support her.

The lamps were dim in the drawing room, and the ceiling fan clicked as it turned. Miranda flopped on the sofa and he sat opposite her.

'Where do you think they are?' She lifted her head and their eyes met across the room. 'I'm so worried.'

'Don't be.' He tried to sound convincing. 'These things happen – I'm sure your husband will be back soon.'

'I'm sure you're right. It's just the not knowing.' She looked like a young girl, gnawing the cuticle of her middle finger. There were smudges of mascara beneath her eyes, and he wondered if she was crying.

'Are you all right?'

'Yes.' Miranda nodded. 'It's been such a long day, that's all. And so disappointing.'

Perhaps, he thought, but he was glad to spend some time with her alone.

'Don't you need to get some sleep?' he asked.

She focused ahead of her, then her face jerked up, and their eyes met once again. Her gaze lingered on his. 'No, I don't think so. Not until Gerry comes home.'

Mei Ling came in carrying a tray of tea. He waited for her to place the tray on the table. She left the room and he could hear her shuffling back to the kitchen.

'Shall I pour?' he prompted.

'No. I'll do it.' She poured out the tea, but spilled it.

'You'd better do it,' she conceded.

He took charge of the pot and handed her a cup, then she yawned.

'Perhaps I should let you get to bed?'

'No. Stay, please. I'm sure Gerry won't be long.'

'All right,' he nodded.

When they'd finished their tea, he watched her curl her legs up on the sofa, and after a time, he noticed how her breathing became shallower and that her eyes were closing. Until he was certain she was asleep, he stayed, looking at the photographs on the bureau. The first was of a fox hunt, the next a wedding snap, then another, revealing a beaming Miranda with a baby in a christening robe on her lap. Was the baby hers, he wondered? It must be. The photograph looked recent, so it was unlikely that the child was already away at school. He hadn't realised, but it was possible that she'd lost a child. He glanced back at Miranda, trying to guess at her past and where her interests lay – she'd told him she'd been in the WVS, but what else? Sewing, perhaps, gardening certainly, but what else she did to occupy her time was a mystery to him. How different women's lives seemed to be, and he wondered if he would ever understand them.

When he was convinced that she was asleep, he placed a blanket over her. For a moment, he wondered what it would be like to be here always with Miranda. He pictured coming home from the hospital and sitting in the chair opposite her. She'd be sewing or reading a book, but, as he came in, she'd lift her head and her face would radiate her pleasure at seeing him. They'd talk about his day, perhaps, or local politics, maybe even about the book she was reading. Then, later ... he closed his eyes, pushing out the thought of them lying next to each other in bed. *Come on, snap out of it, don't be so damn foolish*, he told himself, as he turned out the lamps. He wished that Brendan were there to give him some advice.

But, standing in the doorframe, he lingered for one last moment to look at her and wondered if he was always destined to remain alone.

Fourteen

Miranda woke the next morning on the sofa – her back was aching and her dress crumpled. Someone had switched off all the lights and placed a blanket over her. She supposed it was Mei Ling.

As she stood, she stretched, unlocking each of the stiffened vertebrae in her spine, and moments of the previous night filtered back to her – the high commissioner's assassination, the miserable drinks party, the fact that she'd drunk way too much. And Nick. Of course, it must have been him who'd switched the lights out. She could remember it now, sitting in the drawing room chatting as they'd waited for Gerry. Although the details were hazy, it had been nice, just the two of them. They had spoken like old friends. At some point in the evening she must have fallen asleep, her head swimming from the alcohol. A wave of embarrassment washed over her.

Her mouth felt dry and furry and she stretched again, wondering if Gerry was home. She went to the bathroom, her tread a little unsteady, then cleaned her teeth and after she'd finished in the bathroom went to the bedroom and crawled in to the bed next to him, but she was surprised to see the sheets thrown back and that the bedding was cold. The clock on the bedside table showed twenty minutes past seven. He could be outside drinking a cup of coffee, but, when she looked, the cushions on the sofa were still plump and fresh dew was on the table.

'Mei Ling?' Miranda's head was throbbing as she entered the kitchen. Mei Ling was polishing and putting away glasses from the previous night. 'Have you seen Captain Lewis?'

'He's gone to work.' Mei Ling turned. 'Maybe half hour ago. He said not to wake you up.'

'What? But it's Saturday.'

Mei Ling draped the tea towel over her shoulder and shrugged, then continued putting glasses away in the cupboard.

'You must have been working for hours. Let me make you a cup of tea.'

'If you like, Mrs Gerald.' Mei Ling stretched on her tiptoes to reach the top shelf.

As she waited for the kettle to boil, Miranda set out two cups, a jug of condensed milk and the teapot on the table, then sat down opposite Mei Ling and poured the boiling water over the leaves.

'Tell me about your father, Mei Ling.' She poured out the weak tea into a cup without any milk for Mei Ling, just the way she knew she liked it.

'He's much better. I made him soup. He told me a story from when he was a young man.'

'That's really good. What kind of things did he say?'

'He told me about when he was trishaw driver.' Mei Ling smiled. 'I, Mei Ling, was a young girl. I don't remember it. He showed me a photo. He *jiànmei* – strong, handsome. I didn't know before, but he came here on it all the way from China.'

'Really?'

Mei Ling nodded. 'Many Chinese people walked a long way. They thought leaving China meant they would find a better life Singapore.'

'I didn't know that. But you're not so sure that he did, are you?' She placed her cup back in the saucer and looked at Mei Ling, at the faraway look in her eyes.

'Maybe. He find my mother here. They marry, very happy for a long time before she die. He wanted to go back to China. It made him sad that he didn't go. Then, during the time Japanese people in Singapore, he was prisoner in Changi. Japanese beat him so much there, it make him sick-*lah*.'

'True. But if he'd stayed, his life might have been much worse – think of all the terrible things that have happened during the Civil War in China. And there's no saying he would have survived any of it. And he certainly wouldn't have met your mother – or had you.'

'Maybe you're right.' Mei Ling nodded. 'Best not curse the darkness, better light a small candle instead.' She finished her tea and stood up. 'Now no more talking. I, Mei Ling, will wash up.'

'Here, let me help you.' She stifled a yawn, tiredness finally getting the better of her.

'No-*lah*! You look sleepy. Nearly finish. Nothing left to do.'

Mei Ling was right: there wasn't anything else to do. No clearing up. No Gerry to talk to. No plans made for the rest of the day. She'd have liked to spend a little while longer chatting with Mei Ling, but now her head was pounding, and Mei Ling was busying herself washing the teapot and cups.

'I think I might go back to bed, then. Can you wake me in, say, an hour or so? Bring me some tea and toast?'

She sank into the bed and felt herself longing for her London life – her things, all the familiar patterns and sounds of the day. She missed Socrates, the grandfather clock ticking in the hall, the purr of motors outside on the street, the welcome heat of the coals on the fire when she came in from the penetrating winter cold. More than anything she missed her mother and the company of the women she knew. After a time, she fell asleep and only woke when Mei Ling rapped on the door.

There was still no sign of Gerry. Where was he, and why hadn't he left a note? After her toast, she soaked in the bath for a time, wondering when he'd be back, then she dressed in a pair of slacks and a linen blouse, and made her way out to the summerhouse, carrying a blanket and a copy of *The Straits Times*. Mei Ling and Jinhai had cleared everything away, so she spread the blanket on the ground, kicked off her shoes and spread out the paper.

Yesterday afternoon, Sir Harold Montieffe was killed in a dramatic ambush 60 miles north of Kuala Lumpur. Sir

*Harold was travelling in a military convoy, along with
Lady Montieffe and several members of his staff, when a
force of approximately 40 guerrillas ambushed them. Lady
Montieffe survived the attack when Sir Harold forced her
into the footwell of the car. Sir Harold was killed by a with-
ering attack when the guerrillas fired a fusillade of guns
and rifles.*

*The convoy scout managed to push through the attack
and raised the alert in Kuala Lumpur. The Government has
announced a state of emergency.*

She looked at the photograph of the Silver Wraith riddled with bullets. It was hideous. Poor Lady Montieffe;
how do you get over something as dreadful as that? What
on earth did she, Miranda, have to worry about? Here
in the summerhouse, she was safe, but whatever anyone
had said last night, she was worried about the situation
spreading to Singapore. She lay back and placed her
hands at the back of her head and closed her eyes, wanting to block it all out. Light filtered through her lids, creating an opaque pinkness behind them. The longer she
stared at the colour, the darker the pink became until it
turned blood-red.

Perhaps this was what it was like to be cocooned inside
a shell or an egg? She drifted off and imagined that she
was floating on a raft on a river. But, then, a sound broke
into her thoughts; in and out, backwards and forwards,
like the wind whipping up waves for a storm. She opened
her eyes, trying to work out where it came from. Through

the doorway, she could see the boughs of a ginkgo tree and the magnificent arched branches of some royal palms. A flock of parrots flew down and settled in the branches and a gentle breeze ruffled the leaves, bringing with it once again the sound that had invaded her reverie.

The cries of a baby. It had to be Jack.

She levered herself up and listened, waiting for him to stop. Why didn't someone go and pick him up? The crying grew even louder, reaching a crescendo.

She made her way towards the Yeardleys' bungalow. Jack's pram was outside on the path with a mosquito net draped over the hood and handles. He was bawling; she could hear him batting at the rattles strung across the pram. Where on earth was Charlotte and why wasn't the *amah* doing something? His screams continued, rising higher and higher, and then, mid-scream, he stopped.

His face was scarlet as she reached the pram, scrunched up with a silent scream, but then he let go, bawling with the full force of his lungs. She'd forgotten how babies did that; stored up a cry, frightening the life out of you. It was enough to make the hairs stand up on the back of your neck. She started to jiggle the pram, but he screwed his face up more tightly. She couldn't stand it any longer, so she pulled back the netting and picked him up, cradling him over her shoulder.

'Sssh!' she whispered, closing her eyes and holding his head with one hand. She patted his back with the other, 'Sssh!' and rocked her body from side to side. The scent of talcum powder and soap on his head was more delicious than anything she remembered, and his skin was so soft, like down. 'Sleep now,' she whispered. He rested his head on her shoulder. 'You little darling,' she crooned.

After a while, he moulded his body into her and calmed.

'Excuse me – what you doing-*lah?*'

She looked up. A Chinese woman she didn't recognise was a few feet away, rubbing her eyes as though chasing away sleep. The new *amah*, she supposed. She didn't know her name. The expression on the woman's face was as dark as a rain cloud.

'He was crying, screaming. There wasn't anyone here.' Anger burnt her cheeks. 'You shouldn't leave him alone like this. What would Mrs Yeardley say?'

'She tell me let him cry himself asleep.'

'You shouldn't. You don't know what might happen. He could – I don't know, choke or something.' Miranda kissed Jack on the head, before placing him gently back into the pram. Her gaze lingered for a moment, watching him sleep.

'Well, he sleeping now.' The *amah* walked back to the bungalow, glancing over her shoulder with a look that stung.

Her patience snapped. 'How dare you speak to me like that! I'm Mrs Lewis – a friend of your mistress. And don't you ever let me find you leaving the baby to cry again!' She stormed away, hot tears pricking. For God's sake, she was only trying to help and how dare that woman speak to her like that. And as for Charlotte – well, people shouldn't have babies if they weren't prepared to look after them properly.

Monday afternoon gave way to evening, Nick swung the roadster into the Civil Service Club car park, but he couldn't find anywhere to leave the car.

'Damn,' he said.

Everything seemed to be against him today. Earlier, he'd found Alice Matthews snooping around his office – even lifting up the papers on his desk, of all things. No doubt she was looking for the report he'd written for Longland and Dickie that highlighted the centre's increasing influx of patients combined with their declining funding. Perhaps she was looking for a magical fix to it all? When he'd challenged her, she'd made up some cock-and-bull story about losing an admissions paper and how she'd wondered if he'd picked it up by mistake. As if he couldn't see right through her.

And now the report was ready at last for Longland and Dickie, but there was nowhere to park. He circled around the car park again, and in the distance, he spotted a palm tree with a small patch of grass underneath where he could leave the car.

'Perfect.'

He manoeuvred the car into the shady spot, parked and headed towards the club with the report in a folder under his arm.

It had been a while since he'd been to the Civil Service Club, but he remembered the single-storey bungalow and the Indian food that the club was famous for – fish or vegetable curries that had been simmering in vast cauldrons over charcoal fires all day. The curries were made by Indian chefs wearing loincloths, their dark skin glossy from the heat. They served the curry on banana leaves at long tables and encouraged the Brits to eat local style with their right hand. Hardly any did.

But, over time, he'd got tired of the raucous evenings there, where the spirits and beer had flowed and the cigar smoke had created a thin veil, disguising the men with their arms around a prostitute they might have brought along with them from the Geylang district or the latest pretty little thing from work. Their lewd behaviour got cleared up with the glasses and no one ever spoke about what happened there. Certainly never at work or in front of the wives. He had long ago decided it wasn't really the place for him.

It was a bit of a walk to the building and, when he reached the club bar, he'd already broken into a sweat.

Longland was seated on a high stool at the bar.

'What's your poison?' Longland asked, as Nick joined him.

'A Tiger beer would be great.'

'Nothing stronger?' Longland rolled his eyes at him. Nick placed the document folder he'd been carrying on the counter and wiped his forehead with a handkerchief.

'No. I'm good. It's got to be well over 90 degrees out there today. Had a devil of a job parking. Eventually found a spot miles away.'

'Yes, there's some do going on that involves the new staff. Some young secretaries, I think.' Longland ordered the beer then picked up the folder Nick had placed on the counter. 'Might have something to do with Dickie and Gerry being late.' Longland winked. 'This it, then?'

'Yes.' Nick watched Longland flick through the pages. 'I honestly don't know how you're going to implement this social housing plan, even if you do get all the funding. The locals don't trust us as it is – they only come to St Augustin's if they want food and shelter. It's a devil of a job getting them to be vaccinated or to carry on with treatment. How are you going to persuade them to leave their homes and watch them being knocked down without a fight?'

'We'll see. Besides, we persuaded them in Birmingham.' Longland glanced up at him. 'Don't see why we can't clear all the slums here too.'

'At least they spoke the same language at home.'

'True, but if they know what's good for them, they'll do as they're told. Ah, look, here's Dickie at last.'

Dickie sat next to Nick. 'Missed much?'

'Just started.'

'Whisky, please, with soda.'

'Seen Gerry?'

Dickie shook his head.

'Well,' Longland continued, 'Wythenshaw's just given me his latest report, that's all. Haven't had time to read it all yet.'

'So, what's the score?'

'Well,' Nick took a long sip of his beer, 'we all know that the shanties down by the quays need to be demolished – my research shows that there's been an increase in typhoid in these areas, and if you look here,' he took a map out of the folder and pointed with his pen, 'there's recently been an outbreak of cholera. And here, there's a higher than normal ration of polio.' He took a sip of his beer, then continued. 'Immigration reports suggest that there's been an increase by 20 per cent of Chinese immigrants to this area in the past four months. What's shocking is that the average household now consists of twelve to sixteen people. Bearing in mind that most of these people live in one-roomed shacks down by the docks, it doesn't take much to work out why or where these clearances should begin. Thing is,' he paused and looked at both men, 'where's the government planning on rehousing these people?'

'Come on, do we need to talk about this now? Thought we could have some fun tonight.' Dickie turned his head towards the direction of where music was playing in the other room. *Where all the new secretaries are*, Nick thought.

'Later,' Longland said.

'Well,' Dickie placed his glass carefully on the counter, 'the most popular suggestion is out by Changi.'

'What?' Nick said. 'But that's miles away. You'll be forcing them to move away from their communities – can't see them buying that. What about some of the land around Tanglin or Orchard Road? That's got to be closer – can't we requisition land from some of the bigger rubber plantations and keep these people closer to what they know?'

'You've got to be joking!' Dickie snorted. 'Can't see anyone giving up their land, can you, for a load of housing? Besides, land's cheap out there – because of the Japs' prison camp being out that way, no one wants to live out there now. Only way we can deal with the ever increasing influx of immigrants is to buy cheap. If you ask me, beggars can't be choosers.'

'Surely there's somewhere closer?'

Dickie shook his head. 'Half of the newly settled lot won't care.'

'Let's see if we can find somewhere better,' Longland interrupted. 'Now, I've been thinking how best to market the Singapore Improvement Trust's ideas to the locals. Best try and get them on our side, if we can, find a way to phrase what we're doing so that it sounds less intimidating. Any suggestions?'

'Mmm.' Nick thought for a moment.

'What about "The Reconstruction of Singapore"? Has a nice ring to it as well as making the locals feel they're playing a part in Singapore's future. Get them interested in the rebuilding of Singapore after all the destruction. What do you think?'

'Sounds good to me,' Dickie nodded.

'Great.' Longland jotted *The Reconstruction of Singapore* down on the cover of the report. 'Great work, Wythenshaw. All this information is exactly what we need for our meeting next week with the Trust.'

Nick fell silent. He was conflicted. He liked the idea of calling the housing project 'reconstruction'; it felt proactive and forward thinking, but that didn't mean he liked Dickie's attitude that you had to bully people into submission.

'Staying for a bite to eat, Wythenshaw? They do a great fish curry.'

Despite his earlier plan to do so, Nick shook his head. 'No. I think I'll get off – early start in the morning.'

He downed his drink, then walked beneath the whirring fans to the door.

The sky had darkened now, but the heat was as intense as ever. He lit a cigarette on the verandah and listened to the heavy thrum of the cicadas for a moment, and the music coming from one of the club rooms where the party for the new secretaries must be taking place, then he made his way to the roadster. Red lanterns had been lit along the pathways and he could hear the music and raucous laughter behind him. He could smell incense mingled with the spices and hints of perfume that lingered seductively in the air.

Another vehicle had been parked opposite his and, though it was dark, he could just make out that a man and two women were leaning against the bonnet. He climbed into his car and turned on the ignition, but at the sound of the car starting, the man lifted his face towards Nick. It was Gerry Lewis.

Nick ought to say hello. He got out of the car and went over to greet him.

'Evening. I think you've missed the meeting.'

'Damn.' Gerry swayed as he looked at his watch. Nick caught the smell of whisky on his breath. 'Over before it started, then?'

Nick laughed. 'I'm sure you can get the report from Longland or Dickie. But perhaps I can give you a lift back home and fill you in on the way?'

'Thanks. But I've got one or two things here to finish off first.' Gerry winked.

One of the women laughed and the other rested her hand on Gerry's shoulder.

'Well, good night,' Nick said.

'Goodnight.'

As Nick pulled away, he heard the two women laughing and, in his rear-view mirror, he saw Gerry sitting, with his arms around the both of them, on the bonnet of the car.

Fifteen

The heat became intense. Gerry left for work earlier each morning and came home later in the evenings, explaining to Miranda that it was to make the most of the cool parts of the day. She retreated to the summerhouse more and more, reading or sewing, sleeping when the heat became too strong. It became a sanctuary, a place that reminded her of home.

Sometimes Charlotte would call over with Jack, who loved the wind chimes Miranda had hung up around the summerhouse – when he was fractious, the spangles of light glancing off them seemed to be the only thing that soothed him.

One afternoon, she was dozing and the book she had been reading slipped from her hand. It thudded to the ground, startling her, and as she bent to pick it up, she heard Jack screaming again. Her head on one side, she listened. What was that *amah* up to? She clenched her fists and made her way over to the Yeardleys' to find out.

'Is there anyone here?' she shouted, as she approached the pram, Jack's screams ripping through her. 'Charlotte?'

She was about to jiggle the handle when she saw a snake coiled at the bottom of the pram.

'Jesus Christ!' She grabbed Jack from the pram, held him close and kissed the top of his head, her body shaking. 'There, there. You poor little thing.'

She glanced back into the pram – the snake was about three feet long, shiny and black, with narrow yellow bands across its body.

'Ugh!' She shivered as she clutched Jack closer to her. His sobbing calmed as he rested his head against her shoulder and she could feel his mouth sucking against the fabric of her dress.

She brushed her mouth across his head and inhaled the aroma of baby powder.

'My God, it doesn't bear thinking what might have happened.'

Jack's back arched and his body tensed as he prepared to start screaming again.

'You need something to drink, don't you? Let's find your mummy.'

She glanced back at the pram, as she made her way to the bungalow and shouted, 'Charlotte! Are you there?'

No reply. She headed towards the kitchen. It was empty, but a baby's water bottle was on the counter. She gave it to Jack, who drank in desperate gulps, his body relaxing as he sucked.

When he'd finished, she wandered around the bungalow looking and calling for Charlotte or the *amah*. Then she remembered it was Wednesday – wasn't that one of Charlotte's days for lunching with Jane and Mary? In that case, where on earth was the *amah*? She was nowhere in sight.

Miranda wondered what she should do. Jack couldn't be left alone. What if the snake got into the house and slithered into Jack's cot later? The thought made her blood run cold. She returned to the garden and looked inside the pram to check it hadn't escaped. The damn thing was still there, coiled like a spring but staring at her with such menace, as though at any moment it might strike. Perhaps she could get it out and then it might slither back into the jungle? She looked around for a big stick to fish it out with, but as she lifted the stick towards it, the snake lifted its head and a hood flared open as it hissed at her.

'Bloody hell! It's a cobra!'

Miranda dropped the stick and knocked the pram over, her heart racing. Then she ran, clutching Jack to her. Now the snake was riled she needed to get Jack as far away from it as possible. Fear took over, and she carried on running, holding him tightly as she blindly made her way back to the summerhouse. He liked it here, and the snake wouldn't be able to find them, she thought – she placed him on the floor and curled around him. She listened to his breathing settle as he watched the wind chimes and finally he began to coo. She kissed the top of his head and ran her fingers across his peachy cheek.

'It's all right, Jack. I'll keep you safe until your mummy gets back.'

Up on Bukit Kalang, Nick ran hard. Alice Matthews was driving him mad. Yet again she'd been in his office when he'd been out. Evie, one of the nurses that he was thinking of asking out, had told him she'd seen her picking through the papers on his desk. But instead of confronting Alice after his shift, he'd headed straight out to Bukit Kalang, and now he was angry with himself for not challenging her.

He stopped running and flopped down on the ground to think. There were stones at his feet with orangey flecks of fungi embedded in their rough, pimpled surfaces; Aspergillus or Cladosporium. They reminded him of ones in the alpine gardens he and his grandmother had created at Coombe. To his left there was a rhododendron bush and, beneath its branches, piles of twigs, leaves and stones, and an aroma in the air, like the sweet promise of spring.

It all brought back more memories of when he was a child. Such as how he'd tried woodwork for the first time. He remembered that morning well, the clear blue skies and the daffodils nodding buttery yellow heads as he made his way, with apprehension, with his grandmother to the estate handyman, Cooper's workshop; how he'd watched the old man smooth pieces of wood. Cooper had given Nick a plane and he'd been thrilled by the way it glided over the wood, as white and pure as an apple. He could almost smell the fresh shavings and feel the spiralling, translucent curls tumbling into his outstretched hand while the sunlight streamed fiercely through the windows.

Skills and crafts like that were reassuring – a connection with nature that he had enjoyed regularly after that. On his visits to Coombe, Cooper had taught him how to understand the grain of every piece of wood, in which direction it was correct to plane it and how to prep the pieces of timber. As his skills grew, he learnt how to cut a mortise and tenon joint or to dovetail joints to make a box. He had taken pleasure in finishing wood, applying the correct varnish with the appropriate brush. All the skills he had learnt from Cooper connected him firmly with his time at Coombe. A yearning to restore this contact grew within him, although he knew Coombe was the last place he could return to right now. He wondered if there was a primitive sense of yearning for the place that had developed through generations of his family living there.

He stood up, had a gulp of water from his bottle, then ran down the hill towards the government bungalows. Through a break in the tree line, he saw a small black Ford pulling into one of the drives.

He continued towards the bungalows and passed the crowded drive, noticing a pram, a police radio crackling, the sound of a woman crying and the angry voice of a man.

Sixteen

Nick stood at the end of the drive assessing what was happening, then made his way towards a policeman who was writing in a notebook. The man lifted his head at Nick's approach.

'I'm a doctor,' Nick said. 'Is there anything I can do to help?'

The man was Eurasian, about forty. He looked at Nick suspiciously.

'St Augustin's,' he continued. 'At Tanjong Pagar. I live up the hill, just there. I've been out running.' He pointed in the direction of the red roof just visible through the palm trees.

The policeman stopped writing. 'A doctor, you say. What's your name? Address?'

'Nick Wythenshaw. Belvedere. Just up there.' He pointed again in the direction of the house.

The policeman jotted his details down, then glanced towards the bungalow, from where Nick could still hear a woman crying.

'Perhaps you might be able to help the lady?' the policeman said. 'She's very upset.'

'What's happened?'

'Someone has taken her baby. You haven't seen anything while you were out? A person with an infant?'

Nick glanced towards the pram. 'No. Nothing.'

He entered the bungalow and followed the sound of voices. Two women sat on the sofa. One he recognised: Charlotte, her eyes were red and her face glistened with tears.

A man who must have been her husband rose from an armchair and demanded, 'Who are you?' His face, too, was red.

'Nick Wythenshaw. I'm a neighbour and a doctor. I was passing. I wondered if there was anything I could do to help?'

'Not unless you can find Jack,' Charlotte moaned, then she buried her face in her hands and her shoulders began to shake.

'There, there. I'm sure it will be all right.' The other woman put her arm around Charlotte's shoulder. 'They can't have gone far.'

He felt awkward standing there between them both, conscious of the damp rings of sweat under his arms and his forehead beading with perspiration. He remembered that Charlotte's husband was called Andrew. 'What happened?'

'We're not certain of all the details yet,' Andrew said. 'But we're pretty certain someone's snatched Jack.'

'I was out for lunch with Jane,' Charlotte's voice was weak, her distress punctuating her words, 'and when I got back, the pram was tipped up and there was no sign of Jack. The stupid *amah* had fallen asleep in a hammock at the bottom of the garden – can you believe it?' She wrung her hands. 'I should never have let that woman stay with him alone.'

'Sssh,' Jane said again. 'It's not your fault.'

The policeman entered the room. 'I know it's difficult, but try not to panic. In cases like this,' he said, 'we usually find the baby unharmed. Can you think of anyone who might want to take him?' His voice lowered. 'A friend, perhaps?'

Charlotte gasped, 'Oh God! Miranda.'

'What? Surely you don't mean Miranda Lewis, Gerry's wife?' Nick asked.

Charlotte nodded.

'Good God!' Jane jerked her head up. 'I always thought there was something strange about that woman. Do you remember when I caught her snooping in your house? She's probably been planning something like this all the time.'

Charlotte winced. 'She did it another time, too.'

'Why didn't you say?' Jane's hand touched Charlotte's arm.

'Can you tell me some more about her?' the policeman asked.

'She's my neighbour.' Charlotte clasped her hands again. 'I know she lost a baby.' She glanced up at Andrew. 'Do you think she could do such a thing?'

'Infants are often taken by someone who knows them,' the policeman said. 'And it's better if it's someone closer to home; there's more chance of a better outcome.'

Charlotte paled.

Nick felt helpless standing there watching. 'Perhaps I could go and look? I don't have any experience with this type of thing, but you might need a doctor when you find him.' He glanced from the policemen to Andrew, who nodded, his jaw rigid.

'We'll look together,' the policeman said.

They didn't speak as they walked the short distance to the Lewises' bungalow. On any other day, he would have enjoyed listening to the birds or looking at the shrubs stretching along the path. The garden looked peaceful as they approached, but no one seemed to be about. The policeman knocked on the door, and after what seemed like minutes, Mei Ling opened it.

'Is Mrs Lewis here?' the policeman asked.

'Why do you ask?'

The policeman spoke to her in Chinese. She replied and shrugged.

'What did she say?' Nick asked.

'That Mrs Lewis isn't home at the moment, that the car and driver have been out with Mr Lewis from early this morning. I don't suppose you have any idea where she might be, do you?'

Nick turned and looked across the garden. Of course – the summerhouse.

It was as though something had shifted, causing the air to move. She wasn't certain what it was. Perhaps it was the birds stirring from the branches or the pat of gentle steps across the grass sending a ripple that, like a tsunami, would gather pace and force.

A shadow fell across the summerhouse window, blocking out the light. She lifted her head, her arm still cradling Jack.

'Miranda? Are you there?'

The voice was familiar but she struggled to place it.

'Yes?'

The door opened.

'Nick?' She sat up, wondering what he wanted. A creak. More footsteps. Another man appeared, his features obscured by the sunlight.

'Sssh!' she whispered. 'You'll wake him.'

'Who?' There was a tremor in Nick's voice, as though something were caught in his throat.

'Jack.'

She saw Nick glance towards the other man, who stepped forward, light glancing off the pieces of metal on his shoulders. Now she could see that he was a policeman.

He took Jack from her, then handed him to Nick. The policeman reached for her arm.

'Mrs Lewis?'

'Be careful with her,' Nick said. He looked awkward with Jack in his arms. Strange, she thought, for a children's doctor.

'Would you mind coming with me?' the policeman said. 'I have a few questions I need to ask.'

'Why?' she asked, stiffening at the memory of feeling another policeman's hand on her shoulder. 'I haven't done anything wrong.'

But she stood anyway.

'Stealing a baby is a serious crime, Mrs Lewis,' the man said.

'What?' The shock of his words was like being plunged into an icy sea. 'You can't possibly think that, surely?'

The man held on to her arm more firmly, pulling her towards the door.

'I'll have to ask you some questions to find out exactly why you took him from the Yeardleys' house.'

'Oh come on! What nonsense. I heard him screaming – there was a snake in his pram. I went to have a look, there was nobody there, so I brought him here with me for safe keeping.'

She looked up at Nick, who glanced away.

'You don't believe me, do you? This is ridiculous.'

'Come now, Mrs Lewis,' the policeman said. 'Let's go back to your bungalow, shall we? We can talk better there.'

'Judas! What's wrong with you? I've explained.' Panic consumed her. 'Well, I'm not saying anything more unless my husband is with me.'

She had no option but to follow a policeman back to the house, her eyes trained on Nick's back, which lightly strained as he held Jack, until he turned down the drive to the Yeardleys'.

Mei Ling showed the policeman into the sitting room as he talked into a crackling walkie-talkie. Miranda sat on the edge of the sofa, staring at a patch of dust on the floor, determined not to say a thing. All the time her thoughts kept turning to the thimble, the pocket watch and the chipped jug she had once stolen and which were now concealed in her treasure box. If the police found out what had happened back in England, they'd never believe her about this.

The stealing had started just after Henry had died – that thimble to start with, then a pair of scissors, a jug. Usually it had been items she hadn't wanted and could have easily afforded. Each time she'd felt a thrill and a sense of triumph when she left the shop unobserved. Until the day she'd taken the baby's blanket. It was finely knitted, like lace, and she remembered lifting it close to her face and imagined the scent of talcum powder mingling with lily of the valley. She could almost picture wrapping it around Henry's tiny body and holding him tight to her chest. Then it came, the powerful urge to leave, taking the blanket with her. No one seemed to be looking, and so she rolled it up and stuffed it under her coat.

She shuddered, remembering how it had felt to have a hand on her shoulder, the shame of sitting in the police station, and how cold it had been in the corridor while she waited for her parents to take her home.

'You're lucky you got away with a warning,' her mother had said, as she wiped her hands gently on her apron.

'You won't tell Gerry, will you?'

Her father placed a cup of tea in front of her. She caught the sideways glance her mother gave him.

'Well,' her mother had sat down opposite Miranda and slowly stirred sugar into her tea, 'we know how difficult it's been for you lately, but ...'

The thoughts and memories swirled around in her head. What if they found out? And Gerry didn't know either. She simply couldn't go through all of it again.

And now, as she waited for Gerry for what felt like hours, those thoughts haunted her, and she was so relieved to finally see him, despite the look of complete confusion on his face.

'Oh Gerry!' she rushed towards him. 'This is all so ridiculous.'

The next few minutes had gone by in a strange, horrifying blur; it was as though everything was moving too fast for her to process more than snippets of the scene in front of her. She heard the policeman say, 'This is very serious – stealing a baby,' then the sound of Gerry's voice rising and falling, but she couldn't hold on to the sense of it.

'I didn't,' she muttered, but no one seemed to hear her. So she shouted, 'Why won't you listen to me? I *didn't* steal him. There was a snake.' She began screaming at them, 'I could hear him from the summerhouse. I looked for Charlotte and the *amah*, but there was no one about. They're the ones who are in the wrong – leaving a baby alone. Don't you know that? God knows what might have happened.'

Gerry lifted his head and frowned, then, in the same lowered voice, said something to the policeman that she couldn't hear. He went outside and the policeman followed. She stood at the edge of the sitting-room window watching them talking, then a black police car pulled into the drive, as dark and as threatening as a rook. Another policeman opened the door, followed by Andrew. They both joined Gerry and the original policeman. She drew in her breath, straining to hear what they were saying.

For five minutes, there was much talking and shaking of heads, then the occasional nod between the men. Eventually, Andrew walked away and she saw Gerry take his wallet from his jacket and count out a handful of notes. She stepped back and leant against the wall, crossing and then uncrossing her arms, then looked up at the ceiling. A car door slammed, then the police car's engine spurted into life, followed by the sound of wheels crunching on gravel.

A few seconds later, Gerry's footsteps echoed in the hall. Her throat felt dry as she peeled herself away from the wall and watched him sit on the sofa.

His look scalded her.

'I'm sorry,' she said.

'Well,' he exhaled, his breath loud and long. 'No thanks to that awful woman Jane egging them on, but you'll be relieved to know that the Yeardleys aren't going to press charges.' His voice was kind, and not at all what she had been expecting. She sat down in the chair opposite, her attention on him like a hungry dog.

'Miranda.' He pinched the bridge of his nose.

'Yes?' she whispered.

'You know, when we first met, I couldn't believe my luck. I wondered what I had done to deserve such a wonderful woman. You enchanted me – you know that, don't you? You were so different to all the girls I'd known before, so fresh and enthusiastic about every new experience. I can still picture the way your face used to light up like a child's at the simplest thing.'

She nodded.

'And I did everything in my power to look after you. But now,' he shook his head, 'I don't know what's happened to that woman.' There was confusion in his eyes, as though she were close but he couldn't quite see her. 'I've tried to understand, to protect you. Since Henry died, God knows it's been difficult for us both, but all of this business – taking things that don't belong to you, it has to stop.'

'I told you, I didn't *steal* Jack.' The words stuck in her throat.

'No.' He shook his head. 'I don't mean Jack. I mean the shawl.'

His words chilled her. So, all along he'd known and he hadn't said a thing.

'How did you know?'

'Come on! It doesn't matter how I know, what matters is what drives you to do it. What exactly is going through your mind when you take these things?'

'I ...' Her words trailed away as she looked down at the floor. 'I don't know. I suppose I wasn't myself and then it became a sort of game, I guess. But that's all in the past now. Honestly, this thing with Jack ...'

But he wasn't listening.

'Don't I give you enough? Have I failed you in some way?'

'Look, I've told you, none of this is your fault.'

'But I can't help thinking that it is, that I should have talked to you about it before, instead of sheltering you. You're not a child; you know it's wrong. If you need things, you have to earn them; you can't take them simply because they're there.'

She wanted to tell Gerry that it wasn't about the objects themselves, that it was about something else, her feeling of helplessness and the strange sense of relief that stealing them gave her, but she found that she couldn't say any of those things and so she was silent.

He looked away and then back at her.

'What more could I have done to help?'

'You have to believe me. All of that ... it got out of control.'

Still he carried on. 'Do you know how much all this has cost us?' There was pain in his voice. 'And I don't mean the money I've just given to that policeman.'

'No.'

'Leaving England, giving up my job. We thought that coming here would give you the fresh chance you needed.'

'*We?* Who's we?' She waited, straight and silent, for him to answer.

'You didn't think that moving here just happened, do you? Your poor parents; they didn't know where to turn after you were cautioned by the police.'

His words were like sharp metal.

'I told them not to tell you.'

'Of course they told me. What did you expect them to do?' A vein pulsed in his forehead. 'They knew how much damage this could do to us – my career, my family. We had to think about everyone.'

'Your parents – they don't know, do they?' Not Lily. She hoped desperately that he hadn't told her mother-in-law; it would give her all the ammunition she needed. She could almost hear her telling her friends with smug satisfaction, '*I told you that girl was no good.*'

'How do you think we could afford to do all this if it wasn't for my parents' help?' He indicated their surroundings, then he inched forward in his seat.

And then, it was as though the safety net that was supporting her had broken and she was tumbling down and down.

191

Seventeen

Miranda wanted to scream, to smash her fists against the wall. How could they plan all this behind her back, without even talking to her first? All those words of encouragement her mother had spoken, her father's gentle support. Liars. Deceivers, all of them. It hadn't been about Gerry's job at all; they had wanted to send her far away. Suddenly, the move to Singapore felt less like a fresh start and more like a life sentence.

She ran out of the bungalow, tears swimming in her eyes and her heart hammering. As she ran, rain began to fall. She lifted her face as thunder rattled above her, and the gentle drops turned swiftly into a torrent, creating rivulets in the jungle floor. A flash of white light tore across the sky, followed by another rumble of thunder. As she looked back, she saw a branch being torn from the rain tree and petals from the blooms being dashed to the ground.

On and on she ran – up towards Bukit Kalang, scrambling over rocks, her dress tearing on branches as she went. She was almost halfway to the top, but the climbing was hard and she slipped, falling with a bang. For a while, she hunched over, listening to the racing of her breath, then she began to cry and pounded the ground with her fists. *'Father, Mother,'* she shouted, *'Gerry, Charlotte, Lily,'* and those women who were, even now, she imagined, clamouring together to spread vicious untruths about how she had stolen Charlotte's baby. How she hated them, and how much she loathed herself.

Thunder cracked overhead, startling her, and the rain thickened. Her clothes and shoes were sopping, and she couldn't keep the drops from blinding her. She blinked again, but all she could see was the damp, grey mist sweeping down from the peak. Sliding across the mud, she found shelter beneath the branches of a tree, wondering if her rage would ever burn itself out.

An hour passed and soon she was shivering. It had been stupid to run out like this, blinded by anger. No one knew where she was. There were bound to be snakes in the undergrowth and poisonous spiders or mosquitoes, bringing with them the threat of malaria. She could be injured and then it could take hours, even days, to find her.

The more she thought about it, the more she realised how foolish she had been. Apart from anything else, she would be giving Gerry all the ammunition he needed to prove that he was right. She wondered if he was looking for her now, and tried to picture his reaction if he found her – would he be angry or sympathetic? What was she to do?

Besides, even if she wanted to, she couldn't stay out here for ever. However angry, ashamed and frustrated she was, she'd eventually have to return to the house. The thing to do would be to show Gerry that he was wrong and that she was a better person than he thought her to be. There must be a way to rekindle the embers that still burned. That would be the only way that she would survive.

She wanted to stay a little longer, to wait for the rain to stop and to see the stars appearing from above the canopy of the trees, but now her teeth were chattering.

There was no option but to go home, to tell Gerry he'd got it all wrong and to prove that she hadn't stolen Jack, but most of all, that those days of taking things were behind her. How would she do that? Should she take the high ground, or act as if nothing were wrong? A flying cockroach brushed her face and it landed on its back in her lap, its legs wiggling. She jumped up and brushed it away.

Slowly, she headed down the waterlogged pathways, hugging herself for warmth. Her legs ached and it seemed as though an axe had settled in her head.

The shivering grew worse and she realised that she didn't have a clue where she was. After a time, she was relieved to see a building and a man sitting on a chair under a verandah, obviously watching the rain. It was Nick. And Belvedere. He turned his head to face her and, a moment later, he was coming towards her with a blanket, which he wrapped around her.

'Miranda, whatever is the matter?' His voice was kind and soothing, but she protested, pushing him away.

'Please,' he insisted, and the cold and tiredness forced her to give in. She allowed him to lift her off her feet and carry her through the driving rain back to Belvedere.

'What on earth are you doing out here alone?' His voice was almost drowned out by the roaring rain as they approached the building.

It was then that she started crying.

'Sssh,' Nick soothed. 'It'll be fine. We'll be inside in a moment, then we can get you warm.'

He lay her down on the sofa in the living room.

'Come on,' he said. 'Why don't you rest here for now. And what about those wet clothes? I've got a shirt you can borrow.'

She wiped her face with the back of her hand. 'Thank you.'

He fetched the shirt for her, then left the room as she took off her sopping dress. The shirt was pale blue with darker stripes with the scent of freshly laundered linens. She slipped it on and did up the buttons, then fingered the collar as she lay back on the sofa, noticing again the shells on the bookshelf, and the group photograph of Nick she had examined on her previous visit, before pulling the blanket back around her.

'You know, you don't have to tell me.' Nick had returned with a steaming cup and saucer. Tea. She could smell it. She took the cup from him, enjoying the warmth seeping into her hands. 'But what is going on?'

'It's complicated.' She blew across the cup, cooling the liquid. 'And I'm not proud of any of it.'

'Would you like to talk about it?'

His voice was kind and patient. Somehow it made it worse and the big pulsing sobs started all over again. She shook her head.

'Here,' he gave her a hankie. 'I can see you're not in a fit state to do anything. But if you ever do want to talk, you know where to find me.'

She wiped her eyes and nodded. 'That would be nice. Perhaps another time.'

'Good. When you're ready. Why don't you sleep now?'

'I don't think I can.'

But she lay down and moments later she drifted off to sleep.

She wasn't sure how long she'd been sleeping when she woke to the murmur of men's voices.

Gerry was in the room. Nick must have called him.

'Miranda!' Gerry knelt down next to her. 'I've been worried sick. Come on, let's get you home.'

She sat up, but her head was aching, and instinctively she put her hand to her brow.

'What's the matter?' Nick asked.

'My head hurts a little, and the light's a bit bright.'

'Here,' he said. 'Let me see if you've got a temperature.' He put his hand on her forehead, then he felt her pulse.

'You're a little warm.' He turned to Gerry. 'Get her to bed. She needs rest, and keep an eye on her for a few days.'

'I'm quite capable of looking after my wife,' Gerry snapped, his arm was around her, lifting her up. 'Come on, let's get you home.'

The floor seemed wobbly as he led her through the sitting room and out to the car. The engine was running, she noticed, and Jinhai was at the wheel. She stepped into the puddles of rain, then into the car, grateful to be going home. Back at the bungalow, Mei Ling was waiting.

'Oh, Mrs Gerald, you're so wet!'

'We'd better get her to bed. A hot drink, perhaps, Mei Ling, with a shot of brandy?'

Gerry guided her to the bed and she slipped under the sheet.

'What about your nightie?' Gerry asked.

'I don't have the energy to change. I'm fine with this,' Miranda said. She had started to shiver. 'And it's got long sleeves.'

Mei Ling knocked on the door. Gerry opened it and took a tray of tea from her. He placed it on the bedside table and sat on the bed next to Miranda.

She ran her hand through her still damp hair. 'I wish we'd never come here. Can't we go home?' She tried to keep the desperation out of her voice.

He shook his head. 'This is our home now. Even if we both wanted to, it would be impossible. We've got to stay for at least three years.'

'I don't think I can face it, Gerry.'

'Darling, just get some rest. All this will pass. And I'm sure we can keep this between the Yeardleys and ourselves.'

'Ugh.' She wrung her hands. 'Do you think I could ever face Charlotte again?'

'You will. Give it a day or two. Write her a letter to explain and apologise. I'm sure she has a generous heart.'

'It's easy for you to say that. But you *do* believe me when I say I didn't steal Jack.'

'Miranda,' his tone rose with exasperation, 'just give it a rest.'

If her own husband didn't believe her, no one would. She levered herself up, but the room was too bright, and she winced as pain shot between her eyes.

'It's so bright.'

Gerry sighed and went to close the curtains.

Miranda wriggled down under the sheets and heard the sound of Gerry leaving, closing the door behind him. Her head was still aching, and she tried to focus on the patter of rain against the windowpanes

She listened to the sound of Mei Ling's footsteps and, after a while, Gerry playing Wagner on the record player. She could hear Wotan, Fricka and Brünhhilde's voices rising, then Gin and Tonic calling to each other from the palm trees. Or was it Tommy, calling to other monkeys? She lay there for what felt like hours, listening to the sounds of the house and the jungle outside. Occasionally, Gerry or Mei Ling would open the door to check on her, leaving cups of tea and bowls of soup by the bed, then, after a while, they would come back and remove the offerings from where they lay, untouched.

Was it morning? She could hear the birds singing and a beam of light shone through the crack in the curtains. Miranda lifted her head and tried to drag herself up to sit. The sheet stuck to her, wrapping itself around her legs like a dead thing.

Later, her fever broke. She ought to get up from the bed, but she couldn't. It was so hot and she was so damn tired.

Voices in the corridor. Shadows at the door.

Time passed; how much, she wasn't certain. But then she heard something, or rather felt it, a voice that seemed to be calling to her through the darkness, *Come on. Pull yourself out, Miranda, just like you did before.*

'Mrs Gerald?' Miranda opened her eyes. Mei Ling was standing in the doorway, carrying a tray with a bowl and a pot of tea. 'You awake?'

Miranda still felt lightheaded, but she nodded and pulled herself up against the pillows, watching tiny silver stars dancing in front of her eyes.

'You best eat. I bring you rice porridge with chicken.' Mei Ling placed the tray on the bedside table next to a carafe of water, then began to straighten the sheets. 'It's been three days and you've eaten nothing. I also make you ginseng to drink. Good. Make your body strong.'

'Thank you, Mei Ling, that is very kind of you.'

Had it really been three days? No wonder she was so weak. All she could remember were her feverish dreams. She took the cup from Mei Ling and sipped the woody-tasting liquid, which scalded her tongue.

'You know, I would love a glass of water, Mei Ling. With ice, please.'

Mei Ling shook her head. 'You sick. Best not let the cold get into your bones, Mrs Gerald. Make you not strong. Chinese medicine good – make you better.'

She sipped at the bitter liquid again. 'Is Mr Gerald here?'

'No. He go already-*lah*.'

She missed him and would have liked a reassuring hug.

'But Dr Nick called to see if you better – he wanted to give you some medicine. I told him to go away.'

'Oh. When?' He'd been so kind, so patient, a friendly face when others were clearly staying away, and disappointment flickered through her.

'You asleep. He stay for a while, but not to worry, *I* take good care of you.'

Mei Ling smiled and gave her the rice porridge, placing the warm bowl in her lap. Miranda turned the lumpy mixture with her spoon. It was flecked with small pieces of brown flesh. Chicken. She knew the Chinese always thought the dark meat the most succulent and she pictured Mei Ling salvaging the best pieces for her. There was something green sprinkled on the top – a herb, like parsley, and thin slices of red chilli. She spooned a morsel into her mouth; it was comforting and tasted better than she'd been expecting.

'Thank you,' she whispered, the effort of eating had exhausted her. 'It's good. Spicy.'

'Make you sweat out bad thing. Make you better.' Mei Ling's face was close, her forehead creased with worry. 'Mrs Gerald. Maybe I'd better not say, but why did you cry so much? Mr Gerald say you be better soon, but I don't think so. Crying give you fever.'

A rush of air left her lungs and the spoon shook in her hand.

'But, surely you've heard, Mei Ling? From Mrs Yeardley's *amah*?'

'She's gone, Mrs Gerald. She's a bad girl leaving the baby. Some people say you're bad, but I don't think so.'

'Oh, Mei Ling!' A lump of pain throbbed inside her throat. 'I— I don't know what to say.'

'Don't worry now. You best eat three more mouthful, then you rest, Mrs Gerald.' Mei Ling's voice coaxed. 'You too thin. Like young girl.'

Tears began to prickle, but she swallowed another spoonful of rice porridge and closed her eyes, aching to shut out the world. She felt the touch of Mei Ling's hand on her own.

'Mrs Gerald, I hope you don't mind. I've never show you before, I brought you a photo of my father.'

She looked up to see Mei Ling taking from her pocket a jade-framed photograph that wasn't much bigger than the size of child's palm.

'This his wedding day.' Mei Ling placed it in Miranda's hand. She was surprised to see the bride wearing not a cheongsam, but a knee-length white lace dress and wedding veil, and the groom was dressed in a Western-style suit. Mei Ling was right, her father had been handsome. His features were neatly arranged on a square face while her mother's had been more delicate, with finer features.

'It's beautiful, Mei Ling. They both looked so happy. So young. What did your mother do?'

'She sew. She make dragons, peacock, everything on cloth. I not know how say. Small needle. Small stitches.'

'You mean embroidery?'

'Embroidery. Yes. She very good. Her work was very beautiful. Then she die giving birth. My brother. He die also.'

She held the frame for a few moments longer. Mei Ling must have been very young when she'd lost her mother. Who had looked after her when her father had been out at work, she wondered? Had there been grandparents or aunts or had Mei Ling been expected to cook and run the house from an early age? Was that why she'd never married?

'You look like your mother,' Miranda said, and smiled as she handed the photo back. 'And I think she would have been proud of you. Thank you for showing it to me. I know it must be very special.'

Mei Ling gave a nod as she tucked the photograph back into her pocket. 'You best sleep now. Get better.'

A short while later, Miranda was woken by the sound of heels on the gravel and then a knock at the door. It wasn't long before Georgina entered the room carrying a basket of fruit: a pineapple, some star fruit and a papaya. It was only as she was standing there that Miranda realised how much she'd missed her.

'Hello, stranger.' Georgina entered the room and kissed her on the cheek. 'I called before, but Mei Ling wouldn't let me in. However, this time I wouldn't take no for an answer.' She placed the basket on the floor then sat down in the chair next to the bed.

'It's good to see you.' Miranda held out her hand and smiled. She wondered if Georgina had already heard about what had happened with Jack and the police.

'And me you.' Georgina took her outstretched hand. 'But, I must say, you've looked better. You're as pale as anything – a real *gweilo*.'

'*Gweilo?*'

'Chinese for ghost.'

Miranda let go of her hand and sank back on to the pillows. A ghost. Yes. Alive, but not here. A translucent being lurking in the shadows. If she stayed in Singapore, like this, surely that's what she'd become. Everyone must know what she'd done – she could imagine the gossip in the clubs and whispered conversations at ladies' lunches. People would turn away when she entered a room.

'These tropical fevers can be *awful*,' Georgina said.

'I suppose you know what happened, don't you?' Miranda asked.

'About the baby?' Georgina nodded. 'Yes. But you don't have to talk about it if you don't want to.' Her head was tilted on one side, and her eyes had a softness to them, the way you might look at a child who had hurt themselves.

'Actually, I do.' Miranda pulled herself up. 'I keep going over and over it in my mind. I didn't take him. Not on purpose, but I can see how it might seem. He was screaming and bawling – it's happened once before, and the *amah* wasn't doing anything about it. I couldn't stand it.'

'I believe you.'

'Do you? I'm sure Gerry doesn't.'

'Of course he does.'

'Does he really? You know, it's been horrible since we got here. And he won't talk about anything. He'll tell me what to do, but not properly talk about how I'm feeling.'

And then the tears came in breathless, undulating waves.

'Oh, Miranda.' Georgina took her hand. 'It really isn't such a bad thing that you've done.'

Miranda wiped her nose with the back of her hand. 'It seems unforgivable.'

'Look, I'm sure people will understand when they know the truth. Why don't you write to Charlotte and explain? She'll be angry, obviously, but—'

'It's not just that!' Miranda broke in.

'What is it, then?' Georgina frowned.

Miranda sat up and clutched her knees. 'I've never told anyone this before.' She glanced at Georgina. 'Promise you won't tell anyone.'

She nodded.

'Well,' Miranda picked at the sheet, 'after Henry died, I went to pieces.'

'Of course you did,' Georgina said, and placed a soothing hand on her arm.

'Mother took charge – the house had become a real mess and she made me go out while she got it straight and tidy.

But when I was out, something took hold of me. I started taking things from shops – stealing.' Her cheeks burned. 'I couldn't stop it. It became a need. I can't explain it.'

Georgina tilted her head to one side. 'What kind of things?'

'Stupid things – a thimble, a baby's blanket. For ages I thought that Gerry didn't know, but he did, all along it would seem. That's why he won't believe me about Jack.'

'*I see.*' Georgina's tone was sympathetic. 'But losing Henry – it must have been dreadful; ripped you apart. I can't begin to imagine what you've been through. No wonder you blamed yourself, but it can't have been your fault. You've got to stop blaming yourself for it.'

'I got caught stealing. Did you know that?' She might as well come out with it all. 'It was so humiliating. Thankfully, that's as far as it got. I vowed I'd stop after that.'

'Well, it sounds like they understood. Try to put it behind you now.'

'But that's just it. I *did* try to put it behind me. I carried on helping at the hospital. I felt as though I was doing something, living with a purpose again. And then we came here – and now there's this business with Jack. What if I simply can't help myself – if I'm nothing but a failure and a thief?'

'Oh Miranda, of course you're not. But I wish I'd known how bad things had got.' Georgina's voice was gentle. 'I wish you'd told me all of this before.'

'So, you see, that's why Gerry is unable to trust me.'

'I'm sure he understands.'

'No.' She lowered her voice, 'He's ashamed of me.'

'Don't be ridiculous. He's done everything for you, hasn't he? When you were so ill, he wouldn't leave you. He was so worried.'

'I think he cares more about what people will say.' She lay back on the pillow.

'I'm sure that's not true.'

Miranda sighed and then said, 'To be honest, I'm not sure of anything any more.'

Georgina took Miranda's hand. 'Look, this might not be the right moment, but I'm going to say it anyway. Whatever's happened, has happened. You need to find your old self again. Think about all the good times we used to have at school. You used to have so much spark. So much life. Remember how you used to love dancing on a Saturday night? What's happened to you?'

'Please,' she frowned. 'Things have been difficult.'

'Of course they have.' There was exasperation in Georgina's voice. Miranda jerked her head up, but this time Georgina didn't meet her look. 'But you've got to bounce back, Miranda, be that girl we all used to love.'

'Everyone must think I'm mad.'

'No they don't, but even if they did, what the hell does it matter? Time will pass. I know you won't feel like it now, but the sooner you get well and get out, the sooner this spell will blow over. I'll help you write to Charlotte and explain it was all a misunderstanding. It will take her time to forgive you, but she won't be angry for ever.'

Georgina's eyes were bright. 'How about we go for lunch in a couple of days? At my club?'

'I don't think I could bear it.'

'Yes, you can. It will be absolutely fine. And, you know, you really don't need to face this alone.'

Eighteen

Over the next two days, physically, Miranda began to feel much stronger, but emotionally, she was still feeling fragile, and although she was looking forward to seeing Georgina again, she was dreading having to go out in public.

Georgina arrived a little before eleven, bringing with her a red silk dress for Miranda to wear. She helped Miranda wash and style her hair, then applied her make-up and some lipstick: fire-engine red.

'I look so glamorous, almost like Princess Margaret,' Miranda said. 'Are you sure this is such a good idea?'

'Yes.' Georgina nodded her head. 'And you don't look like Princess Margaret. You look like yourself, which is much better. Ready?'

Georgina's car lurched as Adi, Georgina's driver, swung the car into Stevens Road, then they progressed up the drive to the Tanglin Club, and he parked beneath a banyan tree. Miranda opened the door and stepped out – the only sound she could hear was the crickets thrumming.

She looked up and caught Georgina's smile and the slight, reassuring nod of her head. But still, she stumbled slightly and was relieved when Georgina tucked her arm into hers as they headed towards the open doors of the Ladies' Club Room.

'Table for two?' the waiter asked.

'In the corner – by the window?' Georgina suggested.

Miranda followed Georgina, studying the heels of her friend's sandals. Why had Georgina chosen that table? The distance across the restaurant floor seemed far too long. Silence fell across the room. It wasn't her imagination; she was certain she could feel them all staring at her, but she dare not look. They reached the table facing the courtyard. Relief washed over her as the waiter pulled out a chair. She watched a man outside sweeping bougainvillea leaves and brushing them into a neat pile.

'Some water, madam?'

She nodded, grateful to have something with which to occupy her hands.

'We've sole today, fresh from the port, if you're interested.'

'Two of those, please, then.' Georgina ordered without consulting her, but she didn't mind.

'You *do* look nice,' Georgina said, a gentle smile on her lips. 'And that red suits you – even matches the Christmas decorations.'

Miranda placed her glass on the table and ran her finger around the rim. 'Is everyone looking at me?'

Georgina lifted her head. 'No. Stop worrying about it.'

When their food arrived, she could only pick at it.

'Mmm. Perfect.' Georgina dabbed at the corner of her mouth with a napkin, then ordered some wine.

'Do you fancy going to the beach later?'

'I don't know. Perhaps.'

'We could have tea at the Sea View. It's glorious sitting on the verandah, watching the world go by.'

'Dessert, madam?' The waiter hovered at the side of the table. 'There's chocolate mousse, apple pie with custard, or fruit.'

'Share the pie, Miranda?'

She shook her head.

'Just two teas and the bill, then – will you please add it to my account?'

Their teas arrived.

'I told you, didn't I, that Poppy, my niece, is coming out? Well,' Georgina poured out the tea into their cups, 'she's arriving tomorrow. When you're well enough, we should do something together.'

'That would be lovely,' Miranda smiled. 'I still remember her as the little girl we used to push on the swings.'

'Or played hide and seek with all afternoon.'

'Indeed, now she's, what, twenty?'

Georgina nodded.

'Then I'll expect she'll want new dresses and parties when she's had time to settle in.'

'Parties are what I need to keep her away from. Bloody impossible, if you ask me.' Georgina finished her drink.

'Ready?'

Miranda nodded and then they made their way to the foyer.

'Great, we'll pick up some stuff from my house for the beach, then head off to the Sea View, but,' Georgina said, 'I need to nip to the loo first. Won't be long.'

Miranda waited, looking at the noticeboard: cookery classes for *amah*s, bridge for beginners. A woman she thought she knew stood next to her. She smiled at her, but the woman ignored her then brushed past.

I'm a *gweilo*, she thought, and I don't want to be. Everything heals, she knew that, but today it was hard. With her hand shaking, she took a packet of cigarettes from her handbag and lit one. Immediately, the nicotine gave her a surge of strength. But as she looked up, she saw Charlotte and Jane blocking her line of vision.

'Oh God!' she moaned.

'Look at her!' she could hear Jane hiss. 'She's got a cheek showing up here.'

'It's fine, Jane.' Charlotte placed her hand on Jane's arm.

'How can it be? Swanning around here, tarted up to the nines, as though nothing was wrong. Rubbing your face in it, if you ask me.'

It was as though nails were clawing at her stomach. 'I'm sorry,' she whispered, gazing at Charlotte, wanting to be able to tell her the whole truth. 'Did you get my letter?' she asked, stepping closer to Charlotte. 'I wanted to explain. There was no one there. I couldn't leave him by himself and I thought I was doing the right thing.'

Jane came close, pushing her face right in Miranda's. 'Do you think anyone cares what you think? I know all about women like you,' she snorted. 'The isn't the first time you've taken something, is it?' There was a look of triumph and hatred in her features, which stunned Miranda.

'Leave it, will you?' Charlotte's voice was firm.

Miranda's throat tightened and she stared at the ground, trying to keep her breathing calm, willing the women to go away and longing for Georgina to come back.

'I should leave,' she muttered.

'Good. Make sure you don't come back in a hurry.' Jane brushed past her; her words stung. 'Your name's mud here as it is.'

'Charlotte, please, I didn't mean any harm.' Miranda lifted her head.

'While I'm still bloody angry with you, there was no need for her to be so rude,' Charlotte said, her voice rising, 'but what the hell were you playing at? You had absolutely no right to take Jack – you, of all people, should know the pain you'd be inflicting.'

The words cut deep.

'I was in a panic – I didn't think.'

'Well, perhaps you should have. Look, I don't want to talk about all this now.' Her voice softened a little, 'I know you've been ill – I hope you get well soon.'

Charlotte left and Miranda's breathing became longer and calmer. She stood there alone for a moment, before she heard the sound of Georgina's heeled sandals clicking towards her.

An hour later, Miranda and Georgina sat beneath the coconut trees on the beach, watching long shadows fall across the sand. A radio was playing at a small beach café and the laughter of children rolled back to her as they ran along the surf towards the Sea View Hotel.

'Thank you,' Miranda said. 'It's been a tough day, but it was good to get out.'

'I'm so pleased.'

'Even meeting Charlotte – it's actually made me confront a few things.'

'Well, that's a step forward, isn't it? And now you can put it behind you, surely?'

Miranda nodded, trailing her fingers in the sand.

'You know,' Georgina said. 'You don't have to tell me if it's too painful, but what exactly did happen with Henry?'

Miranda picked up a foxtail shell and dug it into the sand. 'It was just before Christmas.' She swallowed, picturing in her mind how she'd been sitting by the fire. 'I was so tired and all I wanted to do was to fall asleep. I'd left him to cry, like my mother suggested. The crying stopped and I must have dozed off, but I woke suddenly with a feeling that there was something wrong.'

She dug the shell further into the sand.

'When I went to his cot I could tell almost straight away.'

'Why?'

'It was a warm day for December, but there was a coldness to his body that didn't feel right. A silence that didn't fit the day.' She shut her eyes, remembering the stillness of his body as he lay there, the shadow of blue around his mouth. 'I didn't have to pick him up to know. I could see he wasn't breathing. I didn't know what to do, so I picked him up and ran to the hospital.'

'That must have been dreadful.'

'No words can describe it.'

She watched a ball roll towards them, a little girl running in its wake.

'You know, I blamed my mother for ages. But, in the end, I was angrier with myself. I shouldn't have left him. That's why I got so cross with Charlotte's *amah*.'

Miranda picked the ball up. 'Here you are.' She smiled at the girl, who ran back to her mother.

'They told me later that he had a hole in his heart. I know now that nothing could have stopped it, but I should have been with him all the same.'

She watched the woman rub Nivea on to the girl's back and plant a kiss on her forehead.

'What about your mother? Have you forgiven her?' Georgina asked.

'I suppose so. It wasn't really her fault, was it?' Miranda brushed sand from her legs. 'You know, I think I'd like to go for a walk.'

'Would you like company?'

She shook her head.

'Don't forget your hat, then. It's a scorcher.'

She picked it up but didn't put it on and she let the ribbon trail in the sand as she walked. Deep in thought, she stumbled on a piece of driftwood and watched it tumbling towards the waves. The truth was that she still felt so much guilt. It tripped her up umpteen times a day. No one knew how it pained her, how she replayed that moment over and over again. Of course, she longed to laugh, to feel free, to dance in the sand, not to drag the past around like some awful deadweight. No one wanted Miranda to be the person she used to be more than she did. But somehow she couldn't find her way back.

Nineteen

Nick watched the waves frothing against the shore. He could make out what looked like giant speckled stones, a shoal of grey fish basking in the shallows and the blue outline of an island on the horizon surrounded by a halo of afternoon light. A gull screeched overhead. He looked up, following the flight of the bird, as it ducked and dived then headed inland. Along the shoreline, he could make out the figure of someone walking towards him, head bent down, shoulders forward, as though battling against an imaginary wind. A woman; her hair was flapping across her face. He could see a hat in her hand, the ribbon trailing and grazing the sand.

It was Miranda.

'Hello,' he called.

She lifted her head. Her gaze was distant, as though she were looking at him from a long way away.

'Nick?' Her features focused when she saw him.

He made his way quickly towards her. 'How are you? I tried to visit but your *amah* wouldn't let me in.'

'I heard.' She passed the rim of her hat slowly between her fingers. 'I'm all right.'

'Good. But, surely, you're not here alone?'

'No.' She glanced towards the sea, then back at a space in front of her. 'I came with Georgina.'

'And are you thinking of going back or walking on?'

'I don't know. I might go back.'

She looked pale and tired.

'Well,' he paused, uncertain. 'Would you like company? I could walk with you?'

'If you like. You decide.' She set off again, her hat ribbon trailing once again in the sand.

He caught her up. 'You can see where the Japanese surrendered from here.' He pointed across the sea. 'And Jurong is up there, further up the coast.'

She slowed. 'So many islands.'

'You know,' he began, 'I really did try to call.'

She stopped hard and swivelled round, her dark eyes flashing.

'I wish Mei Ling had let you,' she said.

Me too. His heart beat faster; he could feel it fluttering – like the wings of a baby bird.

'I was so grateful for your help the other day,' she said.

He could see tears in her eyes. 'It will get easier, you know. All of it.'

'Will it?' She flopped down and brushed the sand away from her feet. 'From where I am, it's only getting worse.'

'You'll find something; you'll come through it.'

'I wish I could. Right now, I don't know where to start.'

'Anything that is worth doing is hard.'

'That's easy for you to say.'

'Believe me, I do know. You're not the only one to live each day overshadowed by grief.'

He could hear her shallow breathing as she drew slow circles in the sand, then he watched her brush away a strand of hair that had blown across her face.

'You?'

'I had a brother, Freddie.' His ribs felt like a tightening cage around his heart. 'He was two years older than me. Freddie was everything that I wasn't – academic, good at sport, popular. The only time I was better than him was when we visited my grandmother at Coombe. She had a house by the sea, large garden, rolling fields down to the cliffs. We used to visit her all summer, to get away from London. Great place for two boys.' He paused for a moment, looking at her face, at the frown that was forming.

'One day my grandmother was sick. Freddie and I were left to entertain ourselves. We spent the day on the beach, racing along the sand, crabbing in rock pools, all kinds of things. Freddie always ran faster, caught the biggest crabs. But he wasn't as good at climbing as me. On the way back to Coombe, I climbed up one of the cliff faces and taunted him. Said he was a coward. So he took the challenge – I could see in his face how much it scared him, but he was almost at the top when his foot slipped. I tried to reach out and grab him, but it was no good. I watched him fall and saw him hit the rocks. He was just eighteen.'

'That's awful.' He could see the shock on her face.

'Yes. So, you see, even though I'll never understand what you've been through, I do know what it's like to blame yourself. And, don't you see, it doesn't matter if it's your fault or not. However hard it is, you've got to carry on?'

'But how do you come to terms with something like that?'

'You have to keep busy, to try to keep the pain at bay. Turn something bad into something good.'

He saw her flinch. 'Is that why you became a doctor – some kind of atonement?'

'I suppose.' He finished his cigarette, then stood and made his way to the water's edge. The sea was surprisingly cold as he paddled and he noticed how little pieces of seaweed floated on the top, crashing on to the sand with the breaking waves. The tide was going out.

'Sometimes you can see little flashes of phosphorescence in the water,' he said, as she joined him.

'I'm sorry, Nick.' Her hand brushed his arm. 'About your brother.'

'Thanks. Perhaps we should go back?'

She nodded, and they walked side by side in the outgoing water. He lifted his head and their eyes met.

'You're stronger than you think.' He was about to reassure her further when something rough caught the sole of his foot. He bent down; it was a starfish.

'Look.'

'Is it all right?' She took it from him. 'It feels strange, all dry and scratchy, like sandpaper.'

'Yes.' He took it from her. 'But I think it's still alive. I'm going to throw it back into the sea.'

'Oh no! There's another.' He looked up to see her pointing to a smaller starfish. 'And another!'

He began to collect them up.

'I wouldn't bother, if I were you,' she said. 'They'll only come in again on the next tide.'

'I know, but they might not, and if only one survives, then it will have been worth it, won't it?'

A frown flickered across her face, then she knelt down and helped him throw them back. When they'd finished, they carried on walking in the surf, but still she looked broken and diminished – he knew all too well how that felt. He wished he could do something to help her and then an idea occurred to him.

'I've just been thinking about what you said about the volunteering you did in England, how you were missing it and wanting to help other people.'

'So?'

'There's a patient at the centre, Martha. She's more of a political refugee, if I'm honest. She needs some company, someone to look after her. I don't suppose you could help?'

She pressed her lips together. He wasn't sure what she was thinking, but he saw a slight movement of her head, confirming that she'd heard.

'Martha Hollande? I've heard of her.'

'Yes.' He waited, but she didn't reply, and so they walked on in silence.

Finally, the Sea View came into sight. 'My car's parked at the back,' he said. 'Will you be all right if I leave you here?'

'Yes. Thank you.'

'Here – I almost forgot. Close your eyes and hold out your hands.'

Miranda did as he told her, and he saw her flinch as he placed a tiny starfish in the palm of her hand. 'One that didn't survive, I'm afraid.'

'Oh,' she said, opening her eyes.

'Will you think about what I said? About Martha?'

She didn't reply, but at last he caught the stirring of a smile.

Twenty

The following morning, Miranda stood in the bathroom doorway watching her husband. He caught sight of her and smiled, then he lathered up shaving soap with his badger brush and peered in the mirror, his head poised as he scraped his chin with the razor.

'It's good to see you looking so much better,' he said. 'And it was good of Georgina to take you to the club yesterday. It won't be long before the incident is forgotten, now you've written to Charlotte, and everything will return to normal.'

But her thoughts weren't with the club and their social life – they were at the beach, thinking about Nick's suggestion. About Martha.

'What do you know about Martha Hollande?' she asked, leaning against the frame.

He paused, razor suspended. 'Why? What do you want to know?'

'I've heard about her a couple of times, that's all.' She picked at her nails.

'It's a complicated and unusual adoption case.' He rinsed the blade in the water and stared at it, as though examining the soapy foam. 'Martha's parents were in Malaya before the Occupation. They left Martha with a local family for safe-keeping. Now they want her back, but the local family claim she was legally adopted.' He swirled the water with his hand. 'It will be going to the Supreme Court soon.'

She listened to the scrape of metal on hair as he resumed shaving.

'It's all become a little divisive, if you ask me.' He was working on his upper lip, concentrating as he worked the blade in neat rhythmic strokes.

'How do you mean?'

Their gaze met in the mirror. 'Well, Catholics against Muslims; expats against locals. Word is that the Chief Justice will be harsh.'

'But what do *you* think will happen?'

He shrugged. 'I'm not a lawyer – how can I answer that?' He rinsed the razor in the sink again, shaking it before moving on to his sideburns. 'But, if you ask me, her father was doing the right thing at the time. Can you imagine what it was like – the prospect of being rounded up and sent off to a Jap concentration camp?' He paused, not waiting for her to answer. 'You'd be bloody terrified, of course, you would. No doubt about it, he thought he was doing the best thing for the kid.'

'Poor girl. But, after all these years, shouldn't she stay put?'

He finished shaving, picked up a flannel and rinsed it under the tap, then held it over his face, muffling his voice. 'Well, without proper documents, there isn't a case to answer, I suppose.'

She shifted against the doorframe, folding her arms. 'Surely it's the right thing, morally, I mean?'

'Emotions and morals aren't what the court will be looking at.' He pulled the plug out of the sink, the gurgling of water breaking into their conversation.

'What if it were the other way around – if she were a Malay child adopted by a European family, do you think the situation would be the same?'

She watched him applying Brylcreem to his hair and smoothing it down with a comb.

'Honestly, Miranda,' he placed the comb on a shelf, 'I don't know.' He picked up his watch. 'I'd better get on.'

He walked past her into his dressing room. She could hear drawers opening and closing, the bang of a wardrobe door.

Poor Martha. What a bloody awful situation.

All morning, her thoughts drifted back to the girl and to Nick's suggestion on the beach. She touched the starfish on her dressing table. What was it that Nick had said? *You have to keep busy, to try to keep the pain at bay. Turn something bad into something good.*

After lunch, she asked Jinhai to drive her to Tanjong Pagar.

'Here we are,' he said, as he pulled up outside the crumbling building.

'Thank you.' She got out and walked towards the entrance and passed a sign for 'St Augustin's Mission Hospital' before she pushed open the creaking door. Inside, it smelt of boiled cabbage and antispectic, which conjured up memories of the sick bay at school. The corridor was empty and voices filtered down from a staircase, then a door banged, startling her. Which way should she go? Along the corridor, she heard rubber-soled heels squeaking, and she turned her head.

'Can I help you?' a Malay nurse asked.

'Yes. I've come to see Dr Wythenshaw. Can you tell me the way?'

'I'll show you – I'm heading that way myself.'

Miranda focused on the large circles of sweat beneath the nurse's armpits as they drew closer to the sound of voices and the tapping of a typewriter.

'Are you family?' the nurse asked.

'No. I'm a friend – just visiting.'

'Oh. It's a bit unusual to get visitors during the day.'

They turned a corner and passed a group of patients waiting on chairs, a small ward of children and then, opposite the ward, an office door with Nick's name on it.

'Wait here.' The nurse indicated a chair, then she knocked on the door and gently turned the handle. Miranda sat down; her stomach knotted as she waited for the nurse to return.

'He said you should have made an appointment. Is there any chance you could come back later?'

'Oh. Please, could you tell him it's Miranda Lewis?'

The nurse frowned, as though weighing up exactly what it was that Miranda wanted and whether she'd get into trouble for not doing what Miranda asked.

'Please?' she asked again, her tone firmer.

The nurse went back into the office, and a few moments later she returned.

'He said all right – if it's quick.'

She stepped across the corridor and pushed open the door. His office was smaller than she expected, crowded with books and journals. On the walls there were photographs from his university days; the humidity had speckled the edges of the mounts with mould. Documents teetered from every surface and a tea tray with tiny cups balanced on the desk.

'Miranda I'm sorry. I didn't hear properly when the nurse told me who it was.'

'It's me that should be sorry, disturbing you when you're busy – I shouldn't have just turned up like this.'

'Why don't you sit down?' He removed a stack of papers and a pile of books from a chair. 'So,' he began, 'what can I do for you?'

She sat down, clutching her bag. 'I keep thinking about what you said at the beach. About Martha. I thought I could help. If you still want me to, that is.'

Her throat was dry as she waited for his reply.

'That's excellent. Wonderful. I'm so glad you want to help. How much time would you be prepared to give?'

'A few hours a week. I could easily manage that.'

'That would be perfect.' He glanced at his watch. 'I'm sorry, but I've really got to dash.'

'I'll come back tomorrow, then?'

'Great. How about ten o'clock? I'll meet you here.'

As Miranda made her way home, a warm glow radiated through her body, although she was a little nervous about telling Gerry about her plans. She suspected he wouldn't be as excited as she was. She spent the rest of the day in the summerhouse, reading *The Pursuit of Love*, but she couldn't concentrate, so she wandered around the garden and cut some scarlet peonies, which she arranged in a vase. At six o'clock, she sat in the drawing room with her book until she heard the car pull up and Gerry walking through the hall.

'You seem happy.' He put his case on the floor, poured himself a whisky, then sank into a chair.

She closed her book. 'Actually, I am.'

'Any particular reason?' He swirled his whisky gently in the glass, before looking up at her.

'I wasn't going to tell you until it was all settled,' she began, 'but I've decided to volunteer at St Augustin's. You know, where Nick works?'

'Mmm. Doing what?' He waited for her to continue, his glass in his hand.

'A little bit of teaching.' She ran her finger over the edge of her book. 'That girl we were talking about this morning. Martha Hollande.'

'Martha Hollande.' A frown flickered across his features. 'So that was what all the questions were about, then?'

'Yes.'

'Why didn't you tell me?' His voice was stony.

'I hadn't made up my mind, and nothing firm was planned.'

'But you should have talked to me first.'

'I thought you'd be pleased, that I'm feeling like my old self again.'

'But after everything we've discussed, and Martha Hollande to boot!' He knocked back his drink.

'Yes. Why not?'

'Lots of reasons. Is it wise, working with children? You'll get fond of her, of course, you will. Then she'll leave. And what would that do to you? Losing yet another person you care about?'

She was about to object, but he raised his hand. 'Then there's the question of loyalty. Her case is sensitive. We have a position; we can't be seen to be showing sides. Think of what people would say.'

'Don't be so bloody ridiculous. She's a child. Anyway, I don't see what's it got to do with anyone else.'

'That's not the point, Miranda. And I've told you so more than once.'

'Well, I'm sorry, but you can't stop me.' She stood. 'And I don't agree that it's a problem. It's not just that doing this will make me happy, it's also good for the child.'

Gerry looked at her as though she had knocked the air right out of his lungs.

The following day, Miranda went to St Augustin's and sat down on a chair opposite a girl who was gazing out of the window, watching some boys kicking a ball around a dusty patch of ground. A pile of books was at her feet, none of them open. Sunlight streamed through the window, almost blinding her as the girl turned towards her.

'Hello. You must be Martha.'

Martha was smaller than she'd been expecting; the girl was slightly built and fair skinned, with blue eyes. She had an air of dignity and maturity that surprised Miranda.

'I'm Miranda.' She placed her brown leather case at her feet. 'I thought you could do with some company,' she smiled. 'I'm not one of the nurses – Dr Wythenshaw,' she glanced towards the door, where Nick was waiting, 'suggested I could spend some time with you, so I brought you this.' She bent down and opened her case, then handed the girl a bag of kuih. Martha leant forward and took the bag, her face lighting up when she saw the coconut cakes. She took one of the pink gelatinous rectangles and nibbled on it, like a mouse.

'I thought I could start by telling you some things about myself.' Miranda took a photograph out of the briefcase. 'And then perhaps you can tell me something about yourself.'

'This is me – Miranda.' She touched her image, then herself, and repeated her name slowly. 'And you,' she pointed to Martha, 'are Martha. And that,' she indicated Nick, 'is Dr Wythenshaw.'

Martha nodded, then slowly repeated, 'Martha,' then pointing at Miranda and Nick, she said, 'Miranda. Doctor.'

'But the doctor has to go now,' Nick said. 'I'll see you later.'

Miranda continued, 'I like to eat bananas. Do you?'

She took a banana out of her suitcase and peeled it, then broke the banana in half.

'Banana. That's good.' She gave the other half to Martha.

For the next half an hour she sat with Martha and they took it in turns to name objects in Malay or English until Martha grew tired.

'Shall I visit again tomorrow?' Miranda asked.

Martha frowned, but eventually she understood and nodded.

The next morning, Miranda returned to St Augustin's, this time with a selection of fruit and vegetables she'd bought in the market. They took it in turns naming the vegetables or fruit as well as the colours. Afterwards, they went for a walk in the grounds.

Over the next few days, she continued to return to St Augustin's, despite Gerry's disapproving comments. On each visit Martha grew bolder and they quickly began exchanging words or phrases in English and Malay. Miranda's heart swelled with satisfaction, knowing that it was *she* who had helped the girl progress so quickly.

And Miranda really liked her: the way a toothy smile would break out, illuminating her entire face when she got something right, how she placed her hand over her mouth when she giggled, her neat handwriting and careful drawing, all the time wanting to please. But there was something more: a connection to Singapore, through Martha, that she hadn't felt before, and it was wonderful to feel it. She wondered how long it would last.

Two weeks passed. Nick heard from the nurses how Martha was growing less shy and frightened, and the nurses also told him how her English was improving quickly, thanks to Miranda. He caught fleeting glimpses of Miranda in the corridors of St Augustin's, but every time he'd taken a moment to go and find her, she was out walking with Martha, chatting with the nurses or she'd gone home.

He was walking along the corridor towards the staff canteen when he finally saw Miranda alone.

'Hello, stranger. How's Martha?' he asked.

'Great,' Miranda replied. 'It's going really well.'

'You look happy. It suits you.'

'Thank you. She seems to like me and she remembers most of the things I've taught her.'

'Good,' he nodded. 'I'm on my way to grab a bite to eat in the canteen. Do you want to join me? We could catch up a little more, if you like.'

'Do you know, that would be really nice.'

They found a table by the window and she waited while he collected some tea. There were slices of pandan cake and he wondered if she might like some. He put two slices on a plate then returned to her, carrying everything on a tray. As he approached the table, he was struck by the way she looked: taller and more confident. She was wearing a sunny yellow dress that seemed to light up her face – the way the reflection of a buttercup did against skin. Once again, he wondered what it would be like to reach out, to trace the line of golden light on her face, to feel her breath on his hand, or to run his fingers through her hair.

When he sat down, he placed the slices of cake between them, then he stirred sugar into his tea.

'What's this?' she asked.

'Pandan cake, or chiffon cake – it's a bit like sponge, but the green comes from the leaves of a plant called the Pandanus amaryllifolius.'

She picked up a fork that he'd brought over, sliced into the cake then ate a piece.

'It's nice. As you say, just like sponge, despite the rather alarming colour.'

She laughed and glanced up at him, the corners of her eyes crinkling. Her laughter lit up her whole face, and he smiled back.

'You know, I'm glad I ran into you – it's been pretty manic here.' He picked up his cup. 'I've been meaning to drop in to see how you're both getting on.'

'I wouldn't worry,' she replied. 'But I'm sorry you're so run off your feet.' She lifted the fork to her mouth, then paused. 'Is there anything else I can do to help? I've got more than enough free time.'

'Well,' he thought for a moment, cutting into his cake, 'there *is* something.'

'What?'

'The other children on the ward could do with visiting too. One or two should have been transferred to the orphanage that's attached to the hospital by now, but it's the same old story: not enough space. I worry about the overcrowding, how the children are unsupervised, and how they could easily have an accident. I don't suppose you'd like to help?'

She placed her cup in the saucer. 'I suppose I could.' She paused again. 'What if I came three times a week – I could combine a class with all the children.'

'That would be fantastic. If you're sure?'

'Yes. More than.'

He finished his cake, then his tea. Really, he ought to get back to the ward, but he picked up his teaspoon and played with it between his fingers, trying to think of something to say that would delay his return.

'What will happen to Martha?' she asked, her forehead furrowed with concern.

'I don't know.' He put the spoon back on the saucer. 'But I suspect she'll be taken away from her Malay family for good.'

'Any idea when her case might come to court?'

'No. I think there might be a hearing soon, though. Because of the press interest, you don't get much warning for these kind of cases. Sometimes they're held in camera.'

'Poor kid.'

'Indeed.' He glanced at the clock on the wall. He really needed to get back.

'Well, I guess I'd better head off,' he said.

'Me too.' She picked up her bag. 'Thank you for the tea and the cake.'

'My pleasure.' He pushed back his chair and stood. 'And thank you for offering to help with the other children.'

He watched her leave the canteen. The brightness of her yellow dress seemed to take the sunshine with it.

A week passed where Nick's thoughts kept returning to Miranda – to the way she tilted her head when she looked up at him; how the skin around her eyes crinkled when she laughed; the slight overlap of her teeth; the mole on her throat and the freckles on her face; the light reflecting from her dress on to her skin and how she had looked by the window with sunlight falling around her. She seemed happier too, lighter, not at all like the lost soul of the previous weeks. The work she was doing at the hospital must surely be helping her, and he was glad that he'd been the one to suggest it.

Sometimes, he thought he heard her voice in the corridor or that he'd caught a glimpse of her as she went through a doorway. It was as though she was everywhere and, however hard he tried to push the images of her from his mind, they kept returning, stronger and more clearly than before.

Twenty-one

Saturday came and Miranda sat at the breakfast table with Gerry while she read a letter from her mother:

My dear Miranda,

How lovely to get your letters – the post is so unreliable – I was saying only the other day to Dad that we hadn't heard from you for ages, and now two letters from you arrived on the same day.

I'm so pleased that you've started to volunteer at St Augustin's and I'm sure you'll get lots from it. Since you told me about Martha, I've been noticing the occasional snippet about the case in the papers. It would seem that her case is causing quite a stir both in Singapore and at home. Your father thinks she should go back to her Dutch parents, but, like you, I feel she'd be better staying with the people who raised her.

Did I tell you that Lily Lewis contacted me again? We had afternoon tea, and guess what? She told me that her daughter is going to have a baby – so you're going to be an aunt, but I expect you know this already.

Miranda folded the letter and thrust it on to the table. No, Gerry hadn't told her about the baby.

'You didn't tell me you were going to be an uncle,' she said to Gerry. Her tone was short and curt.

'Didn't I?' Gerry glanced up from *The Straits Times* at the other end of the table.

'No. In fact, you hardly tell me anything these days.'

He put the paper down and looked at her.

'Well, if you weren't so busy at St Augustin's perhaps we might have had the chance to speak about it.'

Miranda let out a short laugh. 'What about you? You come home from work so late more often than not – you're exhausted and all you want to do is go straight to bed.' She knew he'd be annoyed by her answering back, but, this time, she didn't care.

'I told you. There's a lot on – takes me all over the place.'

'Well, Dickie and Longland seem to cope.'

'What's rankled you, Miranda?' he sighed. 'I'm sorry if you think I forgot to tell you about the baby, but that isn't enough to make you so emotional.'

'I'm not emotional!' She tried to keep the snap out of her words, but tears filled her eyes. 'It's been a difficult week – one of the children I've been looking after died. I wanted to tell you about it, but you came back so late. And now I'm worried about Martha – she's become withdrawn. I'm sure her case is due any day.'

The tears she'd felt stinging fell and she wiped them away with the back of her hand.

'I told you, didn't I, that I was concerned about you helping at that place? I knew that you'd get too attached to the children. Isn't it time to stop?'

'No.' She shook her head. 'I love helping there.'

'So what's wrong – is it hearing about the new baby?'

'No.' She blew her nose into a handkerchief that she'd taken from her pocket. 'It's that I had to find out from my mother – from Lily. That's what hurts the most.'

'Come on, now you're being ridiculous.' He stood and left the room.

'For God's sake!'

Would he never understand? It was as though they were like two poles pushing each other away.

She decided to go for a walk. Her route took her along a shaded path towards Belvedere, but despite the shelter of the branches, she soon broke out into a sweat and cursed the fact that she hadn't brought any water. As she got to closer to Belvedere, her thoughts returned to Martha. Nick might have some fresh news about her case, and perhaps if she called in on him, she could also get a drink.

Khalish, the house boy, was feeding chickens as she approached. He stopped with his hand in a bag that hung from his shoulder and watched as she came towards him.

'Is Dr Wythenshaw in?' she asked.

'*Tuan* not long waking, I think.'

Khalish went inside the house, and she waited with the chickens – some clucked and paced about while others pecked at the grain Khalish had scattered on the ground. A few moments later, Nick came out. He was wearing a pair of shorts and was busy buttoning up a navy linen shirt. His hair was rumpled, and she could see the imprint of a crumpled sheet on his face. She remembered that she still had his shirt at home and that she ought to return it.

'Goodness, did I wake you up?'

'Yes, actually, but it's already ten o'clock – high time I was up.' He smiled and indicated that she should sit down on a cane chair on the verandah. 'Would you like some tea?'

'That would be lovely, please.'

Khalish brought out tea, water, freshly squeezed mango juice, toast and a pot of something that looked to Miranda liked a green version of lemon curd.

'Kaya,' Nick explained, when she asked what it was. 'Khalish is very fond of his chickens and uses the eggs to make this custardy jam. Would you like to try some?'

'Yes, that would be lovely.'

He took a piece of toast and spread the butter on it, then added a dollop of kaya. He held it to her mouth, and she took a bite, holding her hand up to stop the bread falling. Their fingers grazed and his touch blistered through her.

'What do you think?' he asked.

'Delicious. A bit sweet.'

'It's infused with coconut, vanilla and brown sugar. Some more?'

She took another bite, conscious that his gaze was on her.

'Not sure if I'd want that every day. Think I'd put on about half a stone a week.'

He grinned at her. 'I doubt it.' There was something in his tone and the way he looked at her that flustered her.

'So,' she took a sip of her tea, confused by her feelings, 'I had a letter from my mother this morning – looks like Martha's case has caught the press's eye over there. Do you have any news about when the trial might be?'

'My feeling is that it will be any day.'

'I hope she can go back to her Malayan family.'

'Me too, but, whatever happens, I'm concerned about how this will affect her.'

'I know. She's been so quiet recently and I noticed that she's hardly been eating.'

Miranda stared into her cup. He was looking at her, she was certain of it.

'It's good of you to volunteer, but if it becomes too much, you don't have to. You're not paid to take the stress and the worry.'

'I know.'

She liked doing it. It made her feel valued and complete. But now, as she sat here with Nick, she realised how much this was combined with the enjoyment of his company and his approval. If she stopped volunteering, she might not see him so much. And that wasn't something she wanted, not only because she had fought so hard to get her freedom, but that she had won.

'Did you see that doctor dress up as a nurse the other day?' Nick asked.

'Yes,' she laughed. 'It was so funny. Those big hairy legs of his – and that wig.'

'Alice didn't find it at all funny.'

'She doesn't find anything funny – what's the deal with you two anyway?'

'Mainly, I don't think she likes the work I've been doing for Longland and Dickie – I don't know if she's simply a stickler for doing the right thing, but I certainly seem to annoy her. Sometimes I think she's looking for any excuse to get rid of me.'

They chatted for an hour longer, and then another before Miranda finally tore herself away.

'I haven't laughed so much in ages,' she said, as she stood to leave.

'Yes. It's been fun. Thank you for dropping by.'

As she walked home, the shadows of tree branches cast a speckled light along the path, and contentment enveloped her. But it wasn't simply pleasure of good company, she realised – there was real friendship between them. She wanted to hold on to it, to hug it to her body and to never let it escape. She remembered the photographs on his bookshelf and wondered again which of the women might be his sweetheart. It was strange that she'd never met her, but whoever she was, Miranda decided, she was a lucky woman.

Miranda had arranged to meet Georgina and her newly arrived niece, Poppy, at Georgina's club for lunch and then to go shopping with them both. Miranda looked at her watch: one-thirty. She was half an hour late.

Jinhai dropped her off at the top of the drive and she made her way into the Ladies' Lounge. Georgina sat by the open window, wearing an emerald-green shift dress, a matching hat and a pair of white shoes. A young woman in an ice-blue shift dress sat next to her: Poppy.

'I'm so sorry I'm late.' Miranda felt her face glowing with the humidity as she joined them.

Poppy stood to greet her. She was taller than Miranda remembered; a little frosty and composed, but very beautiful.

'Mrs Lewis.' Poppy held out her hand. Miranda took it. Despite the heat it was cool to the touch.

'You must call me Miranda. How do you like Singapore?'

'I haven't been here that long.' Poppy's vowels were long; a trademark Miranda remembered of Howdean. 'But it seems very pleasant, if a little hot.'

'Yes. I remember when I arrived it took a while to get used to it. All the seasons run together, I'm afraid, so no let up. I remember how defeated by the humidity I felt, and I was very envious of your aunt's bob.'

'Oh, I don't think I'll be getting *my* hair cut.' Poppy's hand drifted to her blonde chignon. The younger woman's eyes matched the colour of her dress. They seemed to cut into Miranda, like a cold and dangerous sea.

'Well,' Georgina leant forward, a cigarette burned in her tortoiseshell cigarette holder, 'we should go in, I suppose.'

The restaurant was buzzing with activity as they entered: Georgina first, then Poppy, then Miranda. Groups of women gossiped over lunch, or discussed the price of rubber or the tax on rice. Heads turned as they passed, and Miranda noticed that their gazes lingered on Poppy.

They sat down at the table, which was beautifully set with white bone china, silver cutlery and crystal glasses. An arrangement of fleshy orange orchids sat in the middle and sunlight danced across the table from the window to their left, making the setting glow.

'This looks lovely.' Miranda picked up her menu. Chicken supreme, she read. She loved it.

'The fish sounds good,' Georgina said. 'Pomfret. What about you, Poppy?'

'I don't know.' She closed the menu. 'Perhaps a salad.'

'When did you arrive?' Miranda asked.

'The day before yesterday.' Poppy put her hand to her mouth as she yawned.

'And Georgina tells me that you might work as a secretary in the Colonial Office, is that right?' Miranda asked.

Poppy nodded. 'Yes. Aunt Georgina is taking me shopping later to get some suitable clothes. I don't think she approves of the ones I've got.'

'You need some things that are a little more formal and comfortable for every day.' Georgina's tone was sharp.

'Wing Loong's?' Miranda asked, noting again the cut of Poppy's dress, how it hugged her figure. If all her wardrobe was the same, then Georgina was definitely right.

'How did you guess?' Georgina said, then beckoned to the waiter to take their order. 'Some loose cotton dresses, I think. Skirts and tops get far too uncomfortable around the waist in this heat.'

'I've brought some *Vogues* with me. Aunt Georgina said that they can copy anything here, and I rather fancied some Norman Hartnell's they did a feature on. There's a divine dress with little bows on, a little like the ones Princess Elizabeth favours.'

'As long as it's not too fancy and they're in cotton, I'm sure that they'll be fine.'

The waiter arrived and they ordered.

'Have you got much secretarial experience?' Miranda asked, before pouring water from a jug into their glasses. Ice cubes clinked as she poured.

'I did a course at Queen's Secretarial before I came.' Poppy smiled. 'I can type sixty words a minute.'

'Excellent. And you're staying with Georgina for now?'

'Yes.' Poppy turned and smiled at her aunt. 'My lovely gaoler.'

'Oh, come on,' Georgina laughed, diamonds glinting in her ears. 'I'm hardly that!'

'When do you start?'

'A week on Monday.'

'Any plans until then?'

'Apart from shopping?' Georgina grinned. 'What else is there?'

'You're incorrigible.' Miranda smiled at her.

'I try to be.' Georgina winked.

'I hear you work in a hospital,' Poppy said.

'I volunteer, really. Looking after children. Locals mainly. I enjoy it.'

'Good for you. Although I'm not sure I could do it myself. I suppose we're all cut out for different things, aren't we?'

'It isn't for everyone.' Miranda smiled. 'But I'm sure you'll enjoy it at the office. Lots of young company, I imagine.'

'That's what I'm worried about,' Georgina muttered under her breath. She gave Miranda a warning look, and Miranda wondered if Poppy had heard, but she was looking in her handbag and, a moment later, patted her face with a lawn handkerchief that Miranda noted was beautifully embroidered with a delicate 'P'.

Their food arrived and they chatted between mouthfuls. Miranda was starving and ate everything on her plate, but Georgina and Poppy merely picked at their food.

'That was delicious,' she said when she'd finished.

'Tea?' Georgina asked, loading another cigarette into her tortoiseshell holder.

Miranda looked at her watch. It was almost three. Although she was enjoying the company, she sensed that Georgina and Poppy would be better shopping alone.

'I hope you don't mind if I don't come shopping with you. It's been rather a busy week and I'm at the hospital again tomorrow. I'm teaching a group of girls to speak

English and there are one or two things that I need to prepare.'

'Of course not,' Georgina said. 'It was good of you to come and say hello to Poppy. I'm sure that there will be plenty of other times.'

'It's been a pleasure, Poppy. I'm so glad to see you and I'm sure we'll be great friends.'

'Thank you.' Poppy held out her hand and shook Miranda's with a loose grip. 'I'm sure that we will.'

Twenty-two

The door opened. It was Nick.

'Can I speak to you?' The space between his eyebrows was wrinkled and his tone was urgent.

She closed *The Three Bears* and turned to a girl of about eleven who was among a group of six children sitting on the floor.

'Aishah, can you show everyone the pictures in the book? I just need to chat to the doctor for a minute.'

Nick hung back. 'There isn't time to explain. You've got to take the children to the canteen as quickly as you can – try not to worry them.'

'But—'

Before she could ask more, he'd hurried off.

She returned to the children. Nick's demeanour troubled her, and she tried to calm herself. 'Let's finish now and get a drink.'

'Why for, Mrs Lewis?' Aishah asked.

'Dr Wythenshaw asked us to. Come on.' She held the door open, her palm sticky on the handle. 'As quickly as you can.'

They joined others crossing the courtyard. Black smoke billowed across the sky, then a gunshot cracked, followed by a roar and drumming in the distance. Aishah flinched.

'It's probably a funeral,' she said to Aishah.

'I don't think so-*lah*.' Aishah gripped her hand, the nails digging into her palm. 'Funeral make happy sound.'

'I'm sure it's nothing to worry about.' Miranda squeezed her hand back. But all kinds of thoughts rushed through her mind, sparking memories of nights spent in London during the war, the sirens howling as she ran to the Anderson shelter, the hours that passed waiting for the sound of the *All Clear*. She could still recall the smell of onions as she squashed between Mr Culley and Toby Briggins, her bladder stretched to burst. And then the worst of it, leaving the shelter, not knowing if she'd still find her home standing in the street.

She called to a nurse ahead of her. 'Do you know what's going on?'

The woman shrugged.

The canteen was heaving. Children were crying and nurses were organising drinks of water or handing out plates of biscuits. Nick was carrying a wireless with Alice and they placed it in a corner. She heard him ask, 'Any news?'

'Over here.' One of the nurses indicated spaces at a table. 'There's still a little room.'

'No one seems to know what's going on,' she said.

'Another disturbance, I suppose.'

'I thought I heard gunshots earlier.'

'The riots seem to be getting worse, don't they? Last week two women were killed at Raffles Boulevard, didn't you know? It's about time someone took charge.'

'I heard that the army's involved this time,' another nurse joined the conversation. 'Whatever it is, it's out of control.'

Stay calm, Miranda told herself, but her fingers were shaking as she placed Irdinah, another of the children, on a bench next to Aishah. She didn't know what to do: to stay with the children or to go to Nick.

'Would you mind if I found out some more?' She turned to the first nurse.

'Be my guest,' the woman replied. 'But make sure you let us know what's going on.'

The noise and the heat were overwhelming as she made her way to Nick. He was leaning over the wireless, his ear close to the amplifier.

'Nick?'

His eyes flickered towards her. 'Just a minute.'

She waited.

Finally, he lifted his head.

'It's Martha.'

'What? I'm confused – what's Martha got to do with any of this?'

'She was taken to a hearing at the Supreme Court this morning. They've given custody to her Dutch parents and the crowds waiting outside have gone ballistic. Listen.'

'What? I wondered where she was.'

She lowered her head:

After the outcome of the Martha Hollande case earlier today, there are reports coming in of major rioting from supporters, which is moving from the Supreme Court towards Tanjong Pagar. Military police and soldiers have been deployed. Residents are warned to take cover and not to venture into the streets until further notice. We will bring you updates as we receive them.

'Bloody hell! Where's Martha now?'

Nick shrugged. 'At the hearing. I'm going to look outside to see what's going on.'

'Let me come with you.'

'No. Stay here.'

Before she could process what was happening, he'd gone.

Half an hour passed. She paced. She nibbled the cuticles of her fingers. She handed out water, spilling it on the table. All the time, she kept glancing towards the door. Finally, he returned.

'I'm going to see Dr Wythenshaw, Aishah. I'll be back in a tick.' She smoothed the top of the girl's head.

He was carrying a black doctor's bag. The smell of bonfires clung to him and a streak of blood stained his sleeve.

'Nick – are you hurt?

'I'm fine. It's chaos out there – four cars on fire, missiles being hurled at the police.'

'Jesus.'

'And there are barricades along St Andrew's Road. I'm going to get some more supplies – people need help.'

'Shall I come?'

'No.' He shook his head and pushed past her.

Disappointment and confusion wrapped around her as she watched him speak to Alice, then to two of the nurses, who nodded and headed out of the room. She glanced at Aishah, who was watching her, and mouthed, 'I'll be back soon.'

Nick and the nurses were approaching the main gate as she ran to catch up.

'Wait!' she called. 'I'm coming too.'

Nick turned. 'Miranda, you're just a volunteer. It's not safe.'

'I was in the WVS, remember?'

'Let her.' One of the nurses placed her hand on his arm.

'All right.' His voice was brusque as he tugged at the gate before striding ahead of them. Smoke crept across the chaotic street.

'Remember to keep your head down, don't look anyone in the eye and, above all else, don't take sides,' Nick shouted back. They continued past an upturned car and she coughed as acrid smoke slipped into her lungs. Why had she said she'd come? She hadn't been expecting it to be like this. During the air raids, she'd been underground, anxious, but relatively safe. But out here – her fear tasted like metal. She ought to focus on Nick and try not to buckle. He was making his way towards a barricade where soldiers were aiming their guns towards them. It would be so easy to back away and pretend she'd got separated in the confusion.

Nick raised his hands, 'We're medics – come to help.'

Beyond the barricade, fire licked through shattered windows and rocks were scattered across the street. A crowd of men, some carrying flags with green stars and a crescent moon, others with their mouths covered with handkerchiefs, marched through the street, chanting – *'Keadilan! Keadilan! Keadilan!'*

'What are they shouting?' Miranda asked.

'They're demanding justice,' Nick said.

'You'll have to stay behind the barricade,' one of the soldiers shouted.

'Come on,' Nick's voice showed his impatience. 'I told you, I'm a doctor. Can't you let us through?'

'Over there!' the solider yelled, jerking the barrel of his gun, indicating a space behind them.

'For God's sake!' Nick muttered. The nurses glanced at each other; she guessed that they too were wondering what the hell they'd got themselves into.

They sheltered on the pavement behind a stack of boxes and waited. The chanting grew louder and angrier. A group of men rolled a car over while another man picked up a rock from the road and threw it at a café window and a spider's web of glass splintered into the street. Window after window fractured like eggshells.

'I think this is a bad idea.' Her knees were trembling, her throat powder dry.

A machine gun hammered. Nick grabbed her hand, yanking her into a nearby shop, where they stood among baskets of mangosteens and pak choi listening to the noises on the street. Their breath was rapid.

'Where are the others?' She looked around. The shop-keeper was crouching at the back of the shop with a machete in his hand and an elderly Chinese woman in black was squatting behind a sack of rice with her hands over her face. The two nurses had disappeared.

'They're OK. I saw them run back.'

'Jesus, Nick. Shouldn't we get out of here too?'

'No.' He dropped hold of her hand. 'It can't last much longer.'

She sank on to a sack of dried beans, watching Nick peer into the street. No one spoke. She leant forward, her face in her hands, and concentrated on her breathing. She couldn't bottle out now; she'd have to take whatever fate threw at them.

They waited, listening. Five minutes. Ten. Another gun shot. A baby crying. Her heart raced in unison with her watch: tick, tick, tick; thump, thump, thump.

Another ten minutes passed, then Nick turned towards her. 'I think it's safe to go out.'

'I hope you're right.' She stood, praying that her legs wouldn't give way.

The soldiers had left the barricade and she tried to deci-pher the distant sounds and debris around her. Five cars had been overturned, consumed by flames. Stalactites of glass hung from window frames, and the ground crunched, like the first fall of snow, beneath her feet. A few people stood in doorways, dazed, not yet brave enough to face what might lie in the street.

'It's unbelievable.' Her words fell, impotent and inadequate, among the ravaged buildings.

Nick approached a Chinese man in a doorway. 'Are you all right?'

The man nodded.

Nick moved on. She followed, picking her way through shards of glass and the stones strewn in her path. There was a young woman sitting on the pavement, cradling a baby. Blood poured from her head, staining the child's face.

'Nick, look.'

Together they examined the piece of glass half-buried in her forehead. The woman winced as they examined her jagged and glistening flesh.

'I'll have to pull it out. It needs sutures. Can you pass me a needle and some thread, and some small clamps?'

She opened the bag and handed him the tools. His jaw was clenched in concentration as he extracted the glass and laced the woman's skin with neat, horizontal threads.

'You'll have to come to the hospital at St Augustin's to get the stitches taken out. Come next week – ask for Dr Nick. Got that?'

'Dr Nick.' The woman nodded. She was pale and shaking. 'I remember it.'

For the next hour, they wandered around the shattered streets: a broken hand, a bleeding neck. He gave her monosyllabic instructions and the occasional, reassuring nod. She focused, watching his agile fingers, all the time blocking out the danger but keen to help.

In the distance, a clock chimed six. 'We should go back,' he said.

She nodded. Her body ached and she noticed a long rip snaking up from the hem of her skirt. Her whole body seemed to be covered in dust and speckles of blood, and her eyes itched from the rawness of the smoke. There was nothing she wanted more than to down a gallon of icy water, to take a long shower and to change into clean clothes. But as they approached St Augustin's, a group of three men, their leader waving a Muslim flag, ran back into the street. Gunshots ricocheted behind the trio as a soldier chased them, his rifle aimed at the men's backs. Together, the men upturned a car to ward him off, then one of them stuffed a cotton rag into the petrol tank.

'My God, Nick!' Miranda's hand flew to her mouth as she saw the man strike a match and light the rag. 'It's going to explode.' She and Nick were caught between the car and the soldier giving chase, but before she had time to think or to say any more, Nick pushed her to the ground, protecting her with his body as the blast ripped along the street.

They lay for a moment. All around her she could hear the cacophony of voices shouting, gunfire, the car burning. Fumes filled her lungs, and she coughed, not yet able to see through the smoke blackening the street.

'Nick?

'Yes.'

'Can you move?'

'I think so.'

He raised his head slowly, then his body shifted. 'Quick,' he said. 'We'd better get out of here.'

He stood up and pulled her with him. Dust covered, he led her through the chaos. The men were throwing stones at the solider, who was now joined by another two. Nick ducked and guided her through the smoke and gunshots until they were safely through to the other side of the car.

'I thought we were done for,' she said, breathless. Her heart kept company with the gunfire pounding around her. 'And now I can't see a blessed thing.'

'Stay with me. Hold my hand. I know a short cut back to the hospital.'

'Thank God,' she said, as they ran through the backstreets. 'I'm not sure if I can take much more of this.'

At last she saw the roofline of St Augustin's, but there were people pooling around the gates and she realised that, far from being over, their work was just beginning. All that evening, she collected bandages or mopped blood from the corridor, only catching fleeting glimpses of Nick. She did whatever was required of her, losing count of the number of people in the hospital: bodies on stretchers, policemen with guns, reporters pushing for answers. The faces blurred and the evening slipped away.

Around midnight, the influx calmed. She went to the canteen and found Nick, who was sitting at a table with a half-finished cup of tea.

'I guess I ought to be getting home,' she said, sitting opposite him. 'I can't wait for a shower and to get out of these clothes.'

'You can't – just heard there's a curfew.'

'*What?*'

'You'll have to contact your husband and let him know that you'll have to stay the night here. You can use the phone in Alice's office.'

'But where on earth can I sleep?'

'Ask Alice. One of the nurse's rooms?'

'What about you?'

'Slept on many a hard floor in my time.'

He looked her in the eye. 'You know, what you did today – you should be proud.'

'I did what anyone would.' But then she remembered the nurses who'd disappeared at the first sound of gunshots and the skin on her face began to prickle. Perhaps it was simply the glow of the lights overhead grazing her skin, but a new kind of warmth radiated through her, flowing through her veins and making her face feel flushed. She glanced up towards Nick. But this time, as their eyes met, he didn't look away.

'If I'm honest, I didn't know you'd have it in you, but you did.' He finished his tea, then stood. 'You'd better find somewhere to sleep – you don't know when you'll be needed next.'

She watched him go but wanted to call him back. The day had been hell, but still she wanted to hold on to this moment. When the swinging canteen door finally settled, she waited for a while, then went to find Alice.

Somehow, she managed to fall straight asleep and didn't wake until the morning. The bed was uncomfortable, better suited for camping, and her back ached. She sat up and stretched out her arms, the collar of the borrowed hospital gown slipping over her shoulder.

The room was little more than a broom cupboard. In the corner, there was a chair with a broken leg – a small towel hung over the back and a thin blanket was draped over the window for a curtain. She got out of bed, letting the gown fall to the floor.

In the opposite corner, there was a washbasin stained with yellow marks and she had to force the small, dried-out soap out of the dish, where it was stuck fast. She lathered it, washed her face, under her arms and between her legs, then pulled on her clothes again. They stank of smoke, sweat and God knew what else.

She looked in the mirror, running her fingers through her hair; she really did look a mess. Memories of the night before played back to her: the anger of the rioting crowd, the injuries of innocent locals caught up in the turmoil on the street, standing next to Nick as they helped, the way their fingers grazed as she passed him needles or plasters, his breath on her face as they bent over to help a man who was lying on the pavement.

Beneath the residual grime and tiredness, not only was her face glowing, but it was as though something much deeper within her had come alive – like a seed germinating, its shoots reaching through the dark soil and stretching upwards towards the sun.

Twenty-three

Miranda made her way to the gates of St Augustin's to wait for Gerry. The air was suffocating, the way it felt before an electrical storm. When she reached the street, it was empty apart from a woman sweeping glass into a gutter and a man setting up a makeshift vegetable store. Thoughts of the previous night still consumed her; she couldn't stop reliving the scenes on the street, the people she'd helped, and then Nick, the way he'd lifted his head and the burn of his gaze as he'd spoken to her in the canteen. She knew that, however hard it had been, however dangerous, that she'd been pleased to help so many people and that she'd willingly do it all again.

Minutes passed. She glanced up and down the street, looking for Gerry, but there was still no sign of the Vauxhall and now she was getting anxious. An Indian man cycled past and she smiled nervously at him; his eyes flickered towards her, then he shouted angrily at her. Startled, she stepped back from the edge of the pavement.

Finally, the Vauxhall came into view, and as the car drew up along the pavement, the passenger door swung open. It was Gerry.

'Quick – get in!' he shouted.

'Thank you for coming to get me – I'm just so glad I eventually managed to get hold of you at work.'

He frowned, thrusting the gear stick forward and concentrating on the rear-view mirror as they accelerated away from the hospital. Her mood disintegrated, like ice melting.

'I could have got a taxi or a bus if it was inconvenient.' She flopped back in her seat, taking in the smell of stale perspiration, tobacco and hint of whisky lingering in the car. 'Or I could have stayed a little later – until Jinhai could pick me up.'

'You wouldn't have got a taxi.' He double de-clutched and the car jerked forward. 'And Jinhai's gone.'

'What do you mean, *gone*?' She focused on the stubble around his chin and the dark shadow of new growth on his upper lip. His shirt was crumpled and patches of sweat soaked the shirt beneath his armpits. 'Gerry, whatever is the matter?'

He ran a hand through his hair. 'You don't know what's happened, do you?'

'Of course, I know about the riots. I was there, remember? I told you all about it when I rang you this morning.'

'I don't mean all that.' His tone was dismissive. She watched the rise and fall of his Adam's apple as he prepared to speak. 'Apart from spending all night at crisis meeting after crisis meeting, I get home to find Jinhai's disappeared. Arrested.'

'Good God. Surely there's been a mistake?'

'You'd better read the paper.' Her jerked his head back, indicating one on the back seat, so she reached behind and picked up a dishevelled copy of *The Straits Times*.

Five Dead and a Hundred Injured in Riots
Mob rule in Singapore streets as cars and buses burned. British and Malay troops were called to the support of the Singapore police last night to quell the rioting, which took place after the Martha Hollande hearing.
Two Europeans, two Chinese and one Malay have been killed, and more than a hundred injured in the Muslim rioting, which gripped Singapore's city centre last night.

'But I know all this.'

'Carry on reading. The next page.'

'What, this bit about Mrs Evans?' *I saw rioters get on our bus*, she read. *They pointed guns at us, then they started on my husband, beating him with a stick. I was terrified as they began hitting me in the face. I lost sight of my husband when they dragged him off the bus.* 'But what's all this got to do with Jinhai?'

'He got swept up in it all, Mei Ling told me. So, of course, apart from coming to get you, I'm going to have to deal with that.'

'I can't believe it. Jinhai, of all people. And that poor woman. Imagine being slapped in the face like that and not knowing where your husband has been taken.' Fingers of fear slithered down her back. 'Is it safe, to go home?'

'If we keep away from the main roads.' He swung the car into a warren of shadowy back streets. 'I tried to come across town earlier, but there was a roadblock across Dunearn Road. I've heard the causeway's closed too.'

'But how,' she folded the paper, still shocked, 'did it turn so ugly so quickly? I don't understand. Martha's natural parents were Dutch, not British.'

'It doesn't matter. They see us all as Europeans, and they know that Europeans were supporting the claim of Martha's real parents.'

Not all of us, Miranda thought.

'Besides, there have always been tensions between us and them rising in the background. Martha was the tipping point and they haven't forgiven us for the Occupation,' Gerry said dismissively.

Miranda remembered what Georgina had told her when they first arrived – about the European women being marched by the Japanese for miles in the midday sun to Changi prison, and the locals standing back, not even offering them water.

'Surely not all of them feel like that?'

Gerry shrugged. 'Who knows? The point is now no one can tell which way things will swing.' He paused, then the tone of his voice dropped a level or two.

'After all of this, I think a lot of people will feel unsafe. I won't be surprised if some people make the decision to go back to England.'

'But you said yourself that the government won't allow you to leave your jobs.'

'Not the men, of course, but their wives might go home alone.'

'That's a bit extreme, isn't it?'

'Actually, I was thinking that perhaps you should go home too.'

'*What?* That's ridiculous.'

'It will be safer for you. And the more I think about it, I realise it wasn't fair of me to bring you out here in the first place.'

She found it difficult to process what he was saying.

'Are you serious?'

He ran his finger under his collar and thought for a moment.

'Well, it would be a solution, wouldn't it? Aside from the fact that you put yourself in real danger last night, I know you've been unhappy here. It's an opportunity. You could travel home without it looking odd.'

She fell silent. If she went home now, even if she wanted to, surely that would be the worst thing they could do to heal the cracks in their marriage?

'You *are* serious, aren't you?' She looked at him, but he was focusing ahead of him, his features set. 'I think it's a terrible idea.'

'What if you'd been attacked last night?'

'I wasn't, though, was I?'

'That's not the point,' he carried on. 'There are ships most days, but we should get you a passage before they all get taken up.'

'I'm not going.'

'*Please*, Miranda, you've read the papers, seen what's been happening in Malaya. It looks like things are blowing the wrong way here, too. I'm trying to keep you safe.'

'But, what about all the things I've done recently? And what about last night? No. I want to carry on helping here. You can say what you like, but I'm not leaving.'

'I'm not asking you. I'm telling you.' His voice exploded in the car, making her jump. 'I'm tired of your obsessions with these blasted local kids. Do you know what people are saying about you?' He spoke as though the thought revolted him. 'First, it was the incident over Jack, and now it's all this bloody Martha thing. Gossip in corridors all the time. Well, I've got news for you – you can't afford to make too many bad choices out here. It's bad form. Mud sticks. Just do as I say for once, Miranda. Go back home and stay with your parents.'

She clenched her fists, digging her nails into her palms. Why the hell did he always have to trample on her, crushing away all her happiness?

'Huh! Anyone would think you were trying to get rid of me.'

'Come on, Miranda. What kind of a thing is that to say?' He turned the steering wheel too fast, almost clipping the pavement. 'I don't want to talk about this now – you're tired and emotional after last night.'

'You brought it up, not me.' She took a deep breath, trying to stay calm.

They drove on, not speaking. Gerry focused on the road ahead, while Miranda looked out of the passenger window, her frustration building like the pressure inside a volcano. Gerry must have taken her silence as acquiescence, because he gently patted her on the knee.

She pushed his hand away as firmly as she could.

When they arrived home, she showered and changed, then she threw herself on the bed. After a time, she could hear Gerry moving along the corridor, the click of the bathroom door, then the flush of the lavatory. She sat up, then went to listen at the door.

'I might have to stay at the office again,' he called from the other side of the closed door, as if he'd been there waiting. 'No need to keep supper for me.'

She didn't reply.

He began to whistle, setting her teeth on edge. She clenched her fist and hit the doorframe. After a few minutes, she heard his footsteps fading across the hall. Miranda sank back on to the bed and eventually she fell asleep.

Sometime later, she woke and made her way to the kitchen door to see Mei Ling.

'We've not got much food, Mrs Gerald. Today I don't want to go to market. I hear plenty of people got hurt last night.'

'Yes, they did. And the army and police are still out on the streets. But you don't need to worry, I think we'll be safe here. I was surprised about Jinhai, weren't you?'

She nodded. '*Wah!* Very big surprise. I didn't know Jinhai would do something like this.'

'No. Nor me. He never spoke to you about his views, then?'

'No-*lah*. Why didn't he tell me?'

'It's fine, Mei Ling. I'm not cross,' she sighed. 'Right. I suppose we ought to check out the store cupboard in case we're stuck here for a few more days.'

Together they checked the cupboards for rice and preserved food.

'These recent riots have been awful,' Miranda said. 'Far worse than anything before. Do you think it will ever end?'

Mei Ling turned to her, holding a small bag of rice. 'Chinese people have a saying – the ground becomes solid after lots of rain. I, Mei Ling, say it's been raining Singapore too long.'

'I think you might be right,' Miranda said, as she placed a tin of corned beef on top of a container of dried egg then closed the larder door.

She brushed her hand, dusting off some dirt. 'Well, it looks like we have enough in for a day or two. Shall we have fried rice for lunch?

Miranda hadn't eaten since the night before and was starving. She sat down on the verandah while Mei Ling cooked. After a time, Mei Ling brought out a plate of fried rice, scattered with small pieces of chopped chicken.

She dug her fork into the plate of rice. From the far side of the trees she could hear Jack crying, followed by Charlotte's voice. Her fork remained suspended in the air as she continued to listen – to Charlotte singing and soothing Jack, reminding her of Jane's hostility and of the rumours about her that Gerry had hinted at, and which, thanks to Jane, she was more than certain were circulating at the club. Well, stuff them all. Gerry was right about one thing, and she knew which side she was on.

It was five o'clock. Nick sat at his desk, his head in his hands. Tiredness stung his eyes and his body ached with fatigue. His shirt was damp with perspiration, and he realised it was the second day that he'd been wearing it. He longed to go home, to have a soak in the bath, to pull on a freshly ironed shirt, but the deadline was looming for the Nairobi application and he didn't want to miss this chance at running a medical centre. He checked over the letter, satisfied with what he'd written, then lifted his head and ran his fingers over the prickly growth on his chin and his thoughts turned to Miranda. If he went, he would never see her again, and the thought pained him. Still, it was a promotion and a chance to prove himself. He would post it before he changed his mind and before the damn curfew kicked in. He collected his belongings and entered the corridor, which was strangely empty as he trudged towards the exit. He was relieved to see that his car was where he had left it – beneath a royal palm but now covered in a thick layer of dust. At least no one had wrecked or stolen it. He sat down on the scorching seat, started the engine and it fired into life. There was an army Land Rover patrolling the streets outside the hospital, and the marketplace was deserted, as though the lifeblood of Tanjong Pagar had drained away. He slipped his letter into the post box on Craig Road, and then, back in the car, he put his foot down and headed towards Belvedere.

'*Tuan!*' Khalish called out, as Nick walked through the door. He was rolling up the chick blinds and mellow sunlight streamed across Nick's line of vision. 'I worry about you. All these riot make everyone nervous, frightened.' Nick could hear the relief in Khalish's voice.

'I'm sorry, Khalish. There was so much to do at the hospital, and it's been hard to get anywhere with this damn curfew. Has everyone been all right here?'

'Everything just fine here. Mr Brendan and Mr Charlie come home late last night. They tell me you must be at hospital. Not to worry.'

'Really? They made it out from KK?'

'Came back in army truck. Mr Brendan say he know someone in army.'

'That sounds just like Brendan – luck of the devil.' Nick went to the dresser and poured himself a whisky. 'Khalish – I'm going to have a soak in the bath.'

'Then maybe you like I make you something to eat. Nasi goreng? I think you like that.'

'Perhaps, Khalish. I'll let you know.'

He went to the bedroom first, took a long slug of his whisky, then looked at the most recent report he'd been compiling. After he'd bathed and dressed, he went back to pour himself another drink. Khalish had left a pile of letters on the table and he flicked through them. Three for Brendan, two for Charlie and two for himself. One was from his mother. The other, hand delivered. No stamp.

He studied the writing – a cursive blue sprawled across the envelope.

From the words she'd written on the board in her classes, he recognised the script as Miranda's.

He hadn't seen her since last night. He pictured the way she'd looked up at him while handing him a needle or a bandage, her eyes keen to please, the way she'd lugged buckets of water and mopped the corridor free of spilled blood without being asked. And she'd left without him being able to thank her. He pulled out the folded paper and read.

Dear Nick,

I wonder if you could call? I need to speak to you about something.

Miranda.

He knocked back his whisky.

'Khalish?'

'*Tuan?*'

'When did this arrive?'

'Just before you come home.'

Nick glanced at his watch. Six o'clock. An hour left until curfew.

'I'm going to go out for bit, Khalish, but I'll be back by seven. Then I'll have that Nasi goreng.'

He walked, glad to be out and to see the cobwebs of clouds lacing across the sky, to hear the rustle of monkeys in the trees and the thrumming of crickets. As he approached the bungalow, he inhaled the musky aromas from mosquito coils and incense, while from within the bungalow he could hear the murmur of Miranda's voice, the click of what might have been a game of mah-jong, then Mei Ling's laughter. He hesitated a moment, then knocked on the door. The conversation stopped, followed by the sound of heels clicking along the hall.

'Nick!' To his surprise, Miranda opened the door, not Mei Ling.

'You got my note, then?' she said, as she stepped aside, and he followed her to the living room.

'Excuse the mess,' she nodded towards the coffee table. 'Mei Ling's been teaching me mah-jong, but I still can't get the hang of it. Martini, whisky, gin?' she asked.

'Martini, thanks.'

He looked around. Mei Ling had gone.

Miranda poured vermouth from a bottle into a cocktail glass and mixed his drink. 'Well,' she handed him the cocktail, 'I don't suppose you know what happened to Martha?'

'No.' He shook his head. 'But I expect she's on her way to Holland.'

'I'd hoped that I might have been able to see her one more time before she left.' She scrunched her mouth, as though she were trying to contain her disappointment. She took a handkerchief from her pocket and dabbed her eyes. 'I was really fond of her, you know. These past few weeks were really quite special. I can't believe I'll never see her again.'

'I know it doesn't help, but I'm sure she won't forget what you did for her.'

She looked down and he wondered what it was that she wanted to tell him.

He watched her light a cigarette, then cross her legs as she leant back into her chair.

'You left St Augustin's before I had a chance to thank you for your help,' he began.

'You don't need to thank me. I suppose it's wrong of me to say I enjoyed it, but I did. Being useful, I mean, not seeing those poor people who were injured.' A frown flickered across her forehead.

'I know what you mean.'

'Last night made me think that I'd like to do more to help – even train to be a nurse. I think I'd be good at it.'

'I think you'd make a wonderful nurse.'

'Do you know if there might be any more work at St Augustin's? I've heard that there's a programme for training nurses. Do you know more about it?'

'Not really. My understanding was that it is mainly for the locals or recruiting from England, but I could find out.'

'Meanwhile, I'd like to do some more volunteering – would that be possible?'

He turned his glass in his hand, watching the drink cling to the side. 'I can ask.'

'Good. Can you let me know, then?' She flopped back further in her chair. 'Oh. There's one more thing. We don't have a driver any more. Would you be able to take me in when you go?'

Their eyes met, and the lines of her mouth creased into a gentle smile. He nodded, then he looked away. Again he wondered if he had done the right thing about applying for the position in Nairobi. He thought about telling her of his plans, but changed his mind, not wanting to spoil the moment.

He returned to Belvedere in the remaining moments before the sky turned suddenly black. It fascinated him how the sun rose and set regularly at the same time virtually every day of the year, as though someone had flipped a switch from day to night – so different to the lingering sunrises and sunsets of home. It occurred to him that Miranda was like that: a light that had been hidden and then emerged from beyond the horizon, dazzling with a brilliance that he had never expected.

Back in the living room, he sank into a wicker chair and lit a cigarette. A trail of burning tobacco rose from the cigarette balancing in his hand as his thoughts remained on Miranda; the way she'd held her head; how she smiled whenever their eyes had met. He poured a finger of whisky into a glass and knocked it back. The bitterness made his teeth tingle. He took another sip, then finished the glass and poured another shot. He finished that glass, then poured out a third, setting the bottle in his lap. He needed to pull himself together. Miranda was a married woman. He could only guess at what Brendan or Charlie would say if they knew what was going on in his mind – 'You're a bloody fool, mate, playing with fire, you'll only get burned.'

Still, his thoughts wandered, and he imagined placing his hands around Miranda's waist, listening to the soft rhythm of her heart, feeling her breath sweeping over his skin. And then there were her eyes – every time she looked at him, it seemed to electrify him. Was it possible that she felt the same?

Twenty-four

Each morning, Miranda waited for Nick on the corner of the street, and every evening he brought her home around six. Gerry had been coming back later and leaving earlier than usual; sometimes, he even stayed overnight at the club. There had been another crisis in Malaya followed by another. Every day it seemed there was another attack on a rubber plantation or another guerrilla attack on the road that called for Gerry's immediate attention. His absence suited her. And when they did meet, they barely spoke, giving each other a formal nod or leaving hurriedly written notes on the hall table.

Christmas Eve crept up quickly. The corridors at St Augustin's and her classroom felt empty without Martha, but she kept busy teaching the children Christmas songs and decorating the room with snowflakes cut out from newspaper.

At lunchtime, the door opened, and a small shadow fell across her desk

'What are you doing?' Aishah asked.

'Making snowflakes,' Miranda put down the pair of scissors and unfolded the newspaper cut-out in her hand, 'to decorate the windows. Would you like a go?'

'What is snowflake?'

'In England, sometimes it is very cold and the water in the clouds freezes. As it falls to the ground, instead of rain it comes as snow. It covers the ground with a fine layer of white, which looks like ice kachang.'

'Really?' Aishah scrunched up her face. 'Is it sweet? Can you eat it with a spoon?

'No.' Miranda smiled. 'But sometimes the water in the rivers and lakes also freezes, and a long time ago people used to collect the ice to keep food cold. And,' she added, 'the snow is made up of millions and millions of snowflakes, each one different, like tiny, glittering stars.'

'I like this snow and snowflake. Maybe one day I might see.' Aishah paused, 'Maybe can you ask someone to send me some from England?'

Miranda laughed. 'I don't think that they would survive the journey, I'm afraid. Ice melts, Aishah, and so would the snowflakes. They might be pretty, but they don't last. Tell you what, why don't you make one of your own – you can put your name on it and keep it until you see real snow.'

Aishah nodded, and together they made half a dozen more newspaper snowflakes and added them to the collection on the window.

The afternoon drew to a close, ending with the Christmas Eve service in the chapel. Miranda sat at the back, half-listening to the carols as her mind wandered back to a previous year, when the wireless had been playing 'Hark the Herald Angels'. She thought of Henry and how she'd never celebrated a Christmas with him. It was almost as though he was there with her now; she could almost feel the rise and fall of his chest, his soft, blond hair as she ran it through her fingers. She pulled out a handkerchief and quickly wiped away a tear before anyone saw.

'The singing's lovely, isn't it?' A woman next to her offered her a peppermint. Miranda shook her head and wiped her nose. When the service finished, she saw that Nick was waiting for her outside.

'I hope you don't mind,' he said, leading her to the car, 'but I promised Brendan I'd collect a few things from Cold Storage. It's a bit of a trek, though.'

'That's fine. I don't mind going shopping.'

As they drove, the streets grew busier and the buildings grander.

'You know,' he said. 'I never did thank you for what you did the day of the riots.'

'Didn't you?' She raised her face to his. 'I thought that you had.'

'Not properly.'

'It doesn't matter now. And I'm glad I did. Otherwise ...'

'Otherwise what?'

His voice was low, almost a whisper.

'I wouldn't ...' She wasn't brave enough to tell Nick what she truly felt, that the best part of her days was the time she spent with him.

'I wouldn't be helping at St Augustin's, would I?'

Was she imagining it or had Nick's face fallen just a little?

'Well, it suits you,' he said.

She smiled at him, and the way he grinned back caught her off guard. She watched his hand shifting the gear stick as they slowed and turned a corner, resisting the urge to reach out and touch his fingers, to spread her hand over his. She turned her gaze away.

'So,' he said, parking the car at the side of the road opposite Cold Storage, 'you haven't told me what you are doing for Christmas.'

'Oh, I don't know,' she hesitated, not wanting to tell him that she was dreading it. Gerry was taking two days off and they hadn't got much planned – they were bound to argue and, to be honest, she didn't know if she could be bothered to make the effort. 'I've been so busy, I haven't even had time to get a tree.'

'They might have something left in here.' He held the door of Cold Storage open, and she stepped in, their bodies bumping into each other.

'You go,' he smiled, his face close to hers.

'No. After you.'

'No.' He shook his head, and she entered, then she wandered up and down the aisles beside his tall, reassuring form. She picked up Hershey bars and Oreo biscuits, then examined strange, plastic boxes with lids called *Tupperware* until she came to a stand of glass baubles.

They were like red and green jewels, reflecting the overhead lights.

'My goodness, look at these!' She couldn't resist picking them up, turning them as they glittered and sparkled. Next to them was a stand of patterned paperchains, with images of balloons stamped along their length. 'It's been years since I've seen anything other than brown paper ones.'

'Then you should get them.'

'But I told you, I haven't got a tree.'

Nick put the decorations in her basket, then pointed out a small pawpaw tree that would do for a Christmas tree. 'And what about these?' He picked up a box of fairy lights. 'That should do the trick. Now, I need to get those six bottles of Château Latour for Brendan, as well as two bottles of Glenlivet.'

After they paid for their goods, they headed back to Alexandra Gardens.

'Is your husband at home or shall I'll give you a hand?' Nick asked, as he parked the car on the corner of the road.

'No, he isn't – and that would be kind.'

He handed her the bag of decorations, their fingers brushing once again. It intoxicated her, but she dropped her gaze from his, for a new hunger was beginning to gnaw inside her; it thrilled and it bewildered her. Much as she longed to follow the feelings growing within her, she knew that they were wrong, but yet they overwhelmed, almost blinded her.

He picked up the small tree and followed her to the bungalow.

'Where would you like this?' He hung back.

'Just there would be fine.'

What could she do or say to hold on to this moment?

He placed the pawpaw next to the front door.

'How about a Christmas drink?' It was as though a fault line was opening ahead of her; small to begin with, but, if it opened, she knew that the crevasse would suck her in. Her breath slowed as she waited for his reply.

He hesitated. 'I'd better be getting back.'

'Oh!' Baffled, she couldn't think of another reason for making him stay, and he obviously wanted to leave. Whatever she was feeling, he clearly wasn't feeling it too.

'Good night, then,' she said. 'Happy Christmas!'

'Yes. Happy Christmas.'

As he walked off, her spirits floundered. More than anything, she wanted him there and for the touch that lingered on her hand never to go away, but she couldn't form the words to call him back.

Instead, she called after him, 'I didn't ask you, what are you doing for Christmas lunch?'

'Oh,' he turned back to face her, 'I'm with Brendan and Charlie. Thought we might head over to the Sea View later.'

'Well,' she fingered the rim of her shopping bag, 'if you're passing, why don't you call in for a drink?'

'I might. I'll see how it goes.'

She wished more than anything else that he would.

At that moment, a taxi drew into the road. She watched as it pulled up outside the bungalow. When she glanced back to Nick, he'd already gone.

The door to the taxi opened. 'Georgina! What a lovely surprise!'

'I know, but just you wait. I've got so much to tell you!'

'Really?' Miranda opened the door to the bungalow. In the distance, she could hear Nick's car pulling off. She pictured the set of his features, his hands on the wheel, and the dent in the seat where only minutes ago she'd sat.

'Yes. What a day!' Georgina followed her into the hall. 'I don't know where to start.'

Miranda placed the decorations on the hall table. 'How about at the beginning?' She brought in the pawpaw as Georgina leant against the table and lit a cigarette.

'Well, the first thing is that Peter's uncle wants the house back.' She exhaled smoke into the hall as Miranda dragged the tree into a corner next to the table. 'There's been one hoo-ha after another in Malaya, and he's decided it's safer back here. They're coming back at the end of the week.'

The tree was damp, and Miranda wiped her hands on her skirt. 'Why? What's happened this time?'

'Their plantation was attacked the night before last – the workers' houses were torched and the foreman was beaten. He's still in hospital. The attacks have never been so close to their property before.'

'That's terrible.'

'And that's not all.' Georgina took her arm. 'Peter's handed in his notice.'

'*What?* Why?'

'Well,' Georgina let go of her arm. 'Lots of reasons, really – but the short of it is, we're going to America. Chicago. Peter says the future's there. That the Colonies are over.'

'Jesus. I need a drink. This is all so sudden. What's he going to do?'

'Community housing.'

'And what about Poppy – doesn't she still live with you?'

'Ah, Poppy!' Georgina rolled her eyes.

'What's that supposed to mean. Is she not adjusting to the life here?'

'The opposite, in fact – she's a little minx. Always out late. Never know where she is or what she's up to. There's a flat share with some of the other girls that she's adamant she wants to get involved with, but, if I'm honest, I don't think they'd be a good influence on her. I'm in such a turmoil, and I know she won't come with us. I don't suppose you'd mind awfully, just keeping an eye on her for me until I get it sorted out?'

'Of course. I'll do my best. But when are you going?'

'Two weeks.'

'But— I don't know what to say. So many changes!'

'Oh, Miranda.' Georgina folded her arms and glanced away. 'That's not all! You've been so busy with yourself, I didn't want to tell you before. I'm pregnant. We've been trying for ages and ages. I've had so many miscarriages.' Her voice lowered. 'It's been tearing us apart.'

'I had no idea.'

'Well, you do now.' Georgina looked up at her, radiating happiness. 'New start all round. Hug?'

'Of course!' As they embraced, she shut her eyes as though closing them could block out her growing pain. 'But I probably won't see you again. Or the baby.'

'Perhaps not for ages. But don't say never. You'll have to visit me in Chicago. Promise?'

'I'll miss you.'

'I'm not dying.'

'I know. We should be celebrating.' Miranda pulled away. 'How about a drink? And I could put up these decorations to celebrate.'

'All right, if you insist. But let me help you.'

'No!' Miranda made her way to the bureau and began mixing vermouth and gin. 'You should be resting.'

'For heaven's sake, not yet. Plenty of time for that when I can barely move.'

'Here,' she handed Georgina a martini. 'To the future.'

Georgina took her glass. 'To the future – whatever it may hold.'

Miranda sipped her drink. 'Look at these.' She opened the box of coloured lights. 'I got them in Cold Storage.'

'They're beautiful.'

'When you're in America, you'll be able to get things like this all the time.'

She took the lights out of the box and wound them around the tree. Georgina gasped as Miranda switched them on: red, blue, green and yellow lights glowed like fireflies between the branches. Then she took a bauble out of the box and held its delicate eggshell body in her hand, running her finger along its bumpy, glittery surface. This is what life is like, she thought. From the tiny baby growing inside Georgina, to Martha's and Aishah's futures. It wouldn't take much to destroy any of it. She hung the bauble on a branch, then took out another and positioned that until the tree was covered in glorious, sparkling orbs.

'Is there anything I can do?' Georgina asked.

'You could help me make the paper chains.'

'Great.' Georgina picked them up. 'I love paper chains. The way one scrap of paper links to another, creating something strong. But I haven't seen anything as pretty as these for years.'

Together they sat threading narrow bands of green and red until the chain was complete. It was long enough, she estimated, to hang on the far wall. She pushed the chair into the corner of the living room and stood on it, straining to reach the picture rail to attach the chain trailing from her hand.

'Mrs Gerald, you be careful.'

'Mei Ling – I didn't see you come in.'

'No. I was just passing. Seeing you made me worry.'

'I'll be fine. In fact, you can help me – pass me a tack, would you?' Miranda attached the end loop to the corner of the room, then pushed the chair to the middle of the wall and waited for Mei Ling to pass her another pin. Finally, she moved the chair to the far corner of the room and secured the final piece.

'Don't they all look pretty?' She looked down at Georgina and Mei Ling.

'Yes. Red ones good. Red Lucky,' Mei Ling said.

'They're all lovely. Everything's so lovely. So perfect,' Georgina murmured.

'Isn't it just?' Miranda stood on the chair for a moment longer, looking down, trying to imprint this moment on her memory. In a few months' time, all of this would be gone and Georgina would be halfway around the world, with a new life and a baby on her lap.

Nick had parked the roadster around the corner from Belvedere and lit a cigarette. His hand shook as he inhaled. The last week had been akin to torture as Miranda had sat next to him in the car. He'd wanted to touch her hand, to stroke her hair. He couldn't stop thinking about her, dreaming about her at night. Even now, he could smell her perfume in the car. And when their fingers had touched just now, he had wanted to pull her towards him so much that the depth of his feeling had panicked him. He hadn't even felt this way about Daphne. While the cigarette burned in his fingers, he pondered what to do. The trouble was, if something happened it would be doomed from the start. And then it would be like recovering from Daphne all over again. He pinched the bridge of his nose, trying to ward off his emotions with reason.

To keep out of her way here would be impossible, as their lives had become so entwined. There was only one thing for it, he decided: if he still hadn't heard from the mission in Nairobi by the end of next week, he would scour *The Medical Journal* again. Let fate play a hand.

He flicked the stub of his cigarette out of the window and drove on to Belvedere. As he pulled up, he could see Khalish in the distance, feeding the chickens. Khalish raised his hand in greeting and, slowly, Nick returned the gesture.

In the hall, there was a pile of letters and a small parcel. He picked the parcel up, immediately recognising the spidery writing. Guiltily he pulled open the string and brown paper and opened the card that fell out:

My dear Nicky,

Happy Christmas!

It is too long since I have written to you and even longer since I have heard from you. I do hope that you are well. Your father came to visit me last week and told me a little of your news, but not enough to let me know when you might return home.

Although I know you have no need for presents, and given that I don't know when I'll see you next, I thought you might like the enclosed – some Gaillardia seeds from the tropical garden at Coombe. If you have somewhere to plant them, you might grow them to remind you of here. If not, you might find someone that might like them instead.

I often remember the first time you and I planted Gaillardia grandiflora seeds, your delight at seeing them grow, and wonder if you do too?

Well, write to me when you can,
The best of love,
Gangy
xx

Nick opened the small blue envelope and sprinkled the seeds into his hand. It was as though his grandmother were standing by his side, and he longed to see her again. She would know what to do, for it had always been she who had been able to guide him when he was troubled as a child, and there was nothing he longed for more right now than her wise words.

Tomorrow morning, he decided, he'd wake early and climb Bukit Kalang. He'd plant the seeds up there, where there was a beautiful view. It had been too long since he'd thought of his grandmother, and even longer since he had been to Coombe.

Twenty-five

Georgina was late. Miranda sat in the crowded P&O waiting room for fifteen minutes, then paced along the quayside for another ten.

A little after half-past two, she saw Georgina's car moving slowly through the crowded dock, then it pulled to with a sharp stop outside the waiting room. Georgina got out and gave flustered instructions to her driver, who found a porter. Never-ending trunks and suitcases were unloaded from the car on to a quayside trolley. Miranda walked towards them.

'Georgina?'

She lifted her head. 'Oh, I'm sorry I'm late. I didn't forget. Just a million and one things to do. But we've still got time, haven't we, for a quick drink?'

Georgina handed the porter some money, instructing him to take her baggage to First Class, then they went to the café next to the waiting room and sat among groups of travellers seated at wooden tables. Georgina ordered some cake, but Miranda only picked at the sponge, as her stomach had stirred up in the same way it always seemed to do the night before she returned to school.

'So,' Miranda began, 'Chicago. Are you excited?'

'Nervous.' Georgina picked up a porcelain teapot and poured out a cup of tea.

'Have you somewhere to live yet?'

'Yes.' Georgina lifted her head – her bob swinging gently back into place. 'I have a cousin who lives in the suburbs. I'm going to stay there for a bit, then look for an apartment.'

'And Poppy?'

'She'll move in with those girls I told you about for now.' Georgina frowned. 'You know, it's awfully good of you to keep an eye on her for me.'

'I don't mind. I've always been fond of her. Will she join you eventually, do you think?'

'I don't know. Maybe. From what I can see, she's doing her secretarial work really well, but it's her social life I'm worried about – all those parties at the Civil Service Club.'

'Not exactly what her mother sent her out here for, is it?'

'No. I think I failed on that front.'

Silence fell between them. There was so much Miranda wanted to say.

She cleared her throat.

'I'll miss you, you know that, don't you? It's such a long way to go.'

A horn sounded from the ship. Georgina glanced at her watch. People began to stand up in the café.

'I'll have to board soon.'

'I know.' Miranda nodded, a knot forming in her stomach.

'But before I do, there's something I want to say.'

'Go ahead.'

'When you first came here, you were *so* unhappy.'

Miranda hesitated. Surely now she could tell Georgina the truth?

'It's hard losing a child,' she began. 'And, if I'm honest, it has taken a toll on my marriage. I thought coming out here would help, but now I'm not so certain if anything can. Sometimes, I think our marriage is over.'

'But you seem to be coming through it.' Georgina paused. 'But if I think about why, now I realise it's because of the hospital. Because of him.'

Miranda looked up and their eyes met.

'Oh, Miranda, I think you could be so much happier than you are.'

'How?' Her breath shallowed and the moment lengthened as she waited for what Georgina would say.

'I've seen the way he looks at you.'

'I don't know what you mean.' She felt herself blush, for she'd guessed what Georgina was suggesting.

'I think you do.' Georgina gently patted her hand. 'I think you do.'

For a second or two, she sat as though frozen. Her thoughts raced but she was unable to summon what she wanted to say.

'You only get one life, Miranda,' Georgina said, her voice urgent as she stared deep into her eyes for a moment, before she smiled. Then stood up, hugged Miranda and made her way towards the door.

Once Georgina had boarded, Miranda sat on the quay watching the ship edging away while mulling over

Georgina's words. Even when the ship was out of sight, she continued to sit there, drawing in her mind the line of Nick's face, the shape of his hand, the sound of his voice. She had struggled for a while with her own conflicting feelings, but Georgina had articulated what she had been unable to openly admit. And now that the words had been spoken, it was as though, like Pandora's box, something both shocking and wonderful had been let out into the world. Something that, once opened, it would be impossible to put back.

There was a letter waiting for her when she returned home – a creamy white envelope containing a ribbed card edged with gold and a brief note:

In Aid of The Sick Children's Society
Chinese New Year Celebrations, Friday, 17th February
At Raffles Hotel, 7.30 for 8 p.m.
Carriages at dawn
RSVP Charlotte Yeardley
Tickets twenty-five dollars

She trailed her finger over the rippling grain and the embossed lettering, lingering over the curves of Charlotte's script as she read the accompanying note:

Miranda, I've recently become involved in the setting up of a new charity for sick children here. I wonder if you and Gerry would like to buy tickets for the charity dinner?

She could hardly believe that Charlotte had forgiven her, let alone that she was inviting her to a party.

And Raffles – the name alone conjured up images of a bygone era; rakish self-indulgence mixed with extravagant elegance. She'd been there once before on one of her shopping trips with Georgina. There was something magical about the white façade and the rosewood interiors, the covered terraces surrounding the Palm Court, to say nothing of quiet corners, where secret conversations played out in the jasmine-scented air.

She smiled and placed the invitation on her desk. There had been so much surprise and too much change in just one day. She poured herself a whisky then sat on the verandah, smoking a cigarette as she watched Gin and Tonic settle in the rain tree.

January gave way to February – each day as long and as hot as the last. Georgina might have left, but the seeds of her words had taken root and were growing rapidly in Miranda's heart. Every night she would tell herself that she was being foolish, that it was reckless to consider throwing her life away on a doomed romance, but every time she saw Nick, her thoughts took her down a familiar path.

On the afternoon of Charlotte's party, Poppy called round unexpectedly.

'Oh, hello,' she said. 'I wasn't sure if you were in or not.'

'Just back from the hairdresser.' Miranda put her hand to her hair. 'Can't you tell?'

'Oh, yes. It's very nice.' Poppy clutched her bag and looked around her.

'Sorry, would you like to come in?'

'Well, I suppose, but not for too long.' Poppy looked at her watch. 'I'm meeting a friend in about half an hour.'

Miranda asked Mei Ling to prepare a tray of tea and they sat on the verandah, politely sipping from china cups. Poppy sat on the edge of her seat. She looked awkward, Miranda thought, as though she really didn't want to be there, and it puzzled her why she had called.

They chatted about Poppy's new flat and the girls she was sharing with, about a dress Poppy had seen in a magazine, a secretary at Poppy's office who had left a sensitive government document on the bus and who had been given the sack. Poppy mentioned that she too was going to the charity dinner that evening along with some colleagues from work and that she had a tonne of things to do before she got ready.

'I'd better go now,' Poppy said, placing her teacup and saucer gently down on the tray.

'We should meet up next week, perhaps?' Miranda said. 'Over lunch at the club?'

'Yes. If you like. I mean, that would be really nice.'

That evening, Miranda took a newly made dress out of the wardrobe; it was scarlet satin, with a low cutaway back that she'd had copied at Wing Loong's from a picture in *Marie France*. It fitted perfectly, and she slid her hand over the fabric as she looked at herself in the mirror.

Her pearl necklace, she hoped, added an air of sophistication to the softly draped neckline. She applied some red lipstick, picked up her evening stole and her satin bag, gave one final glance at herself in the mirror, then went to find Gerry.

He was in the sitting room, listening to *The Pirates of Penzance* on the wireless.

'I'm ready.'

He nodded and stood. She wondered if he would compliment her on her dress or how she looked, but he walked ahead of her to the car, not even holding the door open for her. She knew that, once they were at the party, Gerry would act congenially towards her for the sake of appearances, but she had come to realise that her husband in public and her husband in private were as different as night and day. They drove in silence. When they arrived at Raffles, candles lined the path from the foyer towards the foot-tapping rhythm of the band. Couples danced in the Palm Court, their bodies almost touching in the drowsy heat. Waiters drifted between tables, their trays laden with exotic cocktails. Even the palm trees seemed to follow the beat, their branches floating elegantly in the breeze.

Charlotte was sitting at a table towards the centre of the court. She looked both beautiful and elegant in a long peacock-blue dress with ropes of pearls draped around her neck.

Miranda waved, and muttered, almost to herself, 'It's something else, isn't it?'

Gerry nodded. For a moment, as he stood in the warm light, with the violet in his eyes brought out by the white of his evening jacket, she thought that, if only he could be how he had been when they had first met – kinder, more thoughtful – that it would be so easy to love him again.

As they walked across the court towards their table, Gerry caught sight of Longland Fraser and Dickie Mackintosh standing at the bar as they passed.

'Longland! Dickie!' Gerry slapped Longland on the back. 'Might have guessed I'd find you at the bar.'

'Miranda – don't you look lovely in that dress?' Longland kissed her on both cheeks. The smell of cigars and too many whiskies lingered on his breath.

'Thank you.' She glanced across at Gerry.

Dickie smiled. 'The red suits you.'

'It's my favourite colour in a dress.'

'Now, what's your poison, Gerry?' Longland grinned.

'Oh, I'll have a Tom Collins.'

'Miranda?'

'Nothing for me, thank you.' She looked across the court to Charlotte. 'I think we ought to join our table.'

'Nonsense. It's a party. You got to have a drink.' Longland raised his finger at the barman to get his attention. 'Three Tom Collins and a Gin Sling.'

'Gerry,' she hissed.

'I thought we'd come out to enjoy ourselves.'

'Of course we have. But ...'

'Well, then.' His back stiffened. All the magic of the evening crackled away. She hoped the others hadn't heard, but she noticed Dickie looking at her.

'Why don't I bring your drink to your table?' Dickie asked.

'Thank you,' she gave him a thankful smile. She hadn't always liked Dickie, but right now she could have hugged him.

'I'm sorry we're a bit late.' Miranda sat down in the chair next to Charlotte. 'Fabulous dress,' she added. 'You look gorgeous – where's Andrew?'

'Oh, he's over there somewhere.' Charlotte indicated beyond the bar, to a small group of men smoking cigars. 'He'll be along in a minute.'

As Miranda looked up, she noticed Poppy, who had joined Gerry and the others. Her dress was the colour of lemons and she wore a matching ribbon in her hair. She slipped her arm around Longland's shoulder. Laughter cascaded towards them. There was the flash of a camera as someone took photographs, then more laughter.

'Lively little thing,' Dickie said, as he brought her Gin Sling to the table and saw where Miranda was looking.

The laughter rippled towards them again and she saw Gerry bend his head towards Poppy's as she whispered something in his ear. Strange, Miranda thought, that they seemed so familiar with each other, but then she realised Gerry would most probably have come across her quite often as a secretary at work.

Miranda sighed. She had promised Georgina that she would look out for her niece. *I should say something to her, about flirting with all the men like that, but I know she won't listen.*

'Ciggie?' Dickie offered her his cigarette case.

She took one, but noticed Poppy slip her arm into Gerry's. Then she thought she saw him put his arm around her waist, but when she lifted her head from the flame Dickie had offered her, both Poppy and Gerry had gone. She strained to see where they were, but there were people and shadows everywhere.

'Well, better be getting on.' Dickie winked at Miranda, then left.

She stood to go and look for Poppy and Gerry, but Charlotte touched her arm.

'You know, I'm so glad you came this evening.'

'Yes,' Miranda replied, turning her attention back to Charlotte. 'It means a lot that we can be friends again.'

'Well,' Charlotte ran her finger along the rim of her glass, her gaze fixed on the bottom, 'if I have to be honest, it was Andrew's idea.'

'Oh.' She drew her hand away from Charlotte's arm and returned it to her lap.

'But,' Charlotte was looking at her now, 'that doesn't mean I didn't want to. I can see how hard you've tried to change, helping at the hospital and all that. It's a way of putting things right, isn't it?'

'I suppose so. Yes.'

'And I can see that perhaps I was too harsh. You gave us all a fright, but I think I now believe you.' She paused. 'You don't know, do you, that Jack has been so ill?'

'No. Is he better now?'

Charlotte nodded. 'Yes. But it made me think – that I couldn't imagine what it must be like to lose a child.'

'No. It's a mother's worst fear, isn't it? Still, I'm grateful for your understanding.'

'Why should life be harder for you out here because of me?'

Before Miranda had a chance to reply, the band started to play the 'Woodpecker Song'.

'Look who I found!' Andrew approached the table with Jane, in a green dress, on one arm and Mary, in pink, on the other. Behind him walked a couple of men, who Miranda assumed were their husbands. 'What, not dancing yet?' He smiled at Miranda and held out his hand. 'We'll have to put that right.'

She looked at Charlotte.

'Go on,' Charlotte smiled. 'You have the first dance.'

She stood and joined Andrew. Really, she ought to find Gerry, and as they moved across the dance floor, she tried to see him in the crowd, but, instead, her attention kept returning to Charlotte, her head bent low, deep in conversation with Mary and Jane.

When the music finished, Andrew took her back to the table. She sat down. Mary had already joined her husband on the dance floor and now it was Charlotte and Andrew's turn to dance. They walked off, arm in arm.

'So,' Jane said, her cat's eyes flickering in the candle-light, 'I see Charlotte's forgiven you.'

'Yes. I can't tell you how relieved I am.'

'Well, don't expect the same from all of us. I, for one, have always maintained that you're hiding something.'

'What do you mean?'

Jane ran her index finger around the rim of her glass and purred like a cat toying with a mouse. 'A little bird told me something about you. A secret you'd rather for-get – and some gossip you don't yet know.'

'Like what?' Miranda frowned.

An old sense of panic rose within her.

Jane's husband placed a hand on his wife's shoulder.

'There you are, darling – I wondered where you'd go to.'

Jane pushed back her chair and took her husband by the arm. 'Let's dance, shall we?' As she left, the look she cast back at Miranda was dark, and it unsettled her.

Miranda picked up a glass of wine – she wasn't certain if it was hers or not, but she drained it anyway. *She doesn't know anything*, she told herself, *she's playing with me.*

The wine both numbed her and made her feel strong. She signalled to the waiter for another glass, which she drank more slowly, observing the other guests, as though everyone were actors on a stage. Couples had their arms wrapped around each other as they swirled across the floor, their faces radiant with the heat. It was hard to imagine her dancing days; how she used to be so popular and would out-dance almost every other girl in the room. She turned away.

'Sitting all alone?'

She turned, surprised to see Nick.

'My goodness! I hadn't expected to see you here.' She wondered if he was here with his sweetheart, and if at last she'd meet her. 'Are you with a group?'

'Brendan and Charlie organised a table.' He sat down.

'Just the three of you, then?'

'Along with a group of nurses Brendan knows,' he smiled, avoiding her eyes. 'Where's Gerry?'

'I'm not sure.' She glanced towards the bar again, but couldn't see him.

'It's busy, isn't it? Difficult to see everyone.' He followed her gaze, then asked, 'Are you staying for the fireworks later? I've heard they're quite something.'

'Yes. Are you?'

'Plan to.'

A waiter brought some champagne and they took a glass each.

'Cheers!' She raised her drink, clinking her glass. 'To the year of the Tiger.'

'To wisdom, energy and making the world a better place.'

'Hear, hear.'

As they raised their glasses, she thought she saw the dizzying flash of a yellow dress on the dance floor and Gerry's face among the dancers. She tried to follow their movement, but the floor was too busy, the night too dark.

'Are you all right?' Nick asked. 'You seem a little distracted.'

'I'm fine. It's nothing.' But she was feeling disturbed and overwhelmed and all she could think of was the image of Poppy and Gerry earlier. Had she been imagining it – that Gerry's arm had been around her waist? Their laughter unsettled her, along with the way Poppy's features shone. She looked at Nick, the concern and kindness on his face.

Georgina's words echoed in her mind, *'I've seen the way he looks at you.'*

Oh, the times she had thought of *that* conversation. Ever since, she'd been alert to Nick's every gaze, the meaning of his words, which lingered long after he had spoken them. How many times had she struggled with her conscience, wanting to be near him, but then thinking once more of her wedding vows? That love she'd had for Gerry had faded and was probably gone for ever – was it possible there was a chance for her to love again? With Nick? How much she wanted him, dreamed of him – would acting on her desire be so very wrong?

'Live a little,' Georgina had said. Perhaps it was because of the wine flowing through her veins, the intoxicating scent of jasmine, the slow, sensual rhythm of the band that resonated in each fibre of her body, the knowledge that Poppy was feet away dancing in Gerry's arms, but she could no longer hold back her feelings.

The band began to play 'The Tennessee Waltz'.

'Oh! It's my favourite song. Come on, Nick, let's dance.'

They danced, not speaking, their faces close. Slowly, she rested her head on his shoulder and closed her eyes, taking in the aroma of him, enjoying the pressure of his hand against her back. As the dance progressed, she leant into the curve of his body, and he responded, holding her tentatively at first, then his arm grew stronger and more supportive.

She wished he'd never let her go.

Nick sat down in a club chair inside the Long Bar. The room was spinning, and he realised he'd had too much to drink. The dancing hadn't helped. He should have told Miranda to stop, but she'd wanted one more dance and then another. And then there was the meal. Every time he reached for his glass, he'd noticed someone had topped it up.

He loosened his collar and tie, walked back through the Long Bar and out into the night. The riverbank was crowded. Groups of people were sitting or standing, all clustered along the bank; some had bottles of champagne, others held cigarettes or cocktails.

'Nick!' It was Miranda, only feet away. 'I can't find Gerry – have you seen him?'

'Gerry? No.' He felt himself sway.

'They're about to start the fireworks.'

'Ah. Well, never mind.' He hiccoughed as he gave her his arm. 'I'll help you find him.'

'No. It's all right.' She hooked her arm in his, and he felt her lean into him. 'Shall we go over there? It's nice and quiet.' She guided him to a space on a rock away from the crowd. 'I think we should sit down, don't you?'

'I'm fine,' he said. 'Just a bit wobbly. I think I've had a few too many drinks.'

'Don't worry about it.' She sat down next to him, her leg brushing his. 'No one can see you anyway.'

'Where *is* Gerry?' he said. 'All those white jackets in the dark, make us look the same.'

Miranda said something, but he didn't catch it. On the far side of the river, an explosion of gold and silver fireworks cascaded through the sky.

They sat together watching, listening to the *'oohs'* and *'aaahs'* of the crowd as firework after firework catapulted through the darkness, trailing tails of sparkling light. A volley of firecrackers exploded, then another and another; it was electrifying. Miranda leant into him, and instinctively he placed his arm around her waist.

She turned her face towards him. 'Happy New Year, Nick.'

Was he imagining it? Were her fingers interlocking his? He squeezed her hand and felt pressure return. Her face turned to his, and her earrings – rubies, matching her dress – caught the light.

'You look very beautiful,' he whispered.

'Thank you.'

But then she took a sharp in-breath and stood.

'Look, there's Gerry. And Poppy. I wondered where they'd gone.'

Nick followed the direction of her gaze. A little in the distance, he could see Gerry standing with a young blonde woman among a group on the riverbank.

Nick followed Miranda, who was making her way towards them, but he was still feeling unsteady. Someone thrust a glass of champagne into his hand. He knew he shouldn't take it, he'd had far too much, but he drank it as he walked.

'Evening, old chap! Happy New Year!' He patted Gerry on the shoulder, trying to steady himself, but Gerry was speaking to Miranda, his voice sharp and angry.

'Where've you been? I've been looking for you everywhere.'

'Just dancing.' Miranda shrugged. 'And watching the fireworks.'

'Come on,' Nick said. 'It's a party, no need to be like that.'

Gerry muttered something.

'Sorry, didn't quite hear that.' Nick leant in closer.

'Leave my wife alone,' he hissed. 'Do you hear?'

Gerry grabbed Miranda by the wrist and pulled her towards him.

'Gerry, please—'

Nick saw the tears in her eyes as Gerry walked away from the group, pulling Miranda with him, along with the stares of the group standing on the riverbank following Gerry and Miranda as they disappeared into the night.

*

When Nick opened his eyes, Khalish was standing by the window, and sunlight streamed across the room. He lifted his head, trying to work out where he was, but it was as though something heavy was lying on his forehead, forcing him back. His shirt was on the floor, along with his white dinner jacket, which seemed to have acquired a browny-orange stain.

'What time is it?'

'Eleven o'clock, *tuan*.'

The previous night filtered back to him and he groaned.

He watched Khalish pick up his trousers and jacket, his shirt and his bow tie. 'I think, *tuan*, that perhaps these need a good wash.'

Nick nodded and lay back on his pillow. 'Khalish? Do you know how I got back last night?'

'No, *tuan*. Perhaps Mr Charlie or Mr Brendan?'

'Are they still asleep?'

'No, *tuan*, They are up already – gone out. Perhaps, *tuan*, I make you breakfast – some eggs, black coffee? Something nice and hot. Make you feel better.'

'Yes, that would be good.'

When Khalish had gone, he had a cold shower and dressed. The aroma of coffee drew him through to the dining-room table. He sat down and picked up the letters Khalish had placed by his cup and saucer.

'Here, *tuan*.' Khalish placed a coffee pot on the table, next to a jug of condensed milk, then brought through a plate of scrambled eggs on toast.

Nick drank his coffee and, as he ate, picked up his letters. There was a familiar blue envelope. Mother, he assumed, but as he picked it up, he saw his father's handwriting. Father never wrote.

My Dear Nick,
I thought you ought to know that your grandmother is not well. Your mother and I were called down to Coombe – a stroke. Mother is still with her. The doctor is vaguely optimistic, but she's eighty-two and, to be frank, I don't think it's looking too good.

He placed the letter down on the table. Of course, he had known it would happen one day, but he'd half-assumed she'd always be there, simply because she always had been. Father didn't say how bad the stroke was, but, at her age, he knew it wouldn't be good. He pictured her: the cobweb of lines across her face, the pale blue of her eyes, the way she always smelt of lavender, how tall she was and so fiercely proud.

He had to clear his head and so he decided to walk to Bukit Kalang. After he finished his coffee, he collected his hat, and then a canteen of water from the kitchen.

He walked along the back of the government bungalows, thinking about his grandmother and Coombe; running along the beach with Freddie on endless summer days; picnics on the rocks; riding on his grandfather's shoulders along the coastal path; at Easter, the flowering of the first daffodil bulbs he had ever planted. Strange how Father hated Coombe – and soon it would be gone. He wondered what would happen to it all when his grandmother died.

As he passed the Lewis home, more fragments of the previous night returned: dancing with Miranda; sitting with her watching the fireworks; knowing that, after the scene with Gerry, he'd had too much to drink.

And then, suddenly, there she was, walking towards him, her hand shielding her eyes from the sun.

'Nick?' She lowered her hand and squinted. 'Where are you going?'

'Up there.' He nodded towards Bukit Kalang. 'For a hike.'

'Oh.' She glanced towards the hill. 'I don't suppose I could come with you? Gerry's still sleeping off last night and I'm at a bit of a loose end.'

He nodded. He'd have rather walked off his headache alone, but it looked as though she wouldn't take no for an answer.

She chattered on, pointing out flowers or asking about the birds. The midday sun pounded down on them, making him think of that Noel Coward song about mad dogs. It was foolish to be out in such heat, and soon she lagged behind. He looked back. She was struggling up the hill in his wake, her forehead bathed in perspiration.

'Are you sure you want to come?' he asked.

'Yes.' She wiped her forehead with her hand.

'Here.' He handed her his flask of water. 'Have a drink.'

She unscrewed the top and drank, then handed it back, their fingers grazed.

'Honestly, I don't know how you run up here, it's so damn hot!'

'We can go back, if you like.'

But she seemed determined, and they carried on, Miranda still lagging behind. He waited for her to catch up, and then they reached the top.

'Wow!' She stood with her hands on her hips. Through the fabric of her shirt, he could see her chest rising and falling. 'This is amazing! It's so beautiful. So—'

'Peaceful?"

'Yes.' She smiled. 'I love it.'

They stood together, observing the sweeping valley below. The heavy jungle canopy was gilded with light, while thin threads of wood-fire smoke trailed upwards.

'When you're above it all like this, it gives such a sense of scale, don't you think?'

He nodded. 'We're just tiny specks in the massive universe.'

'That's not really what I mean.' She looked up at him. 'I've always been on the lower level before and hadn't appreciated the size of the island. And I know it's a stupid thing to say, but the sea is all around us! I've never seen that here before.'

He grinned. 'Up here, it makes me feel like I'm Robinson Crusoe.'

'And I suppose that makes me Girl Friday, does it?'

He glanced at her, trying to assess her, all his senses alive – to the tilt of her head; the sound of her breathing; the aroma of her scent, like gentle lilies borne across the breeze. Her hand was raised to block out the sun as she scanned the panorama below. Her proximity took him back to the previous evening, to the way she had fitted so perfectly into him as they danced, like two pieces of a puzzle that clicked and belonged; how, at the fireworks, she had taken his hand. Was he imagining her actions or merely willing her feelings to echo his?

She sat down under the shade of a coconut tree.

'I could sit up here all day, simply watching. It's hard to think that in England it's winter, the rain or snow lashing against the darkened streets.'

He joined her, his back leaning against the trunk.

'I know. Me too.'

They were inches apart, but still she didn't look at him, but he was conscious of her, watching him from the corner of her eye. His breath was long and shallow as he pondered what to do.

'Look!' she said, leaning forward. 'There's something here.'

He looked to where she pointed. Now she was kneeling, her hands brushing the soil to reveal something that was buried. Something was poking up, with the glint of burnished metal.

'What is it, do you think?'

He knelt beside her, and she smiled at him as their fingers simultaneously touched as they brushed away the soil.

'It looks like a figure – a dragon.'

She leant forward to get a better look. A bead of perspiration hung to her lip, then trickled towards her neck. He fought the urge to wipe it away.

Their faces were close; he could feel her breath against his cheek and smell the muskiness of her perfume. Together they released the dragon from the ground.

'It looks like a lucky charm,' he said. 'Bixi – a turtle dragon, it brings strength and prosperity to the owner. Here. You should have it.'

He placed it in her hand, and she looked at him, her face alight with the pleasure of it. Their fingers lingered on the charm and he covered her hand with his.

Time suspended. She didn't move.

He waited, then he inched his face nearer to hers and placed his mouth close to her lips.

Then, he remembered Gerry the night before, watching them at the fireworks, and the look of anger on his face.

He turned his face away.

Twenty-six

Miranda woke early and sat by the window rubbing her wrist. There were still bruises from where Gerry had grabbed her so fiercely the night of the party. She closed her eyes, trying to blank it all out – the way Gerry had dragged her down the path towards their car; how he'd shouted at her, telling her she was a flirt and that people were staring at her. She had fought back the tears, not wanting to let him know how much he had hurt and humiliated her, that he was no better, really, that she'd seen the way he'd been acting with Poppy, but there was a look in his eyes that frightened her and she hadn't said a thing.

She took the lucky charm from her drawer, ran her fingers over its curving back, and placed it on her dressing table. Once again, she thought of Georgina's parting words about Nick. Why was she playing with fire? Was it just that she knew this was right? And, yesterday, he had been going to kiss her, she was certain of it. They had been inches apart, so why had he turned away?

She paced her room, going over and over the scene in her mind. At that moment, it had been what she had desired more than anything in the world, but now trepidation took hold and her courage faltered. Something creaked on the window ledge, and she raised her head. It was Tommy. His face cocked towards her, as though he could sense that something was troubling her.

'What do you think, old chap?' she said. But Tommy simply flashed his teeth at her, then scampered away.

She looked out of the window in the direction of Bukit Kalang, shut her eyes and pictured his face close to hers, then gently brushed her lips with the edges of her fingertips as she thought of the longing in his eyes.

There was only one thing for it – she had to speak to him, but the hard thing would be finding the words to tell him how she felt.

She got a taxi to Tanjong Pagar, then she wove through the crowded walkways of the market to get to the hospital. The aroma of garlic and chillies wafted from hawker stalls busy with lunchtime diners, while housewives hurried by, searching for last-minute bargains. She continued on past a hawker selling fish, another with bags of rice and a group of women dropping eggs into buckets – testing their freshness by seeing if the eggs could float.

Surely this was folly? No, just wrong. Immoral. She should go home, but she kept expecting to hear his voice or his footsteps on the path and so she lingered. At a fruit stall, she dithered and bought some lychees, watching intently as the storekeeper put them into a paper bag.

Finally, she reached the market exit and paused beneath the awning, then turned right and walked for three hundred yards to the end of the street. She stopped and turned back the way she had come. She clenched her fists, then retraced her steps and made her way through the back door of St Augustin's.

Nick was sitting in his office, his back to the glass in the door; something must have alerted him to her presence because he turned, then he stood and opened the office door.

'Miranda! What are you doing here?' His shadow fell across her. 'I didn't think you were in today.'

'No. I wasn't meant to be.'

She hesitated, uncertain whether to enter the room or not. 'I had some shopping to do, so I thought I'd call in. Look, I bought some lychees.'

He avoided her eyes and glanced at his watch. 'I was about to have a break – would you like some tea?'

'Please.' She squeezed passed him as he stepped back. He put a small kettle on a gas ring to boil, and she moved some books in order to sit down in the chair in the far corner.

He held a small tin awkwardly in his hand. 'It's green tea. You drink it without milk. Not everyone likes it – it's a bit bitter.'

'I'm happy to try it.' She watched him pour hot water into a pot, then, minutes later, she took the small egg cup-like bowl he handed to her, which was full of golden-yellow tea.

'Do you like it?'

She sipped it. It was how she imagined straw to taste or grass cuttings.

'It's better than I thought. Lychee?' She opened the bag and the small, crinkly red orbs scattered across his coffee table. They sat for a while, chatting about this and that, peeling lychees, sipping tea, the unsaid hanging between them.

'Well,' he said, 'I suppose I ought to be getting back to work.' He picked up her cup, avoiding her eye. 'It's been nice talking.'

'Yes. It has.'

She stood and brushed out the creases in her skirt, then she picked up her bag. He was close to her, and she could feel his breath on her skin, and she couldn't hold out any longer.

'Nick, I have to ask you something,' she said, uncertain of her ground. 'At Bukit Kalang,' she hesitated, waiting for a sign that she should carry on, 'something happened between us and I have to know – did you feel it too?'

It was like watching a coin spinning; while the coin turned, there was still the thrill, the agony of both pos-sibilities, but once the coin settled, the outcome would be decided and there would be no turning back.

She saw him stiffen. 'I'm not sure that I know what you mean.'

'I think you do.'

He looked away from her and down at the floor.

'Supposing, just supposing I did.'

'So?' She knew she'd been right.

'What good would it do? You're married. I can't destroy you – your happiness.'

'My happiness?' she laughed. 'Do you know how "happy" I've been these past few months?'

His eyes fixed on hers. 'When Henry died, something divided Gerry and me and it doesn't seem able to heal.'

'Perhaps it needs more time?'

'No.' She shook her head. 'It's hard to explain, it's not something that was said or done between us, it's more what *hasn't* been said or done, if that makes any sense?'

'I think so.'

'And now, it's as though we're travelling on two separate paths and going through the motions of being husband and wife.'

'But,' he began, shifting in his seat, 'that is between you and your husband. I can't interfere with that.'

'But what if we both want it?'

'It doesn't make it right.'

'I love you, Nick, I know I do. And I think you love me too.'

His gaze shifted from hers.

'Nick?'

'Miranda, I'm sorry. I can't. It's not right.'

'Well,' she hesitated, 'I suppose that's that, then.'

He didn't reply. She waited a moment longer, hoping he would say something or change his mind.

Eventually, she nodded. 'I guess I'd better go.'

Before she left, she turned back to look at him one last time. 'Goodbye, Nick.'

'Goodbye, Miranda.'

He didn't look up.

She headed back towards the market and pushed through the shoppers and the crowded stalls to the streets beyond. What a bloody fool she'd been. Tears scorching, she bumped into a group of tourists standing by a leather goods stand.

'I'm sorry,' she said, with cold politeness, but, really, she wanted to scream.

The tourists smiled and nodded. She blustered on – not knowing where to go, not caring about a thing. As she wiped the tears away, she realised she had wandered away from the main streets that she knew. She tried to orientate herself by looking for familiar shops, and as she searched, she heard a bird singing. It was beautiful, a brave, forlorn melody. As she listened, it seemed to rise and fall, the tune obscured by the bustle of the crowded streets. But it drew her, and she followed it, weaving between people until she found a small stall where an elderly Chinese man sat cross-legged on the floor. He was repairing shoes, but next to him, on a stand about three feet high, hung a cage with a single bird.

She stood in front of it. The bird was slightly bigger than a robin, dull brown with a reddish tail. It began to sing, and its song was the most beautiful she'd ever heard.

'It's glorious,' she said out loud. 'Exquisite. I wonder what it is?'

'It's a nightingale.'

She spun around.

It was Nick.

Twenty-seven

'We can't talk here.'

He led her by the arm through the crowded streets. Without speaking, they squeezed through the hawker stalls set up in the shade of the covered pavements, their bodies bumping into each other as they walked. Traders called to women in saris, who were examining rolls of brightly coloured fabric stacked with precarious nonchalance next to bulging hessian bags of spices.

'Here?' He indicated a *chai-wallah*'s cart on the walkway. It was shaded by the five-foot-wide awning spanning the pavement and tucked away from the main road and out of sight. The cart was brimming with steaming urns and, on the pavement, a small collection of wooden tables and stools were crammed close together.

She sat down at the rickety table in a corner behind a pillar, away from the street, convinced that everyone would be staring at her, but when she lifted her head, no one was. His heart beat faster as he leant towards her and gently his lips brushed hers; softly at first, then harder and more insistent as she responded. They kissed again. He knew he should stop, that someone might see them, but it stole his breath away and it was as though everything around him had dissolved or turned upside down. In that moment, all that mattered was Miranda and the space that encompassed them.

Then he pulled away.

'Miranda, is this really what you want? If we start on this journey, we don't know what might happen.'

'Can't you see – I've already made up my mind?' She covered his hand with hers. He didn't pull away.

'And what about your husband? It's crazy, but I haven't been able to stop thinking about you,' he said. 'Day and night. Night and day. I can't believe you're sitting here, opposite me, that you feel the same.'

'I know,' she squeezed his hand. 'Me too.'

Over the next few weeks, they visited the beach at Changi and ate prawns cooked on a barbecue on the sand. In Chinatown, he taught her to use chopsticks by picking up peanuts from a plate. Whenever they passed each other in the corridor at St Augustin's, it was as though her heart almost stopped and, as her body prickled with desire, she wondered if anyone noticed.

Sometimes, when Mei Ling was out, they stole an afternoon together at the bungalow, or a morning at Belvedere, whenever Brendan or Charlie were out. Their liaisons were brief and passionate, but she was hesitant and nervous, and longed for a time and a place when she would be ready to consummate their love. 'Don't worry,' he told her, kissing the top of her head. 'We can wait until you're ready. I fully understand.'

'Have you been to the Sri Mariamman Temple?' he asked her one afternoon. 'We really should go – it's the oldest and most important temple in Singapore. I think you'd like it.'

'How about next Friday?'

They met at the corner of South Bridge Road and Temple Street.

'Is this a good idea?' she asked. 'Gerry's office is just around the corner.'

'But you really have to see it.' Nick took her hand as they stood to go. 'It's not far.'

She gasped at the vast tiers of rich carvings towering ahead of her.

'That's a gopuram,' Nick explained. 'See all those figures carved on the tower? They're all Hindu gods.'

They stowed their shoes in open lockers and, as they passed through the huge double doors into the compound, she could hear bells ringing. She looked around, making sure no one was watching her.

Inside, there were inner courtyards encompassed by a high perimeter wall decorated with brightly coloured mouldings and sculptures of both male and female deities.

'That's Krishna, and that is Sita over there,' Nick pointed. 'And that blue figure over there is Rama.'

He knew so much about the culture. Hearing Nick talk about Singapore was intoxicating.

'It's so vibrant and lovely,' she said. 'All the bells ringing and the incense. It's just how I imagine India.'

They continued looking at the figures of sacred cows and monkeys, Krishna and Shiva, and she watched from a distance as priests in loincloths gave food to beggars sheltering in the temple courtyard.

'I can't tell you how much I loved it,' she said, as they left.

'It's wonderful, isn't it?' Nick placed his arm around her waist. 'Come on, let's go and get something to eat.'

She drew her arm away. 'Careful.'

'Sorry.' His face fell. 'I forget sometimes to be careful.' He fiddled with his watch strap, then glanced at the time. 'Well, I suppose I'd better get back to the hospital. Shall I walk you to the bus stop, then?'

'No. It's too close to Gerry's office. Anyway, I thought I might explore a bit first.'

When he'd gone, she walked beneath the covered walkways around the temple and the market, gazing into shop fronts with rattan displays, stacks of shoes and sandals, and roll upon roll of brightly coloured fabrics. There were cured ducks, flattened and waxy, hanging in windows; jars of curious herbs and strange objects that both intrigued and unnerved her. Red lanterns were strung across the roads, crisscrossing the chaos of the labyrinthine streets.

In one of the shop fronts, she noticed a mannequin wearing a long red Chinese-style silk dress with a high collar and tiny buttons knotted like delicate crowns. She could just make out the impression of lizard-like dragons on the silk as she stared at it and was wondering how the fabric was made when the door opened. A young woman came out of the shop and greeted her.

'You wan' come take look?'

The woman was wearing a similar red dress and had dark, glossy hair that fell to her shoulders like silk.

'No, I don't think so.' She turned to go.

'Yes, you come look. I got what you wan'. Can give you good price. Please, you come.' The woman's voice was lyrical and enticing. Miranda hesitated, then followed her inside.

There were polished counters with ladies underwear – underpants, petticoats and silk stockings. Red, blue, black and gold dresses hung from rails. Miranda ran her hand over them, there were more dragons embroidered in the fabric, along with chrysanthemums and peacocks, all decorated with tiny pearls or coloured jewels. Some had bell-shaped sleeves; others ruffled collars or lace frothing from the neckline.

'These are so beautiful.'

'Cheongsam.' The woman clicked her long red nails against the counter. 'Very expensive. I got new silk night-dress if you wan' take look.' She opened a drawer and spread a collection of pale blue, peach and creamy silk nightdresses on the counter.

Miranda touched the silk. 'They look lovely.'

'Wait.' The woman began to sort through them. 'This one your size. Look nice with your hair.'

The fabric was sensuous as it slipped through her fingers. She held it against her chest and examined her reflection in the mirror. The woman was right. It was beautiful; just holding it against her body made her feel seductive and a longing to own it crept through her.

'Best quality.' The woman was close now and Miranda could smell her perfume, sultry and enticing. 'Make you look like Rita Hayworth.'

Inside the changing room, she slipped out of her cotton dress and the nightdress rippled over her skin in a delicious wave of pleasure. She turned to the left, observing in the mirror how the silk swung, and felt its buttery softness slip across her legs.

'How much is it?' she called through the curtain.

'I give you good price. Ten dollar.'

'Oh.' In the mirror, she saw the smile fall from her face. She'd already spent too much of her month's allowance – she didn't see how she could justify buying this. One more time, she ran her fingers over the bodice and admired how it was cut to show off her waist and breasts. With a sigh, she took it off. 'I'm afraid it's too much.'

Her cotton dress was damp and unflattering as she put it back on.

'I'm sorry, it's absolutely gorgeous, but far too expensive. Perhaps another time?'

The woman gave a curt nod.

As she reached the door, she heard the woman's voice coaxing her back.

'OK, lady. I give you nine dollar.'

'How about five?' Her hand rested on the door handle, her heart racing.

'*Aiyo!* Cannot-*lah*! Best price seven dollar.'

Her heart thudded. 'All right. I'll take it.'

She paid and watched the woman wrapping the night-dress carefully in layers of tissue paper.

'You come back,' the woman said. 'Bring your friends next time. I give you extra special price.'

'Thank you.' Miranda placed the parcel under her arm and opened the door.

'You not regret.' The woman gave a slight bob of her head. 'I'm sure your husband like very much.'

She smiled to herself as she closed the door, the door-bell ringing behind her. Gerry was the last person on her mind.

When she got home, she went to the bedroom and laid the nightdress on the bed, then slipped off her dress. She ran the silk through her fingers, then pulled the night-dress over her body, wrapping it around her skin. She swayed in front of the mirror with a gentle movement, bare feet skimming over the bedroom floor as she began to dance. Slowly at first, her feet came together, one-two-three, one-two-three, then they picked up the strains of an imaginary band.

In her mind, the light softened and the music quick-ened and she found it hard to keep the pace of the beat. The music grew faster and wilder and, as she swirled on her toes, the nightdress fluttered, like butterfly's wings in a dangerous wind, until finally, exhausted, she collapsed across the bed. She watched the ceiling fan revolving above her, as though it were a reflection of her imagination and waited for it to cool the beads of sweat prickling across her head.

She started when she finally sat up. Gerry was standing in the doorframe. His arms were folded and the look on his face terrified her.

'Oh! I thought you were at work.'

He swallowed, but kept his arms folded in front of him. Dread crept over her.

'So, is this how you pay me back, is it, Miranda?' The way he pronounced her name was as though he had eaten something bitter. 'After all I've done for you.'

'I'm not sure I know what you mean?' she whispered, noting the way his jaw was set.

'I think you do.'

She glanced away.

'Oh, come on, you could at least have the decency to look at me – I doubt you feel that ashamed.'

He spat the words out. 'The incident with the baby was bad enough, then Martha, but now this! What on earth do you think you were doing with *that* man. Did you think someone wouldn't see you wandering around town today like a pair of lovebirds?'

She shook her head. 'We went to see the temple. There was nothing wrong with that.'

'Not today, maybe, but what about yesterday, the day before and last week? Do you think I haven't guessed? The lifts to the hospital and now this.' He indicated the nightdress. 'Jesus! You look like a tart.'

He stepped further into the room. His face was red and beads of perspiration covered his forehead. She backed away.

'Do you know how close I am to a promotion?' He thrust his hand in front of her face, pinching his index finger and thumb.

'This close. First Secretary from Second. What if Longland finds out?'

'I ...' she didn't know what to say. Shame washed over her and his anger scared her. 'It's all gone wrong for us, hasn't it?' She paused for a moment. 'So, what do we do next?'

'I don't know.' He looked so tired; she hadn't noticed how much before. She reached her hand out to him, but he flinched.

'I don't know what's right for us any more.' He frowned, then he sat on the end of the bed and placed his head in his hands.

'We've come to a dead end, haven't we?' she whispered. 'We're not happy, not suited to each other any more. Perhaps we should come to terms with how things are.'

'What?' He jerked his head up, eyes narrow. 'You mean we should separate?'

She nodded. 'Yes. Even if this hadn't happened, our marriage is over, isn't it?'

He shook his head, taking her hand and then tightening his grip.

'I won't allow it.'

'Then, I'll leave. I'll move out.'

'Don't be so bloody stupid, Miranda.' He laughed. 'How on earth would you live? That doctor of yours wouldn't take you in and you have no way of supporting yourself, no real friends, no prospect of getting a job. Let's face it: you need me – you can leave, but give it two weeks and you'll come running back.'

He took hold of both her hands and pushed her on to the bed, holding her arms above her head.

'You're hurting me! Get off. Please, stop.' She clenched her teeth and pushed him off. Anger seared through every fibre of her body.

'For God's sake!' he shouted, and he slapped her hard across the face. 'Don't say I didn't try.'

He stormed out of the bedroom, slamming the door on his way out as her face stung. She raised her hand to where it burned, unable to believe what he had just done.

In the bathroom, she switched on the light and splashed water on her smarting face, trying to suppress the tears. She leant against the basin, trying to calm herself, and, after a time, she turned on the shower, pulled off her nightdress and washed. How dare he say those things to her? The lather dripped from her body, spiralling down the plughole, then, with all her force, she hurled the bar of soap against the floor.

When she'd dressed, she sat on the bedroom floor with her back against the wall, wondering what she was going to do next. Shadows of leaves danced across the window and she glanced up to see Tommy watching her from a nearby tree. He made her think of Socrates, the way he curled in her lap whenever she was down and how he'd purr as she stroked the back of his ears. She huddled forward, wrapping her arms around her knees, and buried her face as deeply as she could into the circle of her arms and waited for tears to form, but they didn't come. A memory surfaced of when she was in the WVS, of a woman whose husband had just been killed in a bombing raid and how calm the woman had stayed in the face of the shock – collecting all her husband's belongings from the hospital as though nothing were amiss. Shock. That was it, she realised, what she must be feeling now. Was it a need to survive, she wondered? Whatever it was, she now needed to decide what she was going to do next.

Eventually she stood, then she went to their room, gathered up her clothes, and moved them to the guest room.

Then she sat down at her desk in the living room and wrote:

Gerry,
    It is clear to me that we no longer feel the same way about each other as we once did. For the time being, until a better solution can be arranged, I suggest that we have as little to do with each other as possible.
    For that reason, I am sleeping in the guest room.
    In public, I will, of course, continue to support you – but, in reality, I wish to see as little of you as I possibly can.

I seem to remember that you always wanted to spend more time out with your friends or at the club, so perhaps you might find the occasion to do so now unhindered?

I may be your wife, but you do not own me, so I will continue to volunteer at St Augustin's, and I will do what I like. For the first time since Henry died, I feel happy and worthwhile, and I'm certainly not going to let you take that away.

Miranda

She sealed the letter in an envelope, then placed it on the rosewood table in the hall, her heart a kaleidoscope of butterflies. The sun cast long shadows across the tiles, and she could hear the sound of Mei Ling moving saucepans across the hob and plates clattering in the kitchen, as though nothing in the world had changed.

Twenty-eight

That morning, Nick woke to a frantic knocking.

'*Tuan*, wake up! Telegram!'

It was dark. He got out of bed, fumbling to open the door. Khalish stood with a worried look on his face, which was exaggerated by the glow of light from the hall.

'I hope, *tuan*, that everything is good.

Nick took the telegram and read:

GRANDMOTHER DIED THIS MORNING. FATHER

Nick ran his hand through his hair. He should have been expecting it, but over the past few weeks, he'd been so absorbed with Miranda that he'd pushed all thoughts of his grandmother to one side.

'It's fine, Khalish. Thank you.'

Nick closed the door and leant against it. Regret roiled through him. It wasn't as though he could have been there or done anything, but perhaps he should have sent one last message to show he cared. She was eighty-two; she'd had a good life, but in his memory she was still the woman from years ago – holding his hand at Freddie's

327

funeral, stroking his head when he'd woken screaming in the night.

He shouldn't have neglected her, and he was angry with himself for doing so. It was time to rein back in, to focus on his work again, like a snail, pulling into its shell and withdrawing from the world.

It was just before seven when he left Belvedere. He drove along the coast road to Tanjong Pagar, watching the sun rising over the sea: a golden-orange disc emerging over the steely water. He pulled the car over to watch the brightening world and a pair of motionless whimbrels standing in the waves that were breaking on the shore.

He'd lost track of how many mornings he had watched the sunrise at Coombe – and now he knew that he'd never see them again; that the life he had known there, the house, the land, would all soon be gone. He lit a cigarette and listened to the monkeys calling to each other. When he finished his shift at the hospital, he'd go back to Bukit Kalang and plant something special there as a memorial for his grandmother. He tried to remember what her favourite plant was. A camellia. That was it. He would buy one on his way to work.

After a time, he got back into the roadster, and pushed the accelerator pedal hard against the floor as he headed off.

In the end, he didn't have much time to think. The day was jam-packed with appointments and ward rounds, timetabled and executed with military precision.

At five, he sat down in his office and started writing the end-of-day reports.

'Dr Wythenshaw?'

Alice stood in the doorframe, a sheaf of papers in her hand.

He stiffened.

'There's been another board meeting and I thought you should look at these.'

She stepped towards his desk and placed the papers in front of him. A waft of carbolic and peppermints reached him.

'This,' she began, 'is a list of the centre's expenses. You will see here,' she turned over a page and pointed to a column of figures, 'that our income is lower than our expenditure.'

He leant forward to take a look. 'Yes. By rather a lot.'

'And this,' she turned over another page, 'is our forecast for how many more children will need supporting in the next six months – vaccinations, here,' she tapped the paper sharply, 'beds, here, meals per day within the hospital and at the feeding centre, here.'

She took a step back and looked at him. 'We can't afford it. We haven't got the funds.'

He crossed his arms. 'What about fundraising?'

'We're still well below target. Something more drastic has to be done – such as redundancies.' Her eyes narrowed and her lips set for a moment, then she said. 'I hate to bring this up. I'm not one to gossip, but there have been rumours.'

'About what?'

'About you, Dr Wythenshaw,' she paused. 'And Mrs Lewis.'

His full attention was on her now. 'Such as?'

'As I said, I'm not one to gossip, but it would seem that the board knows about it too. Carrying on with a married woman – what kind of an example is that? That kind of behaviour goes against the very ethos of the centre. In light of the need to make some serious job cuts, you might like to consider your position.'

'Are you threatening me?' He picked up a pencil, curling his fingers around it, avoiding her gaze.

'No – just stating facts.' She raised an eyebrow.

'I won't be spoken to like this.' He stood up, pushing his chair back so hard it nearly tipped over.

He pushed past her, noticing her satisfied smile.

In the corridor, he sensed people staring at him, but he didn't care; he forced his way through them and headed to the main entrance, punching open the door, which swung back, thudding against the wall.

He sat in the chapel courtyard on a bench beneath an arching palm. The pressure of his anger made his ears throb; he wanted to hit something, to punch a hole in a wall – this rising, uncontrollable anger was the same as when Freddie had riled him over winning a game of chess or getting better marks at school.

When his anger had subsided enough to drive home, he made his way to the roadster and headed along the coast road back to Belvedere. When he got there, he threw himself down on a chair to think.

'Everything all right, Nick?'

He looked up. It was Brendan.

'No,' he glowered. 'It's been a lousy day. The worst.'

'Want to talk about it?'

Nick's leg was restless. He tried to calm it, placing his hand on his knee.

'Listen,' Brendan said. 'I've got some damn good whisky tucked away. Purely for emergencies, mind you. Would that help?'

'Fine. If you like.' Nick watched as Brendan poured whisky into two glasses. Sun streamed through the window, illuminating the amber liquid in the bottle.

'Cigarette?' Brendan sat down and passed a packet of Pall Mall to Nick. Nick lit one and watched the smoke curling through the air.

'Thanks.' Nick picked up his glass. The whisky was good, peaty, and it warmed the back of his throat.

'I had a telegram today,' Nick began. 'My grandmother died.'

'I'm sorry to hear that. Were you close?'

Nick nodded. 'Very. Much closer than to my parents.'

'Often the way,' Brendan swirled the whisky around in his glass, 'with grandparents and grandchildren.'

'She was the kindest person I have ever known.' The tears were coming now, he could feel them. His shoulders began to shake, and he took a handkerchief from his pocket to wipe his nose. 'Sorry.'

'You've got no need to be sorry.'

'But that's not all.'

'Go on. You can tell me.' Brendan leant back. 'Just take your time.'

'When I came out to Singapore, I had a sweetheart. I hoped that we'd get married, that she'd join me. But it didn't work out. So, for a while, I've been unhappy here,' Nick began. 'I've been uncertain whether to stay or not. In fact, I've been applying for other posts. But I've been distracted, recently, by Mrs Lewis. Miranda.' Nick glanced up to see Brendan nod, showing that he understood. 'And, just now, well, Alice told me that people know, that I should consider my position here. It was like she was threatening me – I lost my temper.'

'That's certainly a lot to be worrying about.' Brendan topped up their glasses. 'I guess you could either give up seeing Miranda, give up your job or make a stand. Or you might like to move on, start something fresh and new.'

'And what about Miranda?'

'That's for you to decide, Nick. But a married woman? Does her husband know, have you considered that? I can see you're upset, but I think you need to think carefully about it all.'

Nick placed his hand over his face. 'But, you see, I think I love her. I don't want to live without her.'

'All I'll say is that once you've made a decision, you'll have to stick to it. There won't be any second goes at this.'

After their conversation, Nick's thoughts were still muddled, so he decided to head up to Bukit Kalang. Before he set off, he took a spade from the store at the back of the house and the potted camellia he had bought earlier. Light filtered through the trees, giving the footpath an ephemeral feel as he clambered.

Eventually, he reached the summit. It was so beautiful and peaceful in the golden light. He chose a spot for the camellia and then began to dig. When the hole was big enough, he placed the plant inside, spreading the soil with his fingers and carefully patting it into shape. He sat on the ground next to the camellia and crossed his legs.

'Well, Gangy, I hope you're at peace, now.' He looked up at the strands of cloud feathered across the sky then down at his fists clenched in his lap. 'But I wish you were here. Do you remember how I always used to ask your advice and how you always had an answer for everything, even if it wasn't what I wanted to hear? Well, I wish that I could talk to you now, because it's all such a bloody mess. I'm sure that if you were alive you'd be able to tell me what the right thing is to do.'

He stayed for half an hour, thinning out the Gaillardia seedlings, which had grown thick and tall, picking up stones and creating a small trig-point-like pyramid as a memorial. A swan flew overhead. He watched it descending with wide outspread wings, then it landed close by. How magnificent it looked with the sunlight just behind it. Like firebird, he thought, or the Goddess of the Sun.

It was breathtaking, and this place, this moment, was the closest he could imagine to being in heaven. The light was magical; he could see the valley bathed in light, while all around him he could hear birds singing. Above, the bamboos rustled, and he was certain he could smell jasmine.

As he sat, he lost track of time, then small droplets of rain began to fall and thunder rumbled overhead. He didn't want to, but he ought to go. The droplets grew thicker and heavier as he descended the hill, and puddles had already begun to pool on the tracks, but his feet were light, his spirits lifted, making him feel strong and invincible. The warm rain trickled down his collar, soaking his neck and back, and he hurried towards Belvedere, his body braced against the coming storm.

As he ran up the front steps, lightening split the sky. It startled him. But what startled him more was Miranda, sitting alone next to a suitcase, her clothes dripping with raindrops and her face wet with tears.

Twenty-nine

As he approached, she stood up and threw her arms around him. Her body seemed so small and fragile.

'Sssh!' he whispered, stroking her hair, waiting for her breathing to calm down. 'What's the matter? Tell me what's wrong.'

'I've left him,' she gasped, shivering. 'I couldn't stand it any longer.'

'What?'

She began to sob.

'It's all right. I'm here.' He held her closer, wrapping one arm around her shoulder, the other around her waist. 'Look at you; you're soaking. We'd better go in, get you out of those wet clothes.'

She nodded, and he opened the door, letting her go before him and dragging her case behind them.

'Let me get you something, a blanket – or a hot drink.'

'A brandy, please.'

He sloshed some into a glass and watched her as she sunk on to the sofa.

'Here,' he sat next to her, his arm around her in her sopping dress. 'Better?'

She took a gulp, but her hands were still shaking.

'Tell me what happened.'

'Gerry saw us. At the temple. But he'd already guessed.'

'I see.'

'We'd already had a massive row. It's been awful, and then, just now, I finally realised I simply couldn't stay with him any more. I grabbed a few things and left before I bottled out. I can't believe I've done it.' A faint smile crept across her face. 'Could I stay here, with you, for a bit?'

'Oh Miranda, of course. Yes. You don't need to ask.'

'It won't be for long – until I've sorted myself out.'

'Are you going back to England?'

'No.' She clutched the glass. 'Nick, don't you see?' Her eyes were shining; whether it was tears or happiness, he couldn't tell. 'We can be together.'

'So, he's divorcing you?'

'No. Not yet. But he will. I know he'll come round.'

He stood and got himself a brandy too, then sat next to her once more.

'Of course you must stay here, Miranda, but you know, don't you, how this will look for you until you're divorced? He'll have ammunition against you, and then he can divorce you, not the other way round. You'll be a pariah, not a victim. I hate to raise it, but there are things that need to be thought about – like protecting your reputation.' And, he thought, his own. Here was Miranda, offering to come and live with him. It was what he wanted most in the world, but if anyone at the hospital found out that Miranda was staying with him, he'd most certainly be let go and then where would they be?

'I know. I've thought of that. What should we do?'

'Well, there's Brendan and Charlie to think about. And Khalish.' He was probably standing by the kitchen door listening to them right now. 'Until we get something more suitable sorted out, for appearances, you'll be seen to be using my room – I can sleep on the sofa.'

He turned to her; she wasn't shaking as much now. 'But, darling, for now, I think you should have a bath, don't you, and something hot to drink? Let me worry about the details.'

'Yes.' She wiped her face with the back of her hand. 'Thank you.'

He ran her a bath. 'Here, you can use this.' He gave her his dressing gown and a large towel. 'I can ask Khalish to dry your clothes. Would you like tea or coffee?'

'Coffee,' she said. She took off her damp clothes and sank into the bath. 'With brandy.'

While she bathed, Nick sat on the sofa thinking. He had to protect Miranda, had to save her reputation, which meant she couldn't stay at Belvedere for ever. If Gerry knew about the two of them, then he was bound to know where she was right now. He had a little money put by, enough, he thought, for her to stay in a hotel for a couple of weeks. He wondered if he knew anyone who might have a spare room she could stay in.

'Excuse me, *tuan*?' He lifted his head to see Khalish standing in the doorway.

'Khalish, Mrs Lewis will be saying for a while. Can you cook some extra food, and find me some pillows and a blanket – I'll be sleeping on the sofa.'

PAULA GREENLEES

Khalish gave him a puzzled look, then nodded and returned to the kitchen, leaving Nick to his thoughts. Whatever happened now, Miranda couldn't go back to St Augustin's and neither could she stay at Belvedere for long. He'd look for a hotel. Somewhere that he could afford, that wasn't too expensive, and then they'd see where fate took them.

'It's not much, I'm afraid.' Nick held the hotel door open to reveal a double room, which was dominated by a cast-iron bed. Above, a light flickered intermittently; the shade was mottled with brown stains. At the far end of the room, the shutters were still shut, closing in the heat, while a small oscillating fan struggled to create a breeze. 'But hopefully it won't be for long.'

Miranda entered the room as he placed her case at the bottom of the bed.

'There's a shared bathroom at the end of the corridor and breakfast is included. Evening meals are extra.' He felt guilty that he couldn't afford a better hotel than The Excelsior.

Miranda opened the shutters and looked down at the street. A hint of jasmine and cardamom filtered into the room, and, in the distance, she could hear sitar music playing.

'Is this the Indian Quarter?' she asked. 'Only, I've never been to this part of Singapore before and there are so many women in saris. Is that a temple at the top of the street?'

338

'No. The Indian Quarter's a few blocks down. It's a quiet street, though. Not much traffic.'

'I'm sorry,' she said, turning to him, her frame silhouetted by the window.

'What for?'

'Causing you so much trouble.' She left the window and sat on the bed.

'You're not.' He sat next to her and took her hand. 'Don't worry about it.'

She lay down and he joined her, pulling her towards him with one arm, glad when she nestled into him.

'You'll stay the night, won't you?' she whispered. 'I don't think I could bare to stay here alone.'

He stroked her head. 'Of course. Do you think I'd leave you?'

Her hand rested on his chest and he kissed the top of her head.

'If only it could always be like this. Just the two of us, no other cares in the world.'

Her hand slid under his shirt and she kissed him. Slowly, he rolled her over and placed his hands beneath her head, gently holding her, then he moved his hand to her back and unbuttoned her dress. He wanted to ask if she was ready at last, but he knew it, as he felt her breasts, her waist and the curve of her hips responding then melting and moulding into him.

After, they lay on the bed, watching the light filter through the shutters. He picked up her hand and traced the outline of her fingers, then ran his finger along her lips and kissed her chin and her nose. She smiled at him and they curled into each other, his arms around her.

'I love you,' he said. 'That was wonderful.'

'I love you too. And, yes, it was.'

He kissed her once more, pulling her close, and they made love again, before falling asleep. When they woke it was dark. They bathed and changed, then wandered around the area in search of somewhere to eat.

'What about this?' Nick indicated a bustling restaurant. 'Banana-leaf curry? You eat it with your fingers straight from the banana leaf.'

'Why not?'

Inside, diners made room for them as they sat down at one of the long tables. *Dhobi*s in loincloths ladled out rice, followed by fish and vegetable curries. They ate to the sound of sitars filtering through the open windows over the jasmine-infused air.

'You don't mind the hotel, do you?' he asked again.

'How could I? To be honest, I don't think I've ever been so happy. And as you say, it won't be for long.'

'And St Augustin's – won't you miss helping there?'

She smiled at him. 'Yes, but I'll find something else. I've got a feeling that from now on everything is going to work out.'

And he smiled back, hoping that she was right.

That night, Nick couldn't sleep, tossing and turning in the poorly ventilated room. When the fluorescent hands on his watch pointed to five thirty-five, he gave up and crept with his clothes and shoes towards the door. As he opened it, a shaft of light from the corridor fell on to the bed. He could make out Miranda lying on her side with her back to him; she was sleeping like a child with her hands clasped beneath her cheek. He quickly scribbled a note telling her that he'd woken early and that he would see her later, then he placed it on her bedside table for her to see it when she woke.

It was still dark. As he walked towards the car, he noticed that shutters were closed in the windows of the shops and houses. He heard a baby crying and a light flicked on in one of the windows above his head.

He sat in the roadster deciding what to do next. There was already heat in the breaking dawn and the short walk had made him sweat. He ought to see if there was any mail for him, so he decided to drive back to Belvedere. He was still officially living there, even if it was for appearances only, and he could have a shower, get some clean clothes and find out how Khalish was getting on. It had been ages since he'd had a catch up with Brendan and he missed their chats over a glass of whisky, his jokes peppered with matter-of-fact conversation.

It seemed as though the world was sleeping as he drove back through the streets – even the shoreline looked deserted, the only objects with any life were the lights sparkling on the ships at sea.

Belvedere was in darkness. As he entered, everything was silent – not even Khalish was awake. As he passed Brendan's room, he could just make out the sound of Brendan snoring. He washed and changed, then made his way to the kitchen to look for something to eat. Nick flicked the lights on in the hall, and his eye fell on an air-mail letter addressed to him.

The stamp was unusual; there was an image of the king's head in the corner, and a ghostly outline of a traditional sailing boat dominated the front.

He tore it open.

Dear Dr Wythenshaw,

Thank you for your application to work at Nairobi Mission Hospital. The board has carefully considered your application, and it is with pleasure that we can offer you the position of Senior Doctor specialising in Childhood Tropical Diseases.

We wait to hear from you by return with your acceptance, and we look forward to welcoming you here.

Meanwhile, if you have any questions, please write to the Chief Medical Officer at the above address.

Miranda stirred at eight. She turned over, running her hands towards Nick's pillow and opened her eyes with disappointment to discover he had gone, but then she saw a note on the bedside table explaining that he'd woken early. As she lay in bed, she contemplated the day stretching ahead of her like a long, dark tunnel. She had finally done it. She had left Gerry. For a while, she lay with her hand resting on the imprint of Nick's head on the pillow, listening to the whirr of the fan turning.

Eventually, she got up and surveyed the contents of her case.

In her haste to get away, she had left the bungalow with a variety of shoes and clothes, but without much money to her name. Nick had told her he could pay for her to stay here for a week or so – but what then? Even if she could get a job, she'd still have to find a place to live, and then there would be rent to find.

She lit a cigarette, then lay back against the pillows, fiddling with her wedding ring. The ring was worth something, but she expected that it wouldn't fetch more than ten dollars. In any case, it was as well to have it, especially staying in a hotel, where people assumed Nick was her husband. Her engagement ring must be worth more. How happy she had been when they'd bought it – going to Collingwood's, trying on all the biggest diamonds that Gerry could afford. That day, they'd been on cloud nine, and although she wasn't supposed to, she knew how much he'd paid.

If she were lucky, she might get as much as five hundred dollars for it, but if she misjudged it, no more than three. The problem was, she had no idea where to sell it.

She stubbed out her cigarette and went down to breakfast.

'Would you like tea, madam?' the waiter asked.

'Please.'

The waiter smiled, and a moment later returned with a silver teapot and some toast. 'Anything else, madam?'

'Yes. A question. If you had something to sell, where would you go?'

'Is this something of value, madam?'

'Yes, it is.'

The waiter thought for a second, then replied, 'Have you tried Change Alley?'

'Change Alley. Yes, of course.'

She'd heard about it: the pickpockets who might steal your wallet and would sell it back to you for twice the price, about the moneychangers and the roving dealers who ambushed tourists with anything from tin artefacts to leather bags.

It was just the place to go.

After breakfast, she headed towards the bus stop.

'Excuse me, does this bus go to Change Alley?'

The driver nodded. 'Clifford Pier. Not far to walk from there.'

When they reached the pier, she was glad of the slight breeze coming in from the sea and stood for a while on the promenade watching the sampans and the boats. Eventually, she walked towards a red awning squeezed between two buildings, where people crowded into a warren of shops.

It was heaving inside. There were stands crammed with wirelesses, watches and handbags. Between the stalls hawkers were selling fried rice and noodles, while sailors mingled with shoppers and tourists. It was noisy, the heat unbearable, but the buzz thrilled her. Large red signs with gold Chinese characters hung above the shops' doorways announcing what they sold. She couldn't understand a word and wondered how on earth she would find what she wanted.

Clutching her handbag, she wove through the crowd. To her right, she saw someone selling jewellery – a small collection of gold chains, watches and bracelets.

'Do you buy rings?' she asked an elderly Chinese man sitting on a stool. He shook his head.

She tried two more shops, entering further and further into the alley. Mosquitoes lurked in places like this, she was sure of it, and she wanted to run when she saw a rat rummaging through one of the hawker's bins.

'Do you buy jewellery?' she asked a man at a third stall.

The man nodded. 'Buy rings, watches, plates, pictures. Anything you not wan' I take.'

'What about this?' She held her ring out to him, the diamonds glinting in the shadowy alley.

'Lem'me take one look.' He took it from her, placed the band between his teeth, then took a jeweller's loupe from his pocket, placed it in his eye and held her ring towards the light. 'These good quality diamond. Where you buy?'

'England.'

He stroked his chin. 'You sure you wan' sell ring? Very nice.'

'Yes.' She wondered if he could hear her heart pounding. 'Absolutely. I have no need of it any more.'

'I give you,' he twisted his mouth, continuing to examine the ring, 'three hundred dollar.'

'It's worth a lot more than that. How about five?

'But hard for me sell. People might think stolen. Maybe I give you three fifty?'

'I'm not sure.'

'Three seventy-five. Take or leave it.' Poker-faced, he gave her back the ring.

'Fine. I'll sell it.' She handed him the ring again. Her fingers trembled as she watched him go to the back of the stall. A few minutes later, he returned with a handful of notes that he counted out slowly.

Her hands prickled with sweat as she put the money in her wallet, then she pushed her way out of the alley.

Thirty

Kandang Kerbau Hospital was vast: five floors at least, and it dominated the surrounding buildings. Nick had always liked this part of town: the shaded pavements packed with Indian traders in loin cloths, women in saris and children playing in the streets. There were more fruit trees than he had thought possible, and stalls with red, green or yellow bananas ranging in size from a couple of inches to over a foot long. Groups of old men sat in chairs under shop awnings sipping cardamom-infused *chai*, putting the world to rights, while all around them the gentle aroma of jasmine punctuated the air.

He was early. Brendan had said he'd finish at five, but Nick was eager to speak to him. He sat in his car and watched women at various stages of pregnancy coming and going through the main doors of the hospital. Obstetrics had never appealed to him, but at least Brendan and Charlie had steady jobs. They were always saying KK was the place to be, really going somewhere.

He got out of the car and headed along Bukit Timah Road towards Winston's Bar, where Brendan said he'd meet him.

'Tiger beer,' he ordered, as he sat down at the counter.

He glanced about. There were two English doctors, still wearing their white coats, sitting close to the door. They were leaning across the table, their heads close, as though exchanging a confidence, then one of them laughed. Nick turned away.

The waiter brought him a glass and a bottle of Tiger beer. He poured the liquid into the glass and watched the bubbles settle in a thin line of foam. He heard footsteps, but when he looked up, it was only two nurses, all smiles, who were joining the doctors.

Someone had left a copy of *The Straits Times* on the counter. He picked it up and began to skim-read over the pages: *Famine Spreads to Half of China – Parents Sell Their Children to Buy Food; Australia Will Not Refuse Aid; Royal Crisis in Belgium; British Petrol Rationing Rumoured to End.* No further mention of Martha and the riots, then. It was only a short time ago, but how quickly things get forgotten. It was as though none of it had ever mattered. Five-thirty came. He'd finished his beer ages ago and so he ordered another. He should have known Brendan would be late.

The doctors and nurses stood to go. He looked at his watch, wondering if he'd come to the wrong place. It was a quarter to six.

'I'm sorry I'm late.' Brendan loomed next to him. 'Emergency caesarean – you know how these things are.'

Nick gave a gentle nod.

'Another beer?' Brendan raised his hand. 'Two Tigers and a packet of Pall Mall.'

He sat down. 'So, what did you want to talk to me about that couldn't wait until we got home?'

Nick rested his hands on the counter and watched the waiter pour their beers. He was uncertain where to start. 'I don't want Charlie to know yet. But I've just been given the sack.'

'Jesus Christ!' Brendan's attention was fully on him now. 'What the hell happened?'

'For a while now, St Augustin's has had to make cuts.' He didn't want to mention the real reason; that Alice had finally got her way over his relationship with Miranda and that she'd managed to persuade the board to get rid of him just an hour ago on grounds of 'conduct unbecoming to a doctor'. 'But it's all right, I've been looking around for other posts. I've been offered a post in Nairobi. It's a promotion, really. A step up.'

'Nairobi? Bloody hell, Nick.' Brendan rolled his eyes.

'I know. But a job's a job. Unless,' he turned his glass, examining the foam, 'you might be able to have a word with someone for me about a post at KK?'

'What a bugger.' Brendan shook his head. 'I happen to know that all the vacant posts they had are full.'

Nick took a swig of beer straight from the bottle. 'Jesus. I'm sunk. And then there's Miranda. If I go to Nairobi, the pay might be better, but I can't take her. Accommodation is provided – you know what Catholic missions are like.'

Brendan scratched his head, thinking. 'Are Miranda and her husband getting divorced?'

349

PAULA GREENLEES

Nick shook his head. 'And I can't imagine her husband will allow it.'

'Blimey. What *are* you going to do?'

Nick shrugged. 'Seems like I only have one choice. I'll have to go – without Miranda. At least, for now. It's so brutal.'

It felt as though a tonne of lead were crushing him. 'You'll look after Khalish for me, won't you? Make sure he keeps up his English, and that he tries to get into a good school?'

'Of course. But when will you tell Miranda?'

'Tomorrow. I can't face it right now.'

The next evening, the monsoon rolled in from the east. Rain fell in steady rods, pounding the pavements outside The Excelsior Hotel. Through the windscreen, Nick watched lightning illuminate the horizon; then the sky turn a darker shade of pewter. He glanced at his watch. Six-thirty.

A sea of umbrellas came and went, and then he saw Miranda leave the hotel and look around. She smiled as she caught sight of the roadster, then she crossed the road, stepping around the puddles and skirting the perimeter of the car. She opened the door and slipped inside.

'So you got my message, then?' he asked.

'Yes.'

'Good.' He started up the engine, feeling like a traitor.

'Where are we going?' she asked.

'I thought we could go to the Fullerton for a drink.'

She placed her hand on his knee, but he couldn't look at her and concentred on the traffic instead as they headed towards Maxwell Road. White light exploded across the sky and lightning forked above them, followed by a crack of thunder. The rain began to hammer against the windscreen and the car began to steam up, insulating them from the outside world.

He drove north, on to Boat Quay, past the government offices and the Fullerton Building, until they reached the river and parked along the quayside. And then, just as suddenly as it had begun, the rain stopped and the low sun broke through, staining the clouds pink.

'Look – they never stop, do they?' Miranda nodded towards the river. Sampans and junks jostled on the water, along with fishermen and deliveries at landing stations. Sunlight glinted from office windows, reflecting the trail of fire in the thundery sky.

'Come on.' He opened his door to let Miranda out. Her face turned towards him as she stepped out and she placed her hand lightly on his arm. He could smell her perfume: lilies, and fought the urge to pull her close.

As they walked, she pointed out pillars and arches on the buildings. He nodded, half-listening. He couldn't bear it – he'd been awake half the night trying to think of a solution and, right now, he knew he was going to break her heart.

They passed through the courtyard of the Fullerton and she stopped to watch the mailbags being brought in from the quay. The pleasure on her face was almost too much for him to watch.

The lift took them to the clubrooms at the top, where they found a table on the sun deck outside.

'I didn't know you could come here,' she said, her hand over her eyes as she looked down at the boats on the river below.

He swallowed, unable to reply.

'What is it?' she turned to him. 'Something's wrong.'

He reached across for her hand and stroked her fingers. She smiled, waiting for him to go on.

'I've lost my job at St Augustin's,' he began.

'God, that's awful. Why? What's happened?'

'There was a board meeting. They've had to make some cuts and my head was on the block.'

'You must be devastated.' She put her hand on his. 'What are you going to do?'

'I've been applying for other jobs – out of Singapore.' He looked away, down at the table. 'And I've accepted one.'

'Where?' There was fear in her voice.

'Nairobi.'

'Nairobi,' he heard her whisper. 'So far away.'

'They want me to begin at the end of the month.'

Her hand tensed in his, then her lips began to quiver, and she pulled her hand away, placing it over her mouth.

'I'm sorry.' His words sounded hollow and inadequate.

'And what about us?'

'Oh, Miranda.' He'd known that question would be coming, but as she asked, the full knife-thrust of it hurt.

'Take me with you.'

'I can't. Not now.'

She raised an eyebrow, tears brimming in her eyes. 'Why not?'

He waited for a moment, carefully forming his thoughts, but it was as though he were suffocating. 'You're still married, and—'

'And Gerry won't divorce me,' she finished his words, and he saw her body bristle. 'Think of the scandal,' she mimicked his voice. 'Your reputation.'

'Come on, you know that's true. I love you, but it's a Catholic Mission – I simply can't take you. Not while you're still married. Perhaps if Gerry divorces you?' He placed his hand on hers again, but this time her withdrawal was fierce. 'Think about it – what kind of life can I offer you now? But I'll be running the mission in Nairobi. Think about the long term and how much better I'll be able to look after you in a year or two.'

'A year or two? I just left my husband for you.' She took a packet of cigarettes from her bag and lit one, her hand trembling. 'Surely we could find a way to make it work?'

He shook his head, then placed it in his hands. 'I can't see how.' The words were choking him now. 'But when the obstacles have been removed, when you're divorced.'

'But if you loved me, you wouldn't go. You'd find a way for us to be together.'

353

'I've tried. But I can't seem to find a way to make it work.'

'Honestly,' she said, crumpling, 'I don't believe it. I thought ...' She shook her head, unable to complete her words.

Telling her was worse than he had feared. He saw himself as an executioner taking away someone's life.

'Well,' she said. Her face was pale, the shock still stinging. 'It appears you've made up your mind.'

He lowered his head in shame, but when he lifted it, she was walking back towards the lift.

'Miranda!' he called. 'Please. Come back.' He leapt out of his chair and followed her, putting his hand against the lift door to stop it closing. 'For goodness sake! Miranda!'

She shook her head, unable to speak, and pushed his hand off the door.

'At least let me give you a lift home,' he insisted, getting into the lift before it closed.

They drove through the darkness, Miranda crying and pushing his words of comfort away. Finally, they reached The Excelsior.

'Well, goodbye, then,' Miranda's voice croaked, as they pulled up outside the front door.

He heard the car door click open.

'No. Let me walk you up.' He placed his hand on the door, ready to join her. 'We can't part like this. Please.'

'No, Nick. I don't want to see you again,' she sniffed. 'If it's over, then it's over; no need to prolong the pain.'

She got out and slammed the door. He watched her heading towards the entrance, listening to her footsteps. He willed her to look back, but, blinded by tears, he could only just make out that she simply carried on up the steps and pushed open the door. There was no way he was going to leave it there. He ran out after her, following her through the foyer and up the stairs towards their room.

'Miranda!' he shouted. 'Wait!'

But she was quicker than him. She slipped into the room and slammed the door in his face.

'Miranda.' He leant against the door. 'Please. Let me in.'

He waited. He thought he could hear her breathing on the other side.

'I know that you're upset and you don't want to speak to me now.' He pressed his forehead against the door, imagining her face an inch away. 'But as far as I'm concerned, this isn't over. Wherever I am, whatever I do, I'll always love you. However long it takes, I'll be waiting.'

He heard a sob, but she didn't speak. He waited, but after a few minutes, he knew he had to leave. Each step he took away from the door felt heavier than the last until he left the building and, eventually, he reached his car.

He sank into his seat with his hands clasping the steering wheel, knowing that he would hold this moment with him for the rest of his life. Slowly, he depressed the accelerator and, blindly, he swung the car away from the street into the all-enveloping night.

*

She couldn't bear it. From the window, she watched the car turn the corner, then she flung herself on the bed. Big shuddering sobs shook through her. All around her, she could feel Nick's presence lingering: the touch of his hand, the scent of his cigarettes, the sound of his voice. How could he do this? Just at the point when she thought everything seemed to be working out, her world had fallen apart. She scrunched up the pillow, then thumped it. He'd taken her heart and crushed it. There wasn't anything she wouldn't have done for him and she'd believed the same of him. Georgina had made her believe that following her heart would make her happier, but, in pursuing her happiness, she hadn't calculated the cost. Everything had fallen apart and she didn't know what the hell she was going to do. She had nowhere to live, no job and not much money of her own. And she didn't even have Georgina to turn to any more.

Exhausted, and still fully dressed, she fell asleep hugging the damp pillow. Loneliness seared through her. She tossed and turned, imagining him lying next to her, the touch of his body like silk against her skin; she could almost hear his voice in her ear, whispering that he loved her, the taste of his kiss. She must have fallen asleep, for, in the hour before dawn, she woke with her arm lying across his side of the bed and her leg hooked to where his should have been.

Her head hurt from crying, her mouth was dry, and she poured herself a glass of water from the carafe on the bedside table. After she'd drunk it, she sat up properly and curled her arms around her knees. Her body felt numb.

She thought for a moment about going home, but then the memory of Gerry hitting her snapped her out of it. What was it that Georgina said had? That she was living in the shadows? A *gwelio* – a ghost. Well, she was damned if she was going to be.

She decided to count the money in her purse. She was getting through it too quickly. At this rate, she could afford to stay at the hotel for another week, then that was it. Nick had mentioned the possibility of sharing a room or a flat with some secretaries from the Colonial Office. It seemed as though she had no option but to look, and she'd have to find some kind of job, but she hadn't a clue what she could do. Nick had written the name and telephone number of the flat-share in her diary: Janice Edwards. She'd telephone her after breakfast.

'Come after five o'clock,' Janice said, and her voice was firm, almost brusque. 'Nassim Road. We're on the ground floor, first flat on the left.'

It was twenty-five past when Miranda got off the bus on the corner of Nassim Road and headed towards the Botanical Gardens, where there was a collection of two-storey buildings. From the open windows, she heard pacey, loud music that sounded like Frankie Laine.

She had to knock twice. When the door opened, it revealed a slender woman in her early twenties wearing beige slacks. The way she had tied her hair up with a scarf reminded Miranda of a land-girl.

'I'm Miranda Lewis.' She held out her hand.

'Oh, yes, of course. Come in. I'm Janice.' She stepped aside and Miranda followed her to a small living room where a caged parrot began to squawk.

'There are four of us, and two rooms,' Janice began. 'Daisy, Annabelle, Dora and me. Dora is moving out at the end of the week. You'd be sharing with me.'

'I see.'

'Lav's down here. Bathroom's just here. Kitchen's just there.' Miranda followed Janice as she pointed out the flat. 'Small, but it does the job. *Amah* comes in two hours a day. This one's Daisy and Annabelle's room. This is Dora's and mine.'

The room was smaller than she'd been expecting. Two single beds were at either side, with a chest of drawers separating them. A washbasin was in the corner of the room, cluttered with makeup and hairbrushes, and there was a small wardrobe with the door swinging open, crammed with clothes. The room smelt strongly of a sweet violet perfume.

'It's twenty dollars a month, including the *amah*. She does shopping and light cooking. And a twenty-dollar deposit up front.' Janice led her back to the living room. 'Cup of tea?'

'Please.' Miranda looked around the room while Janice disappeared into the kitchen. There was a collection of *Marie France* magazines; lipstick-covered cigarette ends in an ashtray; a Philip's portable gramophone and a collection of records: Sinatra, Doris Day, Crosby. The parrot watched her, pushing its beak through the bars of the cage.

'Sugar? Wasn't sure if you did or not.' Janice returned, carrying a tray with two green teacups and saucers, the standard colour Miranda associated with school. 'And I've run out of biscuits.'

'No sugar, thanks.'

'Tell me a little about yourself. What do you do?' Janice handed her the cup.

The tea was milky, and a globule of condensed milk floated on the top; Miranda took the cup with her left hand, inwardly grimacing. Her wedding ring glinted in the light.

'Oh. You're married.' Janice frowned. The parrot began to bob up and down, shrieking 'Pretty boy, Toby. Biscuit. Biscuit. Biscuit.'

'Separated.'

'Divorced?'

Miranda shook her head.

Janice pursed her lips.

'Look, I don't want any trouble, and it's none of my business, but how do I know he won't come looking for you? Or that you'll stay, for that matter? If you did move in, I'd want six months' rent up front. And no trouble,' she said again.

'I'm sure there won't be.' Miranda looked at the tea and placed her cup down on the coffee table.

'Can you let me know tonight? Flat-shares are hard to get around here, and there's another girl that might be interested. I put her off until tomorrow.'

'Of course. I suppose I ought to be getting along. I'll call you later. And thanks for the tea.' Miranda placed her cup on the table, knowing, deep down, that she wouldn't telephone.

For the next week, she continued to look at flats, each as depressing as the other. She applied for jobs: housekeeper, receptionist, secretary, but each time she was turned down, and eventually someone told her that word had got around about her and that she'd never get a job in Singapore if Gerry had anything to do with it.

On her way back from looking at yet another disappointing flat, she waited in the rain for the bus for almost half an hour. When she boarded, the bus was crowded, and she had to stand. Good God, she'd had enough. She really couldn't do any of this any more. Gerry had won. She would go back to England and live with her parents; she'd write to them as soon she reached the hotel.

It was well after seven when she got back.

'Can I have a double gin and tonic?' she asked at the bar. 'In my room, please.'

'Of course, madam.'

She drank it by the open window, before having a bath. It was too hot to get properly dressed, so she sat on the bed in her bra and knickers, a writing pad and pen in her hand. It would take two weeks for the letter to get home, she guessed, and six weeks for her to sail back to England. Two weeks would be more than enough time for her to plan a voyage home and to sort out the rest of her affairs.

She tapped the pen against her mouth and began:

Dear Mother and Father,

By the time you receive this, you should have already received my telegram telling you I am coming home, and so I thought you were owed an explanation. I have left Gerry – I don't know if it was because of Henry, or Singapore, or that we simply just weren't right for each other any more, but our relationship is over. I can't live with him, nor he with me. I am not sure what to do when I return, but I am longing so much for your love and support,

Miranda

xx

She read the letter, placed it in an envelope, then picked up her pen again:

Gerry,

So, you have got what you wanted. I have decided to go back to England. I am going to book a voyage for a couple of weeks' time. Meanwhile, I shall be staying at The Excelsior in town. I'd be grateful if I could come back to Alexandra Gardens to collect some of my belongings; there are a few things that I didn't have time to pack – my passport among other things. I was thinking about Friday of this week? Obviously, you don't need to be there. In fact, it is probably better if you're not.

Miranda

She sealed the letter, then pulled on a dress and went downstairs to the concierge.

'Madam?'

'Could you post some letters for me?'

'Certainly, madam.'

'This one's airmail for England. And this one is for Singapore. Can it go express?' She placed a dollar in his hand.

'Of course.'

'Thank you,' she nodded.

The following morning, she woke at seven. At breakfast she began a list: P&O office, she wrote in bold, underlining it twice. Passport.

'Telegram, madam.'

She lifted her head. A waiter was standing next to her.

'Thank you.' She took it and read:

IT'S OF NO CONCERN TO ME WHAT YOU DO. G

She scrunched it up and threw it to the floor.

Thirty-one

When she finally went back to the bungalow, she prayed that Gerry wouldn't be there. The light was blinding, and the sun was high over the trees when she arrived at Alexandra Gardens. She walked along the path, carrying a bunch of jasmine for Mei Ling. Earlier, the P&O offices had been busy, but, finally, she'd managed to secure a passage home.

It was strange arriving at the house like this – a visitor. Her body tensed as she walked towards the door, not knowing what to expect when she got there. She contemplated entering by the front door but decided to look for Mei Ling at the back of the bungalow, where there was a pair of pillowcases, a set of sheets and three of Gerry's shirts drying on the line. A little way off, there was a sound of sweeping and water running.

'Mei Ling?' she called.

Mei Ling came towards her, wiping her hands on the front of her clothes, a look of surprise and pleasure on her face.

'Mrs Gerald.' She bowed her head. 'It good see you back.'

'I ...' A lump caught in Miranda's throat. 'Here,' she shifted the jasmine in her arm, 'these are for you.'

'Thank you, Mrs Gerald. But why have you brought me flowers?' Mei Ling took the jasmine and inhaled the aroma coming from the blossom. 'Smell very nice.'

'Is Mr Gerald here?' Anxiety made her stiffen; she could feel it in her jaw as she spoke.

'No. Go to work already.'

Relief washed over her. 'Shall we go inside? Have a cup of tea?'

Mei Ling followed her into the kitchen. Miranda sat down at the small table, watching as Mei Ling put the kettle on to boil, filled a vase with water and then arranged the jasmine so that it cascaded around the side.

She wondered whether the Colonial Office would allow Gerry to continue to live in the bungalow as a single man, and what would happen to Mei Ling. The distance between them all was already lengthening, and she felt a heaviness settling within her. Eventually, the kettle boiled, and Mei Ling brought a pot of tea, teacups and saucers over to the table.

'You look well.' Miranda picked up the teapot, concentrating hard on pouring the tea into the cups. 'Mei Ling,' she began, 'I have something to tell you.' She handed her a cup, taking more care than was necessary to place it on the table.

'I'm sorry, but I'm not coming back. I'm going home, to England. I've come to say goodbye and to collect some of my things.'

'What about Mr Gerald? He go too?'

'No, Mei Ling. Mr Gerald will be staying here. We won't be living together any more.'

'I glad, Mrs Gerald.'

Her hand shook, spilling her tea; she watched it bleed on to the table.

'You've been too sad for too long. Better you not here any more. I worry about you for a long time.'

'Really?' She jerked her head up. 'You're so kind, Mei Ling. Sometimes, I think you're the only one that ever really cared for me in Singapore. I'm certainly going to miss you.' She put her hand out, covered Mei Ling's and squeezed it gently for a moment.

'I see you not happy,' Mei Ling hesitated. Her expression was a little shy as she continued. 'Maybe Dr Nick would make you happy?'

'I once believed he might, but now I don't.' Miranda spread the spilt tea with her finger. 'I'm better off by myself, really.'

'Maybe you think so, but don't think like that.' Mei Ling picked up her cup and blew across the top. 'I didn't think you were so foolish.'

Miranda shook her head.

'In any case, Dr Nick's leaving Singapore. He's going to Nairobi – to Kenya, to work in a hospital there.'

'Maybe you best join him?'

'I can't.' Miranda sighed. 'Once I would have thought you were right, but we have a saying in England, *Let sleeping dogs lie*, and that's exactly what I'm going to have to do.'

'Chinese people also have saying, *Pluck flower while it blooms, if you wait too long you will only have a twig.*' Mei Ling pursed her lips.

Miranda looked down at the tea cooling in her cup. This was exactly how she felt; like a cold cup of tea – once longed for but now forgotten until someone remembered it, picked it up and flushed the dregs down the sink.

'I should start to pack.' Miranda stood. 'I'll let you know if I need any help.'

In the bedroom, she pulled a case from the top of the wardrobe, then glanced around the room. The bed was made up with fresh sheets, the pillows propped up and the mosquito net trailing to the floor. It was hard not to think about when they'd first arrived, Gerry sitting on the bed, the excitement and hope she'd felt as they had explored the bungalow.

There were only two dresses left hanging in the ward-robe – a fuchsia silk evening dress that she had hardly worn, and a blue-and-white polka-dot shift dress that she didn't like. She folded them up, and put them in the case, wondering if, now that she was so short of cash, she might be able to use the fabric for something else. Then she turned her attention to the chest of drawers, where she found the old tin box. She lifted the lid, took out the thimble and for a moment considered giving it to Mei Ling as a gift, before dismissing the idea and collecting the starfish that Nick had given to her, placing it with the thimble on top of the pile of clothes on the bed, before heading off to the drawing room.

She stood in the doorframe, looking at the cobalt-blue curtains she had made with silk from Dhobi Ghat, the cushions she'd sewn with the remnants, and the Chinese brush-stroke paintings she'd bought in Holland Village. It was so strange to stand here; her house, but her home no longer. The picture of the sparrows was her favourite; she took it off the wall, then sank on the sofa, placing it on the cushion next to her and picked up her sewing basket.

Each spool of thread told a story: cream for Henry's christening gown, powder blue for his baby pyjamas, dark blue for a winter dress she had hemmed for her mother. There were greens, pinks, oranges and yellows, each like precious jewels and all of them bringing back memories of the past.

A screech startled her. Tommy was sitting on the window ledge; she'd miss him, and Gin and Tonic too. Tommy bared his teeth at her, then scampered away. She went to the window, hoping to see him for one last time, but he'd gone.

She ought to carry on sorting; apart from anything else, there were her photographs to collect. Leaving the sewing box, she went to the drinks cabinet and picked up the one of Henry sitting on her lap. She ran her finger over his image; far, far too precious to leave behind, she placed it next to the sewing box. Then, she went through to the hall, where she sifted through a pile of letters: an invitation to a ladies' lunch from a friend of Charlotte's, a letter from a friend in England.

For the next half an hour she opened drawers, examined books and peered in cupboards, adding to the pile growing on the sofa. When she had finished, she remembered she had to collect her passport, which was still in Gerry's desk.

Slowly, she opened the study door, half-expecting to see him sitting in the chair. There was a smell of stale tobacco in the room, along with the hint of whisky, and one of his linen jackets was draped over the back of his chair. She felt like a trespasser.

Everything was as she remembered it: the photograph of Henry, another of Gerry at the Sidcup hunt, and the tray with a brass paper knife and a collection of pens lay in the middle. There were letters stacked in a leather rack. She flicked through them. They were mainly letters from his mother; the writing on the wafer-thin envelopes as bold and as sharp as she remembered Lily's tongue. There was a postcard from someone in Penang, and an invitation to a garden party she'd long forgotten.

After she'd placed them back, she turned her attention to the drawers. There were six in total: a long middle drawer, and then, on either side, two smaller drawers above a larger bottom one. She couldn't remember which one the passports were in, so she began to search. The middle drawer contained a bottle of ink and block of air-mail writing paper and matching envelopes. The smaller drawers on the left held a collection of drawing pins, a stapler, two bulldog clips, along with a government stamp and a pad of ink. As she pulled the bottom drawer, it stuck.

'Damn!' She looked for the key, sifting through the tray of pens. From the corridor, she heard someone's foot-steps, and a shadow fell across the doorway.

She jerked up her head. 'Who's that?'

The floorboard creaked again. 'I, Mei Ling. I bring more tea.'

'Thank goodness. Mei Ling, do you know where the key is for this drawer?'

She hesitated. 'Yes, Mrs Gerald.'

'Can you get it for me, then?'

Mei Ling placed the tea tray on the desk, then went to a bookcase and opened the lid of a tobacco pot. She took a key out and handed it to Miranda.

'You wan' I get anything else, Mrs Gerald?'

'I don't think so.'

'I made kee tsui – your favourite.'

'Go on, then,' she smiled.

Mei Ling nodded and left the room.

She unlocked the drawer and pulled it out only to see a lawn handkerchief and a bundle of thirty or forty envelopes tied with a white ribbon. The handkerchief was edged in delicate lace and embroidered with the let-ter 'P'. She lifted it to her nose – a musky perfume clung to the fabric; there was something familiar about the scent. She frowned and picked up the bundle of envelopes as though they were glass, untied the ribbon and pulled the first letter out. It, too, was scented with the same musky perfume.

Darling Gerry, she read, her breathing became shallow and laboured, then she glanced at the signature – *For ever yours, Poppy xxx*

Shockwaves tore through her. She knew that Gerry was a flirt, and had suspected it, but an affair? With her friend's niece? She really hadn't suspected that. Her palms were sticky and her ears were throbbing with fast-pumping blood as she read the letters, dropping them in turn to the floor, where they surrounded her like fallen leaves. Gerry had been cheating on her with Poppy and although she was sure that she no longer wanted to be married to her husband, their betrayal was as bitter as poison oak.

When had it started? She'd seen them at Raffles laughing, then talking in a darkened corner. Nausea roiled within her as she remembered Gerry's hand on Poppy's back, the way their heads had been too close over drinks. She'd chosen to ignore it, but was that the reason for all his nights away, and why he was so keen on getting Miranda back to England? She stared at the photograph of him on the desk. His expression looked smug; she'd never thought of that before. Anger boiling, she lifted her hand and swiped the frame hard to the floor.

Mei Ling opened the door, holding a plate of kee tsui. Slowly, Miranda looked up to see the concern on her face.

Pointing to the floor, Miranda demanded, 'What do you know about these letters, Mei Ling?'

'I not know what you mean-*lah*.'

'Poppy Fanshawe – young, blonde hair. Surely you know?' Her blood was up now and she couldn't keep the anger and shame from her voice.

'*Aiyo!* I not want to say.'

'But you have to. How long has it been going on?'

Mei Ling shrugged and looked away. 'I don't know for sure. Maybe few weeks. Maybe more.'

'Has she stayed the night?'

'I'm sorry, Mrs Gerald, I not want to say too much.'

'Mei Ling, you have to tell me.'

Mei Ling put the plate of biscuits down on the desk. 'Maybe five, six times she stay here.'

'And where did she sleep?'

'In you room.'

'Alone, Mei Ling?'

'No, Mrs Gerald. Mr Gerald stay with her.'

Miranda ran her hands through her hair and laughed.

'I can't believe it. She was like a niece to me – and as for Gerry, he's old enough to be her father.'

The shame of it burned and she sank into the chair, burying her face in her hands. Outside, the parrots were chattering, and she could feel sunlight falling across the desk and on to her back.

'Oh, the irony of it all,' she moaned, then she realised that she of all people has no right to be so self-righteous. 'And now, everything else has fallen apart, don't you see?'

'Mrs Gerald?' Mei Ling interrupted, her voice gentle. 'You mean Dr Nick?'

Miranda lifted her face from her hands. Mei Ling was inches away.

'You like him. Maybe you best find him. Stop him go without you.'

'I can't. It's too late. I told you!' Miranda wrung her hands.

'It's never too late if he's a good man. Only big fool let him go.'

Miranda looked up at Mei Ling's concerned face. 'I think you might be right.'

She gathered up the letters from the floor then waved them at Mei Ling.

'Because you know what this means, don't you? Everything's changed. Gerry might think he's got what he wanted, but now the ball's in my court. Whatever he thinks, however much he tries to refuse, I can make him give me a divorce, the bastard. With all of this evidence, *I've* got exactly what I need.'

She put the letters in her bag, but then her thoughts turned to Nick. Could there be the slightest hope that he hadn't left already, or that he would even want her back? As she lifted her head and looked through the study window, she saw something was scattered across the ground. Tommy was busy emptying the contents of her sewing basket over the grass. She must have left it open in the living room.

'Oh, for God's sake, stop it, you stupid, stupid monkey!' she shouted as she ran outside, but he bared his teeth at her, then scampered up the trunk of the tree still clutching something. She gathered up cotton reels one by one, followed by a pair of scissors and, cursing, she threw them back into the basket. The leaves rustled overhead; then something tumbled through the air.

It was the starfish, and, as it landed, it hit a stone and split in half.

Thirty-two

Miranda sat on the floor of her hotel room with her passport and Poppy's letters. As she sifted through them, an expression of her mother's sprung to mind – what's good for the goose is good for the gander. Lord, how she'd always hated that saying, but there was more than a grain of truth to it now.

Her thoughts buzzed around like a swarm of bluebottles. What was it exactly that galled her the most? It wasn't Poppy's love-struck words, which in any other situation she would have found amusing, nor that Gerry had found comfort in Poppy. It was the complete betrayal, not only of their friendship, but also of her friendship with Georgina too. As for her youth – it was such a cliché, but it was more than that, she realised: Gerry had made a choice, one that didn't include her. It was as though she didn't matter any more, like a belonging that had been discarded and easily replaced with something better and new. She pictured Gerry at the bungalow, sitting on the verandah with Poppy, or in bed, their faces and bodies close.

And what did she have? Nothing. She knew that some would say she'd got what she deserved, that she had started it. Perhaps Mei Ling was right; she was a fool to let Nick go. And the more she thought about it, the more her thoughts spiralled until she couldn't think straight. She needed to get out, to give herself time to think.

She gathered up the letters and tied them with the ribbon before placing them in a drawer.

The hotel was quiet as she left, and, in the distance, she could hear the soft chime of temple bells. A bus was idling at a stop on the corner of the street, it's destination Haw Par Villa. She'd always meant to visit, and as the door was open and only a few passengers were sitting inside, she got in.

She found a seat next to an open window. As the bus stopped and started, she focused on the passing streets and the passengers getting on or off: an elderly Chinese man and his daughter, a housewife in her thirties, who smiled at her as she sat on the opposite seat.

The bus chugged on and the scenery changed. Grand houses gave way to shanties, and the bus grew emptier until she was the only passenger left.

At the final stop, she got off and saw ahead of her a large gateway spanning the entrance to the gardens. Four or five graded roofs rose one above the other, their edges curling in a way that made her think of upside-down gondolas. A huge carving of a tiger stretched across the middle of the arch; the same image she had so often seen on the lids of Tiger Balm that Mei Ling kept as a cure for all ailments.

She walked on, through the gateway into the gardens. There were collections of brightly coloured statues; scenes from Buddhist stories, she guessed. Instinctively, she thought of Nick. He would know which they were from. Still, she decided to continue through the gardens, until she came to the entrance to a tunnel, guarded by two stone warriors; one had a horse's face, the other an ox's head.

It looked like a grotto, but darker and more sinister. She followed the path, to discover a large chamber with flickering lanterns dotted in the walls, which cast eerie shadows on human figurines. On a plaque, she read:

The Ten Courts of Hell

In the first court of Hell, King Qin'guang conducts preliminary trials, and each prisoner is judged according to his deeds in his past life. The good are distinguished from the evil, and the king recommends appropriate rewards or punishment. Punishment is then carried out in the various courts. Those with virtuous conduct in their past life will be led over the 'Golden Bridge' to reach paradise.

Those whose past good deeds outweigh crimes committed will be sent to the 'Silver Bridge' to reach paradise.

Those who were evil doers in their past life will be sent to repent before the 'Mirror of Retribution' and then taken to a subsequent Court of Hell to be punished.

Sin. Punishment. Death. *You've made your bed*, she thought, *now lie in it*. Was she to be punished for ever for her mistakes? Always to be childless, labelled a thief, confined to loneliness or a loveless marriage? If only there were a way forward. A way to put it all right. But, as she stood there, it seemed to her that the bridge to paradise was way beyond her grasp.

She examined the images: the king in judgement; figures dangling over a volcanic pit or having their hearts cut out; a collection of limbs piled next to a severed torso. It seemed that there was a gruesome punishment for every type of sin, followed by forgiveness and paradise. Losing Henry had been awful: surely she'd suffered enough. But even if Gerry did allow a divorce, she'd leave the marriage without any money. Why was a happy ending beyond her reach?

Outside, she found a drinking fountain and splashed her face with cool water, before gulping from the spout. Nearby, there was a sprawling ginkgo tree, and, under it, a bench. She made her way to it and sat and looked at the view, which stretched all the way out towards the sea. In the band of water between Singapore and a distant island, there were ships heading towards the shimmering horizon. She wondered where they were going – Java, the Philippines, Australia, perhaps?

Australia. It had always fascinated her. She recalled hours spent staring at the globe as a child. She loved the way half of the continent was shaped like a rabbit, the other like a dog, and she had poured over the images of kangaroos and koalas in the picture books at school. Once she'd seen a painting of a mass of rock caught between gold and red in the evening sunlight. It seemed magical, a place of escape and distant dreams. For a moment, she imagined herself heading there with Nick.

The more she tried to stop thinking about him, the more she felt his presence: the memory of his voice, his smile, even his touch seemed as fresh and as real as if he were sitting right next to her. She turned her concentration from the sea to where she thought Belvedere might be, hoping to catch sight of the red Malacca-tiled roof, but all she could see was the jungle.

Perhaps it was time to put everything right before it *was* too late. She didn't know how she was going to do it, but it was time to cross her bridge, to do whatever it took to get to a better place. For all she knew, Nick had left, he could be sailing to Nairobi as she sat in the gardens, but, then again, he might not. She would do what Mei Ling said. Start with finding Nick. However long it took.

For a while longer, she sat listening to the children playing and to the birds singing in the trees overhead. The air was still and infused with mimosa or jasmine. Eventually, she picked up her bag and headed back to the hotel.

It was midday when she got back. Her head was throbbing, and her feet swollen and chaffed from walking in the heat. She ate a cheese sandwich in the dining room, looking out across the bustling street, at the couples walking side by side, their bodies not quite touching, at the families with children, all smiling and laughing. For a moment, she thought she caught sight of Nick's roadster turning left at the end of the street. Her head buzzed, the way it did if she'd drunk a fizzy drink too quickly. She was about to stand, to run out into the street to follow it, when the waiter approached.

'Is there anything else I can get you, madam?'

She wanted to tell him to get out of the way, to let her run after the car, but she told herself she was an idiot for thinking like this – imagining Nick's presence everywhere she went.

'A pot of tea, please.' She picked up her napkin and concentrated on winding the cloth around her fingers.

'Of course.' He cleared her plate. 'By the way, madam. There's a letter come for you.'

He returned with a pot of tea and an aerogramme, which he placed on her table. It was from England, but she didn't recognise the writing. She tore it open. It was from Lily.

'Of all the nerve...' She tossed it to one side, but then curiosity got the better of her and she began to read it.

My dear Miranda,
    You will no doubt be very surprised to hear from me.

You can say that again, she thought.

However, your mother, to whom I have become very close of late, has told me that you will be returning home, and I can't say I wasn't surprised. I have also received some rather nasty letters from Jane Curtis – as you might know, I am a friend of her mother's and the daughter is nothing but a troublemaker. She wrote that you are no longer living with Gerry, along with some rather horrible bits of gossip that I won't repeat here, but, somehow, she found out that you are staying at The Excelsior Hotel.

*I feel I owe you some explanations. I know now, from
your mother, that you have always thought I didn't like
you. Quite the opposite, in fact. I have always liked you and
found you to be a strong and interesting woman. However,
it is true that I didn't want you to marry Gerry, but not for
the reasons you might think.*

*I haven't been entirely honest with you. Gerry has
always been a bit of a charmer, and I was angry with him
for it. Not long before he married you, there was another
girl – she became pregnant. She lost the baby, but we had to
pay her off to keep her quiet. Gerry had no money, of course,
and so it fell to us. Once you'd left for Singapore, she tried
blackmailing us again, and we had to sell your house in
Camden to buy her silence – her father is something high
up in the Foreign Office and the fallout from the news
would have damaged my husband's career, to say nothing of
Gerry's.*

Miranda paused, tentatively trying to process Lily's
words. The wound she carried within her from Gerry
and Poppy's relationship was beginning to heal, but now
it threatened to bleed again. She took a calming breath,
then braced herself to continue reading.

*When you met Gerry, I didn't want him to let you down
and I hoped things would work out between you. He told us
that he'd changed, and I wanted to believe him. But then,
after Henry died, I had my suspicions about his behaviour
again, and I had to sort it out.*

What I'm trying to tell you is that it was me that arranged for you to go to Singapore in the first place. I knew about your depression after Henry, how it affected you, and about your situation with the police. And who could blame you? But you were so prickly with me – I wanted to help, but you didn't need me. After the incident with the police, your dear mother confided in me at the time, as they didn't know what else to do. I thought it might help you and Gerry start afresh if you went abroad, so we used some connections to help us arrange it.

Believe me, Miranda, I am very fond of you. My aim was only ever to do what I felt was right at the time, what I believed was best for the greater good of my family, but I see now that all I have done is to make your situation worse. I do hope that you can find it within your heart to forgive me and to start on a new life without my son. I have heard all kinds of gossip via Jane's mother – that Gerry's been up to his old behaviour again. And I also heard hints of your romantic connection with a young doctor. Well, I am not angry with you, as I have failed you before, and I don't want to fail again.

Now, all I can do is to wish you the very best.

The aerogramme fell from her hands and Lily's words echoed around her head as Miranda sat there, trying to take it all in. However misguided, Lily had been trying to help, but confusion mixed with anger pulsed through Miranda as she absorbed the shock of Lily's words. *A new life without my son … I wish you the very best.*

A black-and-pink butterfly landed on the table: a Common Rose. She cupped it in her hands and the fragile wings beat with such force against her palms. She opened them, and, for a moment, the butterfly remained before rising towards the ceiling light, where it spread its iridescent wings. As a child, she'd been told that butterflies only lived for a day, and she'd always wondered, if it were true, how on earth the species managed to exist. This one was spectacular – its wings like black silk embroidered with the finest thread. She admired the colour, it's determination; however small and fragile it was, it had grown from an even tinier mass of cells – it had lived and it was perfect. And even if it were only for one day, well, that day was glorious.

She turned her attention back to Lily's letter, which she folded and placed back in her bag, her thoughts focused on what to do next.

'Is everything all right, madam?' The waiter had returned.

'Yes. No. I don't know. Can you bring me a large gin, please?'

'Of course, madam. Anything else?'

'I don't suppose you have a telephone directory, do you?'

'I'll see what I can do.'

A few moments later, he returned with a well-thumbed directory and a gin. She took a large gulp from the glass, then she licked her index finger as she turned the directory pages until she found what she wanted.

Mayfield and West, Partners in Law, 24 Raffles Place.

She gazed back out of the window, at the corner where she thought she'd seen Nick's car. She'd go now. Before she changed her mind. She collected Poppy's letters, then she caught a bus to Raffles Place.

When she got off the bus, she paused beneath the covered walkway, looking for number twenty-four. In front of her, there was a building with crumbling plaster; a spray of bullet holes pockmarked the walls, a souvenir from the Occupation, she guessed. There were twenty windows, some had the shutters closed, while others were open, and she could see the frenzied rotation of ceiling fans.

She took a deep breath and crossed the road. Number twenty-eight, she noted, then she walked on, twenty-six, twenty-four. Drifting from one of the open windows above her was the tap-tap-tap of someone typing, interrupted by an exchange between two male voices. She pushed the door open.

The dimness engulfed her and she could smell incense – sandalwood and something that reminded her of the mustiness of churches. Voices filtered down from upstairs; then she heard a door bang and the typing start again.

As her foot struck the first step, her throat went dry. She gripped the rail and continued climbing and listening until she reached the first floor, where she saw a teak door. The floorboards creaked as she made her way towards it and she read *Mayfield and West* written in gold.

Her fingers rested on the handle, and then, slowly, she turned it.

A Chinese man in his early twenties was typing at an old mahogany desk. To his left was a filing cabinet, to his right a door to what Miranda guessed were offices.

The man lifted his head. 'Yes? Can I help you?'

'I've come to see either Mr Mayfield or Mr West.'

'Do you have an appointment?' The clerk frowned. 'We're extremely busy today.'

'No, I haven't.'

The man picked up a black diary from the desk and turned the pages. 'Can you come back tomorrow?'

'Would it be possible to wait, to see if one of them can fit me in? I didn't think of making an appointment.'

'You should telephone first. We can't let people just turn up when they feel like it.'

'I'm sorry. Perhaps you could ask?'

He hesitated, frowning for a second. 'All right. I'll ask if Mr West might be able to see you; his last meeting finished early. What's the name?'

'Mrs Lewis.'

'You can wait over there.' He indicated a leather chair in the corner of the room next to the window. Miranda sat down while he opened the door and went into the connecting room.

From the window, she watched a steady stream of bicycles in the street, weaving between shoppers who were laden with kai lan and mangoes from the market. Beyond the rooftops, she could see the Sri Mariamman temple, the entrance tower overflowing with the colourful statues that had fascinated her on her visit with Nick.

It looked like any other day – the people in the street were unaware of her watching them, of the questions she was planning to ask. Minutes passed, marked only by the sound of a clock ticking in the room, and as she waited, doubt and uncertainty began to take hold. She stood to leave, but the connecting door opened.

'Mr West said he can see you for a few minutes,' the clerk said, returning to his desk. 'If it doesn't take long.'

A man in his forties leant against the doorjamb, his sleeves were rolled up, and his tie was loose.

'Mrs Lewis?' his voice was weary as he stepped to one side to let her into the office.

There were law books and journals crammed into an overflowing bookcase, and in front of the window stretched a desk covered with piles of documents.

'So,' he nodded towards a battered rattan chair, indicating that she should sit down, 'what can I do for you?'

'Thank you for seeing me,' she began. 'I know you're busy – so I won't beat around the bush. The thing is, I want to know if I can get a divorce from my husband.'

Mr West puffed out his cheeks as he sat down, then he scratched his head, looking at her. 'Divorce is a nasty business, Mrs Lewis. Are you completely sure? Often, you know, disagreements can be patched up, or couples learn to reconcile themselves to each other.'

Miranda remembered the bruises on her wrist from Gerry's fingers digging into her skin, the slap on her face that smarted for days, and said, 'I'm absolutely certain.'

'I see. And what about your husband, have you spoken to him?'

'Not yet. That's why I'm here – so I know what to tell him.'

'And what grounds were you thinking of?'

'Adultery.'

'Have you got proof?'

'What about these?' She opened her bag and handed him Poppy's letters, and the one from Lily. She watched him flick through them.

'I should be candid,' she said, when he'd finished skimming them. 'My husband is not the only one to have had an affair.' She felt herself blushing and looked away.

'It's not my role to judge.' Mr West handed back the letters. 'But is there any way you could try to patch things up?'

'No. Our marriage has got beyond that.'

'Any children?'

'No.' She fingered her locket.

'And how long have you been married?'

'Three and a half years.'

'These letters make it clear that your husband has, with the utmost certainty, committed adultery, but it would be better if you could provide more tangible evidence.'

'You mean photographs in a hotel bedroom type of thing?'

'We've progressed beyond that, but if he could agree to admission, in court, say, in front of a judge, you would certainly have a case. But you know, don't you, the whole process will take up to at least two years – you haven't been married for five years yet, which is the earliest point at which you could get a divorce, I'm afraid. And the courts take a dim view of a woman leaving her husband, unless it's for insanity or battery, of course.'

'Is it really that long? I wasn't certain. The thing is, I'm going back to England next week – if he agrees, I don't know whether to start proceedings here or over there.'

'The law's the same. Mrs Lewis, it's up to you – Singapore or England, the case still needs to go before a judge. But I should warn you: it will be an unpleasant business.' He handed her back the letters. 'Keep these safe. Meanwhile, we should see if your husband might agree to a divorce. It would be easier for you both. Would you like me to contact him on your behalf? If not, I can recommend someone to you in England. I take it that your husband is staying in Singapore?'

'Yes, he is.'

'Good. Here's my card. Let my clerk know what you want to do. And, by the way, I should warn you that if you do go ahead, you should avoid contact with your husband. Judges can be a bit suspicious of collusion between couples, and we need to show your marriage has broken down beyond repair. Is that understood?'

'Yes.' She stood and took his outstretched hand; his grip was firm and reassuring. 'It most certainly is.'

Thirty-three

Nick yawned. There seemed to be more boxes of books and papers to sort from St Augustin's than he had imagined: sheets and sheets of questionnaires about what people ate, household incomes, illnesses and childhood diseases. All of it was redundant now. He carried the last box from the roadster to the back garden at Belvedere and placed it on the ground next to the others, then gathered up a selection of twigs and leaves, which he shaped into a mound. Next, he scrunched up balls of paper from the box and buried them in the heart of the bonfire. Finally, he lit a match and placed it in the centre and then watched the flames lick around the edge of the sheaves of paper.

He coughed as he watched the fire start; it snaked like lava through the pile. Next, he gathered up a handful of paper from one of the boxes and dropped sheet after sheet into the flames. His jaw tightened as he watched columns of data singe and burn. The flames consumed all the paper, and he waited until it finally died back. All his research in Singapore had turned to ash in front of his eyes, soon all that would be left would be embers.

After, he returned to the house. On the hall table, there were the usual piles of letters. He sorted them into three piles, then poured a shot of whisky before collecting his mail and sitting on the balcony. There was little movement among the branches of the trees, and he could hear the mellow, soothing 'Woo-Ooo, Woo-Ooo' of a koel bird. He wondered what he'd miss the most about Belvedere – the birdsong, the fresh papaya and lime in the morning, Brendan's level-headedness or Charlie's humour?

The whisky was peaty with a lingering aftertaste. He was in no hurry to open the letters in his lap and sat back and closed his eyes as he savoured the flavour.

When he'd finished the glass, he lit a cigarette, then he turned his attention to his mail. One letter in particular stood out: the handwriting on an aerogramme was his father's yet again.

My Dear Nick,
As an executor of your grandmother's estate, I am writing to you with news of her will.

He sat up, concentrating on the words.

You are to be sole beneficiary of her estate. You will inherit Coombe in its entirety.

He read the letter again from the beginning, pondering over each sentence as he processed the information.

After the recent Finance Bill and the uncertainty of future death duties, your grandmother and I spent many weeks

discussing the future of Coombe. It was our joint decision
that you should inherit – I have no wish to live at Coombe
and why pay these escalating death duties twice? I am
aware that this will come as a great surprise to you. Your
grandmother always hoped that, as a younger man, you
might one day return to Coombe, and that you might be
able to make something of the estate. However, I am aware
that this might not be in accordance with your future
plans. Indeed, you might wish to sell. Therefore, I would
ask you to take your time considering what you wish to do
before you let me know what your answer will be.

Too damn right it was a surprise. He'd always assumed
his father would inherit and that he would sell it. The
news was thrillingly unexpected as well as alarming.

He imagined his father sitting with his grandmother
– their telephone calls and letters discussing it. He had
always been aware that, since Freddie's death, his father
had no desire to set foot in the place. But what his father
couldn't have known was that, since that time, Nick had
also been unsettled by Coombe. He had always been
looking for a reason to run away from it, but, at the same
time, he was also looking for a reason to return. Perhaps
his grandmother knew him better than he thought, perhaps she wanted to force his hand, to make him return to
the place that, deep down, they both knew he loved more
than anything.

All his life, he'd been trying to escape from the legacy
of Freddie and the shadow of Coombe. But now, holding

his father's letter, it was as though, however much he fought against it, Coombe would always pull him back.

Was this his grandmother's last act of wisdom, which he'd asked her for that day on Bukit Kalang?

A day passed. Nick kept the letter in his desk, and, in quiet moments, he re-read it. Coombe or Nairobi? Nairobi or Coombe? He knew his father would be expecting a reply, but he couldn't send one. Not yet.

He drove down to the Sea View Hotel and walked along the shore, the waves weaving between his ankles. It was easier to think here with nothing but the emptiness of the horizon and the cool water on his skin. Children were playing in the distance, and he pictured Freddie and himself as young boys, racing along the sand, and he realised that, in leaving Coombe to him, his grandmother had given him the biggest gift of all. Faith. In *him*. She was giving him a reason to believe in himself, a reason not to run away any more.

He decided to make one last visit to Bukit Kalang.

When he had climbed the hill, he looked around him. Convolvulus had already crept through the small rocks and was choking the Gaillardia he'd planted. And now, as he planned to go, he knew that, after he had left, it would only take a few weeks for the jungle to reclaim this spot, and that his story, his time here, was finished. What mattered, he realised, was what he had taken from this place, what was in his heart, and he promised himself that, wherever he lived next, he would remember the peace and harmony he had found here. He sighed. It would be perfect, though – complete – if he had Miranda by his side.

'I suppose,' he sat down next to the Gaillardia and tugged at the weeds, 'that it's farewell for now, Gangy. I never thought you'd leave Coombe to me – and I'm touched and scared by the thought of owning it. But whatever happens, I promise I will do my best to make you proud of me, to see the good in this world, just as you used to.'

He was still torn, but he had decided, in the end, that he would return to Coombe. The pull was much stronger than to Nairobi, and it was a duty of a different kind. One that he found hard to articulate, or even to come to terms with. And yet, as he made his decision, grief tugged at his heart. If only he had known this, the past would be different and the future would have been one of hope. If only he had known, then he could have taken Miranda with him. Should he try to find her, to persuade her to join him? Would she even listen? How could life be so bitter-sweet?

He walked back along the track to Belvedere, determined not to look back. It was the same track that he had run along the day he'd hurt his ankle and called on Miranda for the first time, the one they had walked up together when she accompanied him to Bukit Kalang. How lovely she had looked then. He wanted to find her, to tell her the news, to beg her to forgive him. But he knew he should have fought for her earlier, and that the likelihood was that she'd merely push him back.

He walked slowly, listening to the monkeys calling and the screech of parakeets far above in the jungle canopy, then he made his way down to the lower levels, deliberately avoiding Alexandra Gardens. There was a narrow path to the back of Belvedere, which he followed, past the hen coops and the single-roomed hut where Khalish slept, and finally through the rows of sheets hanging on lines. The sun was directly above him, almost at the highest point in the sky.

Inside Belvedere, he called for Khalish but got no reply, so he quickly showered and put on clean clothing. In the kitchen, he filled a long glass with water, then he lifted his head at the sound of a car approaching. He listened to the engine idling and footsteps falling outside, then he closed the faucet and concentrated on the unmistakeable sharp, quick tap of heels. It couldn't be, but it sounded like Miranda.

There was a light knock at the door, and he placed the glass carefully on the table. It could be anyone, he told himself, as he made his way to the hall, anyone at all. He shouldn't wish for too much, but, still, he turned the handle, hoping.

'Miranda?' He couldn't believe it was her.

'May I come in?'

'Yes, of course.' He blustered, awkward with confusion. 'Would you like a drink?'

She shook her head.

He stood, looking at her. 'I was just thinking about you – but I didn't think I'd ever see you again.'

'I wasn't sure if you had gone.' She clutched her bag in front of her.

'No. Not yet. Shall we sit down?' He sat on the edge of his chair, taking her in. She looked pale and tired.

'Are you well?' he asked. He longed to touch her, to stroke her hair, to tell her how much he had missed her and what a bloody fool he'd been to let her go. He examined her expression, the curve of her neck, the mole in the dip of her collarbone, hardly daring to believe that she was there.

'I'm well enough. And you?'

He nodded, his palms prickling with perspiration. She sat opposite him on the sofa; familiar, yet almost a stranger.

'I'm glad you're still here,' she began. 'That I can see you before you head off for Nairobi, because there's something I have to tell you.

'Miranda,' he interrupted, but she raised her hand to silence him.

'I've been to see a lawyer. You see, I'm going to divorce Gerry after all.'

'I see. That's good, isn't it?'

'It is,' she nodded. 'It will take time, three years, I think, for the divorce to come through, but,' she looked straight at him, her face flushed, 'I can't stop thinking about you, and I wondered if you could wait. That is, if there is the slightest chance that you would still consider it, I mean, could I join you in Nairobi?'

'Miranda,' he paused, 'I'm not going to Nairobi.'

'You're not?' The space between her eyes creased.

'I'm going back to England. To Coombe.'

'What? I don't understand.'

'I've just this moment heard. My grandmother – she left it all to me. The house. Her money.'

'Really?'

He saw in her expression that she didn't fully grasp the meaning of his words.

'It's a large house, Miranda. I never really told you how big.'

'How big?'

'Ten bedrooms, some farm cottages – five hundred acres of farmland, part of the coast.'

'It sounds idyllic, like something from another world.'

'It is. Was.'

'Was?'

'It was commissioned during the war for a rest home. I haven't been there for a long time; I really don't know what it's like now. After my grandfather died, my grandmother continued to live there, but she was struggling and, gradually, it's been falling apart.'

'Oh. I see. I like a place with character,' she smiled.

'Do you?' He stood up and sat on the sofa next to her and took hold of her hand. He'd forgotten how soft it was.

'Come with me.' He pulled her towards him, his face almost touching hers. 'We can start a new life together, can't we? It's not too late, after all, is it? It's what I want, more than anything. Please. Say that you will.'

As he waited, he could see her eyes shining, then she wrapped her arms around him and they kissed.

The P&O office was muggy and crowded. Nick dabbed at his head with a handkerchief as he stood at the counter.

'There'll be a penalty of five dollars, sir, I'm afraid, but the good news is that we do have two second class cabins available on the *Princess Margaret* next Saturday.' The clerk lifted his head. 'Seven o'clock departure.'

'I'll take them, please.' Nick took out five dollars, placed them on the counter and waited for the clerk to write out the tickets.

'Here you are then, sir. Two cabins to Portsmouth – stopping at Calcutta, Alexandria and Lisbon. Have a pleasant voyage.'

Nick nodded his thanks, then tucked the tickets in his wallet and joined Miranda, who was sitting on a bench in the waiting room.

'Success?' She looked up from the *Marie France* she was flicking through. He still couldn't register that she was with him, that they were leaving in less than seven days.

'Yes.' He smiled at her and touched her fingers lightly. 'I think we should go for a celebratory drink.' He held out his arm, waiting for her to stand and to link hers in the crook of his elbow.

'Anywhere special in mind?' She leant into him.

'Let's just wander around the quays, shall we? There'll be something.'

Outside, a ship was docking at the quay with its gang-plank lowering and horns blasting. He'd always liked this area of town: the ripples of activity, the cranes swinging crates to the ground, and men rushing around on trishaws touting for business from the incoming passengers. But now, as they walked towards the shanties, watching the women washing vegetables in the dirty river, a shadow of despondency began to envelop him. When he'd first arrived in Singapore he'd been full of hope and ambition. Perhaps he'd been naïve, but he had thought he could change the lives of the children by offering medical help to the disadvantaged. But now, even with Miranda at his side, a small concern niggled him – how would he adjust to a new unstructured life?

'How about this?' Miranda indicated a small hotel overlooking the harbour. 'There are little tables on the street – we can see if we can get one with a view.'

There was a table in the corner, under a palm tree, which cast a welcome umbrella of shade over them as they sat down.

'Two Gin Fizzes, please,' he asked the waiter, lightening the tone of his voice.

'What will you miss the most about Singapore?' Miranda asked. 'I've heard it's more of a culture shock going home after all this time than it is coming out here, and I'm prepared to believe it.'

He leant back in his chair – could he tell her that he'd miss it all, that he had no idea how he would adjust to this new, wealthy life in England?

'I'm not entirely sure.'

'Is everything all right?' She was looking at him, her head on one side. 'You seem awfully quiet.'

'I've been thinking about Coombe, that's all. It's a big change and it doesn't feel right. And then,' he raised his hand in front of him, indicating the shanties, the children playing in the river, 'I'm not sure how I feel when there are still people in this world who have so little.'

'It's not your fault, though. You'll drive yourself crazy thinking like that.'

The waiter brought them their drinks. He watched teardrops of condensation slither down the side of the glass and waited for the man to leave before replying.

'I know.' He picked up his drink. 'But I've been used to helping people all my life. I'm not sure if I'm ready to be the lord of the manor, a completely different person.'

'You don't have to be.'

'What do you mean?'

'You might think it a foolish idea,' A flush of red coloured her cheeks, 'but I've been thinking about Coombe too.'

'Go on.' He nodded, wondering where her thoughts were leading.

'Just because you've been given this money doesn't mean you should stop doing what you love. You could take in refugees and, in return, they could help restore Coombe; do up the gardens, help with the harvest. There must be plenty of trades: carpenters, builders, farmers to take on, women who can sew, cook, teach. You could give them somewhere to live in exchange for their skills. I was thinking along the lines of a community. I've heard about something like it before – in Dorset.'

He tried to picture it, imagining his parents' reaction. They would think he had gone mad.

'I don't know. It sounds a good idea, but I'm still trying to take it all in.'

'Think about it. See how you feel when we get back to England.'

She picked up her drink and looked at the bottom of the glass.

'It would need a lot of planning and I wouldn't know where to start,' he said.

'So you might consider it?' A smile broke across her face.

'Yes, but I haven't even been back to Coombe yet.'

'But we've got six weeks on board, haven't we, to discuss it?'

He picked up his drink and sipped it. 'I suppose. But let's take one step at a time, shall we?'

Still, there was something in it. He could imagine the house full of people, the cottages and the barns turned into workshops or teaching rooms.

'But, for now, we haven't even left Singapore – and there are plenty of other things to think about first.'

Like selling the roadster.

And making plans for Khalish.

Thirty-four

Miranda was sitting on the bed at Belvedere watching Nick take his shirts out of the wardrobe. He folded them and placed them in his case.

'I'm almost done packing.' He lifted his head towards her. 'But there are still a few things I need to do, and then there's the roadster to take to Pagoda Street. You can come with me, if you like.'

'I've got some bits to finish off before we leave.' She picked up a book from the bedside table, *Tropical Birds of Singapore and Malaya*, curled up on the bed and flicked through the pages, half-listening to the opening and shutting of drawers. 'So I think I'll leave it.'

Suddenly, the temperature in the room seemed to drop and everything became quiet. Miranda glanced towards the window, at the heavy drops that were beginning to fall. She stood, and went over to look out, wondering how long it would last.

Her eyes wandered up towards the branches of a rain tree and she noticed how the flowers had folded. She knew that the locals used the condition of the petals to determine the weather, but she'd never quite caught the gradual tightening of the blooms. Perhaps, on this one last day, she might just catch them unfurling when the rain stopped.

'Right. That's me done.' Nick stood beside her. 'I'll meet you later, then, on board the ship – the American Bar at six-thirty.'

She kissed him on the cheek. 'Try not to be late.'

He pulled her towards him, but she broke away. 'I'd better go.'

Halfway along the drive, she stopped. Bullfrogs were croaking, and she could imagine their bubble-gum cheeks as they called for a mate. From under the shelter of her umbrella, she looked back at Belvedere one last time. The rain was easing now, and everything seemed so clean and transformed. Almost new.

She waited, and after a time the rain stopped completely. Drops of water dripped from the branches overhead, and then the sun came out. As the water began to evaporate, she could finally see the pink flowers unrolling, as though they were stretching out in the sun. A dog barked in the distance and she could hear the engine of the bus grinding as it strained to come up the hill. No time to linger. She needed to run.

When the bus reached the hotel, she could hear a sitar and bells playing from one of the temples, and there were tables and chairs in the courtyard of the Indian restaurant where she had eaten with Nick the first night she'd stayed at The Excelsior.

The street was so vibrant, and she wondered if she'd ever see these scenes again. She walked along the street and, drawn by the red-coloured lanterns strung around banana trees, she decided to eat lunch at one of Chinese street cafés.

She sat down at a table, aware of the other diners looking at her. There was a Chinese family, and a young couple who sat with their fingers almost touching across their table. But she didn't care how odd it might seem to them that she was sitting there alone. When she'd first arrived in Singapore, she would never have dared visit places like this unaccompanied.

'What I get for you?' a waiter asked. 'Fried rice, noodles?'

'Noodles, please.'

Gerry had never liked eating fried rice, let alone noodles. She tried to imagine him here and what he would say to her. For a moment, she imagined him walking along the street and his surprise at seeing her. And, then, she wondered if he knew she was leaving, or if he even cared. Perhaps Poppy had already moved into the house. She tapped her fingers on the table. Despite what the lawyer said, she wanted to let him know she was going. Whatever had passed between them, deep down she still cared. Perhaps she should write to him before she left Singapore for good.

After her meal, she wandered about for half an hour, then returned to her room, where she settled on the bed and began to write.

Gerry,

I suppose you will be surprised to hear from me, but I thought you should know I am leaving Singapore today.

Despite everything that has happened between us, it makes me rather sad to think that I may never see you again, and I don't wish to leave you on the worst possible terms.

You will, of course, have heard from my solicitors, Mayfield and West, by now. I really do believe that this is the right decision for us. I hope that you will agree, and that perhaps one day our separation will mean that we will both be happy again.

Do you remember when we first arrived in Singapore? How long ago it seems now. I never told you what I wished for when we arrived, when I added my coin to the others being thrown into the sea. I wished for us to be happy, for everything to work out just fine. And I suppose, in a way, it has.

I also want you to know that, once, I really did love you and that, despite it all, I wish you all the very best,

Miranda

She sealed the envelope, then placed it in her bag and went downstairs. There was just enough time for her to take the letter to Gerry herself.

'Can I have a taxi, please?'

'Yes, madam. Where to?'

'Alexandra Gardens.'

For the last time, she walked up the path, then placed the letter beneath the door. There was music playing – *Turandot*, she recognised it, as well as the aroma of Gerry's cigar creeping through an open window. She rested her hand against the door until she heard laughter and a woman's voice, and then she recoiled and returned silently to the taxi that was waiting for her.

As she travelled through the now familiar landscape, she told herself she had to look forwards and not to look back. Even though she wanted a clean slate, she knew that it would be hard to come to terms with the fact that their marriage was finally over and that Gerry had a life with Poppy. She tried to focus instead on the steering wheel, on the driver's long, yellowing nails, the hair curling in the nape of his neck and on the cars and bicycles ahead of them.

But, later, she panicked. She shouldn't have written to Gerry. Apart from what the lawyer had said, she imagined him reading her note, laughing over it with Poppy, then scrunching it up and throwing it into the bin.

As the afternoon drew to an end, she wandered back through the Indian Quarter, stopping to run her fingers over the bolts of silk or to inhale the jasmine hanging in doorways. When she had first arrived, it had been so strange to see the banana trees growing on the side of the road, as everyday as a sycamore in England. And now, everything had changed: what once had been unfamiliar was no longer so.

She tried to imagine England – wearing winter coats again, the spark of logs burning in the grate, Mother and Father, freshly baked bread, Socrates, afternoon tea at the Lyon's Café on the Strand. Before she left the Indian Quarter, she decided to buy her mother three yards of pale-blue silk and a selection of spices she knew would be hard to get in England: cassia bark, turmeric, cloves and cardamom.

Back at the hotel, she squashed down the lids on her cases to make sure everything fitted, then she glanced at her watch.

It was time to go.

At reception, she asked, 'Can I have a taxi, please, and some help with my cases?'

'Of course, madam.'

She watched the taxi driver load her cases into the car.

'You want Collyer Quay-*lah*?' the driver asked.

'Yes. The P&O dock.'

'I know it-*lah*.' The driver nodded, and they set off. She saw, but she didn't see, the details of the buildings they passed. She heard but couldn't listen to the driver's conversation. She sat clutching her bag. How tired she felt, on this last journey, and how long it seemed to take.

Eventually, they reached the mouth of the Singapore River and the harbour crammed with boats and ships.

'Collyer Quay, always busy.' The driver hooted his horn as the car slowed almost to a walking pace. 'P&O over here.' He indicated to the left as the car joined others queuing to reach a passenger ship docked at the end of the quay. She leant forward, scanning faces in the crowd, looking for Nick.

'You like I help you find porter?'

'Please.' Disappointment jerked her into action. 'I don't think I can manage all these by myself. Perhaps we can get a move on?'

405

'Plenty time-*lah*.' The driver frowned as she fussed over her bags, and he bustled ahead, looking for a porter to take over. A clock chimed six in the distance as she walked up the gangplank, following the porter, to get her papers checked.

The officer handed her passport back. 'Right. Cabin C, Floor 2. Take the first flight of stairs to your left.'

She followed the porter along the narrow passageways to the carpeted floors and polished walnut walls of the cabin deck. There were two single beds in the cabin, a washbasin and a small chest of drawers. After she had tipped the porter, she unpacked her cases, then sat on the bed and emptied the contents of her tin box on to the covers. She fingered the lock of Henry's hair from her locket and his hairbrush. These she would always keep, but the other things – the thimble and the other items, they all reminded her of a time when she was far from happy, and she knew that, not only was there no need for them any more, but it was time to let them go. Next, she took off her wedding ring and held her hand up to examine her ring finger in the light. The ring had left a ridge, and she wondered how long it would take to fade. She placed the gold band into the box and snapped the lid shut.

She made her way to the promenade deck carrying the box and watched as a couple of sailors carried their kit bags up the gangplank, then she walked towards the stern, where the waterfront sprawled in front of her. There were rows of cars parked in front of the Maritime Centre. She could see the curved façade of the Hong Kong

Shanghai Bank, trams and bullock carts travelling along the Bund, and hawkers' stalls leading down to Johnston's Pier. It was so vibrant, and she loved it, and she ached, wondering if she would ever see it again.

She pictured all that was still taking place there: Mei Ling in the kitchen, preparing an evening meal for Gerry and Poppy; Charlotte with Jack – it wouldn't be long now until he was drawing and colouring, then, in a few years time, reading. Then there were the friends that she had said farewell to, Georgina in Chicago, the nurses at St Augustin's, who would be beginning their evening shift. And then her thoughts moved to Martha, wondering how she was coping in a strange country, far away from the family she had always known.

There was so much that she had learnt from the children at the centre too. It wasn't just their warmth and their innocence; it was their ability to give and to love. She pictured how Aishah's face had lit up with curiosity on Christmas Eve, when they'd made paper snowflakes together for the ward.

But now it was time. Not just to depart, but to leave. She placed the box on the rail, sunlight glancing off metal as she opened the lid. Her fingers picked up her wedding ring and, holding it out between her forefinger and her thumb, she examined it for one last time, before throwing it into the water and watching its trajectory as it plunged into the sea. She imagined the ring plummeting through the water and resting in the mud beneath. Next, she took out the thimble and threw that, too, into the water, then she discarded all of the contents of the box, until at last the box was empty. She gave it one final shake, then threw that over the rail.

For a moment, the box floated on top of the water, then it sank.

She peeled herself away from the rail, her gaze fixed ahead. She walked on, her hand gliding over the polished handrail, until she reached the viewing deck.

A steward was sweeping the deck. 'Been a lovely day, hasn't it? Should make for a calm departure.'

'Yes. It's been glorious. Could you point me in the right direction for the American Bar?'

He rested his hand on the back of a deck chair. 'First on the right – can't miss it.'

There was jazz playing as she entered, and she recognised the soothing tones of a saxophone.

'Champagne, madam?' A steward held a tray of glasses towards her.

'Thanks.' She took a glass and sat in one of the chairs close to the door, alert to every movement and sound as new passengers began to filter in.

Where on earth was Nick? She glanced at her watch, fiddled with her hair and waited. After a time, the bar was full of rustling dresses and boisterous voices. It was then that she detected a gliding movement, which forced her to look towards the door. She was stunned to see that the cityscape was receding behind them and stretches of water were appearing between the ship and the shore.

Thirty-five

The streets in the Chinese Quarter were like a maze, weaving and coiling back on themselves. As soon as Nick thought he'd escaped, he'd realise that he'd doubled back and was where he'd started. The impenetrable expressions of strangers unnerved him as he passed. Having just sold the roadster, he was conscious of the large sum of money inside his jacket pocket, of the thieves and beggars he knew inhabited the complex of interconnecting passageways.

On his third circuit around, he noticed a small bric-a-brac shop jammed between a herbalist's and a money lender. A window display of incense burners – squat lions and dogs with their mouths open, ready to spew perfumed vapour – drew him. He'd always wanted one.

The shop was brimming with clutter: wooden carvings, pieces of embroidery, rickety cane chairs, opium weights shaped like cockerels or elephants, along with rolls of parchment and a yellowing painting of koi carp and dancing butterflies. He picked up one of the opium weights and turned it over.

'I give you good price.' A Chinese man he hadn't noticed earlier stood in the doorway that connected the shop to a room at the back.

'Actually, I'm more interested in the incense burners – the one of the lion in the window.'

'Ah, this one very special.' The man glided towards the window. 'From China. Very old. See here. Copper. Cannot find copper like this for new one-*lah.*'

Nick picked it up and weighed it in his hand. It was heavy enough. Probably copper, but he doubted it was as old as the shopkeeper was telling him.

'How much is it?'

'Ten dollar.'

It wasn't a bad price, but he put it back in the window, thinking he might try to get it for less. 'But I can only afford five.'

'Cannot. Very old. Very special. Eight best price.'

'Five-fifty?'

The man shook his head.

He browsed around the shop, hoping that the shop-keeper would meet him at six. There was a table covered with a collection of earrings, bracelets and jade necklaces, which he picked over, watching the shopkeeper out of the corner of his eye. One of the bracelets caught his attention. It was made from a gold chain, each link shaped like a crescent moon, and the clasp was formed in the shape of a dragon's head with ruby eyes.

'This tells ancient Chinese story.' The shopkeeper was beside him, his bony fingers on Nick's sleeve. 'The legend of Wei Gu.'

'That's funny. I've just been reading that story.'

'You have? Maybe you like to buy?'

It was pretty and he wondered if Miranda might like it. 'How much is it?'

'I give you both twelve dollar.'

'Ten?'

The man nodded again. Nick watched him take the incense burner from the window and wrap it in brown paper, then he found a black velvet box and placed the bracelet inside.

'Which is the best way to get out to Rangoon Street? I seem to keep turning the wrong way.'

'Keep turn left. Three minute.'

He'd have to hurry now. The delay would make him late, but there was one last thing that he wanted to do before he went to the quay. He needed to say farewell to Khalish. Before he left the shop, he felt the money in his jacket pocket, then opened the door and headed out into the street to find a taxi home.

Khalish was feeding the chickens when he found him. His back was to him, his arm outstretched as he scattered feed on to the ground.

'Khalish!'

'*Tuan* – I am glad you have not gone already.'

'Khalish, I've asked Mr Brendan and Mr Charlie to take care of you when I'm gone.'

'Thank you, *tuan*.'

'But,' Nick paused, taking on what he hoped was a casual stance. 'I have a leaving gift for you.'

'There is no need.' Khalish smiled, still clenching a handful of grain. 'I never forget how much you help me. I learn English. You help me, so now one day I am hoping to become a teacher.'

'That's what I mean, Khalish. I want to leave you a gift, the chance to do exactly that.'

Confusion clouded Khalish's features. 'I am not sure what you mean, *tuan*.'

'Look,' Nick slipped his hand into his jacket pocket and took out the money he'd got from selling the roadster, 'I sold my car this morning. I have no need of it now – there was no point in me taking it back to England again. I want you to use this money to go to school. You can learn to be a teacher, just as you want to. I've asked Mr Brendan to help you, but here,' he held the money out to Khalish, 'I want you to take this.'

'But *tuan* …' There was complete bewilderment on Khalish's face, and Nick saw the grain falling from his hands. 'I can't.'

'Yes, you can, Khalish. Promise me that you will.'

'I don't know what to say.'

'Say nothing for now, but write to me. Let me know how you are getting on, and who knows, one day, you might come and visit me in England?'

Khalish took the money from Nick's outstretched hand, then he lowered his head. 'I promise I will do good, make you proud.'

'I know you will. I know.'

Nick patted him on the shoulder, then walked away. A crimson sunbird rose from the branches of a chiku tree. He watched the bird climb into the sky. He heard the sound of a car approaching; it would surely be the taxi waiting for him on the drive.

But when he got there, it wasn't the taxi. It was Gerry. He opened the car door and got out, and his expression told Nick that his visit wasn't going to be an easy or pleasant one.

'So,' Gerry said, 'you're leaving today?'

'Yes.'

'Coincidence, that – so is my wife.'

'Yes.' Nick scraped the ground with his shoe. 'We're off together to England, but you must know that.'

'In that case,' Gerry stepped forward, 'here's a leaving present.'

The blow was hard to his chest. Nick staggered back, but he managed to deflect the left hook that Gerry threw at him next.

'You really are a piece of shit,' Nick shouted, as he returned the blow, striking Gerry on the chin.

'That makes two of us, then.' Gerry hit again, but this time his fist felled Nick. The kicks that came were hard: in the chest, then one to the head, his face.

'I told you to leave my wife alone,' he hissed. 'But you damn well wouldn't listen, would you?' There was another kick, then a searing pain shot across his face and Nick realised that his nose had cracked.

'*Tuan!*'

Nick lifted his head, blood dripping from his nose to the ground, to see Khalish running towards him.

'I'm fine,' he said, staggering back, but his face was burning, and he thought he was going to be sick. He wanted to slam Gerry, to bury a punch into his smug face, but Khalish was pulling him back.

'No, *tuan*!' Khalish said. 'He not worth it.'

'For God's sake,' Gerry sneered, 'don't tell me you need someone like him to look out for you?'

Rage brewed inside Nick. His eyes connected with Gerry's; for all he wanted to pin him down, he realised that Gerry was merely goading. Although it mortified him to see Gerry walking away with a smirk on his face, he knew there was no point in pursuing him, and he was prepared to allow him this one small victory.

The air was cooler outside. Miranda told herself she'd got it wrong, that Nick must be in another bar waiting for her, just as she'd been waiting for him.

She walked towards the bow.

'Excuse me,' she asked a waiter who was carrying a tray of drinks. 'This *is* the American Bar, isn't it?'

'Yes, it is.'

'Is there another bar?'

'No, just this one.'

'I don't suppose there's a way I can find out if someone is on board?'

'You could try asking the Chief Steward, miss. He'd have a passenger list, but he might not be at liberty to tell you.'

'Where might I find him?'

'I'm not entirely sure, miss. Could be anywhere, seeing as we've just set off. But if you're looking for someone, perhaps I could keep an eye out – what's your friend look like?'

'He's six foot, brown hair.' She could be describing anyone. 'And he's called Nick.'

'Rightie-o, then,' he smiled at her. 'I wouldn't worry too much. This kind of thing happens all the time. People get lost. It's a big ship.'

She watched him pick up the tray, walk along the deck and open a door into one of the gangways.

For a while she sat on a step, listening to the hubbub of voices from the bar along with the piano playing and the soft crooning of a female voice.

She decided to check his cabin.

The problem was, she couldn't remember which was his. Was it two along from hers, or three? The cabin corridors were heaving with passengers squeezing up and down, doors banging and children crying. She knocked on the door that she thought was his.

'Yes?' A woman in her late sixties, who was pulling on an evening dress, opened the door.

'Oh. I'm sorry. I think I have the wrong cabin.'

The woman frowned, then said, 'Well, seeing as you're there, I don't suppose you could fasten my dress, could you? It's so hard to get my arm around the back.'

'Of course.' Miranda's fingers fumbled on the hooks, desperate to get away and to find Nick, then she knocked on the next door and the next.

It was no good. There was only one thing she could do – go back to the bar.

Couples were dancing in front of the band, and most of the tables were full. Three men, dressed in dinner jackets, were leaning against the bar. They looked her up and down as she passed.

'Can I buy you a drink?' one of the men asked, as she walked back towards the door. 'Champagne, perhaps?'

'No, thank you.' She shook her head.

Outside, she stood at the rail, looking at the layers of stars just beginning to appear in the sky. The longer she looked, the more stars she believed she could see. And then she imagined her parents, walking through Bloomsbury on an evening out, glancing up at the same sky. It made her feel closer to them, as though the sky were encompassing them all.

As she waited, she pondered what lay ahead of her. There was Coombe, and all that needed to be done there. Perhaps Nick would agree to her suggestions and turn it into a centre for refugees. Perhaps he wouldn't.

But as she thought about it, she knew she needed more than Nick and living at Coombe. A part of her had been woken up, like the petals on the rain tree after the rain, and it would now be impossible for her to let this feeling go. There had to be something that she could make her own; something that no one could ever take away from her. As she thought about it, she wondered if she could train for a profession – a nurse, or as she had once considered before, a teacher. She pictured herself standing in front of a class of girls, reading, say, from *Pride and Prejudice* or Hardy, or listening, perhaps, while they discussed their written work – and she liked the thought of that.

She lit a cigarette, enjoying the feel of the smoke slipping into her lungs, as a new feeling of contentment and purpose grew within her.

A footstep fell nearby. She lifted her head. It was Nick. He had a strip of plaster over his nose, his lip was bleeding and bruises were forming under his eyes.

'Nick! Thank God you're here, but what the heck has happened?'

'Miranda.' He pulled her to him. 'It doesn't matter now.'

'Yes, it does.'

'Sssh!' He shook his head and put his finger to her lips. 'Let's just say, it's the price I've had to pay for being with you.' He kissed the top of her head and she relaxed into the warmth of his body. 'And every blow was worth it.'

'Gerry?'

He nodded.

She touched his face. 'He really is the limit. It must hurt like hell. Shouldn't you put something on it?'

'Khalish sorted it.'

'I can't believe Gerry did this to you.'

'Best leave it in the past – all that matters is that we're together now.'

She leant into him, not wanting to argue. There were gentle lights below the handrails, which created a festive air; she could hear the sound of the engines humming and the waves slapping against the side of the ship. A couple laughed somewhere in the distance.

'Come on,' he said, after a time. 'Let's find somewhere quiet.'

They sat between the lifeboats, gazing at the moon. Nick placed an arm around her, and they watched the wisp of cloud trailing across the moon's surface.

'It's strange to think that this water runs all the way back to Coombe,' he indicated the sea in front of them. 'First, as the Andaman Sea, then the Indian and, finally, the Atlantic Ocean. One massive piece of water connecting the Empire.'

'And we're just tiny little specks or flotsam tossing about on the waves.'

'When I was small, I found it hard to picture a world beyond London and Coombe. Whenever I saw the sea, I wanted to be a pirate.'

'I think you'd make a useless pirate.' She nudged him affectionately. 'But will you find Coombe so very dull, do you think, after everything we've left behind?'

'I'm not worried – are you? Coombe will be what we want it to be.'

She looked out at the silvery-tipped waves. She tried to picture a place that she had never been to, knowing that it may well be where she was to spend the next few years of her life. If there was one thing she had learnt in her time in Singapore and her marriage to Gerry, she was absolutely certain that she didn't want to return to her feelings of remorse and inadequacy.

'I'm sorry I was late,' she could hear Nick saying. 'Apart from Gerry, everything seemed to be against me. Earlier, I got delayed in the Chinese Quarter. Talking of which, I got you this.' He put his hand in his pocket and took out a small black velvet box. 'Open it.'

She took it from him and opened the lid. 'A golden dragon. It's beautiful. You shouldn't have.' She took the bracelet out of the box, and the dragon's eyes glinted in the half-light.

'I think the eyes are rubies.'

'Where did you say you found it?' she asked, placing the bracelet around her wrist.

'In the Chinese Quarter – a little shop tucked away at the end of a passageway. I'd been trying to find my way out for ages. See those interlinking moons on the chain? It's to do with a legend I've been reading, about the man in the moon. As soon as I saw it, I knew I'd have to get it for you.'

'You'll have to explain.' She turned the bracelet.

'It's a long story, but, once upon a time,' he began, 'there lived an old man in the moon called Yue Lao.' He pointed to the night sky, to the moon overhead.

'During the day, you see, he used to sleep in the crook of the moon, but when the sun went down and when the night sky was at its darkest and all the world was asleep, he would get out of his bed and drop long, silken ropes to the earth and climb down.'

He placed his arm around her and together they looked up at the moon.

'Those ropes were no ordinary ropes: they were precious cords that unite couples. No one knew when Yue Lao might come, or whom he might choose, but when he did, he would tie a silken cord to each person and, whatever happened, however far apart they were or however long they had to wait to be united, once those cords had been tied, no one could break them.'

Miranda stroked the dragon's head.

It was a nice story. But with him or without him, she knew that, with all the experiences she'd gained, all the dangers and disappointments she'd undergone, that not only was she willing, but that she was now able to face anything that came her way.

She looked back at the harbour, taking in the day that was finally coming to a close and the lights that were just coming on along the coast. Then she turned her face in the direction of where they were sailing; tomorrow was a new day, bringing with it nothing but hope and new beginnings. She leant her head on Nick's shoulder and smiled.

Acknowledgements

There are so many people that I'd like to thank for help-ing me to write this novel – I wouldn't have been able to produce it without the support of you all.

Firstly, I'd like to thank my wonderful agent, Caroline Hardman, and all the team at Hardman & Swainson. Thank you for believing in my novel and sending my manuscript on its way to a publisher and, ultimately, publication. A huge thank you also to Sonny Marr for your enthusiasm, time and for shaping this book into the form it is in today, and thank you, also, to all of the team at Arrow, Penguin Random House.

Then, of course, I must say a big thank you to all my tutors and fellow students on my MA course at Sheffield Hallam University. To Susan Elliot-Wright, for your ever-welcome help, expert eye and unfailing support. You were there from the beginning, when my novel was a tiny seed in your evening classes, and at the end, when it had flourished into a full-sized novel, ready to be launched into the world.

I would also like to give a huge thanks to my fellow MA writing students: Lizzie Maskery, Linda Moss, Janet Murray and Kathy Rogers, for their tough critiquing in many a workshop, which has often made me see the error of my ways. I'd like to give a special thank you also to Linda Moss, Margaret Coupe, Emma Greenlees, Leah Carlin and Isobel Greenlees, all of whom have read the entire novel and have provided invaluable comments, editorial suggestions and encouragement at various stages of my work.

And, of course, last but not least, to my husband, John, who has been a constant – not only in providing love, support, help with syntax, spelling and grammar, but also in jogging my memory regarding small details of Singapore, and for always believing in my ability to complete this work.

The idea for writing *Journey to Paradise* came to me after having lived in Singapore in the 1980s, as well as from my mother-in-law's experience of having lived there in the 1950s. I became interested in what it was like for the wives of colonial women, how many marriages suffered, and, until *The Matrimonial Causes Act 1973*, how it was much harder for women to pack up their unhappy lives, head back home and start again.

I was also interested in the political and racial divide, the end of colonisation, and the development of Singapore, along with relationships generally at that time – mothers and daughters, husbands and wives, class and race.

There are several subplots, which include political and social unrest: the rise of communism from China;

cover-ups, as shown by the Batang Kali incident; social injustice (the Martha Hollande case) and poverty; class conflicts as well as the role of women in the 1940s.

Many of the events depicted in the narrative are inspired by true life events. For the purposes of writing a novel, there may have been a little poetic licence in the precise timeline and sequence of events, however. And all of the characters come from my imagination.

In researching setting – geographical, cultural and historical – I found the following works extremely informative: *Nella Last's War*, *Singapore: A Pictorial History* and *Scorpion on the Ceiling*. I also spent a lot of time in the British Library, looking at documents and accounts of life in Singapore post the Second World War, as well as visiting the Imperial War Museum.

Bibliography

Buck, Pearl S., *The Good Earth* (London: Pocket Books, 2005).

Chamberlain, J., *Chinese Gods* (Selangor, Malaysia: Pelanduk Publications, 1987).

Eng, Tan Twan, *The Garden of Evening Mists* (London: Canongate Books, 2013).

Farrell, J. G., *The Singapore Grip* (London: Weidenfeld & Nicolson, 1978).

Golden, Arthur, *Memoirs of a Geisha* (New York, NY: Alfred A. Knopf, 1997).

Last, Nella, and Broad, Richard, and Fleming, Suzie, eds, *Nella Last's War* (London: Profile Books, 2006).

Last, Nella, and Malcolmson, Patricia and Robert, eds, *Nella Last in the 1950s: Further Diaries of Housewife, 49* (London: Profile Books, 2009).

Lip, Evelyn, *Chinese Temples and Deities* (Singapore: Times Books International, 1981).

Liu, Gretchen, *Singapore: A Pictorial History 1819–2000* (Brooklyn, NY: Archipelago Press, 2003).

Martine, Roddy, *Scorpion On The Ceiling: A Scottish Colonial Family in South East Asia* (Moray, Scotland: Librario Publishing, 2004).

Ministry of Information, *Make Do and Mend*, 1943, reprinted (London: Imperial War Museum, 1997).

Paxman, Jeremy, *Empire: What Ruling the World Did to the British* (London: Viking, 2011).

Pearson, Harold Frank, *Singapore: A Popular History* (Singapore: Times Books International, 1985).

Shrimpton, Jayne, *Fashion in the 1940s* (Oxford: Shire Publications Ltd, 2015).

Turnbull, C. M., *A History of Modern Singapore, 1819–2005*, (Singapore: NUS Press, 2009).

Utility Furniture and Fashion, 1941–1951 (London: Inner London Education Authority, 1974).

Wong, Hong Suen, *Wartime Kitchen: Food and Eating in Singapore (1942–1950)* (Singapore: Editions Didier Millet Pte Ltd, 2009).

Electronic Publications

Maria Hertogh: http://en.wikipedia.org/wiki/Maria_Hertogh_riots (accessed 14 December 2014).

The Maker of Moons: http://www.chinatownology.com/old_man_under_the_moon.html (accessed 5 February 2015).

The Matrimonial Causes Act, 1973: https://en.wikipedia.org/wiki/Matrimonial_Causes_Act_1973 (accessed 8 April 2017).

The Straits Times Archives: https://newspaperarchive.com/cgi/The-Straits-Times/?gclid=CK_rm-iNl9MCF-bQyowod78gEWg (accessed 8 April 2017).

YouTube

'Old Singapore's Outskirts in 1951', Michael Rogge: https://www.youtube.com/watch?v=ZXgCtoUaeMY (accessed 15 December 2014).

'Singapore Streets and Ports, 1950s', Huntley Film Archive: https://www.youtube.com/watch?v=_RXXnE2yTUg (accessed 15 December 2014).

'Views of Singapore (1946)', British Pathé: https://www.youtube.com/watch?v=xtbB3hyTfu4 (accessed 15 December 2014).

Miscellaneous

Paxman, Jeremy, *Empire*, BBC/2entertain, 2012.